OF HOPE

OTHER BOOKS AND AUDIO BOOKS
BY AUTHOR NAME:

First Love and Forever

First Love, Second Chances

Now and Forever

By Love and Grace

A Promise of Forever

When Forever Comes

For Love Alone

The Three Gifts of Christmas

Towers of Brierley

Where the Heart Leads

When Hearts Meet

Someone to Hold

Reflections: A Collection of Personal Essays

Gables of Legacy Series, Six Volumes

Timeless Waltz

A Time to Dance

Dancing in the Light

A Dance to Remember

The Barrington Family Saga, Four Volumes

Emma: Woman of Faith

The Sound of Rain

A Distant Thunder

Winds
OF HOPE

a novel by

Anita Stansfield

Covenant Communications, Inc.

Cover image: *Young Couple Holding Hands and Walking on a Pier* © 2008 Dorothy Low / Getty Images

Cover design copyrighted 2009 by Covenant Communications, Inc.

Published by Covenant Communications, Inc.
American Fork, Utah

Printed in The United States of America
First Printing: February 2009

15 14 13 12 11 10 09   10

ISBN-13: 978-1-59811-728-8
ISBN-10: 1-59811-728-9

To the Reader

This is part three of a four-part story. In part one, Jayson Wolfe and his older brother Drew are attending the same high school while their mother, Leslie, works as a waitress. The three of them are a close-knit family as they work to take care of each other and avoid the boys' drunken, violent father, whom Leslie had divorced years earlier. Since money is extremely tight and Leslie's birthday is approaching, Jayson decides that he will learn one of his mother's favorite songs on the piano and have Drew play accompanying drums for the number. Nothing means more to Leslie than her sons' musical gifts, and she has sacrificed considerably to encourage them in pursuing their talents. The birthday gift is a great hit, and Jayson feels immense satisfaction in seeing his skills improve through the intense practice of a difficult number. But that night, Jayson's father shows up, drunk and demanding money. After he hits Leslie, he's surprised to face Jayson, who is much taller than the last time they met. Jayson subdues his father until the police arrive, but the entire situation reawakens his loathing for Jay Wolfe; he especially hates having been named after him.

This violent episode motivates Leslie to make a decision she's been toying with for years. Within days, she and her boys sell practically everything they own and leave Montana to find a new home in Oregon, where a friend of Leslie's has secured her a job as a waitress, along with a suitable apartment. Jayson has no problem with the arrangement, except that he has to leave his grandmother's piano behind, and the new apartment is such that he can't play the guitar without causing a problem for the neighbors. Drew playing drums would be out of the question. Jayson hates his new school, feeling that he doesn't fit in, and he struggles to focus while music plays in his head continually. He gets a crush on a girl named Elizabeth, who is in a school play and a couple of his classes. But he's sure she'd never want anything to do with someone like him. Then Jayson gets an after-school job changing oil, and eventually becomes friends with Derek, who also works at the garage. Jayson is thrilled to realize that Derek too has a musical gift. Everything changes for Jayson when Derek makes him welcome in his home, where there is a soundproof music room in the basement, a beautiful grand piano upstairs, and a kind, doting father, Will Greer, who is thrilled with his son's new friend. But Jayson soon learns that Elizabeth is Derek's sister, and the situation becomes complicated in spite of its advantages.

Jayson, Derek, and Drew quickly do great things with their music and get a job playing on Saturday nights in Portland, but they have to talk Elizabeth into becoming a part of the band in order to make it work. She reluctantly agrees, and Jayson finds himself growing to like her more and more, while she is completely oblivious to his romantic feelings. With the passing of time, the two families become close as Will makes up for a missing father in Jayson's life and Leslie helps compensate for Derek and Elizabeth's arrogant, workaholic mother. When Mrs. Greer announces that she's divorcing Will and leaving the family, they all take it very hard, and the transition strengthens the bonds among the group of friends.

In the spring of their senior year, Jayson and Elizabeth begin dating. Jayson is certain they'll end up married someday, but Elizabeth disagrees. Jayson wants to go to LA and become a rock star. Elizabeth wants to go to college and have a secure, predictable life where she can be the kind of mother to her children that her own mother never was. She cares for Jayson but is certain they could never make it work together.

The magical days of their youth are shattered when Derek is killed in a car accident just prior to graduation. Everyone is devastated, and the relationship between Jayson and Elizabeth becomes strained even while they rely on each other as friends in ways they never have before. When Jayson and Elizabeth both make some bad choices, the relationship has little to hold onto. Elizabeth breaks off their relationship, insisting they could never be happy together, and she tells Jayson she'll be going to school in Boston. In spite of the promise that they will always remain friends and keep in touch, Jayson feels like he's lost everything. He and Drew make the decision to do what they've always dreamed about—go to Los Angeles and find a way to make it in the music business. Jayson can only hope that in doing so he will find a way to get over losing Elizabeth *and* Derek. He's grateful for the closeness he shares with his brother and for the constant love and support he gets from his mother. He is also grateful for Will's insistence that no matter what happens, Jayson will always be a son to him. With little more than that in his heart, he heads to LA with his brother, praying that their musical gifts are good enough to make it work.

In part two, Jayson's arrival in LA assaults him with the reality of how tough it is to break into the music industry, but he and Drew are determined to make it work. Jayson is also determined to put his romance with Elizabeth behind for good, even though they've promised to remain friends forever. Jayson and Drew's mother moves to LA to be near her sons, leaving Elizabeth's father, Will, alone in Oregon.

Meanwhile, Elizabeth goes to Boston to attend college and quickly realizes she made a mistake in letting Jayson go. Once she comes to terms with this, she tries unsuccessfully for days to reach him by phone but is unable to get hold of him. When Jayson finally calls Elizabeth, it's to tell her that he's married to a young woman named Debbie, whom he met soon after coming to LA. Elizabeth manages to hide her shock and grief, and gradually she becomes accustomed to the idea that she and Jayson will never be together. Jayson and Debbie have a baby girl, Macy, and he and Drew continue to take tiny steps in the music business. They start getting hired as background musicians, but they still have to do other menial jobs to keep food on the table.

Eventually Elizabeth meets Robert, a fine man who meets every requirement Elizabeth ever dreamed of in a husband. They marry and move to Phoenix, where Robert gets a great job as an accountant. Elizabeth has a son named Bradley and, a few years later, another named Trevin, while Jayson continues struggling to achieve his goals. Then suddenly it happens, and Jayson lands a huge record deal. The deal includes his brother, Drew, and two other band members he's picked up along the way: Rudy and Barry. Elizabeth observes Jayson's success from a distance, although they talk regularly on the phone, and exchange cards and gifts through the mail. She is genuinely happy for her friend's success, but misses her brother terribly as she often thinks he should have been involved in all of this.

Jayson's heart is broken when he comes home in the middle of a concert tour to find Debbie with another man. His success is tainted by a divorce and his concern for his daughter, who is caught in the middle. Elizabeth remains supportive as a friend, and Jayson wonders what he would ever do without her.

On one of the rare occasions when Elizabeth sees Jayson face-to-face, an awkward moment leads to her tearful confession that there is a complete lack of intimacy in her marriage, and she is very unhappy in spite of Robert being a good man in every other respect. Jayson insists that she needs to tell her husband how difficult this is for her and urges them both to get some professional help. After following Jayson's advice, Elizabeth's marriage takes a turn for the better, and while it's not perfect, she recognizes that she has much to be grateful for in her life. She gets pregnant again and has a beautiful baby girl. Following a bout of unemployment, Robert gets a job in Utah, and there, Elizabeth finds a new way of life.

Macy hits some mysterious difficulties in the midst of her teen years, and Jayson's concern for her consumes him. Then she runs away from home, and his anxiety nearly devours him. Jayson doesn't hear from his daughter at all for a few years, his band falls apart, and his mother dies of cancer. Drew starts playing with another band, and Rudy and Barry both die horrible deaths due to their poor lifestyle choices. The only thing that keeps Jayson from going over the edge is playing music, but in that he feels completely alone.

Jayso is touring as a hired musician with a different band in Europe when he gets word that Elizabeth's husband and son Bradley were killed in a drowning accident. Elizabeth's father sells his home and moves in with her to help her with her remaining two children, while Jayson's life descends into a downward spiral in another state. A freak accident that takes the use of his left hand sends him over the edge. Will's repeated insistence that he come and stay with them is ignored, while Jayson convinces himself that he's better off dead. A miracle prevents him from committing suicide, and he has no choice but to go and stay with Will and Elizabeth in Utah. He's shocked to learn that they have both become members of the Mormon Church and insists that he wants nothing to do with it.

Elizabeth quickly figures out that Jayson has an addiction to prescription drugs and arranges for him to go into rehab at a nearby facility. Jayson is terrified to face withdrawal, as well as the reasons why he turned to drugs in the first place, but he feels an inner peace that gives him hope for coming through this ordeal with something to live for.

CHAPTER 1

Arriving at the drug rehabilitation facility, Jayson felt completely dehumanized as both he and his luggage were thoroughly searched. As humiliating as it was, however, he felt grateful to have Will and Elizabeth with him while he filled out a ridiculous amount of paperwork and endured a frank debriefing indicating what the rules would be. It was made clear that Jayson was giving up both his will and his freedom to these people, and that no matter how much he hated it, he would be governed by them until he became capable of governing his own life. When it came time for Will and Elizabeth to leave, Jayson was reminded of the moment he'd realized his mother would die. He felt like a lost child, alone and terrified. He hugged them each tightly, trying to pull their love into himself. As Elizabeth held to him, she whispered near his ear, "I will be praying for you constantly. God will get you through this, Jayson. Nobody else can. He will give you the peace and the strength you need." She looked into his eyes with tears in her own. "Remember that."

Jayson nodded but couldn't speak. He was determined to maintain his dignity, but he was barely holding onto it. Fearing an inevitable breakdown, he forced himself to step back, then he turned and walked away, feeling as if he were about to literally descend into the depths of hell. And nobody could spare him from the inevitable consequences of the choices he'd made to bring him to this point. Not even God could do that.

* * *

Elizabeth started to cry before she even got to the car. She was grateful for her father's willingness to drive as she completely fell apart once they were on the road.

"You've got to calm down, honey," he said, holding her hand. "He's going to be alright. He's a lot tougher than he thinks he is."

Elizabeth wanted to believe him, but her heart ached so completely for Jayson that it felt almost as if they were literally the same flesh and blood, and his anguish was her anguish. During the following days, she kept her promise to pray constantly for him. During every task she performed, and as she fell asleep and came awake, her thoughts were prayers on his behalf. She called more than a dozen temples and put his name on the prayer rolls, knowing that hundreds of people would be praying for him every day for the next two weeks.

More than once she opened the music box Jayson had given her in high school, encompassed by an almost eerie sensation as she closed her eyes and sang along softly to the love theme from *West Side Story*. It seemed so fitting.

Three days after Jayson had been taken to the rehab facility, his cell phone rang while Elizabeth was in her office typing. It startled her, since she'd never heard it ring before. She picked it up and read on the little screen, *Drew*. She took a deep breath and answered.

"You're not my little brother," he said, but he said it lightly.

"No, I'm not," she said, "but I'm in charge of the cell phone for a while."

Jayson had warned that Drew might call, and that she would need to tell him everything. Jayson wanted him to know, but he didn't want to be the one to tell him.

"Where is he?" Drew asked, still not sounding concerned.

"He's in the hospital," Elizabeth said.

"What happened?" he demanded. "Is he hurt? Is he—"

"One question at a time," she said. "Actually, it's not a conventional hospital, Drew. He's in a rehabilitation facility."

She heard him take a sharp breath. "What are you saying?" he asked a moment later.

"He's got a drug problem, Drew. *Prescription* drugs," she hurried to clarify.

"I can't believe it," he said. "He's seemed just fine when I've seen him."

"Well, he *did* seem just fine, as long as you caught him when the drugs were at a peak."

"I can't believe it," Drew said again, and Elizabeth went on to explain all that she knew of how the problem had progressed, how she had discovered it during his stay in her home, and what he would have to go through to get beyond it.

"So he's going to be alright?" Drew asked.

"Yes, he is," she said firmly. "He's got a great attitude. He genuinely wants to get past this, and his addiction has only been for a matter of months, not years as with some people."

"Well, I'm grateful he came to stay with you. I'd like to know how you managed to talk him into it; I haven't been able to hardly get him out of the house for months."

Elizabeth swallowed carefully. Jayson had told her he wanted Drew to know everything, and Elizabeth knew that it was important. Drew needed to know the extent of the problem; he was family.

"Drew," she said carefully, "my father talked him into coming here because he was suicidal."

Drew gasped. "You mean . . . he was talking about—"

"I mean he came extremely close to doing away with himself." Drew gasped again, and she went on to explain what had happened. She could tell he was crying, and he said more than once that his brother being alive was a miracle. She promised to keep him informed, and when the call had ended, Elizabeth sobbed for several minutes before she could get back to work.

When the day came that they could finally see Jayson, knowing that the detoxification process was over, Elizabeth felt almost as terrified as she had the day they'd taken him in, a week earlier. Her concern deepened when Will came down with a flu and was too ill to go with her. Going into the facility, she endured a search similar to the one Jayson had undergone. They wanted to make certain she wasn't smuggling anything in that might set him back. She was then taken down a long hall to his room. She knew that his affluence afforded him the privilege of a private room, among other things. She held her breath as she entered the room and found him sitting on the floor, leaning against the bed, his head down. He wore jeans and a button-up shirt that was only partially buttoned. His feet were bare. He was nervously rubbing his left hand with the fingers of his right, as if to rub out the pain and stiffness that she knew was there.

"You have company," the attendant said, and Jayson's head shot up. Elizabeth couldn't keep from gasping. He looked more ill than her father who had been vomiting all night. His eyes were sunken, his skin sallow. He looked thinner, more fragile. He looked broken.

"Thank you," Jayson said, his voice weak. The attendant left the room, leaving the door open.

Elizabeth watched Jayson take hold of the edge of the bed and come unsteadily to his feet. She rushed toward him and took hold of his arm to help him, immediately wrapping him in her arms.

"Oh, Elizabeth," he muttered near her ear, holding to her tightly.

She took his face into her hands and pressed her brow to his, just as she'd done the night before he'd come here. "Are you okay?" she asked.

"Better now . . . that you're here." He teetered slightly, and she urged him to the edge of the bed, sitting beside him. "Sorry," he said, "I haven't been able to eat much, but that's getting better."

He folded one leg onto the bed and turned to face her fully, taking both her hands into his as she did the same. Elizabeth looked into his strained and weary eyes. She said intently, "Talk to me. Tell me." She watched huge tears rise into his eyes and then fall before he pressed his face against her shoulder and wept.

"I never imagined the human body could endure such horrors and survive. I've never been so sick in my life. The hallucinations alone were horrid. A thousand times I wished I was dead."

"Oh, I'm so sorry," she said, wiping his tears with her fingers. "But the worst is over now."

"So they tell me," he said.

"But?" she asked, looking at him closely.

He chuckled bitterly and returned to rubbing his left hand. "Today is my last official day of detox," he said. "Tomorrow I start into *the program*. It smacks of military basic training; they're not going to give me time to feel sorry for myself. Private therapy. Group therapy. Heaven knows what else. Now comes the picking apart of my heart and soul to find whatever it is I was trying to bury under the drugs. Well, I know what I was trying to bury, and I don't want to look at it. That almost scares me more than the detox did."

"But you made it this far; surely you'll make it through whatever you have to in order to be whole again."

"Again? Was I ever whole? I don't remember. It doesn't feel like it."

"Yes, Jayson. You were. And you will be again." She took his face into her hands. "You can do this. I know you can."

"I don't know it," he said, sounding angry. Then he wept again. "Tell me what I can do, Jayson. Tell me anything, and I'll do it."

"Just be with me," he said, putting his head in her lap. "I don't know how long they'll let you stay, but . . . just be with me." Jayson closed his eyes and became hypnotized by the feel of her fingers brushing his hair back from his face. A thought occurred to him, and he asked, "Where's my favorite father?"

"He's got the flu, actually; he was puking all night."

"I'm an expert at that," Jayson said. "Tell him to get better good and fast. I expect to see him next time."

"I'll tell him," she said and started to hum.

The music had a soothing effect on Jayson, and he muttered quietly, "Sing me that song."

"What song?"

"The one that Addie sang at family home evening; the one the children sang in the chapel when . . ." He stopped and turned his head to look up at her. "I missed the Primary program."

"You did," she said, a little startled by his obvious disappointment.

He settled his head back onto her lap and asked, "How did it go?"

"Rather well, actually—especially considering how distracted and preoccupied the music leader was."

"With what?" he asked.

"You, of course." He made no comment, and she said, "Drew called. I told him everything."

Jayson groaned but didn't move. "Has he disowned me?"

"No, of course not. He cried."

"Drew?" He looked up. "Drew cried?"

"He did," Elizabeth said. "He loves you. He said to tell you so. And he said he's glad you're alive. I'm glad you're alive, too."

"Me too . . . I think," he said. "At the moment, anyway. Ask me again next week."

He settled himself again and said, "Sing the song . . . please."

Elizabeth cleared her throat and sang through all the verses of "I Am a Child of God" five times. When she tried to quit, he begged her not to. She did variations on the melody for variety, and finally said, "How about a different song?"

"Okay," he said, but before she could think of one he asked, "Do you really believe that's true?"

"What?"

"That we really are children of God?"

"Absolutely. And God loves His children, not collectively, but individually. Think of the love you feel for Macy. That's how He loves you, only more so."

Jayson looked up at her in surprise. "How can He love me when I've been such an idiot?"

"God's love is not conditional on our behavior. It's perfect, constant, absolute. Do you love Macy any less because she made some mistakes?"

"No, of course not."

"So, if we as imperfect human beings love our children so much, why is it so difficult to imagine that a perfect God, who is the Father of our spirits, would love us any less?"

"I never thought of it that way," he said. "And you really think it's true? Does He really exist? Does He care? Because if He doesn't, I don't see any point in even going through this."

"I know it's true, Jayson," she said, and then she sang, *"Heavenly Father, are you really there? And do you hear and answer ev'ry child's prayer? Some say that heaven is far away, But I feel it close around me as I pray. Heavenly Father, I remember now Something that Jesus told disciples long ago: 'Suffer the children to come to me.' Father, in prayer I'm coming now to thee."* She lowered her voice to sing the second verse, which represented a parent's response to the child's question. *"Pray, he is there. Speak, he is list'ning. You are his child; his love now surrounds you. He hears your prayer; He loves the children. Of such is the kingdom, the kingdom of heav'n."*

"Oh, sing that one again," Jayson said, marveling at the tangible warmth that filled him. Perhaps it was true. Perhaps God *did* love him. And if that was true, maybe he could get through this after all.

"What are you thinking?" Elizabeth asked when she couldn't sing any more.

"I've lost everything, you know," he said sadly.

"No, you haven't. Job lost *everything*. He lost all of his children, his wealth, his wife, his friends. You've lost much, granted. But there are people who love you. And you're filthy stinking rich," she added lightly.

"That's true. I am filthy stinking rich. But you can have my money if you want it. I'd gladly give it to you."

"I don't need your money, but I could suggest at least one good cause."

"Like what?" he asked.

"We'll talk about it some other time. Let's talk about Job."

"What about him?"

"He lost everything, but he didn't lose his faith because he had a close relationship with God. That's what got him through." Jayson gave her a penetrating gaze as if he had felt something profound in her statement, but he didn't comment. She simply added, "It's something to think about."

Before Elizabeth left, she took a picture out of her purse that Addie had drawn for him. He took it and smiled at her rendition of herself and Mozie done in crayon, with hearts floating above their heads. "The hearts mean that they love you," Elizabeth explained.

Jayson found it difficult to let Elizabeth go, but he found some comfort in seeing that it was equally difficult for her. It was evident that she loved him too. As if she'd read his mind, the last thing she said to him was, "God loves you, Jayson. And so do I."

The following day Jayson began a rigorous schedule that included intense counseling sessions. He quickly realized that he would never get out of this place if he didn't stick to the program. A part of him felt tempted to just give these people the answers they wanted, if only to convince them that he was fine now. But something deeply instinctive told him that he needed to truly cleanse himself of the underlying pain that had lured him into drug abuse. He didn't just want to get out of here; he wanted to be healthy and strong. He wanted to be happy. He wanted to be a good father to Macy—wherever she might be. And he still held onto the hope that by some miracle, he might yet be given the opportunity to be a husband to Elizabeth—and for her, he needed to be the best man he could possibly be.

The difficulty came when he began to realize the width of the chasm between his present state and his goal. His personal counselor, a woman named Maren, told him he was a relatively emotionally healthy person who simply had some unresolved issues. She felt confident that his road to dealing with those issues was not necessarily long or complicated, but it could be intense and difficult. After a few sessions together, she committed to spending more time with him than the usual two or three hours a week, if only to get him past the initial strain of what he had to face.

He was glad to see Will and Elizabeth on the weekend, but he felt shaky and tense and knew they couldn't help but notice. He couldn't admit to them that while he was grateful to be without the drugs, he ached for the euphoria they had given him. He hungered for the numbness that had protected him from the formless pain that festered inside of him.

Halfway through his second week of counseling, Jayson began to wonder if this was really getting anywhere. At times he felt that Maren had him pegged pretty accurately; at others he thought she was full of a lot of nonsensical psychobabble that had nothing to do with him. He actually felt amused as she went into a lengthy explanation of some theory she found fascinating of an inner Pandora's Box, where people would lock away the pain related to certain issues in their lives. He listened only to be polite, then she leaned toward him and asked intently, "What's in the box, Jayson?"

He chuckled, but a deep trembling erupted inside of him in response to the question. "I don't know what you're talking about," he said.

"There's a part of your brain that knows very well what I'm talking about. All you have to do is ask yourself the question, and you'll come up with the answer. So, what's in the box?"

The trembling inside of him increased dramatically, even before she said, "Do you know what kept the box closed and latched and content to stay closed?"

"Apparently you do," he said, amazed at the anger he heard in his own voice.

"Music," she said gently, and he started to gasp for breath. "And when you became incapable of playing the music that kept the box closed, do you know what did the trick?"

She leaned back in her chair and made it evident she wasn't going to answer that question for him. She expected him to say it, and she would sit there until he did. He knew the answer, and the answer made him sick. "Drugs," he croaked.

"You're a very wise man, Jayson," she said with gentle compassion. "And when we can talk about what's in the box, you'll be able to empty it out and get rid of it. Then you won't need drugs, and you will be able to play music because you *want* to, not to medicate yourself." She watched him closely, as if she were sizing him up, then she asked again, "So, what's in the box, Jayson?"

What's in the box? he repeated silently, and the answer rushed up from the core of himself like a volcanic eruption. He groaned, he gasped, and he slid out of the chair to his knees and doubled over with pain. He spent the next three days trying to cope with the metaphoric evil that had been unleashed inside of him. And then Maren coolly asked him, "Are you ready to talk to your loved ones about this?"

"About what?" he snapped.

"You won't get away with feigning denial, Jayson. You know what I'm talking about. And you know that if your healing is going to be complete, the people who love you have to know what's going on. They need to understand it in order to help you press forward and have a healthy life."

"My brother has little to do with this."

"He has less to do with this than Will and Elizabeth, but he's still your brother."

"Will and Elizabeth are not even family."

"They are more family than most people find in the families they are born into. They love you. They share your grief. They are a part of your grief." She leaned forward as she always did when she needed to make a hard point. "They shared a near suicide with you, Jayson. They saved your life. You owe them this."

"What exactly is *this* that I owe them?"

"You owe them understanding of how it came to that. If you come clean with them, if you let them help you now, there will be nothing to hide, nothing to bury. Are you ready to talk to them? Are you ready to tell them what's in the box?"

Jayson thought about that for a minute while his insides trembled. Then he said, "How about if *you* tell them what's in the box, and *then* I'll talk to them?"

"If you want me to do that, I can do that. Do you think that will make it easier?"

"Maybe," he said. But as the hours drew closer for a prearranged counseling session with Will and Elizabeth, Jayson felt near the brink of insanity. He felt uncontrollably cold; he couldn't get warm, couldn't stop shaking with an apparent shivering that made no sense. And then when he thought he couldn't bear the cold, he became suddenly hot from the inside out, feeling a desire to run barefoot in the snow. He had marveled over the last several days that emotional trauma could cause such literal, physical pain. And he felt sure that his symptoms now were from the same source. He felt terrified, and he found himself praying constantly that they would love him enough to endure this and not lose all faith in him.

* * *

Elizabeth felt deeply terrified as the time approached for their session with Jayson. She had to admit that her deepest fear was the possibility that she was somehow responsible for a great deal of the grief in Jayson's life. She believed intrinsically that if she hadn't given in to her fears at a crucial point in their relationship, their lives would have been profoundly different—profoundly better.

Elizabeth and her father were shown into a room with some chairs and little else. They both sat there for several minutes before a woman near Elizabeth's age, with sleek dark hair, walked in and said, "Hi, I'm Maren. I'm Jayson's counselor. You must be Will and Elizabeth."

"That's right," Will said, and she shook each of their hands, then motioned them back into their chairs.

Maren scooted a chair to face theirs and sat down. "I appreciate your taking the time to come. The healing can be much more effective and long-lasting when family support is involved. Jayson has given me written consent to discuss his case openly with you. He tells me that you're as good as family—the only family he has—and I understand you have more than twenty years of history together."

"That's right," Will said again, and Elizabeth was grateful to have him here, especially when she was finding it difficult to speak. "So, how is he?"

"He's come a long way already," Maren said. "He has a long way to go yet, however. Our goal is to resolve the issues that are the underlying cause for a person becoming dependent on drugs to begin with. And Jayson has many of those. He said that he would prefer I catch you up on the things we've talked about, so that he didn't have to tell you himself. So I'll give you a summary, and you are welcome to ask me any questions that you might have." Maren leaned forward in her chair and went on. "Apparently there was a time when Jayson was quite sensitive; he tells me he was always prone to crying easily."

"That's right," Will said.

"And then one day he stopped crying," Maren said. "He made a conscious decision; in fact, he recalls it very clearly. The pain was too much to bear. He couldn't go on if he had to deal with such loss, so he put it away. Every once in a while he was faced with another painful episode in his life. He'd have a good cry, and then he'd close it off again. My favorite analogy of this is the Pandora's Box. In this figurative box, Jayson has locked away every painful episode, and his coping mechanism for keeping the box locked was—"

"Playing music," Elizabeth provided.

"Exactly," Maren said. "You know him well."

"But when he hurt his hand, he couldn't do that anymore," Elizabeth went on.

"Right again. So, when he couldn't keep the pain down any longer, he found a certain euphoria in the pain medication he was taking following the surgery. The pain in his hand let up, but not the pain in his heart. As his body developed a tolerance to the drug, he had to keep taking more to produce the numbing effect. And these were added on top of the sleeping pills, antidepressants, and anti-anxiety medications he was already taking too much of." She turned some pages on the yellow notepad in her hand and added, "I actually have a list of the things that were in that box, if you're interested."

"We are," Will said. "Does this mean they're not in the box any longer?"

"No, they're not in the box, but . . . a person doesn't deal with that much pain quickly or easily. He's going through a grieving process for many losses in his life; a process that he didn't allow himself to go through when he lost his wife, his daughter, the members of his band, his mother, his brother."

"His brother?" Elizabeth asked.

"Not a literal loss like the others were, but when Drew took a different path, Jayson felt cut off from him as well. Now he's grieving for each of these losses. And as you probably realize, the grieving process is made up of many different stages, and a person can go back and forth among them a great deal. Anger and shock are the most difficult stages, and he's experiencing a great deal of those."

While Elizabeth was pondering Maren's omission of Jayson losing *her* more than twenty years ago, Will mentioned another apparent oversight. "You know about Derek's death."

"Yes, of course," Maren said. "His best friend; your son."

"Was that in the box?"

"No. He grieved well for Derek's death. He's continued to miss him, but that loss has been dealt with appropriately."

Elizabeth deeply hoped that her leaving Jayson fell into that category. She summoned the courage to say, "And you know about my ending our relationship . . . just out of high school. Was that in the box?"

"No," Maren said, but she said it with caution. "Your leaving him, Elizabeth, was the creation of the box."

Elizabeth gasped for breath. She reached for her father with a trembling hand. She fought with everything inside of her to maintain her composure, but finally had to resign herself to accepting the tears that burst out of her. For forty-five minutes she talked with Maren about her emotion, her fears, her love for Jayson, her regret. While her father held her hand and remained supportive, Maren listened and attempted to offer some perspective. And throughout the entire conversation, Elizabeth couldn't stop crying.

"Maybe I need some pretty serious counseling myself," Elizabeth said.

"Not necessarily," Maren said, "but I do think it would be a good idea for you and Jayson to clear the air over this." Elizabeth nodded, even though the very idea was terrifying. The fear seized her every nerve when Maren added, "Jayson is waiting. I'm going to get him now."

Elizabeth wanted to scream at her and stop her, but she knew there was no feasible reason to put this off. There was nothing more to say that would make any difference without Jayson being involved. She squeezed her father's hand painfully tight when the door came open and Jayson walked into the room with Maren right behind him. Will immediately came to his feet and met Jayson with a firm embrace.

Jayson accepted Will's hug and the relief it gave him. He'd been terrified of how they might respond to the report of his emotional state. He had no idea how Maren had presented it, but he knew it couldn't have been good. Will's unconditional love and acceptance were readily evident, and Jayson felt grateful. Then Will moved aside, and he found himself facing Elizabeth. His heart fell. She'd been crying—good and hard. A quick glance revealed a box of tissues and a nearly full wastebasket near the chair she'd been sitting in. Her embrace was as firm and eager as her father's, but he felt deeply troubled over the probable source of her tears.

Elizabeth scrutinized Jayson as he moved to a chair and sat down. The last time she'd seen him, he'd looked significantly better than he had after coming out of detox. Now he looked worse. The evidence of the trauma he'd been through showed in his face. His eyes had a shocked, bewildered quality that she'd first seen there following Derek's death. He was barefoot, and he wore jeans and a dark, button-up shirt. The cuffs weren't buttoned, but the sleeves weren't rolled up. The top four buttons were left undone, leaving a portion of his chest exposed. His hair was more mussed than usual. His clothes looked like he'd slept in them. His face looked gaunt and weary, and he was rubbing his left hand with his right.

"So, Jayson," Maren said, making herself comfortable, "is there something you'd like to say?"

He looked irritated by the question as he sank low in his chair and crossed his ankle over his knee. "I'm just wondering why Elizabeth has been crying."

"Why don't you ask her?" Maren said, and Jayson's irritation increased.

With annoyed sarcasm he said, "Why have you been crying, Elizabeth?"

It took Elizabeth a minute to come up with the right words. "I'm crying for the same reason I was crying the night before you came in here."

"You'll have to refresh my memory," Jayson said.

"I was wondering then if I might have done something to contribute to the problem." She watched him closely as she spoke, wondering how he might react. "Apparently I was right."

She saw him shoot a concerned, confused glance toward Maren, as if to question her on this. Maren just motioned her hand toward Elizabeth, indicating that this was between the two of them. Jayson looked apprehensively at Elizabeth just as Will said, "I wonder if you might be more comfortable discussing some of this without me here."

"No!" Jayson said abruptly. He softened his voice to say, "We got beyond that a long time ago. Please stay."

Will relaxed more fully into his chair. Jayson turned his eyes back to Elizabeth and said with a strained voice, "Apparently you were right about what?"

"That I had contributed to the problem."

"I guess you're going to have to spell it out for me, Lady. I'm lost. There is nothing you did or didn't do that put me in this mess."

"But . . ." her tears began again, "I was the reason . . . you started putting the pain away. What I did was too much . . . too harsh."

Jayson drew in a deep breath as he realized what she meant. But seeing her emotion only fed the anger he was struggling to keep in check. His voice was acrid as he asked, "So, what now? Did you think I brought you here to get you to renege on a decision you made nearly twenty years ago? Do you think I would want you making a commitment to me out of pity? Not in a million years!" His voice raised to a shout. "Not then, not now!"

Jayson heard himself yelling, and he squeezed his eyes closed as if he could block out the source of his anger. Without opening them he said with forced calm, "You did what you had to do. How I handled it is my problem. How I chose to respond to that—and every other situation in my life—is my responsibility. Your being here is simply for the purpose of . . . helping me come to terms with everything that's happened, so I can . . . go on."

"That was a very healthy, appropriate thing to say, Jayson," Maren said, and Jayson shot out of his chair.

"Well it doesn't *feel* healthy! It feels *pathetic,* and I *hate* it! Why do they even have to be a part of this? They have done nothing but love me and care for me, and what have I given them but grief?" He kicked the chair he'd been sitting on, and it slid across the floor. "This has nothing to do with them!" he shouted.

"It most certainly does," Will said, apparently unaffected by Jayson's anger—unlike Elizabeth, who was crying again. "We're family, Jayson."

"How is that, exactly?" Jayson snarled. "You didn't bring me into this world; you have no obligation to see me through it. You just took me in like some stray dog off the streets with no idea about the garbage I would bring with me."

Will stood and took Jayson's shoulders into his hands with a vehemence that was startling. He met him eye to eye, saying in a harsh whisper, "The choices you made *are* your responsibility, Jayson. Just as my choices are *my* responsibility. I made a conscious choice to not only bring you into my home, but into my heart. You brought music and life to both. You have no idea the blessing you have been to me from the very first day you showed up with Derek. I have worried over you as I have worried over my own children. I have loved you as I have loved my own children. I've had times of concern, even some disappointment—just as I've had with my own children. But you have never lost my respect, and there is nothing you can do or say that will ever make me stop loving you." He clenched his teeth and actually sounded angry as he added, "Don't you *dare* try to tell me we aren't family! And don't tell me that *my* choices in regard to you were wrong. I have no regrets. I know you're hurting, and I know you're angry, and you have a right to be. Life has dealt you more losses than any man deserves. But I understand those losses, Jayson. My wife cheated on me and left me. I lost a child. But I'm not going to lose you. I made the choice to bring you into this family, and I'll stand by that. Families stick together no matter what; families carry each other through the bad times as well as the good. Families are forever, Jayson." As if to emphasize his words, Will put his arms around Jayson and held him tightly. Jayson felt hesitant to return the embrace, as if he were somehow unworthy of the incredible love this man was so willing to give him. He finally felt himself relax and lifted his arms to more fully accept the expression of fatherly love Will was giving him. Will continued to hold tightly to him, as if to say this was not some token effort to defuse a tense moment. It was as if he intended to make it clear that he would give all he had to give on Jayson's behalf. And Jayson felt the love and acceptance come into him. The anger dissolved into a harsh, raw sorrow. Jayson pressed his face to Will's shoulder and wept.

Eventually the men returned to their seats, and Maren guided them into a conversation about each of the events that had caused Jayson grief and how Will and Elizabeth were tied into those events. Elizabeth noticed that in the absence of Jayson's anger, he seemed suddenly cold, visibly shivering as if the temperature in the room had dropped below freezing. She was ready to demand that something be done to remedy the problem when Maren gently asked him, "Are you cold again?"

He nodded but said, "I'll be okay; just give me a few minutes." But Maren left the room and returned with a blanket that she put around Jayson's shoulders. "Thank you," he said and huddled tightly in it, but he didn't stop shaking. He cried as the conversation went on, then he receded into a visible shock, and his trembling ceased.

Again Elizabeth cried all the way home, while her father assured her that Jayson was making great strides—and so was she. As they pulled into the garage, Elizabeth asked, "What did you mean when you said your wife cheated on you?"

Will looked astonished, then he turned away as he said, "I thought you knew."

"Knew what?"

"That the biggest reason for the divorce was the other man in her life." Elizabeth felt stunned, then wondered if she'd just been blind. She said nothing, and her father added, "That's why your mother was never home. She worked long hours, but . . . I knew it was going on long before the marriage finally fell apart."

"I can't believe it."

"Well, don't go getting upset over that. It's ancient history, Elizabeth. I just wanted Jayson to know that I have some degree of empathy for what he's suffered. But he's lost much more than I ever did."

Elizabeth couldn't think of anything to say so she just got out of the car and went into the house.

Early the next morning, Elizabeth reached for the ringing phone and noticed on the caller ID that it was the rehab center. She answered, expecting to hear the voice of one of the attendants, or perhaps Maren. Instead it was Jayson.

"Hi," he said, sounding more like himself, "Maren said I could call you, but I only have a few minutes."

"How are you?" she asked.

"A little better, I think," he said. "I just wanted to say that . . . I'm sorry, Elizabeth. I'm sorry you had to go through that yesterday."

"It's okay, Jayson. I'd do just about anything if it would help you."

"Yes, I know you would," he said. "And I'm grateful, but . . . I wish it didn't have to be this way."

"This will pass, Jayson. It will."

"I hope so, but . . . I fear the battle hasn't been won just yet."

"Why? What's wrong?"

"The same," he said. "It's just . . . I'm on a roller coaster here, Lady. I fear what else I might do . . . or say . . . before I can come to terms with this. I guess I just wanted to apologize in advance for whatever grief I might yet put you through. And I want to say that you don't have to come anymore if you don't want to. In fact, maybe it would be better if you just let me work it through, then you can come and get me when they declare me fit."

"Your nobility is touching, Jayson. But I want to be there. I want to see you every chance I get. I want to do everything I can to help you through this."

"Your nobility is touching as well, my dear sweet friend. But it's not necessary." She could hear voices in the background, and he said, "I have to go."

"I'll see you soon," she said.

"Just come and get me when it's over," he countered and hung up the phone.

CHAPTER 2

Two days later, Elizabeth went to see Jayson for the usual visit, since the counseling session had been something extra. She found Jayson stretched out on his bed, leaning his head against the wall.

"I thought I told you to stay home," he said, sounding genuinely angry.

"I thought I told you I wasn't going to," she retorted, setting two pictures beside him that Addie had sent.

He glanced at them and set them on the bedside table. "Where's *Dad?*" he asked almost snidely.

"He's home; he thought it might be good for you and me to talk alone."

"Did he, now?" Jayson asked. "Well, as you can tell, I'm in a rather foul mood. You might be wise to turn around and go home."

"And why is that?"

"For your own good."

"I mean . . . why are you in a foul mood?"

"Oh . . . more therapy," he said. With bitter sarcasm he ranted, "This place is full of drug addicts, you know. These people are crazy. They make my problems look like a piece of cake. I'm grateful for the perspective, but I'm sick to death of listening to everybody else's problems. It's worse than an R-rated movie in there."

"I'm sorry."

"Don't apologize. It has nothing to do with you."

"I wasn't apologizing. I was offering some sympathy."

"Well, I don't want your sympathy, either."

"That's too bad!" she snapped, imitating his tone of voice. "Because you're going to get it."

"Well, I don't want it!" he shouted, coming to his feet. "I want you to leave me alone and—"

"I'm not going to leave you alone!" she shouted back. "I would prefer to actually give you the benefit of the doubt and assume that you're so consumed with grief and confusion that you don't know which way is up, and you're just taking it out on me because you know I'll love you no matter what you say."

"Maybe you'd be better off to make a change of policy and just stop loving me."

"It's tempting," she said.

"It might yet be the smartest thing you've ever done," he said with such rancor that she felt genuinely appalled.

"Who are you anyway?" she snapped. "I don't even know you anymore."

"I'll tell you who I am," he snarled, taking hold of her arm and putting his face close to hers. "I'm the man who held you in his arms when—"

"Don't you dare say it!" she countered tersely.

"Oh, of course not. I wouldn't dare say it. I wouldn't want to offend your sensitive nature by actually *talking* about what happened between us. We could talk about it when Robert wouldn't touch you, but since he died there's some invisible wall between us and it's full of everything romantic that ever passed between us. We can be haunted by it. We can think about it far more than we know we should. But we've become so thoroughly accustomed to forcing such thoughts away, knowing they weren't appropriate, that now we can't think about it at all, let alone talk about it."

"We?" she countered. "*We?* What makes you think you know what *I* have been thinking and feeling?"

Jayson leaned closer and looked into her eyes. "Look at me, Lady, and tell me that it's never crossed your mind, that you've never struggled with it." She glanced down abruptly, and he added, "That's what I thought. I know you better than that. Oh, we were noble and we always did our best to do what was right. For me, keeping such thoughts at bay wasn't a problem when my marriage was good. But loneliness has a way of making you wonder. And I saw the change in you. Robert treated you well, and he was a good man. But I could feel the loneliness in you, and I knew you were struggling. We've spent years pretending and not talking about it, Elizabeth. You had commitments and vows that had to be honored, but that's not the case anymore. I'm tired of not talking about it, and I'm done pretending that I don't think about it." He lowered his voice to a husky whisper, but it was still angry. "We were *intimate* as teenagers, Elizabeth—even if we stopped before it got *too* far out of hand. But the timing and the circumstances were all wrong, and I continue to struggle with wondering how one of the most memorable experiences of my life could be the experience I regret the most. Twenty years and the consequences are still with me. I'd like to personally slap every arrogant teenager and force them to listen to what *I* had to learn the hard way. Whether you believe in God or not, whether you acknowledge a sin as a sin or not, the consequences come and they are *real*. For twenty years I have had to deal with difficult memories, and I have struggled with an inexplicable heartache and confusion, the combination of which has been *horrible*. And now, here we are. We're older and wiser, but we're still acting like children. We've even lived under the same roof with some ridiculous, invisible wall between us. We built it one brick at a time. It's full of shame and guilt and regret. Grief and heartache. And fear. Oh, there are so many bricks labeled fear. You see, I've been going to counseling. And I'm learning the hard way

that you have to look at life, feel it, face it, and deal with it. Like it
or not, you have been tangled into every aspect of my life for more
than twenty years, and we *will* talk about it."

He leaned closer still and asked in a husky whisper, "Do you
think I don't wonder what it would be like to just kiss you
again?" She looked up to meet his eyes, her face so close to his
that she could feel his breath. "Tell me," he said, "that you don't
wonder too."

She could hear a quavering in her own voice as she answered,
"Yes, I wonder, Jayson. But this intense attraction I feel is not
enough on which to base the commitment of a lifetime."

Jayson looked into her eyes and absorbed the fact that she'd just
admitted to being attracted to him, but the same old disclaimer
rang loud and clear. "I know," he said, "it's never enough. What I
have to give you is never enough."

"What makes you so sure?" she countered. "Maybe what you
have to give me is more than ample, but we're just not right for
each other."

"And maybe you're just afraid," he said. "Maybe what you feel
is so overpowering that it scares you, and rather than face the fear,
you run from it."

Elizabeth was startled at how his statement pierced her heart.
Had he just hit the nail on the head? Was that the reason she'd run
from him at the age of eighteen? Was that the biggest reason she
felt hesitant to get romantically involved with him now? Whether
or not it was true, at the moment she felt an insatiable need to just
be with him, to revel in his presence, and to give him whatever he
needed to get through this.

Seeing his expectant expression, she knew he was waiting for a
response. All she could come up with was a quiet, "Maybe." But it
made him smile, if only slightly.

Struck by her nearness, and the desperate, lonely ache he felt,
Jayson spoke close to her face. "On second thought, let's not talk
about it. I don't care if it's enough or not. Right now, I don't want

enough to last a lifetime, Elizabeth. I only want enough to get me through another day, another hour. I don't want it to be complicated with implications and assumptions. I just want to kiss you." He pressed a hand over her face and felt her take a sharp breath, but he sensed no resistance in her at the mention of his intentions, and he prayed he wouldn't regret it as he pressed his lips to hers and drew her fully into his arms. Her eager response urged him on while he marveled at the soothing effect she had on his battered emotions. The tangible evidence of her love for him filled the empty, aching hole inside of him, almost making him believe that he could survive the ordeal still left before him.

Following a lengthy kiss, Jayson drew back and looked into her eyes as they opened slowly. Their wistful quality enhanced the dreamy essence of the moment. She took his face into her hands and pressed her lips to his again. When their kiss ended, she nuzzled her face against his throat, murmuring softly, "What is this effect you have on me?"

"I thought it was the other way around," he said, pressing a kiss into her hair. "What is it about you that makes me feel as if I could be thoroughly at peace if I could only hold you this way every day of my life?"

Elizabeth looked up at him, noting the contrast in his expression as opposed to when she'd first come into the room. The strain was gone from his eyes. He was relaxed and calm. She pressed her fingers over his face, in awe of how deeply she loved him. She felt compelled to tell him that, but there was something more important she needed to say to him.

"Jayson," she said gently, "I love you, and I know you love me."

"But?" he said.

"No buts on that. However, I can't give you the peace you're looking for. I'm far from perfect, Jayson. I'm human. I'm capable of letting you down, as I have done in the past. There's only one source of peace that will never let you down."

She reached her hand beneath the open buttons of his shirt, and he caught his breath, then he looked down to see her holding the cross he'd always worn. "You've worn it for as long as I've known you; it's a symbol of Christianity, but if you really understood what Christ did, you would realize that the real gift He gave us didn't happen on the cross. It happened in the Garden. You claim to be a Christian, but do you really know what that means? As I see it, being a Christian is not just a matter of believing in what Christ did, but accepting it into our lives and making it a part of who and what we are. He paid the price, Jayson, not only for our sins, our mistakes, and our weaknesses, but for our sorrow, our grief, and our *pain*. There comes a point where we don't have to carry those burdens, if we will only give them to Him. He already endured the pain—all of it. I know it, Jayson. I know it's true beyond any shadow of a doubt." Her voice broke and tears rose in her eyes. "In a way, I'm only beginning to understand it myself; I have a long ways to go. But I have felt the peace in my heart, Jayson. I have struggled to come to terms with losing Robert and Bradley; I have struggled to understand. But through it all I have felt an underlying peace that no words can describe. It's so completely different from when we lost Derek. I miss them; the separation is so hard at times. But I know beyond any doubt that it was their time to go. I know their spirits live on. And my pain is tempered by perfect peace. You can have that peace too, Jayson. It's there for the asking. That's the only way you can ever fully heal."

"For the asking," he repeated, only slightly cynical.

"That's right," she said. "It's called the Atonement, Jayson, and it's—"

"I know what it's called," he said. "But you're right, I probably have no idea what it means. I believe God's hand has been in my life; I've had miracles. But being free of this pain just seems too impossible to believe. It's too real; too intense. Maybe I just have to accept that it's part of who and what I am, and I just have to learn to live with it."

"And maybe you don't," she said, putting her hands over his shoulders. "Just break the word down. *At-one-ment.* When you can be at one with God, you will find the peace you're seeking. And remember, I will always be praying for you."

"Then surely I will get through this."

"Surely you will," she said.

"Another kiss wouldn't hurt," he said with a little smirk. "I promise I won't try to read something into it and assume this means you'll want to marry me or something."

She gave him a sad smile. "You know, I might want to marry you . . . one day . . . if I knew it was the right thing to do."

"That's a big *if*."

"So, let's not worry about that now. Just kiss me," she said, and he did.

Twenty minutes later, Jayson watched Elizabeth leave the room. It was hard to see her go, knowing the reality that had to be faced in her absence was ugly and tedious, and he hated it. But he felt more calm, more capable of facing it.

The following day, Drew showed up for a counseling session, and Jayson hadn't even known he was coming. He'd flown into Salt Lake City that morning. He hugged Jayson tightly and told him in no uncertain terms that he would do anything to help him through this. The session was difficult, but not necessarily strained as they talked about the struggles they'd shared, their common grief, and the different ways they had responded to what life had dealt them. Jayson was in awe of Drew's declaration to Maren of how deeply he admired his brother; the drug addiction and the suicide attempt hadn't diminished his feelings in the slightest. He told Jayson that if he could conquer this, he would be all the more amazing in Drew's eyes.

Two days after Drew's visit, Maren ended a session with Jayson by saying, "Would you like to go home for Thanksgiving?"

"You mean I'm done?" he asked.

"No, but you can go home for a few hours for Thanksgiving dinner—if you want to. I think you can handle it. You've gotten past the anger."

"Now I'm just depressed," he admitted, not bothering to point out any of the other obvious facts. He was still shaky sometimes, and felt a longing for what he knew the drugs could do for him. He hadn't adjusted to the hovering pain inside of him that ached to be medicated.

"So, a visit home couldn't hurt in that regard, could it? What do you think?"

Jayson was surprised to realize that it was a difficult decision. He felt almost afraid to leave this place. As much as he hated it, he'd developed a comfortable routine where he didn't have to make any big decisions, and his boundaries were very clear. The day before Thanksgiving, he became distracted during a group therapy session by watching snow fall outside the window. He'd not seen snow since his youth in Montana. And it was beautiful. When the session was over, he stood at the window for a few minutes, noting the equalizing effect snow had. Everything was white. Everything looked the same. It was beautiful. He was startled to hear an attendant say, "You've got a phone call."

He walked down the hall to the phone and wasn't surprised to hear Will on the other end. "So, did you want me to come and get you for dinner? You don't want to miss what Elizabeth can do with a turkey. She's got a gift for making gravy, you know."

"Okay, you talked me into it," he said.

Little was said the following day during the drive to Elizabeth's home, but Jayson felt comfortable with Will. The sun shone from a gleaming blue sky, brilliantly illuminating yesterday's snowfall. The mountains to the east were breathtaking. Jayson had certainly noticed them before, but with his mind clear, they stood out more prominently.

Jayson was unexpectedly reminded of his mother when he walked into the house and the smells of Thanksgiving dinner struck his senses. In spite of limited finances throughout his youth, she had always managed to come up with a feast, while she'd strongly emphasized gratitude for all they had.

Elizabeth heard them come in from the garage and met Jayson with a hug. She wore a full-length homemade apron over jeans and a white turtleneck with little turkeys all over it.

"It's so good to have you home," she said and kissed his cheek. There was something about the way she said the word *home* that elicited a rise of tears. In the absence of his anger and the drugs, his high water table had returned. He hadn't decided if that was good or bad.

"It's good to be home," he said, and she wiped away his tears with a smile that indicated she was well-accustomed to his crying.

"You okay?" she asked.

"Yes, actually. I think I am. Is there something I can do to help?"

"Not at the moment. Just relax. They've been keeping you pretty busy over there. Enjoy some down time."

"I'll do that," he said.

Jayson wandered into the front room and stood beside the piano. He stared at the keys with a deep longing, but he couldn't bring himself to touch them. When he knew that his left hand would refuse to respond the way he wanted it to, trying to play only depressed him. Where music had once eased his pain, now the pain he carried had become such an integral part of him that he feared it would only contaminate the music—even if he could play. His eyes were drawn upward to the painting of Christ. Jayson stared at it for several minutes, contemplating the penetrating blue eyes looking back at him. His mind recounted the things Elizabeth had told him about the Atonement, and he wondered if it were true. Did such a miracle truly exist for *him* with all his weaknesses and shortcomings? Was it truly possible to be free of the pain he carried inside of him? Desperately longing for that very thing, he figured it couldn't hurt to try. *It's there for the asking,* Elizabeth had said. But it couldn't be that easy. Surely it would take time—and faith. The question, then, was if he could come up with enough faith.

In a whisper he heard himself say, "Are you really there? Is it really true? If so, I beg you to take this pain from me. Help me to go on, help me understand."

Hearing someone approach, he ceased his verbal prayer and turned to see Trevin. "Hey there, kid," Jayson said brightly. "It's good to see you. How are you doing?"

"Okay," Trevin said in his usual somber tone, and Jayson's heart ached for him. Jayson knew what it was like to be a kid and lose a father, even though he'd lost his to alcoholism rather than death. But he wondered how he might have coped if he'd lost Drew as well. Drew had been his best and only friend throughout most of his youth. While Jayson was wishing there was something he could say or do to make a difference, Trevin added, "Mom says it's time to wash up for dinner."

"Thank you," Jayson said. "I'll be there in a minute."

Trevin walked away. Jayson looked up once more into the eyes of the Savior, praying in his heart that he could be among the saved.

* * *

Thanksgiving dinner tasted so good to Jayson that he realized how bad the food was at the rehab center. Not horrible, but certainly not like this. He told Elizabeth three times what an amazing cook she was, then he insisted on helping wash the dishes.

While Will went to the basement with the children, Jayson worked on washing the last pan, and Elizabeth wiped off the counters. "Oh, it's always nice to have the kitchen clean after a big meal," she said.

"Especially such a meal as that," he said. "How many days have you been working on it?"

"Just today," she said with a little laugh, "although I did bake the pies last night."

"Pie? There's pie?"

"Of course. But the rule is that we don't get dessert until the kitchen is clean."

"As if I could eat dessert at the moment," he said.

Elizabeth finished what she was doing and took the clean pan from Jayson to dry it with a dish towel while he rinsed out the sink. "Wow," she said, "how many women get the privilege of having a famous rock star washing dishes in their kitchen?"

"Well, I know you *did* have a famous rock star washing dishes in your kitchen in Phoenix at least once, but all you get today is me."

"It was always you," she said.

"That all depends on how you look at it," he said. "I used to be tabloid fodder, now I'm nothing."

"I used to be tabloid fodder, too," she said, "but only because I hung around with you. Am I nothing now too?"

"No, of course not."

"Well, listen to yourself, Jayson. Am I supposed to convince you that you're not 'nothing'? Because if you think you are, there's nothing I can say to convince you otherwise. We've had this conversation before, or at least some form of it. You are the same man you were more than twenty years ago when I first fell in love with you. Rock star might have been temporary. Musician is not. Jayson Wolfe is eternal." She softened her voice. "You're not 'nothing,' you're a child of God, and He loves you."

She walked out of the kitchen as if to end the discussion on that note. Jayson absorbed what she'd said, then hung the dishrag over the tap and followed her down the stairs. In the basement they found Will and the kids digging out the Christmas lights. Jayson spent the next hour on the roof helping Will put them up, then he had some pie before it was time to go back.

Elizabeth drove him back to the city while Will stayed with the children. After miles of silence, she said, "You will be spending Christmas with us, won't you?"

"I don't know. I hadn't thought about it. Maybe I'll still be in prison."

"I don't think so," she said. "Maren gave me the impression it wouldn't be too much longer." She turned to look at him for a long moment, then turned her attention back to the road. "We really would like you to stay for Christmas. You can stay indefinitely, if you like."

Jayson wanted to suggest that if they were married, that would be a feasible option. But under the circumstances, he felt he had to say, "I need to go home eventually."

"But not right away," she said. "Maren said it would be good for you not to be alone until you adjust more fully. And you'll be doing some outpatient counseling for a while. So, you'll just have to stay through the holidays at least."

"I suppose I will," he said. "And you're very gracious; your hospitality is touching. But I don't want you to feel obligated to keep me around just because—"

"We want you there, Jayson," she said firmly.

"We?"

"All of us. The children like you; they've both asked if you'll be here for Christmas."

"They hardly know me."

"They like you," she repeated firmly.

Jayson smiled. "I like them too."

"Then you'll stay?"

"I'd like that very much," he said. "Provided they let me out, we'll plan on it."

"Good." She smiled brightly. "We'll look forward to it."

Returning to the facility was even more difficult for Jayson than he'd anticipated, but spending time at Elizabeth's home had wrought a remarkable change in him. He wanted to get out of here. He wanted to put this behind him and not only be with Elizabeth and her family for Christmas, but for all of the holiday preparations that he'd gotten a little taste of in putting up the lights. Christmas had been so meaningless since Macy left, and even worse without his mother. And Drew would be with friends. The idea of sharing the holiday with these people he loved was terribly inviting.

The following day Maren gave Jayson a projected release date of December eleventh. She told him he was doing well, and barring any setbacks, she felt confident that he would be ready to make it on his own and stay drug-free. Jayson appreciated her faith in him, and for the most part he agreed with her. But he continued to be plagued with a hovering pain that seemed to be a conglomeration of each of the losses he'd endured in his life. He couldn't even think about certain things without being plagued with uncomfortable thoughts and feelings. He wanted them to go away, mostly because at some level they frightened him. At times he couldn't help wondering what he might do when he ended up back in LA, living alone, and still dealing with such impulses. Would he lose his resolve and turn back to the drugs? He talked to Maren about his fears, and she simply said, "If you prepare yourself for your worst fear, then you'll know ahead how to handle it. Picture yourself in the condo in LA. You're missing Macy, worried about her. You're missing your mother, Elizabeth, Drew. The music is doing nothing for you. You seriously consider taking some pills. You have a bottle of Lortab in the medicine chest. What are you going to do instead? It's the middle of the night; you're completely alone."

The scene she described evoked a tangible fear inside of him, but he was surprised at how easily the answer came to his lips. "I'm going to call Will or Elizabeth, and I'm going to tell them the truth." Maren just smiled.

She told him a few days later that she'd talked to Elizabeth and had arranged for him to have another outing. Jayson felt sixteen all over again as he anticipated the day she was coming to pick him up. He had no idea what her plans were; he didn't care. He was going to be out of this place for a number of hours, and he would be with Elizabeth. And this excursion marked one week until he would be released. The reality of having such an enormous milestone behind him filled him with unmistakable hope. If only he could be free of the pain!

Jayson couldn't hold back a little laugh when he saw Elizabeth. She laughed as well and gave him a quick kiss that reminded him of the days they'd been dating in high school. Was that the present state of their relationship? Dating with no definite, long-term commitment? He could live with that.

In the car she held his hand while she drove. "Where are we going?" he asked.

"Well, I thought it might be better to stay close and not waste precious time on the road. There is something I'd like to show you; it's one of the big tourist attractions in the city. So, I figured you should see it—if only so you can say that you have."

"Okay," he said. "What is it?"

"It's a surprise," she said with laughter, and he laughed with her. It felt so good to laugh.

They drove into the heart of the city, and she turned into a multilevel parking garage. She parked the car, reached into the backseat for her purse, and then handed him a long scarf in a dark plaid and some black gloves. "What are these for?" he asked.

"I should think it's obvious. We're going to be outside part of the time, and it's cold. These are on loan from my father."

"Okay," he said, putting them on while she did the same with her own.

They walked outside, down the block and across the street into a beautiful high-rise building. It was old but well kept, and Elizabeth told him, "This used to be a hotel. Now it's called the Joseph Smith Memorial Building, and it has many purposes."

"Who is that?" he asked, pointing at a large statue to their left as they crossed a wide, beautiful lobby.

"Joseph Smith," she said as if he should have known.

They got into an elevator and went to the top, where she announced, "I'm starving. You have to buy me lunch. It's kind of expensive. Can you afford it?"

"I'll see if I can scrape it together," he said with a chuckle.

Before they went into the restaurant, Elizabeth took him to a huge window at the end of the hall, and Jayson caught his breath at the view. "That's Temple Square," she said. Pointing out the huge spired building with a little gold statue on top of it, she added, "That's the temple. The pioneers spent forty years building it."

"Incredible," he said and added with sincerity, "It's beautiful. What's that?" He pointed to an oval, domed building.

"That's the Tabernacle. It's home to the Mormon Tabernacle Choir."

"Of course," he said.

"The acoustics in that building are incredible. You would be impressed."

He made a noise of interest, then said, "So, is this what I needed to see so that I could say I had?"

"Well, you need to see the temple up close, but . . . no. This isn't the highlight of the tour. After we eat we'll go down to the Square and wander around."

Jayson enjoyed the meal they shared, especially since they didn't talk at all about counseling or grief or drug addiction. When they'd finished eating, they went back down the elevator and out a different door where they wandered through some beautiful grounds east of the temple. They stood by a little pool and looked up at the magnificent edifice, then they turned around and she pointed out the high-rise that was the Church office building. He'd never imagined a church needing that many offices. They moved farther north where she pointed out what was called the Conference Center across the street, then they entered Temple Square through the north gate and went into a building that she called the North Visitors' Center. She seemed to be headed somewhere specific as she took his hand and led him past some paintings and displays, paying them no mind. They started walking up a wide circular ramp, then all of a sudden it came into view. Jayson slowed his pace as his focus lifted to the huge, magnificent statue of Christ, His arms outstretched.

"It's incredible," he murmured as they moved to stand directly facing the statue.

"It's called the *Christus,*" she said. "I thought you might like it."

"Oh yes," he said distantly. He was more preoccupied with the way standing there made him feel.

Elizabeth watched Jayson's expression as he took in the glory of the *Christus.* He looked like a child seeing snow for the first time, his eyes wide, full of innocence and awe. The visible effect was so touching that she felt near tears. She prayed in her heart that he would be even more affected within, that he would be able to come to understand and accept the miracle of all that Christ stood for and to allow its healing power to purge his battered spirit.

When it became evident they were in the way of some people wanting to take pictures, Elizabeth urged Jayson back several paces, where they sat close together on a bench, and she kept his hand in hers.

Jayson watched as a family gathered and posed in front of the statue for a picture. He counted seven children, the youngest around Addie's age, and the oldest a girl who looked like she was in high school. He watched her closely for a long minute, missing Macy so much that his heart threatened to break wide open. The antics of the children distracted him, and he couldn't hold back a little laugh as the father teased them while he tried to get them into position and to hold still, with their mother in the middle. When the father moved back to take the picture, Elizabeth stood and approached him, saying, "Here, let me take it, so you can be in the picture too."

"Oh, thank you," the man said with a smile and showed her how to use the camera.

Jayson watched as he moved to stand beside his wife, giving her a quick kiss before he turned to look at the camera. Elizabeth took two shots, then gave the camera back. As she sat next to Jayson, he said, "What a beautiful family."

"Yes, they are."

"How do you get a family like that?" he asked.

"You have lots of babies," she said, and they both chuckled.

"No, but . . . look at them. They practically glow." Just as he said it, two of the younger children started arguing and the mother had to break it up, provoking another chuckle from Jayson and Elizabeth.

"They're probably *Mormons,*" she said facetiously.

"Probably," he said, not finding the humor in it. "But how do you get a family like that?"

"I don't know," she said. "Why don't you ask them?"

Jayson stood up and moved toward the father, mostly hoping to embarrass Elizabeth, since he was certain she'd been joking. "Excuse me," Jayson said, "but . . . I couldn't help noticing what a beautiful family you have. What's your secret?"

The man chuckled comfortably and said, "I think my wife covered the beautiful part." He tossed her a loving glance while she was oblivious to anything but trying to keep the youngest under control. "We were married in the Salt Lake Temple twenty years ago last week. Bringing the family here is part two of our anniversary celebration."

"Congratulations, then," Jayson said and walked back to sit beside Elizabeth.

"What did he say?" she asked.

"He said he stole the children from the North Pole."

Elizabeth laughed and playfully slugged him in the shoulder. He laughed with her and pressed a kiss to her brow. Then his attention was drawn again to the *Christus.* He felt reluctant to leave and was relieved that Elizabeth seemed content to just sit with her hand in his, gazing upward with him while he pondered all he was feeling. People came and went, some posing for pictures, some just gazing. He became distracted by a girl who looked to be about seventeen, he guessed. Good heavens, he thought, Macy would be seventeen by now. He'd missed so much of her life—if she were even still alive. He told himself she had to be. She just had to be! Watching this young woman, who was apparently alone, standing before the statue for several minutes, he suddenly missed Macy so intensely he wanted to curl up and sob. The pain was tangible, intense, excruciating. He hung his head and discreetly wiped tears from his face.

"What's wrong?" Elizabeth asked softly.

"Macy," he muttered. "Why doesn't she call me? Where is she?"

Elizabeth put an arm around him while she produced with her other hand his cell phone to show him that she carried it. "She'll call," she said gently.

Jayson wanted to believe her, but it felt so utterly hopeless. He looked up at the statue and prayed silently with all the energy of his soul, *Please keep her safe and strong. Please bring her home to me. I'll do anything if you just bring her home to me. I will give you the rest of my life, Lord. I'll do anything you ask of me, just give me back my baby.*

While they sat in silence for several minutes longer, the thought occurred to him that for the moment the best thing he could do for God—and himself—was to get through rehab and stop being a burden to the people around him.

Elizabeth broke the silence by saying, "It's not true, you know."

"What's not true?" he asked, wondering if he'd missed something.

"What you said about forever; it's not true."

"I have no idea what you're talking about."

"In one of your songs, on the second CD. You said, 'nothing lasts forever.'" She imitated the way he'd sung it.

"I did say that, didn't I."

"It's not true," she repeated. "There *is* a forever, Jayson."

He looked into her sparkling eyes and said, "Are you going to tell me about it?"

"Maybe someday," she said and turned her eyes back to the image of Christ.

They finally stood up, took another long look at the statue, then started down the ramp. They moved slowly past some of the displays in the downstairs lobby, then back outside. It was dark now and they moved through the Square, which was lit up for Christmas with thousands of little colored lights. They went into the Tabernacle, then saw the temple up close from the other side, and Jayson had to admit he was impressed with the fact that pioneers had built these remarkable edifices, having very little to work with.

Jayson hated going back to the rehab center, but he fought to hold with him the glimmer of peace he'd felt while facing the image of Christ. Throughout the next day he felt as if he were in some kind of fog, as if he were perhaps supposed to understand something he didn't understand. He went to dinner as usual, but as he moved across the room to sit down, his eye was drawn to something he'd seen there every day since he'd first come, but he'd given it no attention; he'd not wanted anything to do with it. But now the little spinet piano called to him. While he ate he couldn't keep his eyes off of it. He knew he could do very little with his left hand, but suddenly that didn't feel like a detriment, but rather a challenge.

Sizing up the situation, he realized he was kept far too busy to have time to play the piano in the midst of all else that he was required to do and attend. He concluded that the best time to do it would be in the night, when everyone else was asleep. And fortunately, this room was a significant distance from the dorms where everyone slept. There were people on night duty, but he just had to placate them a little, and since he was well-known as a non-troublemaker, he figured he could win them over.

Jayson went to bed thinking about the piano, then his mind drifted to the image of Christ he had seen at Temple Square. The peace he'd felt then came back to him, and with it he fell asleep. He woke up in the dark, realizing his plan to stay awake and play the piano had been foiled by falling asleep. He glanced at the clock. 4:42. He still had time. He hurried to get dressed and went quietly through the halls to the room of his destination. He flipped on the light and moved stealthily toward the instrument with a kind of reverence. "Hello, my friend," he said, lifting the cover off of the keys. He sat on the bench and felt his heart quicken with a combination of fear and excitement. He concentrated on the song he'd been hearing in his head, something that had germinated from standing on Temple Square, listening to Christmas music. With his right hand he quickly picked out the melody, hearing himself laugh as he heard music come through his fingers. He worked out a variety of embellishments on the melody, and without even thinking he lifted his left hand onto the keys to play. He stopped abruptly when it wouldn't respond the way his mind told it to. Then the thought occurred to him that all that was really needed to give the song some depth was a very simple bass-line. Surely he could get his fingers—as stiff as they were—to play a two-note sequence over and over. He tried it. It worked. He laughed and kept working at it for a few minutes until it was coming naturally, fluidly. Then he put his right hand into the mix, and music filled the room, but more importantly, it filled his soul. He went through the song three or four times, finding a pattern to his rendition of "O Little Town of Bethlehem." He heard himself singing when he'd not premeditated doing so. The words came out softly, timidly at first. Then with all the energy of his soul, he closed his eyes and lifted his face heavenward, singing the final phrase of the first verse—the only verse he knew. *The hopes and fears of all the years are met in thee tonight.*

Jayson stopped abruptly and took in the contrasting silence around him. And that's when he felt it. A discernible warmth rushed into him, as clearly as if a warm wind had come from nowhere to take his breath away. The peace he'd felt earlier suddenly magnified tenfold, consuming him with a perfect hope and serenity that he'd never imagined possible. He felt as if he could take on the world. He felt capable of overcoming any obstacle in his path. He felt completely devoid of pain. And that was the key. He knew he was capable and strong, because he knew he wasn't alone. He was at one with the Creator of heaven and earth, the Savior of the world; *his* Savior. He laughed through a rush of warm tears and basked in the reality of the sensation filling his heart and soul, then he put his hands on the keyboard—and he played. He played, he sang, he wept. Only through music could he fully express his joy. Only through this gift that God had given him could he articulate his gratitude to God.

He finished the song and sat quietly basking in the peace that echoed through the silence. He looked at his left hand; he opened and closed it, attempting to ease some of the stiffness. He felt angry with himself for not having done the therapy exercises all this time, but he determined that he could start now, and he would do whatever it took to restore it to its full capacity. He simply wouldn't stand for anything less.

While Jayson sat there, another Christmas carol came to his mind; one of his favorites. "Hark! The Herald Angels Sing." He picked it out with his right hand, then worked it into a lush embellishment that just seemed to flow right through him, as if the music came from a source outside himself and he was merely the conduit with enough training and experience to make it happen. Again he used his left hand only enough to give it some depth with some repetitive low notes, while what he played with his right hand almost had the effect of an intricate music box.

Jayson was startled to catch movement in the room. He stopped playing and turned to see a couple of staff members standing in the room, watching him, their expressions pleasant. A quick glance in the other direction told him the sun was coming up; the day was beginning.

"Oh, don't stop," one of them said. "It was beautiful. It would be nice to work to music for a change."

Jayson knew the regime here was strict, for employees as well as residents. He knew he wasn't where he was supposed to be, but he felt compelled to heed their request and said, "Well, then, you'd better keep working, or they'll kick me out."

They both chuckled and began preparing the room for breakfast. Jayson was vaguely aware of the room slowly filling with people, mostly other patients. He just kept playing, trying not to let his audience distract him. He played the same two songs over and over, but nobody seemed to notice. He finally stopped, if only to try to ease the ache in his left hand. He was met with cheers and applause. He turned on the bench and chuckled, saying, "Sorry, I don't know many Christmas songs."

"Oh, there're some right here," a woman said, shooing him off the bench. She opened it and quickly produced a book of Christmas carols.

"So there are," Jayson said. He wasn't terribly fond of playing from a book, but taking a long glance at his small audience, he felt compelled to do so. He'd experienced endless hours of horrific group therapy with many of these people. Some of them had been on hard drugs for so long their brains were fried. He'd seen many of them break down and sob inconsolably; he'd heard many of them scream and swear and throw violent fits. Of course, he'd done all the same things—but he'd managed to keep it corralled into his private sessions. But looking at these people now, they all looked mesmerized, perfectly calm, yet expectantly eager to hear him play something else. Breakfast was being served, but no one seemed interested in the food.

"Okay, well," he said, putting the book in front of him, "let's see what we can do. The left hand isn't working very well, but we'll give it a try."

He picked out the melody for "Away in a Manger," then when he had a feel for it he started over, making it more fluid. He played it twice, then moved on to "What Child Is This?" And then he did a fair rendition of "Sleigh Ride."

The expected intrusion by a staff member came, urging everyone to eat breakfast while they had a chance. But Jayson kept playing and was relieved when no one told him he couldn't. He was asked by a couple of people if he was hungry and wanted to eat, but he politely declined. This was feeding him far more than whatever they were serving for breakfast ever could. He was aware of people finishing their meal and then gathering around him again. Beginning to feel terribly conspicuous, Jayson said, halfway through "Jingle Bells," "Okay, guys, if you want me to keep playing, I think you need to sing. I'm not a one-man band, you know."

He got some chuckles, then a couple of brave voices began to sing, and the others gradually joined in. Jayson smiled and decided that maybe he *was* a one-man band, considering that he'd lost everyone else in the band—and his family. But maybe that was okay. At least it was for the moment. He was making these people smile—and sing. He eased into playing "Silent Night," and he felt hard-pressed not to cry as he realized a room full of dysfunctional drug addicts were singing about one of the greatest miracles that had ever occurred—the birth of the Savior of mankind. Did they feel the peace and the hope that he felt? Did they comprehend that what they were singing about was real? That it was the only thing capable of truly rescuing them from the pits they had dug themselves into?

When Jayson finished the song, he wasn't surprised to hear one of the assistant administrators say in a subtly harsh voice, "Okay, I think that's good. We all have job assignments or therapy sessions we should be in and—"

"That won't be necessary," a different voice said, and Jayson turned in the other direction to see *the* administrator of the place, sitting among the patients. In a gentle voice she added, "I think this is the best therapy we've *all* had in a long time." She motioned toward Jayson with her hand. "Please . . . go on. Let us know when you need a break."

"I'm fine," Jayson said.

"Play the one you were playing when we came in earlier," a gruff male voice said. "The really pretty one."

Jayson assumed he meant the one that had come out sounding like a music box. He began to play "Hark! The Herald Angels Sing," which was far too intricate for anyone to sing along to, but the patients clearly enjoyed it. He moved into one song after another that they could sing, and he wondered why he'd not been able to play this way before now. He was using his left hand very little and was managing just fine. Perhaps it was because he'd always tried to play music that he'd already learned with both hands. And now he was playing music he'd not played for years, and in a completely different way; some of it he'd never played before, so he had no predetermined notion of how it should sound.

It was nearly lunchtime before Jayson finally declared that he was exhausted. His left hand ached like it hadn't for months. But he got a standing ovation, and he got several hugs and hand-shakes as he moved away from the piano. He'd spent weeks in this place, and he'd suddenly made new friends. There would have been a time when he might have been irritated at people only liking him when they learned he had some talent. But he felt differently now. He recognized the ability his gift had to reach beyond the normal barriers of human judgment and caution.

The following day the administrator asked Jayson if he would be willing to play during lunch for the remaining days of his stay. He eagerly agreed. He called Elizabeth and told her nothing about what was happening. He just asked her to call Drew and have a significant number of CDs shipped to him overnight. When they arrived, Jayson got a list from Maren of every resident and staff member, and he personalized and autographed a CD for every person there. He did a few extras with his signature for any newcomers that might arrive in the next few days.

With his Christmas gifts for his new friends tucked away and ready to give out, he looked out the window and watched the snow fall, smiling to himself as he anticipated going home—and being able to take this newfound peace with him.

CHAPTER 3

Elizabeth was chopping vegetables for a salad when an unfamiliar noise startled her. She stared at Jayson's phone, where it was charging on the kitchen counter, realizing she'd only heard it ring once before, when Drew had called weeks ago. Drew had called many times since, but he'd called her home number. She'd carried Jayson's phone with her diligently for weeks, never letting it out of her sight, just as she'd promised him. And now it was ringing. She told herself it could be a wrong number or a telemarketing computer that had randomly dialed this phone. The caller ID gave no information. She grabbed it and pushed the ON button. "Jayson Wolfe's phone," she said and heard nothing. "Hello?"

"Who's this?" a female voice asked, and Elizabeth's heart quickened. Could it really be the call Jayson had been anticipating for more than two years?

"This is Jayson's friend, Elizabeth. May I help you?"

The voice on the other end cracked with emotion as she asked, "Where's my dad?"

"Macy? Is that you?"

"Yes, but . . . where's my dad?"

"He's just not available for a few days, but—"

"Why do you have his phone?" she asked.

"He made me promise that I would keep it with me twenty-four hours a day, just in case you called. He's been hoping and praying to hear from you."

"He has?" she asked with a ring of hope.

"He has," Elizabeth echoed firmly. "Do you remember me, Macy?"

"Dad talked about you a lot," she said. "I know you've been friends for a long time. Didn't I come to your house in Arizona a couple of times?"

"That's right," Elizabeth said. "Macy, honey . . . do you need help? Is there something I can do to help you?"

Following a long pause, she asked again, "Where's my dad?"

"He's in the hospital. It's a long story, but he's fine. He just needs to stay there a few more days. I can tell you all about it later. Right now I just want to know what I can do to help you. Anything, Macy. Anything."

The following silence was riddled with sniffling on the other end of the phone. Elizabeth uttered a silent prayer, then said, "If you were talking to your dad, what would you say, Macy?"

"I want to come home," she answered right away. "But I don't even know where he's living now."

"Your dad's been staying with my family, Macy. Would you like to come and stay here as well?"

"Where is that exactly?" she asked.

"Utah . . . a little place called Highland, to be exact. Where are you?"

"I'm in San Francisco."

Elizabeth breathed some relief; she was talking, and her location wasn't terribly far out of reach. Her first thought was to tell Macy she'd buy her bus or plane fare over the phone and meet her when she arrived, but a different thought crowded into her mind. "Do you want me to come and get you?"

Sobbing came through the phone, intermixed with the broken words, "I'm so scared."

"Okay, Macy, tell me why you're scared and—"

"The phone's going to cut off. It's a payphone. I don't have any more money, and—"

"Tell me the number, quickly, and I'll call you back."

Macy said the number, but Elizabeth still felt panicked about breaking the connection. She immediately dialed the number from her home phone and felt deeply relieved to hear Macy answer it. "Okay," Elizabeth said, "now tell me why you're scared, and then we'll decide what to do to fix the problem."

For the next forty-five minutes, Elizabeth listened to the recounting of Macy leaving home with her boyfriend, Cory, and their various jobs and apartments. But the experiences were spattered with evidence that Cory was abusive and cruel. Together Macy and Elizabeth formulated a plan, taking into consideration Cory's work schedule and Macy's available resources.

"Okay," Elizabeth said, "I'm going to hang up and call right now to arrange the flights. I'll call you back at your apartment with the details in an hour and—"

"Elizabeth," Macy interrupted. "There's one more thing you have to know, and you might change your mind."

"What is it, Macy?"

"I'm pregnant." She started to cry again while Elizabeth squeezed her eyes closed. "He wanted me to get an abortion, but I couldn't do it. I'm afraid he'll hurt me . . . or the baby."

"It's okay, Macy. I'm going to come and get you, and Cory will never find you. When we get you safely home, we'll talk about what to do. Everything will be all right, I promise."

"Do you think my dad will be mad at me?"

"Honey, your dad is going to be so happy to see you that I don't think he'll care. He loves you, Macy."

"I know," she muttered and sniffled loudly. "And I was so awful."

"It's okay. Everybody makes mistakes; everybody has rough times. We'll work it out. I promise."

"Okay." She sniffled again. "You'll call me in an hour?"

"I will. I promise."

Elizabeth got off the phone and got right back on, ignoring her dinner preparations. While she was on hold with the travel agent her father walked into the kitchen from doing errands. She put her hand over the phone long enough to say, "Macy called. She's in trouble and needs help. She's in San Francisco and—"

"Well, you've got to go and get her," Will said firmly. "I'll take care of everything here."

"I knew you would," she said and kissed his cheek. "I'm getting the airline tickets now."

Elizabeth made the arrangements quickly and called Macy back at the apartment where she was living with Cory and two other guys. Three hours later, Elizabeth was on a flight to San Francisco. She arrived and rented a car and drove to the hotel where she'd reserved a room. After getting four hours of sleep, she found the address Macy had given her. Before she got out of the car, she called Macy from her cell phone to make certain all was clear. Cory and his friends had all gone to work, and Macy was packed and ready to go. Elizabeth got out of the car and headed up the outdoor steps to the second story. When she got to the landing, Macy was standing there, a suitcase at her feet and a couple of bags over her shoulders. She looked thin and pale, and her long, dark hair looked more stringy than curly. Her well-rounded belly made it evident she was probably about ready to deliver. Her eyes looked scared. Still, she looked so much like her father.

"Hello, Macy," Elizabeth said and opened her arms. The girl dropped her bags and fell, sobbing, into Elizabeth's embrace. "It's going to be alright," Elizabeth said, putting a motherly hand to the back of her head while she held her. "I'm going to take you home with me, and everything's going to be alright."

"We'd better go," Macy said as if fear suddenly overrode all her other emotions. Elizabeth picked up the suitcase and one of the other bags and led the way to the car. While they were putting the bags in the trunk, Macy kept looking around nervously. In the car, she asked Elizabeth to drive around for a while and be certain they weren't being followed. When she was assured that they weren't, they went to the airport and checked in Macy's luggage. They shared a meal without having much to say between them, then wandered around a short while before they boarded the plane to Salt Lake City. In the gift shop, Elizabeth said, "Go ahead and get yourself a book . . . or a magazine. A candy bar if you like. Anything you want."

Macy looked confused and surprised. She picked out a magazine and got a little bag of M&M's. Once they were off the ground, Macy said, "I don't know why you're being so nice to me. You hardly know me."

"Your father's like family to me, Macy. I'm happy to do anything I can to help you." She took hold of Macy's hand and added, "He made me promise that if you called, I would do whatever I had to in order to help you. I told him that short of engaging in any criminal activity, I would do that. I'm just keeping my promise to him."

Macy gave a sad smile and looked away. "I've missed him so much."

"He's missed you, too."

As if she'd just remembered, she looked up with concern and asked, "Why is he in the hospital? You said it was a long story."

"Yes, but . . . I'll give you the short version. I know he'd want me to be honest with you, even though I know he feels embarrassed over the whole thing. He's been struggling with depression on and off for several months." She wondered if she should tell Elizabeth about her grandmother's death, but she figured it would be better coming from Jayson. She went on to say, "He always managed to keep a handle on it with his music, then he injured his left hand; a freak accident, really. He just . . . fell on it, tore some ligaments or something to that effect. It needed surgery; the recovery was painful, but worse . . . he couldn't play the guitar or the piano." Macy sighed loudly as if she knew how difficult that would be for him. "We invited him to come and stay with us when we realized that he was really struggling." She left out the suicide incident. "When he got there, he admitted that he had a drug problem and—"

"What?" she interrupted, astonished. "Why in the world would he—"

"Now, let me clarify. I'm talking about prescription drugs, Macy. Not—"

"Oh," she said, obviously relieved—just as Elizabeth had been when her first suspicions had been clarified.

"It was a combination of painkillers, tranquilizers, and anti-depressants. It just got out of hand. So he checked himself into rehab—but only when I promised that I would keep his phone with me every minute."

Macy blew out a long breath. "He really loves me."

"He really does."

"I knew my leaving would hurt him, but . . . I didn't know what else to do."

"Believe it or not, I think he understands," Elizabeth said. "But yes . . . it did hurt him, and he's worried terribly." She smiled. "Which means that seeing you again is going to make him a very happy man."

Macy smiled sadly, then looked down. "Until he realizes how messed up my life is."

"I think he'll understand," Elizabeth said. "He's in drug rehab, Macy. I think the two of you will be able to work everything out."

During the remainder of the flight, Macy didn't open her magazine at all. Instead she posed one question after another about Elizabeth's history with her father, their high school days, and the way they'd kept in touch over the years. She asked what had happened in her father's life since she'd left home, and she talked a little more of her own experiences, with a great deal of regret. When the plane landed in Salt Lake City, she became visibly nervous, but Elizabeth assured her that everything would be fine, and she'd have a couple of days to get settled in before her father came home.

"Don't tell him yet," Macy said. "If you talk to him . . . or did you already? Does he know?"

"I haven't talked to him since you called. My father is at home with my children. We agreed that it would be better for him to wait until he got out to know that you were back."

Macy was visibly relieved. She commented on the mountains, just as her father had many times, and she asked questions about the Mormons when she saw a billboard on the freeway advertising BYU football. Elizabeth told her a little bit about the religion and that she was a member. Macy said little but seemed more interested than concerned.

As they approached home, Elizabeth marveled at the timing and silently thanked God for answering Jayson's most fervent prayers. It was truly a miracle.

* * *

Jayson got permission to make a phone call in order to arrange his going home in a couple of days. He called the house, and Will answered. He mentioned his purpose, and Will said, "I've got an appointment with a client, but I know Elizabeth is planning to come and get you. It's all arranged."

"Great," Jayson said. "I don't need to tell you how anxious I am to get out of here."

"Not as anxious as we are to see you, I'd bet."

"That's debatable. Is Elizabeth around?"

"Actually," Will said, "she went out of town for a couple of days. It was kind of an unexpected, last-minute thing. She needed to help a friend."

"Oh," Jayson said, unable to hide his disappointment. "Okay, well . . . I'll try not to be deflated to know I'm not the only friend she goes out of her way to help." Will just chuckled. "So, tell her I called. And I guess I'll see her in a couple of days."

"I'll tell her."

Jayson got off the phone and went to one of his last group sessions. He concluded firmly that he was not going to miss it. After dinner he spoke privately with one of the administrators and asked that his CDs be delivered to all of the patients and staff, according to the names he had on them—but not until after he'd gone. She eagerly agreed and assured him that the gifts would be greatly appreciated. Secretly, Jayson couldn't help but think of the times he'd been told that his music had given people hope and encouragement. And if anybody needed that, it was these people. He truly hoped the music might make a positive difference in their lives—even if he no longer had star status.

With that taken care of, Jayson began counting the hours until his release and anticipating Christmas as he'd not done for years. Surely this holiday season would be memorable.

* * *

Elizabeth helped Macy settle into a spare bedroom upstairs that was used as a guest room, which had a private bathroom. Macy was quiet and overly humble, as if she'd suffered so much that she'd grown to appreciate even the smallest things. She seemed subtly nervous as she met Will and the children and shared a meal with them. Then Elizabeth suggested she take a bath and relax. Macy got a little teary and admitted that her apartment had only had a shower, and she'd not actually taken a bath for a very long time.

The following day Elizabeth took Macy to a doctor to be certain that all was well. Macy was uncertain about a due date, but the doctor estimated from the size of the baby that it was likely due the first week of January. When the doctor asked Macy some routine questions, the visit suddenly became very traumatic. Elizabeth held Macy's hand while she cried and talked of some events that made her behavior of the past make so much sense.

The doctor was gentle and reassuring, and she privately told Elizabeth that it would be good to get Macy into some counseling. Elizabeth agreed and was relieved that Macy was able to calm down and that she seemed fine once they left the office.

After the appointment, Elizabeth took Macy out to lunch, watching the way she seemed in awe of eating in a moderate restaurant. And this was a girl who had spent most of her youth as the daughter of a very wealthy man. Halfway through the meal, Elizabeth said, "If you don't want to talk to me about it, that's okay, but I can't help wondering what your plans are after you have the baby."

"I have no idea," she admitted with an emotional chuckle. Then tears rose in her eyes. "I don't feel ready to be a mother. I just feel scared."

Elizabeth hoped she wouldn't come across as pushy when she added, "Maybe you're not ready. Maybe it would be better for you and the baby if you gave it a home elsewhere."

She was relieved when Macy said, "I've thought about that; I've thought about it a lot. But I feel guilty every time I think of giving it away."

"Allowing your child to be raised by people who have been longing for a baby for years is a very wise and noble choice, Macy. There's nothing to feel guilty about. It would give you a chance to start over, and it would give this child a good, solid family to grow up in."

Macy's eyes brightened as Elizabeth went on about the possibilities. She assured Macy that the decision needed to be hers, but it needed to be an educated decision, and they could arrange to talk with some people at LDS Family Services who could help educate them and support her in whatever she decided to do. Macy eagerly agreed to meet with them. It seemed her instincts had been strong all along about not being ready to have a baby, and she was well prepared emotionally to let it go, of her own free will. She'd simply needed some validation and encouragement. Elizabeth felt deeply relieved, knowing that such a choice would be best for everyone involved—however difficult it might be.

After lunch, Elizabeth took Macy shopping. The clothes she'd seen the girl wearing were pathetic, and she wasn't well-equipped for the Utah weather. While they were picking out a number of different things, Macy said, "You shouldn't be spending money on me."

"Oh, don't worry," she said. "Your dad will pay me back. And he can afford it."

Macy laughed softly and said, "I can't wait to see him."

"I can't wait to see the look on his face when he realizes you're back."

They laughed together and talked about the best way to let him know.

Back at the house, Macy took a nap, then Elizabeth got her involved in helping the children make sugar cookies in Christmas shapes. They talked about plans for Christmas, while Macy became emotional. Elizabeth didn't ask what was wrong. She just put her arms around her and let her cry. She wondered if it was just the pregnancy and the trauma, or if she'd inherited her father's high water table.

Later, Elizabeth found Macy toying a little with the piano. "I didn't know you played," she said.

"Oh, I don't really," Macy said. "I had some lessons when I was a kid, but I didn't stick with it." She chuckled softly. "No musical gifts here." Her expression became sad. "I never told Dad how much his music meant to me, and how proud I was to be his daughter. He's amazing, you know."

"Yes, I know. I'm sure he'll love to hear how you feel when you see him tomorrow."

Macy looked away, seeming embarrassed, then her eye was drawn to Elizabeth's family portrait. She looked at it a long moment, then said, "What happened to them? Your husband and son. Where are they?"

"They were both killed in a drowning accident," Elizabeth said, surprised at how she was able to say it without being assaulted with emotion.

"Oh, I'm so sorry," Macy said.

They talked for a while longer, then Macy went to bed early and was barely up the next morning when Elizabeth left to get Jayson. Driving the freeway, Elizabeth listened to one of her favorite Christmas CDs and cried a few tears. It was going to be a beautiful Christmas. They had much reason to celebrate.

* * *

The night before Jayson's release, all evening activities in the hospital were superseded by a repeat of the Christmas sing-along that had occurred spontaneously some days earlier. Cookies and eggnog were added to the festivities, although there were many jokes going around about how the eggnog would taste better if it were spiked. Jayson didn't appreciate the humor, but he just focused on playing music that lifted their spirits.

Alone in his room, Jayson pondered how far he had come, and how greatly blessed he felt. He removed the chain from around his neck that held the little silver cross he'd worn since his early youth. Elizabeth had been right, he thought, pondering it with his fingers. The real miracle hadn't happened on the cross; it had happened in the Garden. And Jayson knew beyond any doubt that what had happened there was real. He had felt the miracle in his own heart and soul. He set the cross on the bedside table, never to pick it up again. Then he went to bed deeply gratified with his experiences in this place—and immensely grateful to be leaving.

* * *

When Elizabeth pulled up in front of the rehab center, Jayson walked out the door with his luggage. She got out to open the back of the Tahoe for him to put his bags there.

"Anxious?" she asked.

"You have no idea," he said and closed the door before he hugged her and lifted her off the ground, laughing as he did. "Oh, it's good to see you—and to be free."

"In more ways than one," she said and laughed as well.

Jayson opened the driver-side door for her and she got in, then he walked around and got in on the passenger side. She asked him what he'd done with the CDs Drew had sent, and he told her, but he omitted telling her anything about the music he'd been playing. He preferred to surprise her at the right moment with his version of a couple of great Christmas songs.

Elizabeth talked a little about their plans for Christmas as she pulled onto the freeway. When a lull of silence fell between them, she figured this was the right moment. She'd contemplated how many times Jayson had told her that he'd been waiting so long to hear Macy's voice over the phone, that he wondered how it might feel when he did. Macy had agreed that they should give him that experience.

Elizabeth pulled his cell phone out of her purse and handed it to him. "Would you call the house?" she said casually.

"Who do you need to talk to?" he asked, pushing the speed dial for her number.

"Nobody. But there's somebody *you* need to talk to." She smirked and added, "We have a surprise for you."

"Really," he said skeptically, wondering what silly thing they might have cooked up. "It's busy," he said and hung up.

Elizabeth wondered how that could be possible when they had call waiting and their call was being expected.

"A surprise, eh?" he said. "You didn't tie yellow ribbons all over the place, did you?"

"No yellow ribbons; sorry. I didn't think you'd want the neighbors asking about them."

"Good point. So . . . did you bake a cake, or something?"

"Nothing so domestic, I'm afraid. Although Dad's planning your favorite for dinner."

"Chicken enchiladas?"

"That's right."

"I love his chicken enchiladas."

"So do I, but that's not the surprise."

"So what is it?"

"If I told you, it wouldn't be a surprise. But I promise it's a really great surprise." She laughed. "It's going to make you smile."

"I can't wait," he said.

"Try again." She motioned to the phone with her hand. "We have call waiting. It can't be busy for long."

Jayson pushed the redial and put the phone to his ear while Elizabeth's heart quickened painfully. She knew that Macy was well prepared, knowing what she should look for on the caller ID. She watched Jayson as closely as she dared while she continued to drive.

Jayson heard the phone ringing just as he recalled that Will had said he had an appointment during this time. Trevin would be in school, and Addie wouldn't have been left home alone. So why was he calling the house? And then he heard an intensely familiar voice on the other end of the phone say, "Hi, Dad."

"Macy?" Jayson squeaked and abruptly reached for Elizabeth's hand while he pressed the phone closer to his ear, fearing it had deceived him.

"Yeah, it's me," she said, her voice tinged with emotion.

"Oh!" he said and made a noise that was a combination of sobbing and laughter. "Where are you?"

Macy laughed softly. "You called me, Dad. I'm at Elizabeth's house."

Jayson shot Elizabeth an astonished glare, wondering how long she'd been holding out on him. She just smiled with tears in her eyes and held his hand more tightly. "Are you okay?" Jayson asked, squeezing his eyes closed to more fully accept that this was not a dream. Tears trickled down his face, and Elizabeth let go of his hand to give him a tissue.

"I'm fine. I mean . . . my life's a mess, but . . . I'm okay . . . now."

"Oh, baby," he cried, not even trying to hide his emotion, "I can't believe it. I've missed you so much."

"I've missed you too, Dad," she said tearfully. "I'm so sorry."

"It's okay, baby. You're back now, and everything's going to be okay."

"Yeah, I think it is," she said. "So . . . why don't you just hurry home and we'll talk some more, okay?"

"Okay," he said and wiped his tears before taking Elizabeth's hand again. "But . . . how did you get there?"

"Elizabeth flew to San Francisco and got me," she said, and Jayson looked at her again, stunned beyond words. What had Will said? *She'd gone out of town for a couple of days. It was kind of an unexpected, last-minute thing. She needed to help a friend.* "She can tell you everything; I told her it might be better if she did."

"Okay," he said. "I'll see you in a while, then."

"I'll be counting the minutes," she said.

"Yeah, me too." He chuckled through his tears and reluctantly ended the call. With the phone in his hand, he pressed his forearm over his eyes as a burst of emotion overtook him.

Elizabeth had expected Jayson to be emotional over the news, but when he began to sob so hard he was gasping for breath, she pulled over to the side of the freeway, put the car into PARK, and pulled him into her arms.

"It's okay, Jayson," she murmured, pressing her hand to the back of his head.

"I know," he muttered through his tears. "That's just it. It's okay. She really came back. She's really okay. I just can't believe it. God truly does answer prayers, Elizabeth. He does!"

"I know He does," she said, and he cried some more.

A minute later he calmed down enough to say, "What if I wasn't here? What if I had taken those pills . . . and died? What would she do?"

"We've been blessed with many miracles, Jayson," she said.

He sat up straight and wiped his face with his sleeve. "Oh," he laughed, "I can't believe it." Then he turned toward her with a glare that was only partly humorous. "How long has she been there? How long have you known?"

Jayson realized as he asked the question that it couldn't have been too long; she'd only been out of town a couple of days ago. She quickly told him what had happened and when.

"Okay, drive," he said with a little laugh. "I want to see her."

"There's one more thing I need to tell you before I drive," she said, thinking this might be better said face-to-face.

"Okay," he said with hesitance, wondering what horrible thing they hadn't told him yet. Did she have some disease or illness? Was she in trouble with the law?

"She's pregnant, Jayson," Elizabeth said. *"Very* pregnant."

Jayson took a deep breath as a mixture of emotions settled into him. He figured there could be worse things to deal with, but it certainly posed some big concerns. His gratitude to have her in his care deepened as he wondered what had brought her to this end. For the millionth time he thought of the atrocities she might have dealt with and felt a little sick. The possibilities of how this pregnancy might have come about made him nauseous. He wondered if she'd been raped or coerced, or if she had willingly made a choice that had left her unwed and pregnant. But if being pregnant had prompted her to finally make the call that brought her home, he couldn't resent it.

"How is she?" he asked quietly.

"Physically, she's fine. I took her to a doctor yesterday to make certain all was well. They figure it's due the first week of January."

"That soon?" he asked, and she nodded. "Did she tell you anything about . . . how it happened?"

Elizabeth repeated what Macy had told him, pulling back out onto the freeway as she talked. When she had nothing more to say, Jayson pondered all he'd heard and let it settle in. Trying to look at the positive aspects of this, he said, "Well, it looks like we're going to have a baby." He thought of how desperately he'd wanted more children, almost as soon as Macy had been born. And how devastated he'd been when he learned there would be no more. The idea of having a grandchild to help care for had a definite appeal, in spite of the circumstances. "I guess that's not so bad. It might be nice to have a baby around." Elizabeth looked so stunned by his comment that he had to say, "What?"

"I think you need to talk to Macy before you set your heart on that."

"What do you mean?" he asked. She hesitated, and he added, "She said you would tell me everything."

"She doesn't want to keep the baby, Jayson."

He was so stunned he didn't know how to respond. Only one thought stood out prominently enough to get to his tongue. "That's my grandchild!"

"It's the child of a seventeen-year-old girl who is not married!"

"What did you say to her?" he asked hotly. "This needs to be her decision. You can't tell my daughter to—"

"If you'll calm down and listen to me, I'll tell you what I said to her. I simply asked her what her plans were after she had the baby, and she told me she wasn't ready to be a mother. She said she'd been feeling all along that she shouldn't keep it, but she felt guilty for feeling that she didn't want her baby. I told her it was a wise and noble choice to allow her baby to be raised by people who desperately wanted a baby, and would be good parents. I told her it needed to be her decision, and it needed to be an educated decision, and I offered to take her to a place that deals with unwanted pregnancies. They will give her some counseling, and she can decide what to do and do it for the right reasons. You can't raise this baby for her, Jayson. You can't use this baby to make up for the children you didn't have." He looked at her sharply, wondering how she had read his mind so accurately. Her voice softened as she added, "Your desire to keep the baby is understandable. It is a part of you—and her. But it's also the child of some creep who had her scared out of her mind and treated her like dirt. Macy's desire to give this baby a good home is selfless and mature. You need to admire that, not make her feel guilty for it."

Jayson squeezed his eyes closed, deeply grateful that this had come up *now*, and not in front of Macy. "Okay, point taken," he said. "You're right, and . . . I'm sorry."

"It's alright." She took his hand. "This is a lot to take in. And you haven't even quite stepped back into the real world yet."

Jayson turned to look at her. "Oh, but my daughter is back. Whatever we have to face, we can face it together. I don't have to wonder any longer. Do you have any idea what that means to me?"

Elizabeth smiled at him. "Yes, I think I do."

Jayson pressed her hand to his lips. "Thank you for being there for her. You actually went to San Francisco to get her."

"I was glad to do it," she said. "It really wasn't that big of a deal."

"It's a big deal to me," he said. "Obviously it was a big deal to Macy." He quieted his voice and said, "Debbie would have told her to get on a bus, and she *might* have paid for the ticket."

"Well," Elizabeth said, "I think we established a long time ago that Debbie is a fool."

"Why is that?"

She met his eyes and smiled. "She gave up a beautiful family."

Jayson was relieved to realize they were getting off the freeway, and they were less than ten minutes from home. When they finally pulled into the garage, he suddenly felt so nervous he was almost shaking.

"We'll get the luggage later," Elizabeth said and led the way into the house.

Jayson stepped into the kitchen and caught his breath to actually see Macy standing there. She'd changed very little beyond the absence of all the horrible makeup and jewelry she'd been wearing the last time he saw her. And she looked thinner, despite the pregnancy that was noticeably evident.

"Hi, Dad," she said, almost looking scared.

"Oh, my baby," he muttered and wrapped her in his arms, unable to keep from crying. He was grateful for the burst of emotion he'd gotten out of his system in the car that kept him from completely falling apart now. Macy held tightly to him and cried as well. He took her face into his hands and laughed through his tears. "Oh, look at you! So beautiful!"

Macy laughed softly, then cried harder and clung to him again. "I love you, Dad," she murmured. "I'm so sorry."

"I love you too, baby," he said. "And everything's going to be okay. We're together now, and everything's alright."

Wiping at her tears she said, "I'm pregnant, Dad," as if he might not have noticed.

"I can see that," he said, briefly setting a hand over her well-rounded belly. "It doesn't matter, baby. We'll do whatever we have to do to get through it."

The relief in her expression was so immediate and so evident that Jayson couldn't do anything but pull her into his arms again, holding her the way he'd dreamed of doing for more than two years, while she cried against his chest. "I love you, baby," he said, and she cried harder, holding to him more tightly. He just returned her embrace, silently thanking God for granting him the miracle he'd been praying for since the day she'd left. He caught Elizabeth's gaze over the top of Macy's head, and the compassion in her eyes meant more to him than he could ever tell her.

Jayson and Macy went to the front room and sat close together on the couch while Elizabeth did some work, giving them time together. Jayson held his daughter's hand and listened to her version of the story Elizabeth had told him. While they were attempting to catch up on all that had happened in her absence, Jayson had to tell her that her grandmother had passed away.

"I know," she said sadly.

"You know?" he asked. "How could you possibly know?"

"Cory's grandmother told him she'd seen the obituary; she sent me a copy of it from the newspaper."

"Wait a minute . . . Cory had contact with his family?"

"All the time," she said and became emotional. "But he wouldn't let me call you or Mom. He told me my family would cause problems for us."

Jayson let out a frustrated groan. "Did his family know you were a minor, a runaway?"

"Probably; they didn't care. They're all as bad as he is."

Jayson attempted to suppress his anger and frustration. While he'd spent more than two years in anguish over her whereabouts, she'd been living with a manipulative, emotionally abusive creep. He wanted to go hunt the guy down and belt him, the way he'd had it out with his own father when he was sixteen. He knew, however, that no amount of anger would fix anything. He reminded himself that Macy was home now, and she was safe. But he couldn't help wondering, as he'd always wondered, what it was that had changed her. What had drawn her to such an idiot? To such a lifestyle? Had he wronged her somehow as a father? Had his own lifestyle exposed her to something that had planted these seeds of destruction? He wanted to ask, but felt it would be better to save such a discussion for another time. Instead he just put his arms around her and let her cry, murmuring gently, "It's okay, baby. Everything's going to be okay now."

Elizabeth went to get Addie at preschool, and when she returned, the child ran to hug Jayson. He laughed and lifted her off the ground. "Thank you for all the beautiful pictures you sent me," he said.

"You told me that when you came for Thanksgiving," she said.

"Well, I wanted to thank you again. They really helped me feel better."

"Are you going to stay home now?"

"For a while," he said.

Elizabeth urged them to the kitchen for some soup and sandwiches, insisting that Macy needed to eat. They shared a comfortable lunch, then Jayson and Macy went back to their conversation in the front room. She asked about his mother's death and the funeral, and they both cried as he told her how difficult it had been. She asked about the drug rehab, and he told her the simplified version, feeling as if he'd found a new friend who seemed to understand him completely, and accept him without judgment.

He asked her what had finally compelled her to call him. With new tears in her eyes, she said, "I'd been wanting to call you for a long time. I mean . . . things weren't too bad for a while. But after I got pregnant, I kept telling him I should call you and get some help. But he actually frightened me. He threatened me. I started praying. I've never prayed much, even though you had taught me to. But I remembered that you'd always told me to say a prayer if I was afraid or feeling alone. So I started praying . . . a lot. I knew he didn't want the baby, and I was afraid of what he might do after it was born. Anyway, I was driving his car to work. It's not very often I was in the car alone, but . . . a song came on the radio." She smiled through a fresh surge of tears. "It was you," she said. "And it was like you were singing just to me. And I knew that I needed to call you, and that I would be able to come home if I did."

"What song was it?" he asked, knowing there were a few big hits that would still get some radio play.

"'Only My Baby Knows,'" she said, and his heart quickened.

"They *never* play that on the radio."

"I know," she said tearfully.

"I wrote that song for you."

"I know," she said again and hugged him tightly. "It was a miracle, Dad. That song reminded me that you love me and that I needed to come home."

Jayson held her close and absorbed the miracle into himself. His little girl had come home. His brain and body were free of those horrible drugs, and he was home—at least it was home for the time being. And he was grateful. He silently expressed his gratitude to God, then laughed for no reason except that he was feeling completely happy.

CHAPTER 4

Jayson sat at the dinner table with Mozie at his side. Watching Will and Elizabeth interact with Macy, he felt so perfectly happy he wanted to jump out of his chair and shout for joy. After dinner, Macy said she wasn't feeling very well, and she went to bed early. Jayson felt a little panicked until Elizabeth assured him that she was more than eight months pregnant, and she was entitled to feel miserable and exhausted. She'd seen a doctor, and everything was fine. She then reminded him of something he would have preferred avoiding.

"I think you need to call Debbie. If Macy was with Debbie, you would want her to call you."

"Maybe Macy should call her mother."

"I asked her earlier if she wanted to call her, and she didn't. She doesn't want to talk to her."

"Well, I don't want to talk to her, either."

"Yes, but you're the grownup." She took his cell phone off his belt clip and handed it to him. "You're the one who has to do the things you don't like to do."

"How profound," he said with sarcasm. He found Debbie's number in the phone's memory and dialed it. "Maybe I'll get lucky and she won't even be . . ."

"Hello," Debbie said on the other end of the phone.

"Debbie," he said.

"Jayson?"

"Yeah, it's me," he said, and Elizabeth moved away, as if to give him privacy, but he grabbed her arm and urged her to remain for moral support.

"How are you?" Debbie asked.

"I'm good. How are you?"

"The same," she said. "So what's up? I assume you didn't call me just to shoot the breeze."

"No, that's true. I thought you should know that Macy is with me."

He heard her gasp, then she swore as an expression of shock, and he winced. He wondered when she'd started using the really bad words. Apparently she was still hanging around with punk rockers—or the equivalent. "Is she alright?"

"She's fine—relatively speaking."

"Well, tell me what happened."

"She called my cell phone from San Francisco. Her boyfriend—who is an emotionally abusive, manipulative jerk—had her scared out of her mind. He'd threatened her all along against calling us, but she finally got up the courage. I was actually in the hospital when she called, but Elizabeth went to get her."

"Why were you in the hospital?" she asked with what seemed genuine concern.

"It was nothing," he said. "I'm fine now. The important thing is that Macy is here and she's safe."

"Well, when can I see her? I want to—"

"We're staying in Utah, actually. I'm not sure when we'll come back to LA."

"What are you doing in Utah?"

"I'm staying with Will and Elizabeth. We'll be staying through the holidays at least."

"Well, I want to see Macy," she said, beginning to sound like her old demanding self.

"Then you'll have to come to Utah," Jayson said calmly. "Macy's not going very far until after the baby comes."

There was a long pause before she said, "Please tell me I heard you wrong."

"I didn't stutter. Our daughter is pregnant . . . due in less than a month."

"Why, that little—"

"Don't you dare say it," Jayson interrupted. "If you take this conversation into hypocrisy, I will hang up on you. I assume it's okay to do that kind of thing as long you don't get pregnant."

Debbie ignored him and said, "I suppose it's too late for her to get an abortion."

Jayson winced and swallowed his anger. Instead he put his arm around Elizabeth and absorbed the soothing effect she had on him. "Yes," he said with forced calm, "it's too late for her to get an abortion." Elizabeth gasped softly. "I'm sure if she was prone to do something so thoroughly horrible, she would have done it a long time ago. I'm not going to discuss this with you, okay? I wanted to let you know she's with me and she's alright."

"Well, let me talk to her," she said as if she wasn't certain whether or not she believed him.

"She's asleep," he said. "I'll have her call you tomorrow, but only if you promise you will not get angry with her, and you will not tell her what you think she should have done. She's back and she's safe, and we need to keep perspective here."

"Okay, fine," she said. "Thanks for calling."

Jayson hung up the phone and said with sarcasm, "That was even more pleasant than I'd anticipated."

"She really said that about an abortion?"

"She really did." He shook his head. "I wonder sometimes what happened to the woman I married. It just amazes me. I mean . . . we had our problems; it wasn't perfect. But . . . I just cannot believe how thoroughly . . . *horrible* she can be." He shuddered.

Elizabeth laughed softly and said, "It's good to have you home."

"You keep calling it home; this isn't *my* home, you know. I'm company."

"For the time being, it *is* your home. You're family. My home will always be your home."

He sighed deeply. "Well, I'm grateful. And yes, it's good to be home."

Their eyes met, and he wanted to kiss her, but he decided against it, figuring they didn't need any more complications in their lives right now. Not certain how she'd respond, he felt it was safest to just not do it.

"Oh, by the way," Elizabeth said, "you owe me money. And lots of it."

"I probably do," he said with a chuckle. "For what exactly?"

"Plane tickets, rental car, maternity clothes, doctor appointment. Lunch was on me."

"Lunch?"

"I took her out to lunch. That was on me."

Jayson smiled. "And how much for your services?"

"My services are free and given with pleasure. But I'm a single mother. I can't afford to do all that traveling and shopping on my budget."

"I told you before that you could have all of my money if you want it."

"I don't want all of it. You just have to pay me back."

"Tell me how much, and I'll write you a check."

"Ooh," she said, "then I'd have Jayson Wolfe's autograph."

"No, you would have a check," he said. "Did you want to frame it or cash it?"

"I don't know. I'll have to think about it," she said, and he laughed.

Jayson slept well that night without the use of any medication whatsoever. His daughter was safe beneath the same roof, and he was home. The following morning he woke to the smell of bacon and realized it was Saturday. Will always cooked breakfast on

Saturday. He went to the kitchen to find Will cooking and Macy sitting at the table with her feet up on another chair. Mozie was sitting at her side. "Hi, Dad," she said brightly. "I'm not as lazy as I look. I offered to help, but he wouldn't let me. He ordered me to put my feet up, so I'm just doing what I'm told."

"Good girl," Jayson said, kissing her brow. "How are you feeling?"

"Fat," she said, "but not so bad. How are you?"

"I'm great," he said. "Where's Elizabeth and the kids?"

"They went to Wal-Mart actually," Will said. "We overlooked the fact that Trevin has a birthday party this afternoon, and we didn't have a gift. She was planning on going anyway, and just decided to make it early. Addie went along for new shoes."

"Oh, that reminds me," Macy said. "I got new shoes too—and some clothes. You owe Elizabeth some big bucks, Dad."

"She's already informed me," he said with a chuckle. "Don't worry. I'll pay her back. But she said lunch was on her." Macy smiled, as if lunch was a pleasant memory. Jayson couldn't help thinking that perhaps it was an added blessing to have Elizabeth involved in Macy's return. Her mother wouldn't be much good, but Macy needed a woman.

The doorbell rang, and Jayson said, "I'll get it." He opened the door to see a woman he recognized as living in the neighborhood, but he couldn't recall her name.

"Oh, hi," she said, pushing a pie into his hands. "I'd heard you were home from the hospital. I asked Elizabeth if you liked pie. She said you loved pie. I asked her what flavor, and she said you love them all. So here's an apple pie. It's my mother's recipe. I hope you enjoy it. Are you feeling better?"

"I am. Thank you," he said, wondering what Elizabeth had told people. "And thank you for the pie. That's very kind of you."

She smiled and walked away. Jayson closed the door and realized the pie was still warm. He carried it into the kitchen. "The neighbors brought us a pie," he said, genuinely puzzled. He couldn't recall a neighbor ever bringing anything to his home in his entire life.

"Oh, isn't that nice," Will said as Jayson set it on the counter. "You should have seen the food that came in when we lost Bradley and Robert. It was incredible. And then when Elizabeth was sick a few months ago, they did the same thing."

"Elizabeth was sick?"

"Just the flu; but it was a nasty one. And they took good care of us."

"They?" Jayson asked.

"The Relief Society."

"I'm sorry," Jayson said.

"It's the women's organization of the Church. They just do stuff like that; help each other out."

"Wow. That's awesome," Macy said. "And that pie smells heavenly. Is it legal to eat pie before breakfast? I'm starving."

"Have at it," Jayson said, setting it in front of her. He got a couple of plates and forks and a knife and pie server and sat down beside her. "Hey, Will, how about some hot pie before we have bacon and eggs? It smells pretty good."

"You talked me into it," he said and sat down as well.

While they were eating, Jayson said, "Did I ever tell you what we used to do when we'd order pie at the diner where my mom worked?"

"I don't believe you did," Will said, and Jayson told the story of their pie switching, which made Will and Macy laugh.

When they'd finished their pie, they went right into eating breakfast and were just finishing up when Elizabeth came home with the children, and Jayson helped Will put breakfast on for them, even though the children had eaten cereal before the shopping trip.

After breakfast was cleaned up, Will said he was going to the grocery store for a major shopping trip, and he needed Trevin to come along to push an extra shopping cart. Addie insisted she was going, too. Elizabeth said, "Oh, I love it when he does the grocery shopping. I hate grocery shopping."

"Would you like to come along, little lady?" Will asked Macy. "I could use a woman's opinion, I'm sure. And you could let me know some things you like so we can have them on hand."

Macy looked at her father as if for permission. He shrugged and said, "You're a big girl. Go if you want."

Macy looked pleased, and Elizabeth said, "The doctor did tell you to walk as much as possible. It will be good for you."

Jayson pulled some money out of his wallet and handed it to Macy. "Here, get me some Cheetos or something, and don't let Will pay for all the snack food we need to stock up on."

"Thanks, Dad," she said and kissed his cheek.

A few minutes after Will left with Macy and the children, Jayson found Elizabeth in the kitchen doing some advance preparations for Sunday dinner. "Hey there, gorgeous," he said. She turned around and comically looked in both directions. He chuckled and added, "Yes, I mean you."

"Did you need something?" she asked.

"Yes. Since we're actually alone in the house, I wanted to tell you something. And then I have a little present for you."

"For me?" she said with exaggerated drama.

Jayson chuckled and took her hand, leading her to the front room. He sat her down on the piano bench, then he straddled it to face her. He looked above her head at the painting of Jesus, then he looked into her eyes. He took her hand into his and said, "I just wanted you to know that what you told me was true."

"What?" she asked, and he saw intrigue in her eyes.

He glanced again at the painting, then at her. "He *did* take the pain away, Elizabeth. It didn't happen the way I'd expected it to, and it took some time. But it happened. I can't explain it. I only know that the pain is gone, and I know that He is the reason."

Elizabeth smiled with tears in her eyes and put a hand to his face. "Oh, Jayson," she said. "Now I understand."

"Understand what?"

"That . . . sparkle you have in your eyes. It's significantly different from the glazed-over-with-drugs look, or that lost-in-shock-and-pain look." She sighed and smiled. "It's like the real you is back."

"Or maybe the real me was never really here until now," he said.

She laughed and threw her arms around him. Then the buzzer on the stove rang, and she rushed from the room. Jayson waited only a minute before he turned around on the bench and put his fingers on the keys. He smiled as it only took a few notes to realize the stark difference in quality and sound on this piano, as opposed to the one at rehab. He closed his eyes to feel the music warm him as it filled the air around him. He quite liked his music box version of "Hark! The Herald Angels Sing," and he hoped Elizabeth would like it too.

Elizabeth pulled the pan out of the oven and set the hot pads down. She was turning the oven off when she heard lilting piano music from the other room. It was a Christmas song, intricate and melodic. Her first thought was that Jayson had put a CD into the stereo, although she couldn't recall ever hearing that rendition before. He was the only one in the house, and he'd not touched the piano since . . . "Oh, good heavens," she muttered under her breath and hurried back to the front room. She stopped in the hall when he came into view, seated at the piano, playing with all the fluid ease and splendor he was known for. She leaned against the wall and put a hand over her heart. *It was a miracle!*

Once she'd recovered from the shock, she moved slowly closer, wanting to see his face. She sat quietly on the couch while his eyes were closed. She noticed that what his left hand played was simple and repetitive, which explained how he was managing when she knew his hand still needed a great deal of therapy. But meshed with what he played with his right hand, no one would ever imagine there was a problem. She focused on the perfect serenity in his expression. He opened his eyes and watched the keys for a moment before he saw her sitting there. He smiled at her and continued to play. After the song had come to a graceful end, he moved his hands from the keys, looked directly at her, and said, "Merry Christmas."

He stood when she did, and she moved into his arms, hugging him tightly. "Oh, Jayson, it's a miracle."

"Yes, I think it is," he said, looking into her eyes. "I don't know if the peace came with the music, or the music came with the peace. I only know that a great healing took place inside of me."

Again she took his face into her hands, saying simply, "I can see that."

He smiled and added, "I never thought I could be so happy. I've never been so happy."

"Never?"

He shrugged. "Some moments with you and Derek and Drew stand out in my mind, or when Macy was little, but even then I didn't feel what I feel now."

"Life is far from perfect, Jayson," she said with a cautious voice, as if he might not have noticed.

"I know it's far from perfect," he said. "My daughter is unwed and pregnant, my hand hurts like . . . the devil," he said with a chuckle as he purposely corrected himself from cussing. More seriously he added, "And eventually I will probably have to go back to LA and face what might be left of my life there." He saw something sad in her eyes when he said the last. His deepest wish was that she wouldn't want him to leave, that they could make a future together. But he wasn't going to push for that, and he wasn't going to count on it. Still, he had to admit, "Whatever happens, Elizabeth, I know I can be happy."

Elizabeth felt momentarily taken aback, not only by his words, but by the conviction behind them. She realized then that for as long as she'd known him—and known that he loved her—there had always been a certain desperation in him, as if he had needed *her* in order to be happy. The feeling hadn't been there through the years of his marriage, and then hers. But since Robert's death she had felt it from him, as if his love for her was so consuming that he couldn't live without her. She couldn't help wondering if that had, at some level, contributed to her fear of being fully committed to him. Perhaps she'd feared that if he was too dependent on her, she would inevitably let him down. But now there was a new light shining in his eyes, and he was able to admit that he didn't need her—or anyone else—to be healthy and happy. He'd come to learn what she had learned for herself, that having a relationship with God above all else put life into perspective. It didn't take away the struggles or the heartache, but it buffered them and made them bearable.

Not knowing what to say that wouldn't detract from the mood, she simply said, "Will you play it again?"

"I think I could do that," he said.

"I have to check something in the kitchen, but I'll be right back."

Jayson began the song again, and Elizabeth let the music fill her as she stirred the sauce that had been left simmering on the stove; then she moved it off the burner. She heard the doorbell ring, but Jayson kept playing. The chime was actually closer to the kitchen, and she felt sure that he'd not heard it ring. She answered the door to see Sister Gibson from across the street, holding a plate of cookies. With a grin she said, "They're still warm. I hope he's home so he can enjoy them while they're warm. You did say he likes warm cookies."

"He certainly does," Elizabeth said, opening the door wider.

"Oh, what beautiful music!" she said, stepping inside. "You must tell me what it is so I can go and buy it."

"I'm afraid that's not possible," Elizabeth said, motioning for Sister Gibson to follow her. She knew that Jayson would likely prefer to keep his talents a secret, but she felt secretly delighted at tattling on him this way.

Standing in the hall, they had a perfect view of Jayson's back as he played. Sister Gibson gasped softly, then she whispered, "Why, he's very good."

"Yes, he is," Elizabeth said.

"He's not a member, is he," she said with some disappointment.

"No, he's not."

"That's too bad. We sure have trouble keeping a good pianist for the choir."

Elizabeth smiled to herself, imagining Jayson Wolfe playing piano for the ward choir.

Jayson finished his song and was startled to hear an unfamiliar voice say from behind him, "Oh, that was beautiful."

"Thank you," he said as he turned, tossing a subtle glare at Elizabeth, who was smirking.

"Sister Gibson brought you some cookies," she said as he stood.

"I heard you were coming home from the hospital. I asked Elizabeth what your favorite dessert might be, and she said you love warm cookies." She held the plate out, and Jayson took it.

"Thank you," he said. "That was very sweet of you."

"Are you feeling better?" she asked.

"I am, thank you," he said, not certain how he should feel about all this care and concern.

"You really do a lovely job with the piano. Do you have a degree in music?"

"Uh . . . no," he said. "I'm afraid I didn't have the fortitude to go to college."

She looked surprised, but more intrigued than concerned. "So where did you learn to play like that . . . if you don't mind my asking?"

Jayson hesitated, not certain how to answer. Elizabeth piped in and said, "He had some lessons as a kid, and then he just . . . took off."

"A natural, eh?" Sister Gibson said with a wink.

"It would seem so," Elizabeth said.

After Sister Gibson had gone, Jayson said, "Warm cookies? Homemade pie? What did you tell these people?"

"I told the ones that asked about you the truth—just like you told me to."

Jayson sighed. "So I did. Does that mean the whole neighborhood knows I was in drug rehab?"

"I only told a few people, but word spreads. They're all concerned. They just want to help out."

"You might as well just call *The Enquirer.*"

"Oh, I don't think the tabloids would want to bring you warm cookies." Jayson chuckled, and she handed him one. "Eat it while it's warm. You'll feel better."

"I feel just fine. I just don't want everybody knowing I was in rehab."

Elizabeth lowered her voice to mimic what he'd told her. "'I don't care what anybody thinks. I don't care what you tell them.'"

He sighed with disgust. "Okay, point taken. But next time you need to answer the door while I'm playing, warn me."

"What fun would there be in that?" she asked and took a big bite out of the cookie in his hand.

The following day Jayson got up and went to church with the family. Macy declined going, saying she preferred to rest. Of course, she'd never been to church in her life. Elizabeth felt certain that Jayson's biggest reason for going was simply to be polite by showing respect to her family's beliefs, since he was a part of the household. He went to Primary with her, although now that the program was over, the regime was a lot different. Still, he sat at the back of the room through both junior and senior Primary, smirking at her occasionally while she led the music. She wondered what he might be thinking concerning all he was hearing and seeing, but she had no desire to ask him. While she was deeply grateful that he had gained a testimony of the Atonement and had felt its healing balm in his

life, she felt relatively certain that he would never embrace orga-
nized religion—especially this one. His prejudice was deep, and
he'd always held firmly to the belief that he could have a relationship with God without religion.

On their way out of the building after meetings, an elderly lady
stopped Jayson with a hand on his arm and said in a quiet voice,
"It's good to see you back, young man. Are you feeling better?"

"Much better, thank you," he said.

Elizabeth gave him a subtle smirk before the woman leaned
closer and whispered, "You poor dear. I went through that very
same thing when I had my hip replacement."

"What thing?" he asked.

"Why, getting addicted to those awful drugs. Isn't it a wonder
how much better you can feel when you get them out of your
head?"

"Yes, it certainly is," he said, actually finding some comfort in
her validation.

She smiled at him as she walked away.

In the car, Elizabeth asked, "What did she whisper to you?"
Jayson told her, and she said, "Oh, that's sweet."

"Much sweeter than what I was told in Sunday School," Will
said. "I'm not going to tell you who said it, but I figure you ought
to know what's being said. After all, the two of you have been in
tabloids. Surely you can handle a little gossip."

"What did they say?" Elizabeth demanded.

Will gave her, then Jayson, a cautious glance before he said, "A
well-meaning gentleman told me I was a brave man to let a long-
haired drug addict live in the same home with my daughter and
grandchildren."

Will chuckled, but Jayson and Elizabeth exchanged a concerned
glance. "Now, there's some sweet gossip for the sake of concern,"
Jayson said with sarcasm. "Are all Mormons that judgmental?"

"No, they are not!" Elizabeth said. "And calling Mormons
judgmental sounds awfully judgmental to me. This church has

dysfunctional people, just like every other religion in the world. I'm certain every congregation—Mormon or otherwise—has people who are rude or judgmental. But the core of the gospel is good, and most of the members of the Church are too—or at least they're trying to be."

More humbly Jayson said, "Well, I'm sorry if my being here causes problems. If you think I should—"

"It's not causing any problems," Will insisted. "I told him what I'll tell anybody else who has anything negative to say. I said you were as good as my son, and I was proud of you for the positive changes you'd made in your life; that you were a good man and you always had been, and my daughter and grandchildren were all the better off for having you in our home."

"You didn't have to say that," Jayson said.

"I didn't say it to be patronizing, Jayson. I said it because it's how I feel; because it's true."

"I like your long hair," Addie said, which added some comic relief.

"I like it, too," Elizabeth said. "Jayson has pretty hair, doesn't he."

"Yeah," Addie giggled, "Jayson has pretty hair."

Jayson told himself not to let the opinion of one person bother him, but it did. He didn't so much care what people thought of him, but he didn't want his being here to be a problem for these people he cared about so deeply. He was distracted from the issue when they arrived home and he checked on Macy to find her upset. Apparently she had spoken with her mother while they'd been gone, and Debbie had not kept her promise to Jayson. She'd been critical and harsh.

"It doesn't matter what she said, baby. I don't know why she has to be that way, but her attitude isn't about you; it's about her. She's the one with the problem."

"But my life is so messed up," Macy cried. "I've done so many stupid things."

"We all do stupid things, baby. You're talking to a man who just got out of rehab."

She laughed through her tears and hugged him more tightly. He figured his temporary drug addiction might have been worth it if it gave his daughter a reason to feel better about herself.

Macy perked up, but she was quiet during dinner. Then while Jayson was helping Will wash the dishes, he realized that Elizabeth and Macy were both missing. He went to look for them and found Elizabeth's bedroom door closed. He could hear them talking on the other side, but didn't even try to make out what they might be saying. He told himself he was grateful Macy had a woman to turn to, but he wondered what might be wrong that she couldn't come and talk to him about it.

Jayson returned to the front room to find Will listening to Trevin play "Silent Night" on the piano. He missed a few notes, but overall it sounded pretty good. He knew that Trevin was taking regular lessons on the piano and the violin, and he'd heard him practicing some. He wished that Macy had stuck with her lessons, or shown any interest in playing music at all.

Nearly two hours later, Elizabeth found Jayson alone in the front room, reading a travel magazine that Will had loaned him. "Is everything alright?" Jayson asked, setting the magazine aside.

"Relatively speaking," she said. "She's resting. I think you and I need to go for a little drive."

Jayson stood up. "Why?"

"Because we need to talk, and we need some privacy. Come on. I already told Dad we were leaving. He'll watch the kids."

Elizabeth said nothing as she drove. Hating the silence, Jayson finally asked, "Does this have to do with her mother?"

"Indirectly," she said. "But it's complicated."

"Okay, I'm listening."

"Just give me a minute. I'd rather not actually be driving."

A couple of minutes later she pulled into the parking lot of the temple. She parked where they had a good view of the huge structure, illuminated with lights so that it almost appeared to glow in the surrounding darkness. "So, what's this temple called?"

he asked. "If the temple in Salt Lake is called the Salt Lake Temple, then is this one the Highland Temple?"

"Technically it's not in Highland. It's actually called the Mount Timpanogos Temple." She pointed to the east. "That's the name of the mountain straight in front of us."

"You mean the big one."

"The most prominent in this area, yes."

"Okay, you're not driving. The view is good. Let's talk."

Elizabeth said, "The view has a calming effect, don't you think?"

"Do I need a calming effect?"

"Maybe," she said.

"Tell me before I shake it out of you."

"First let me say that Macy asked me to tell you everything she told me. She knows you need to know, and she knows the two of you need to talk, but she didn't want to be the one to tell you."

"Why not?"

"She feared you would be angry. I told her I could deal with your anger, and you could talk to her after you get it out of your system."

"I'm listening," he said, hating this more by the minute.

"The other day when I took Macy to the doctor, I asked her if she wanted me to stay with her through the exam. She said she did. Of course, they handle such things discreetly. There was nothing embarrassing for her. But afterward the doctor—a woman—was asking her some routine questions. And I may be wrong, but I think Macy might have answered them differently if her father had been the one to take her, or if she hadn't had some unbiased moral support in the room. I'd already made it clear that I would help her through this no matter what, and she needed to be honest."

"Okay," Jayson drawled, feeling his stomach smolder.

"When the doctor asked how many different sexual partners she'd had, Macy fell apart."

"Oh, heaven help me," Jayson muttered. "Please don't tell me she has AIDS."

"No, she doesn't have AIDS," Elizabeth said, and Jayson nearly slumped with relief, then he realized he hadn't heard *what* the problem was.

"She finally got the answer out, and it was two."

"Okay," Jayson said again.

"One was Cory, the father of the baby." Elizabeth looked cautiously at Jayson. "The other was the guy who raped her when she was fifteen."

Jayson felt like a fifty-pound anvil had just been heaved against his chest. He couldn't breathe. He couldn't speak. The wind had been completely knocked out of him. While a combination of raging anger and unbearable heartache threatened to smother him, the sharp change in Macy's behavior years earlier suddenly made perfect sense. The shock began to subside, allowing the anger and heartache to take hold of him fully. He gripped the dashboard with both hands and lowered his head to counteract a sudden dizziness. He groaned and hit his fist on the dashboard. He felt Elizabeth's hand on his shoulder, and he muttered hotly, "What happened? Why didn't she tell me? Who did this to her?"

"It's complicated," Elizabeth said, and Jayson lifted his head to look at her hotly. If this had been done by some anonymous attacker, he doubted it would be *complicated*.

"I'm listening," he said.

"Technically it would be qualified as date rape."

"Technically?" he countered, feeling his anger become dominant.

"He was quite a bit older than Macy, but when he started kissing her, she was a willing participant." Jayson groaned and squeezed his eyes closed. "When it started to get out of hand," Elizabeth went on, "she didn't protest. Then it got way out of hand and she *did* protest, but he wouldn't stop."

"And who is the . . . *creep* . . . who did this to my daughter?" he snarled.

"She's not going to tell you. Her reasons for keeping his identity from you are as strong now as they were then."

"*What* reasons?" he demanded. "He committed a crime. Not only was it date rape, it was *statutory* rape. She was fifteen years old!"

"And it was her word against his," Elizabeth said. "Do you have any idea the humiliation and degradation she would go through to have to tell the entire story in detail in a *courtroom,* admitting that she was only too eager to let it get started, but not to finish it? And then to have that creep get up on the stand and testify that she'd been a willing partner? Or he could have said it hadn't happened at all."

"She was fifteen years old!" he repeated.

"And *he* was the hottest item in punk rock," she said.

"Oh, heaven help me," he muttered under his breath as that anvil hit his chest again, this time with more force.

"He was all over the teen magazines, and if this story hit the media, it would have been slathered all over the tabloids." The horror of what she was saying began to sink in with implications that threatened to tear him in half, even before she added, "The daughter of one rock star raped by another, and Macy's face in every grocery checkout line all over the country. And to make matters worse, it was already well-known that he was dating the ex-wife of Jayson Wolfe."

The anger burst from Jayson like a comet that burned a hole right through him. He cursed as he got out of the car and slammed the door. He cursed again, then heaved for breath. He put both hands on the roof of the car and hung his head between his arms. He was fighting to keep his equilibrium when he felt Elizabeth's arms come around him from behind. "Let the anger go, Jayson," she murmured gently. "Just take a deep breath and let it go, and tell me what's beneath the anger."

Jayson fought with everything inside of him to do as she'd said. He knew from experience that the longer he remained angry, the longer he remained miserable. Eventually he had to come to the core of the anger, and that was where he would find the hurt and the frustration and the fear. He felt the anger relent in a rush that was immediately replaced by an equal force of pain. "Oh, heaven help me!" he cried again and fell to his knees on the cold concrete of the parking lot. Elizabeth knelt on the ground beside him, holding him while he cried and cursed and groaned over and over. When he finally calmed down, Elizabeth urged him to his feet, and he walked blindly with her arm around him. "We'll be warmer if we walk it off," she said, and he saw nothing but his feet until she urged him onto a cold bench. He looked up to see that they were sitting directly in front of the east side of the temple. Through aching eyes, he read, *House of the Lord, Holiness to the Lord.* He heard Elizabeth whisper, "It has a calming effect."

Taking in the beauty and majesty of the edifice in front of him, he had to admit, "Yeah, it does." He cleared his throat and added, "It's a good thing you're around to spare Macy from seeing my anger. It seems you know me well."

"Your anger is understandable," she said, and he squeezed his eyes closed with a self-punishing grimace.

"You know the person I'm most angry with?"

"Debbie."

"No. Me."

"Why would you—"

"I clawed my way into that world, Elizabeth. I was determined not to let the fame or the rampant evil destroy me. But it destroyed my family. I led them into a den of ravenous lions."

"Debbie made the choice to let that world become a part of her life."

"And what choice did Macy make?" he asked. "She was flattered by some hot rocker that every teenage girl in the country would die to be in the same room with. Her mother's boyfriend." He shook his head and made a noise of disgust. "They were all way too young for Debbie; she had a new one on her arm every six months. And she let them into her home—my daughter's home. Most of them were vulgar, crude, spoiled brats. And one of them took everything from my daughter and destroyed her life. It's no wonder she went off the deep end. No wonder she ran away with that creep who treated her the way she probably figured she deserved to be treated."

"Her life is not destroyed, Jayson. She's strong. She wants to put it behind her. We'll get her some good counseling. She's going to be just fine. And so are you. The two of you have each other. You've both been wounded by a harsh world, but you're both still standing. And you're going to get through this—together."

Jayson appreciated her encouragement, but there were still some holes in the story that were making him uneasy. He turned to Elizabeth and said, "She told you everything?"

"As far as I know."

"Where did it happen?"

"At the house; he was there when she came home. Debbie was gone."

Jayson nodded, fighting off the anger as much as the pain. "And why did this come up today, after she'd talked to her mother? I realize it came up at the doctor's office, but apparently it was okay not to talk about it . . . until today . . . when she talked to Debbie."

"It's complicated," she said, and Jayson made a noise of disgust.

"Okay, well . . ." his voice was angry, "while you're telling me how it's so blasted complicated, maybe you could tell me why Macy didn't tell me this happened when it happened. I really thought she could talk to me. I had talked to her about such things. I thought she was prepared to handle such situations. I thought she knew that I would be there for her, no matter what. I thought she knew I would love her no matter what. I wouldn't have wanted her all over the tabloids. I would have done what was best for her. Surely she had to know that. I wasn't a perfect father, but I was a darn good one."

"Yes, you were," she said. "You still are. First let me mention something I learned through some of my own counseling."

"You went to counseling?" he asked.

"Yes," she drawled. "You're the one who suggested it, remember? I went with Robert. But I had a few private sessions. I had some . . . issues, mostly with my mother. Let's just say I have some understanding of what may have motivated Macy in regard to her own mother. You see, it's typical when a child has a good parent and a difficult parent, that they will work very hard to get validation and approval from the difficult parent. They already have it from the good one. That's why I was such an overachiever, you know. I wanted my mother's attention and approval. And that's why Macy heeded her mother's threats, even though she knew you would understand."

"What threats?" he demanded.

"Macy told Debbie what had happened. But Debbie didn't believe her. She accused her of making it up because she was jealous. And she told her if she went to you with such ridiculous stories, she would cut her off completely; she would never see her again."

Jayson groaned and pressed his head into his hands. It all made sense now; perfect, horrifying sense. He felt sick to his stomach, and too weary to be angry. But the emotion bubbled out of him in painful torrents. He pressed his face into Elizabeth's lap and cried in a way that was pathetically familiar. How many hours of his life had he spent crying like a baby in Elizabeth's presence? When the emotion subsided into a deep ache, he muttered in a hoarse voice, "I don't know how I will ever be able to come to terms with this. How can I ever forgive myself for what I exposed her to? How can I ever not be angry with Debbie for being such a lousy, rotten mother?"

"You already know the answers to those questions, Jayson," she said, and he looked up at her, keeping his head in her lap. "You told me just yesterday about the miracle that had freed you from your pain. He already paid the price for all of this, Jayson. All the pain, the anger, the mistakes, the regret. It's already been taken care of. You just have to give this burden to the Savior, the way you gave Him all of your other pain. And in return He will give you all of the love you need to carry Macy—and yourself—to a fresh start." Jayson felt her words settle into him, and he knew that she was right. The miracle he'd experienced in being free of his pain did not come in limited supply or for a limited time. It was there now, readily available to get him through this new curve ball life had given him. In fact, he felt better already.

"That's all she needs now, Jayson," Elizabeth said. "Love and acceptance. She is very blessed to have such an incredible father. You did prepare her, Jayson. You did the best you could. Sometimes bad things just happen to good people. And that's where the Atonement really makes a difference, you know. It makes up for those places where our best isn't good enough. And you are a good father. You have the ability to make up for her lousy mother, the way my father made up for mine; the way your mother made up for a lousy father. We didn't turn out so bad."

"Speak for yourself," he said. "I'm a long-haired drug addict."

Elizabeth smiled at him. *"Former* drug addict," she said. "And if you ever do cut off that ponytail, you have to give it to me."

"You want my ponytail?"

"I do actually. Whether it's attached to you or not, I'm really quite fond of it."

"I think I'll keep it attached, if it's all the same to you."

"Okay," she said, and he stood up, holding out a hand to help her to her feet. He took her into his arms and hugged her tightly. "It's going to be alright, Jayson." She eased back and said, "She wanted you to know so that she could truly put it behind her with no secrets between the two of you. You need to talk to her about it, and then we'll get her whatever help she needs."

"I know a good counselor," he said. "If Maren's not available, perhaps she could make a recommendation."

Elizabeth smiled. "Come on. Let's go home."

CHAPTER 5

Jayson found Macy sitting on her bed, hugging a pillow, a box of tissues at her side and several wadded ones on the floor. She looked virtually terrified when he knocked at the open door and asked if he could come in.

"Sure," she said, and he closed the door behind him.

"Elizabeth told me everything," he said. "No more secrets between us."

She whimpered and asked, "You're not mad?"

"Not anymore," he said. "And I was never angry with you, baby. I was just angry . . . that you've suffered so much. I was angry with myself, wondering what I might have done to prevent this from happening to you."

"It wasn't your fault."

"Maybe not," he said. "But . . . my profession didn't necessarily bring good things into our lives." He sat on the bed beside her. "Listen to me, Macy, and listen carefully. I am so sorry for what happened to you, and I'm sorry for all that's happened since then that's been so horrible for you. But it's in the past, and that's where we're going to leave it. I love you, Macy. You are more precious to me than anything else in this world, and we are going to get through this—together."

He pulled her into his arms, and she sobbed with relief. When she calmed down, she asked like a child, "Can we stay here with Elizabeth until after I have the baby? She says she'll help me. I need her, Dad."

He smiled and touched her face. "I need her too," he said. "She's my best friend, you know. That's why your middle name is Elizabeth." Macy showed a smile of enlightenment as if she'd just made the connection. "Of course we can stay," he added. "What would we do without Elizabeth?"

"She's awesome, Dad. She's the way I always wished Mom could be."

"That's how I always felt about her father; he was everything my own dad never was."

"Elizabeth said if I want I can stay here and go to school—if it's okay with you. She said the baby should be here before the second semester starts, and I could go to the high school here, and if I take some tests and do some packets I could probably graduate with the kids my age. I really want to, Dad. I don't want to go back to LA. She said we could both stay at least until summer, and then we'd decide what to do after that."

Jayson couldn't deny feeling some relief as he contemplated this plan. He didn't want to return to LA either, but now that he'd survived rehab and was doing better, any excuse he could come up with to stay beyond the holidays would have been lame. But it didn't take a rocket scientist to see that Elizabeth's influence could be priceless for Macy. If she could go to school and get some counseling in a place distant from old associations, great things could happen. He smiled at his daughter and said, "It sounds like a great idea. I'll talk with Elizabeth and see what we can work out."

"And, Dad, there's something else I have to tell you. I'm not ready to be a mother. I hope you don't think I'm a flake or something, but I can't keep the baby. I can't explain it really, but . . . right from the start I just felt like this baby wasn't supposed to be mine."

Again Jayson was grateful for Elizabeth's insight, and that he'd already had this conversation with her. He wouldn't have wanted to make selfish comments that would have made this more difficult for Macy. He took her hand and said gently, "I think that's a very wise decision, Macy, and I'm proud of you. Tomorrow we'll start figuring out what we need to do."

They talked for a while longer until it became evident that Macy was exhausted. He kissed her goodnight and left her room. Seeing that the door to Elizabeth's room was ajar, with the light on, he knocked, then at her invitation pushed it open to see her sitting up in bed with a book.

"Everything okay?" she asked.

"Everything is fine," he said, leaning against the doorjamb. "Miraculously fine."

"God works in mysterious ways," she said.

"Yes, He does. And one of the many miracles He has sent into our lives is you. I'm thinking now that it was a huge blessing for me to be in rehab when she called. I think she needed a woman. Not just any woman; she needed you. To say thank you sounds so trite. But thank you." In that moment he found it ironic that while they'd not married twenty years ago, the way he would have preferred, she was still in the position to be a mother to his daughter. And he was grateful.

"She's a wonderful girl, Jayson. She's a great deal like you."

"I don't know if that's good or not, but I love her." He took a deep breath and added, "She told me you'd invited her to stay until summer, to go to school."

"I hope that's okay; she seemed so concerned about what she would do. I wanted to give her an option."

"It's a good option," he said. "Perfect, in my opinion. But I don't want you to be burdened by any of this."

"It's not a burden, Jayson. We're family. And I assume you'll be staying, as well. She needs her father."

"I was hoping the invitation included me," he said. "Quite frankly, I love it here. But I'll try not to get too comfortable. I insist, however, on helping pay expenses. And I won't take no for an answer. I know you hate that typing job. So, why don't you quit and take in a couple of boarders to make up the difference? Some

room and board should bring in the same amount, don't you
think? Besides, Macy's going to need someone to help her get
through having this baby. I'm a man. You know what insensitive
jerks we men are when it comes to such things."

Elizabeth chuckled. "Some men are, perhaps. I always thought
you were the sensitive, tender type—with a high water table."

"I'm not sure I'd qualify those as strengths."

"As I see it they are," she said.

"I'll let you get some sleep," he said and left the room.

Back in his own room, Jayson called his brother.

"Hey, it's you," Drew said.

"It is," Jayson chuckled.

"You're out of the hospital."

"I am."

"And how are you doing?"

"I'm doing very well, actually," Jayson said and was surprised to
realize he meant it. Even with this evening's trauma, he felt an
underlying peace that kept everything in perspective.

"I'm glad to hear it."

"Thanks for sending the CDs, and for enduring therapy with
me. You're my hero."

"Oh, brother," Drew said with comical disgust.

"Yes, you are, actually . . . my brother, that is," Jayson said, and
they both laughed. "And my hero."

"Therapy was good for me too, I think," Drew admitted. "I
believe we could all use a little here and there."

"Most likely," Jayson said. "Hey, I have some good news."

"Oh, I love good news. What is it?"

"Macy is back; she's here with me."

Drew made a noise of disbelief, then he laughed. "She really is?
She's okay?"

"Yeah, she's okay," Jayson said and went on to tell him all that
had happened. They talked for over an hour, and Jayson finally
slept, grateful for evidence of one more blessing. He had a brother

who was a good man, and even with the distance between them, the bond they shared was incomparable.

The following morning Jayson called Maren's office, and she called him back before noon. He explained the situation, and she eagerly agreed to meet with Macy once a week for as long as she needed. They set up an appointment for Thursday, and she asked that Jayson join her for the therapy, at least to begin with. That afternoon, Elizabeth went with Jayson and Macy to LDS Family Services. While Jayson knew he could never fully embrace Elizabeth's religious beliefs, he'd been able to see that the Church had a strong family ethic, and they had some wonderful programs to help people in that regard. He was impressed with the way Macy was treated and the education and information they were given.

Afterward in the car, Macy expressed some concern in being able to make the right decision. She felt fairly confident in knowing that the baby should go elsewhere, but there were other choices she needed to make—most specifically *who* her baby would go to according to the information she'd been given about a number of different couples, even though any identification was omitted.

While Jayson was pondering what advice he might give her, Elizabeth said, "You know how to pray, don't you, Macy?"

"Well . . . sort of," she said.

"Okay," Elizabeth went on, "as I see it, we as human beings can't possibly know the long-range outcome of such a decision, but God knows. He knows what's best and right for everyone involved. In the scriptures it tells us that the Holy Ghost will let us know what's right, and He speaks to us through our feelings. If you make a decision and it's wrong, then you will feel confused, maybe even upset and afraid. But if your decision is right, you will feel peace. So, you get all the information you can and make a decision. When your heart and your head agree, then you'll know you're on the right track."

Macy made a noise of interest. Elizabeth glanced at Jayson and wished she could read his mind. She could almost imagine him being displeased to have her preaching to his daughter. But his expression was unreadable, and he said nothing.

Jayson listened to Elizabeth's advice to Macy and felt in awe of her wisdom and insight. She'd always been amazing, but he had to admit that religion had brought something out in her that made her even more incredible. In that moment, she reminded him very much of his mother. How many times had he heard Leslie say that the heart and the head had to agree? He was truly blessed to have such great women in his life.

After supper they all gathered for family home evening. After an opening prayer that was given by Addie, they discussed plans for the holidays, including ideas for doing some anonymous service projects for a couple of families they were aware of who were struggling with health and financial problems. When their plans had been made, Trevin told a Christmas story with the help of some pictures that he stuck on a flannel-covered board. Will suggested they sing some Christmas carols. Elizabeth played some simple songs on the piano while they sang, then Macy urged her father to play. He managed rather well, considering the practice he'd had with his drug-addicted friends. He could see that the exercises he'd been doing with his left hand were showing some good results already, although his hand still functioned far beneath its normal capacity. Still, he'd rarely found such joy in his ability to make music. To be gathered around the piano with these particular people, singing Christmas carols and laughing, he doubted he'd ever felt more happy. A couple of times he glanced up at the painting of the Savior, and he silently thanked God for blessing his life so richly.

After the children had gone to bed—including Macy, who was easily exhausted with her pregnancy—Elizabeth found Jayson in the basement watching the news with Will. "Can I talk to you?" she asked, looking directly at him.

"Sure," he said and stood up. They went upstairs to the front room and sat on the couch. "This isn't bad news, is it?" he asked.

"No, of course not," she said with a smile. "There's just something I wanted to tell you, and something I want to ask you about before I go forward with it."

"Okay."

"First of all, I'm going to take you up on your offer to help with some expenses." He smiled, and she went on. "Truthfully, I've hated the work I've been doing. We're really doing okay, but if I didn't do it, then the money would get so tight that it would just be . . . stressful. After the holidays, Dad will be doing lots of taxes and that will help us get ahead, but . . . I've actually been dreading having to work through the holidays. I also got a new church calling, so—"

"I don't understand," he said.

"I've been leading the music in Primary, but they will be releasing me from that, and I will be a counselor in the Primary presidency, which will require a great deal more time and energy on my part; one more reason why the work would be stressful. So I called the woman I work for today and gave her my notice. I'll be finishing up within a week."

"That's great," he said.

"So, I just wanted to thank you for making that possible. I enjoy having you and Macy here, but this is an added blessing."

"It's not a big deal," he said. "I'm glad I can help. My mother taught me not to be a freeloader." Elizabeth laughed softly, and he asked, "What else did you need to talk about?"

Elizabeth took a deep breath, hoping Jayson would feel okay about what she was going to propose. "I spoke with a woman in the ward today. Sister Lansing. She's the Young Women president." He looked confused, and she explained, "The Church has an organization for girls from ages twelve to eighteen. They meet one evening a week and do activities and service projects. They also have a class on Sunday during the usual meeting time. They have lessons, work on setting goals, personal things as well as spiritual things. Anyway, Sister Lansing is the president. We have nearly fifty young women in the ward. I talked to her about Macy's situation, and she would like to come over and visit with you—and Macy. She's a wonderful woman, Jayson. She's not one of those that will be pushy or insensitive or judgmental. She just wants to help Macy through this transition. And if Macy can get involved with the activities, then she could have a few familiar faces around her when she starts school next month. But I didn't want to do anything without discussing it with you. If you're not comfortable with it, then—"

"I'm okay with it if Macy is."

Elizabeth sighed. "Sister Lansing just wants to come over and talk with the two of you, and from there you can both decide what you're comfortable with."

"Sounds reasonable," he said, then he chuckled. "Why were you so nervous to ask me that?"

"I don't want you to think I'm trying to push religion on you, or anything. I just want to do everything I can to help."

"I know that," he said. "Don't worry about it. I can assure you I have no intention of joining your church, but I can appreciate that there are some good programs. If it can help Macy while she's here, that's great."

"Okay," Elizabeth said. "I'm going to call her back right now."

She left the room, and Jayson heard her on the phone in the kitchen. When he could tell that she'd ended her call, he found her there making red Kool-Aid.

"Isn't it bedtime?" he asked.

"Technically," she said, "but I don't want to go to bed." She repeated one of her firm adages. "Once in a while I just want to revel in the peace and quiet of the children sleeping. I want to watch a movie that makes me cry, and eat crackers and smoked oysters, and drink red Kool-Aid, and fall asleep on the couch."

Jayson watched her gather everything onto a tray while she thought of the many times she'd tried to coerce Robert into joining her for such escapades. In spite of their differences, she suddenly missed him. She was startled from her thoughts when Jayson said, "Would I be intruding if I joined you? I mean . . . if this is some solo ritual or something, I'll just go to bed, but . . . I'm great at crying over movies."

Elizabeth stopped what she was doing and looked at him hard while she seemed deep in thought. Then she smiled and said, "I would love to have you join me."

"Okay, good," he said, crossing the kitchen. "But we need microwave popcorn."

Ten minutes later they were in the basement sitting at opposite ends of the couch, watching *It's a Wonderful Life,* the black-and-white version. Jayson ate popcorn with Mozie at his feet while Elizabeth ate oysters on Ritz crackers, then he leaned toward her and said, "Let me try one of those. I haven't had oysters for years."

She put one on a cracker, and he said, "They look really disgusting, you know."

"I know, but they taste heavenly," she said and put it into his mouth.

They laughed as they fed each other, not paying much attention to the movie. But then, they'd both seen it at least a dozen times. When the oysters were gone, they focused more on the movie. Elizabeth was pleasantly surprised when Jayson took her hand, and when she started to get sleepy, he urged her head to his shoulder. "Oh, this is nice," she admitted.

"Yes it is," he said and pressed a kiss into her hair.

At the end of the movie they both cried, then Jayson carried Elizabeth up the stairs and put her on her bed. He kissed her brow and left the room, wishing that his whole life could be like this. Although he'd prefer actually sharing a room with her.

The following morning when the doorbell rang, Elizabeth was in the bathroom, Will was in the basement, and Macy was lying down in her room. Jayson answered it to see a woman younger than Elizabeth, holding a large gift bag with colored tissue sticking out of the top. She looked well put together, and her smile was kind.

"Brother Wolfe," she said.

"Yes," he answered. It was far from the first time he'd been called that during his stay in Utah, and he was almost getting used to it.

As an apparent afterthought, she said, "Oh, I hope you don't mind my calling you that. I know you're not a member, but I have seen you at church."

"It's not a problem," he said, motioning her inside. "You must be Sister Lansing."

"That's right," she said, and he closed the door.

"Come in. Sit down," he said. She took a chair, and he sat at one end of the couch. "Elizabeth said you wanted to talk to me, and to Macy. She's lying down right now, but I can get her if—"

"I'd really like to talk to you first, if that's alright."

"Of course," he said, then Elizabeth appeared.

"Oh hi," she said. "Is it all right if I join you or—"

"Yes, please," Jayson said, patting the couch.

She sat down, and Sister Lansing said, "First of all, let me say that we're truly glad to know that Macy is here with us, and we hope that we can get to know her better during her stay here. Elizabeth has made me aware of the challenges Macy is up against, and a little bit of what she's been through. I can assure you that the things she's told me are completely confidential. Her pregnancy is readily evident, and some girls in the neighborhood have already seen her coming and going, but it's not the first time we've dealt with such things."

Jayson felt surprised at this. Did that mean good Mormon girls had unwanted pregnancies too? He refrained from asking, and she went on.

"I've spoken only to the bishop and to one of my counselors about the other things Elizabeth told me. Our only purpose is to help Macy in the best way possible. I can't promise that all of our young women will be perfectly gracious and appropriate. Most of them will be, but there are some who have their own struggles. The women who serve with me, however, are all marvelous, and they are all willing to do whatever they can to support Macy."

They talked some about Macy's plans, and Sister Lansing explained the Young Women program and some of the upcoming activities. She pointed out the gift bag she'd brought and said that all of the leaders and some of the girls had each contributed something to help Macy get through the coming weeks. She also handed Jayson a little booklet, and on the cover it said, *For the Strength of Youth.* She explained that these were guidelines established by the leaders of the Church to encourage youth to stay strong and be happy. She told him it was certainly up to him how much he applied these guidelines with Macy, but it might give them something to talk about.

Jayson was feeling extremely good about their conversation and was about to go and get Macy when she appeared, saying, "Oh, there you are. Just wondering. I'll leave you to—"

"No, it's okay," Jayson said and came to his feet. "There's someone here you need to meet."

Introductions were made, then Macy sat holding her father's hand while Sister Lansing explained to her about the Young Women program. She gave Macy the gift bag, provoking a stunned expression and a mild, "Thank you."

Sister Lansing spoke frankly and kindly with Macy about her plans. Macy told her about their visit to Family Services and explained that she would be getting some counseling as well. This good woman spoke encouraging words, expressed genuine concern, and told Macy how glad she was that they would have the opportunity to get to know her better. She invited Macy to church and to their activities. Macy politely told her that she would rather keep a low profile until after the baby came. "It's not that it's any great secret or anything," Macy said. "I just don't feel well and . . . I think I'd rather wait."

"I understand," Sister Lansing said. "In the bag you will find a list of names and phone numbers. Mine is at the top. If there is anything at all we can do, please feel free to let us know."

"Thank you," Macy said and excused herself to use the bathroom.

While she was gone Sister Lansing said, "Now, if either of you observe a need that we might be able to fill, please let me know."

"Thank you," Jayson said. "Your visit is very much appreciated."

Sister Lansing then said to him, "So, Elizabeth tells me you're practically family. You've known each other a long time, then."

"Since high school," Elizabeth said. "He and my brother were best friends. When my brother was killed, we kind of adopted him."

"Oh, you lost your brother," she said with compassion. "How difficult that must have been!"

"Yes, it certainly was," Elizabeth said.

Sister Lansing rose to leave as Macy returned, and she said, "It was a pleasure meeting you, Macy. You take care of yourself, now. And make certain your father waits on you a great deal." She smiled at Jayson as she said it, and he smiled back.

"I'm doing my best to spoil her," he said. "It's just so good to have her back."

He hugged Macy, and Sister Lansing said, "You have a beautiful piano, Elizabeth. Do you play?"

"Some," Elizabeth said. "Nothing spectacular, I'm afraid. Trevin's taking lessons, and Addie will start soon."

"That's wonderful," Sister Lansing said. "There's no musical talent in our family."

"You should hear my dad play," Macy said.

Jayson scowled at her and comically put his hand over her mouth. "That's a secret. You shouldn't tell my secrets."

He moved his hand, and she said, "It's hardly a secret when your CDs were all over the—"

Jayson covered her mouth again and said lightly to Sister Lansing, whose eyes were wide, "The pregnancy is making her delirious."

"You're not supposed to hide your candle under a bushel," Elizabeth said with a smirk. "It's in the Bible; you can look it up."

"I'll do that," he said, then turned to Sister Lansing. "Thank you again. It's been a pleasure."

After Sister Lansing left, Macy sat at the kitchen table and unloaded the gift bag. She kept laughing with pure delight as she discovered its contents. There was bubble bath and shower gel, lotion and hand cream. There was a CD of instrumental Christmas music and a couple of novels that Elizabeth declared were clean and uplifting. There was a little bag of homemade cookies, and two of homemade candy, and some other treats as well. There was a journal with a picture of Jesus on the front and a beautiful pen. And there was a little booklet that Elizabeth explained was used by the Young Women program to set goals and achieve awards. She was welcome to use it or not. There was also a candle that smelled like cinnamon and a little plaque that said, *Friends are like angels that watch over us.*

"Boy, you can say that again," Jayson said as he read it.

Later Jayson read the *For the Strength of Youth* booklet and was amazed at how it covered every facet he'd ever been concerned about in raising his daughter in such a crazy world. He couldn't help being impressed.

During the days leading up to Christmas, Jayson and Macy settled more fully into life with Elizabeth and her family. The counseling with Maren went well. She expressed her joy on Jayson's behalf that he was doing so well and that his daughter had come home. She handled Macy's tender emotions with all the gentleness and expertise with which she'd handled Jayson's, and Macy seemed to respond well to her.

Jayson thoroughly enjoyed the Christmas preparations. As they put up the Christmas tree, decorated the house, baked goodies, and made homemade candy, it almost felt like a dream. Macy appeared happy and content, and he was grateful to have her at his side.

Debbie called a couple of times, which always upset Macy. The next time she called, Jayson answered the phone and told Debbie that if she couldn't talk to Macy without giving her grief, then her calls were not welcome. She was angry, but she didn't call again.

Jayson appreciated Elizabeth's determination to make service and giving a part of their Christmas celebrations. He enjoyed quietly contributing to the project of helping some struggling families, and it was apparent that Macy enjoyed it as well. They all went to the ward Christmas party, which included an elaborate turkey dinner and a beautiful program. People were kind and friendly—to him as well as Macy—and Jayson decided he really liked living here.

"People like you," Elizabeth whispered to him following a typical encounter with a friendly woman.

"Even though I'm a long-haired drug addict with a daughter who is unwed and pregnant?"

"Most of these people realize they have their own problems, and they're only too glad to be compassionate toward yours."

A few days later, Elizabeth said to Jayson, "They've asked me to do a violin number in church this Sunday; it's the last Sunday before Christmas, and they're having a special program. And I need to practice. But the woman who usually accompanies me is sick. I don't suppose you could help me out. I mean . . . I heard a rumor that you play the piano."

"A little," he said. "I'd be glad to help."

He sat down at the piano, and she set some sheet music of "O Holy Night" in front of him. She set up a music stand but stood at his shoulder with the violin, saying, "I only have one copy of the music, so we'll have to share until you memorize it."

He gave her a basic rhythm to follow, and she came in with the melody. "Very nice," he said after they'd gone through it once. "Will I throw you off if I put in a little embellishment?"

"No, of course not," she said. "I was hoping you would. How's the hand?"

"Getting a little better," he said and began to play. He started out with a few simple notes then moved fluidly into a lush accompaniment that harmonized beautifully with the violin. They stumbled over a couple of places when he wasn't sure where she would come in. They laughed over it, clarified what they were doing, and started over.

"Okay," he said, "I don't need the music anymore."

"Really?" she asked, thinking she shouldn't have been surprised.

"Really," he said, and she moved the sheet music to the stand so that they could see each other as they played, which actually made it easier to stay together.

This time as they played it through, Elizabeth felt something magical happen. She'd felt the magic before in the basement in her home in Oregon and onstage in Portland. But they had been young, and the music they'd played together had been so different from this. It had always been good music. But this song seemed to perfectly express the miracle that had taken place in healing Jayson's heart and her own. They were making music together, with an unspoken unity in the way it flowed, as if they were somehow of the same mind. The years they had shared, the struggles, the heartache, the grief and the joy, all seemed to emanate through the notes they played, filling the air around them with a tangible warmth. It felt so natural, so perfect, so completely matchless that she could almost believe they had shared this experience in the life before this one. Elizabeth focused on Jayson as much as she could while still reading the music, then the intensity of her feelings for him felt suddenly so overpowering that she couldn't look at him at all. Through the last few bars she played, tears trickled down her cheeks, but her hands were occupied and she couldn't do anything about it. When the last note on the violin was completed, she turned to look at Jayson and found him staring at her while he played the last few bars—tears streaking his face, as well. Had he felt it too? Had he recognized this sensation that was filling the air around them, that seemed to whisper of some everlasting connection, some eternal scheme that had brought them together and would keep them that way? He finished the song and lifted his hands from the keys while the gaze they shared remained unbroken. She dropped her arms but kept hold of the bow and violin, not wanting to look away to put them down. She stepped toward him as he came to his feet, still holding her eyes with his. She moved into his arms as if some power greater than her own will had compelled her to be there. In one agile movement he wrapped her in his arms and pressed his lips to hers. She put her arms around his neck, holding the bow and violin behind his back while he kissed her as if they had both been born for this moment.

"Elizabeth," he murmured close to her face, looking into her eyes as if they could tell him what had just happened. In a way, the feelings were so familiar. He'd felt this way the first time he'd laid eyes on her and a thousand times since. But something about this moment felt strangely new and different. Was the change within himself or in the circumstances surrounding them? While a part of him felt deeply tempted to drop to his knees and beg her to marry him, to share her life with him, something more compelling told him that the time wasn't right, and maybe it never would be. The strength of his feelings did not necessarily mean that marriage was the right course. He suspected that the intensity of his own feelings had once contributed to frightening her away. If they were meant to be together, it would work out. And he needed to be patient and remember his place. Still, looking at her now, holding her in his arms this way, it was difficult to comprehend that life could take any possible course beyond their being together. But he'd felt that way twenty years ago, and he knew better than to believe that his feelings alone could dictate the future.

In spite of a torrent of battling thoughts, Jayson felt deeply comforted when she said in a dreamy voice, "I love you, Jayson."

The phone rang in the distance, but she ignored it, and he muttered softly, "I love you too, Elizabeth, and maybe—"

"Elizabeth!" Will called. "The phone's for you."

She sighed and eased reluctantly away, but they both laughed softly as the spell was broken. She handed him the violin and the bow and hurried away. Jayson closed his eyes and attempted to absorb the last few minutes more fully into his memory, then he placed the instrument gently on the couch and returned to the piano. He'd barely begun to play when she returned, and he stopped.

"That was the woman who is supposed to accompany me Sunday. She's not going to be able to make it at all. I told her not to worry about it; I thought I could probably dig up an adequate accompanist." Jayson smirked, and she added, "So, it looks like you'll be playing the piano in church this Sunday."

Elizabeth saw his brow furrow, and she asked, "Is that a problem?"

"Then everyone will know I play, and I'll never hear the end of it."

"I think you can handle the fame; you've had training in that."

He chuckled and said, "Okay, well . . . I think we'd better omit that last part."

"The last part was lovely," she said in protest.

"Elizabeth, darling," he said with mock severity, "I don't think the congregation would appreciate seeing a passionate embrace conclude the number."

Jayson laughed softly when she visibly blushed and looked away. "Since you put it that way, we should probably omit that part."

"We could practice it that way, however," he said.

Elizabeth met his eyes, and a deep longing filled her—accentuated by her ongoing loneliness. She said in a soft voice, "It's tempting, but . . . maybe we should just play the song."

Jayson smiled and began to play, reminding himself not to read anything into any of this. It was safer just to play the song. But he doubted they could ever duplicate the perfection of that last time through.

When Sunday came, the number went beautifully, and both Jayson and Elizabeth received many compliments afterward. Jayson especially liked it when someone said, "The two of you play so well together."

On the way home from church, Jayson said to Elizabeth, "There's only one thing that could have made it better."

She blushed and said, "As you pointed out, that wouldn't go over well at church."

"I was going to say that you should have been wearing red shoes."

She looked at him in surprise, then said, "I can't. You stole one of them from me."

"Stole? You gave it to me," he said, and she just laughed.

Christmas ended up being one of the best of Jayson's life. It was filled with music and laughter and gifts from the heart. Jayson found it purely delightful to observe the children, and Trevin even came out of his usual somber mood once in a while. Macy began to feel increasingly uncomfortable with her pregnancy, but she seemed happy and content, and Jayson felt the same, just having her safely in his care.

Four days after Christmas, Jayson came awake in the middle of the night and realized Elizabeth was nudging him. "What's wrong?" he demanded.

"Macy's in labor. Get dressed."

Five minutes later he was driving to the hospital while Elizabeth kept her arm around Macy, uttering words of encouragement. Jayson was deeply grateful to have her with them, now more than ever. He felt scared out of his mind. Memories of Macy being born crowded into his head. It had been one of the most wonderful—and horrible—experiences of his life. Could he bear to see Macy suffer the way Debbie had?

At the hospital everything went smoothly. The nurses took good care of Macy, and the labor progressed slowly. When her pain became intense, they gave her an epidural and she was able to rest. He and Elizabeth took turns resting and sitting with her until two o'clock the following afternoon, when she was finally taken into delivery. Macy had actually told Jayson he could stay with her, but he felt it would be more appropriate if he waited elsewhere. Elizabeth went with her, and he felt sure she was in good hands.

A beautiful baby girl was born just past two-thirty. Macy slept the remainder of the day while Jayson stayed near her side, and Elizabeth went home to take care of things there. The following day he and Macy spent several hours with the baby. The counselors at Family Services had told them that it had been proven much better and more healthy in the long run for a mother to let the baby go if she first had the opportunity to become acquainted with her child. It was easier to say good-bye if you've first said hello, they'd been told. Jayson hoped they were right as he observed his baby with her own baby. He held the infant himself a great deal, not willing to admit how difficult it was for *him* to let her go.

Elizabeth came by in the afternoon. She entered the room to find Macy sleeping and Jayson leaning back in a recliner, holding the baby. He looked up with sad eyes as she closed the door and leaned against it. Their eyes met in a way that reminded her of their experience in playing music together. She knew he desperately wanted another child, and she couldn't help wishing that she might be the one to have that child. A practical, logical part of her wondered if the idea was ridiculous, but still, she couldn't help wishing. In her heart she knew she was destined to have at least one more child; a deeply profound experience following Robert's death had given her an undeniable conviction about that. Whether or not it would be with Jayson remained to be seen.

"You okay?" she asked.

"I'm sure I will be," he said, then turned to look at Macy. "If she'll be okay, I will be too."

"She'll be okay. She's got a wonderful father to get her through."

"And we both have you," he said.

The following morning, New Year's Day, Jayson sat beside Macy while she signed the papers to relinquish all rights to her child. She tearfully said good-bye to the baby, then they cried together, knowing that somewhere in the same hospital, a very happy couple was now receiving the New Year's gift of a lifetime. Jayson imagined *their* tears—tears of joy—and it was easier for him to find peace as he took his daughter home from the hospital.

CHAPTER 6

The next few days were difficult for Macy, but Elizabeth did well at keeping her distracted, as well as allowing her to vent and cry as much as she needed to. Jayson was surprised when Elizabeth produced a partially finished scrapbook and a box full of photos and clippings from his career. Much of what she had he'd never seen. He had mixed emotions about seeing them now, but Macy became engrossed in looking through them for hours, reading every article closely. She commented to him a number of times that she'd had no idea how amazing her father really was. He laughed it off and told her she was the most amazing thing he'd ever produced. But somewhere inside he was surprised to feel oddly comforted. His success had been real, and it had been profound. He'd gained much—and lost much. But he was still standing, and he was happy.

Sitting beside Macy while she read an article, he rummaged through the box a little, then pulled out a paper and looked at Elizabeth with disgust. "You joined the fan club?"

"It was the best way to keep up on what was going on."

"You could have called and asked."

"I did. But you didn't send me all those great autographed pictures and stuff."

"No, I sent you autographed letters and birthday presents."

"So you did," she said with a smile.

"I have to admit it's good to see this stuff. Sometimes it seems like a dream. It's nice to know it was real."

"Oh, it was real. And I have videos to prove it."

"You have videos?" Macy asked, looking up abruptly.

"Oh, boy," Jayson said. "I'm going to find something else to do besides watch myself on television."

After Macy had watched everything Elizabeth had on video a couple of times, she embarked on a project of actually organizing all the pictures and clippings and finishing the scrapbook that Elizabeth had never had the time to do.

While Jayson was feeling helpless on how to help out, and he had far too much time on his hands, he was pleasantly surprised when Macy came to him and said, "I have a favor to ask you, and you're probably going to think it's weird, but . . . well . . . I mean, I know I don't have any great talent or anything, but . . ." her voice cracked, "would you teach me to play the piano?"

Jayson laughed and hugged her tightly. "I don't know if I'm much of a teacher, but I can't think of anything I would rather do."

They spent time together on the piano bench at least twice a day, and Macy spent many hours there on her own, working through the simple exercises in some books that Elizabeth had for her own children. What little Macy had learned in her early childhood had been lost, but it was quickly coming back. And she was apparently enjoying it.

Macy quickly regained her health and her figure, although her emotions were understandably tender. The Young Women presidency came by to check on her, and they gave her a schedule of the month's activities and encouraged her to come as soon as she was feeling up to it. The next day Macy had a difficult session with Maren as the grief of letting go of the baby overtook her, but by the beginning of the next week, she was actually doing much better. She admitted readily that she knew she'd done the right thing, and she felt confident that she would adjust with time. She went to the youth activity on Tuesday evening and came home saying she'd really enjoyed it.

Will became especially busy doing taxes in his office in the basement, and Jayson did his best to help Elizabeth with the house and the children, since Will didn't have the time to do much. And he got into a regular habit of walking Mozie.

Elizabeth went with Jayson to register Macy at Lone Peak High School. They met with a school counselor and arranged for Macy to take some tests, and they soon had a schedule in place that, along with a combination of classes and doing some extra packets at home, would allow her to graduate in May. At the next youth activity, Macy discovered she had some classes with a few of the girls in the ward who had been very kind to her. One of them, a girl named Jamie, offered to pick Macy up for school since she drove right past the house every morning, anyway. On the first day of the new semester, Jayson felt a little lost to have Macy gone all day. He changed the oil in both cars in the garage, which surprised Elizabeth, but he reminded her that it had been his first profession. He did some errands and was thrilled to see Macy come home smiling.

Over the next few weeks, Macy settled comfortably into school and was pulling good test scores. She went regularly to the youth activities and then started going to church with Jayson and the family. She clearly enjoyed going to church, as did Jayson. He liked the association there as much as he enjoyed being a part of the ward and neighborhood. For the most part, people were friendly and accepting, and much of what he heard at church impressed him. But there were certain aspects of what they taught that he had to just let roll off. He quit going to Primary when Elizabeth was no longer leading the music, and instead he went to a scripture study class and the men's meeting with Will.

Elizabeth kept busy with her home and children, and he noticed that every couple of weeks she went to the temple. She said nothing to him except that she was going, and he didn't ask any questions. He figured it was better that way. He did find her in the laundry room once, pulling a long, white dress out of the dryer. When he asked why he'd never seen her wear it, she told him she only wore it in the temple. She briefly explained that when attending the temple, everyone changed into white clothes. He found the idea intriguing, but he let the conversation drop there.

Jayson bought a car for himself that Macy could also use, which gave them both more freedom. He didn't like having to rely on Will and Elizabeth for everything, and having his own car meant that they didn't have to work their schedules around each other quite so much. They joked about the fact that they now had three cars in the three-car garage, and therefore the household was complete.

Macy made a few friends at school and started going out with them to movies and shopping. Jayson felt deeply gratified to see her living the life of a normal high school senior. He thought of himself at that age and found it difficult to believe how the years had passed. And he couldn't help thinking of how Derek had been killed at that time in his life. Thankfully, Jayson had come far since then, but he never could have comprehended the paths his life would take.

Macy continued to get regular piano instruction from her father, and she practiced almost daily, although she was so busy that she didn't put a lot of time into it. Jayson was glad to see her life so full and to see her doing so well, but he felt a little lost himself. At one time his empty hours had been filled with music, and while he played the piano regularly and worked hard on improving the dexterity of his left hand, he felt hesitant to take other steps in that direction. He often wished that he could write music again, but it felt dried up inside of him. He could only play what was already written. His own work felt old and boring, so he mostly played work by other people. And for reasons he couldn't quite explain, he felt hesitant to pick up the guitar.

Jayson felt a great relief from his ongoing sense of uselessness when an announcement was made at church concerning an elderly couple in the ward who needed some help with repairs on their home. Jayson got involved with the project and enjoyed getting to know Bert and Ethel, who had been married more than sixty years. When the project was completed, he still stopped by once in a while to see how they were doing.

One day out of the blue, he recalled something Elizabeth had once said to him about causes he could benefit with his excess money. He found her in the basement, organizing the videotapes and DVDs.

"Hey," he said, handing her a copy of his first CD, "I owe you one of these."

"You do?"

"I think I might have scratched your copy," he said, "when I threw it in the backseat."

"Oh, it was all right," she said.

"Take it anyway. It's autographed. You never know when you might need it."

She chuckled. "Thanks. I'll treasure it always."

"Hey," he said again, "you told me once there were some causes I might be interested in. I'm interested."

"Really?"

"I wouldn't have asked if I weren't."

"Okay," she said, and the next day she took him on a tour of the Church's humanitarian center. He was both dumbfounded and awestruck to see the collecting and distribution of goods that went all over the world to aid humanitarian causes with no restrictions according to race, color, creed, or religion. He also learned a great deal about the Church's welfare system that was set up to help its own when they were in need. On Sunday, Jayson gave the bishop two substantial checks with the request that one go to the welfare program, and the other to humanitarian aid. And he asked that his contribution remain confidential. The bishop agreed and thanked him profusely.

Romance suddenly seemed to come out of the woodwork when Will started dating a divorced woman in the ward whose youngest child had just started college the previous year, and Macy started dating a guy she'd met at a church dance. Aaron was a year older than Macy and preparing to go on a mission. Jayson had learned through his time living in Mormondom that most young men went on missions at the age of nineteen, going wherever in the world they were asked to go to share the gospel. When Aaron came over for Sunday dinner, Jayson learned that he was the oldest of seven children. His parents were divorced; he never heard from his father, who had run off with a younger woman, and his mother worked hard to support and care for her family. Jayson liked Aaron and admired his determination and enthusiasm over serving a mission. When Jayson was that age, he'd been married and expecting a baby and playing rock music. He wondered how much different his own life might have been if he'd taken two years out of it to wholly serve God. Whether Jayson believed the Church was true or not, he couldn't help but be impressed with such conviction. And Jayson liked the way Aaron treated Macy—with the respect and honor that any young woman deserved. Macy told Jayson privately that Aaron knew all about her past—the rape, the baby, everything, including the tattoo— and it hadn't changed his opinion of her in the slightest. In fact, he'd only seemed to respect her more for having endured such things and yet doing so well. Macy didn't know if she would still be around after Aaron got home from his mission, or if they would have any interest in each other by then, but she was enjoying his company and wanted to help him prepare for this great event in his life.

Jayson found a new service project in a secret personal challenge to help Trevin get beyond whatever kept him so somber. Jayson had come to know Elizabeth's children well. He helped them with their homework and their chores. He'd taken them to movies and shopping. He played games with them, and tickled and teased them. Addie had warmed to him completely and behaved like a normal, healthy five-year-old. But Trevin, in spite of his occasional smiles and laughter, had a dark cloud hovering around him, and he kept a certain distance—not only from Jayson, but from everyone. He'd lost his brother and his father tragically, but a significant amount of time had passed, and his depression didn't seem normal. He'd turned twelve and had started going to youth activities, but he didn't enjoy them the way that Macy did. Elizabeth told Jayson he'd had some minimal counseling, but there didn't seem to be any obvious problems or concerns that could be helped in that way. So, Jayson decided to put an extra focus on getting to know Trevin better, and to see if there might be something he could do to make a difference during his stay in their home.

On a rainy Saturday afternoon in early March, Jayson found Trevin sitting on the couch, absorbed in a book. He sat down across from him and asked, "What are you reading there, kid?"

Trevin didn't answer; he just lifted the book so that Jayson could read the title. The Book of Mormon: Another Testament of Jesus Christ. He knew the book was written in scripture form, and he found it difficult to believe a boy this age would be interested in such reading.

"Wow," Jayson said, "do you read that stuff because you like it, or because you have to?"

"I like to read it," he said. "I feel better when I read it."

"Well, that's good then," he said. "So, what's it about?"

Trevin looked mildly disgusted. "It's got lots of stories in it. I can't tell you about all of them."

"Okay, what's your favorite?"

Trevin's face became animated. "I like the part where Nephi and his brothers go back to Jerusalem to get the brass plates from Laban. Laban was a bad guy but he had the plates and they had the scriptures on them, like the Bible. Laban wouldn't give them the plates, even when they gave him all of their money and stuff. And

Laman and Lemuel said they weren't gonna go back in the city 'cause Laban was gonna kill 'em, but Nephi went back by himself and he knew that the Lord would guide him because he said that the Lord wouldn't give any commandment without providing a way for it to be accomplished, and the Lord had commanded them to get the plates. Nephi found Laban on the ground and he was drunk, and the Spirit of the Lord told Nephi that he needed to kill Laban, and he didn't want to, but he did it. He took his sword and he chopped off his head, and he put on Laban's clothes and he pretended to be Laban, and he got the plates. And even though you're not supposed to kill somebody, Nephi knew he had to because the Lord told him to do it, and the Lord told him that the people needed the scriptures. He told Nephi that it was better for one man to perish than for a nation to dwindle and perish in unbelief."

Jayson was stunned. He hadn't heard Trevin say that many words total—ever. "Wow," he said again, "that's quite a story. Do you think that stuff really happened?"

"Of course it did," Trevin said. "It's just like stories in the Bible, like Moses parting the Red Sea, and Daniel in the lions' den. Before I was baptized I asked Heavenly Father if the book was true, and He let me know that it was."

"How did He do that, Trevin?" Jayson asked, if only to make conversation.

"The Holy Ghost made me feel warm all over, kind of, only kind of cold, and I started to cry, only I wasn't sad. I felt better than I ever felt in my life, and sometimes I feel that way when I read the book. And when I knew the book was true, then I knew that the way we got the book was true, too."

"And how was that?"

Trevin looked amazed by Jayson's ignorance, but Jayson appreciated the way he could get some questions answered without any assumptions or veiled agendas, as he might get with Elizabeth.

"Well . . . Joseph Smith did it," Trevin said matter-of-factly, and Jayson felt himself bristle.

"What did Joseph Smith do?"

"He was given the gold plates that had been buried in the mountain, and he translated them and had it printed so we could have the book."

Jayson felt his skepticism deepening as he asked, "And how did he know where to find these gold plates in the mountain?"

"The angel Moroni showed him."

"An angel?"

"That's right. Before he died, Moroni was a prophet. His father was Mormon, who put all the records together and gave them to Moroni before the big war. Everyone died in the war except Moroni."

"Everyone?"

"Well, the bad Lamanites were still around, but Moroni was the only good guy left. He buried the plates in the mountain before he died. Then hundreds of years later he appeared to Joseph Smith as an angel and told him where to find the plates." Jayson said nothing, and Trevin said with a maturity that defied his age, "You don't believe me, do you?" He sounded more than insulted; he sounded hurt.

"It's a pretty amazing story," Jayson said, not wanting to challenge what Trevin believed. If believing in this helped him cope with the losses in his life, so be it.

"It's not just a story; it's true," Trevin said vehemently. "But you don't have to believe me. You can find out for yourself. Moroni wrote down how to do that. And that's what I did, and I knew it was true."

Trevin thumbed through pages, then turned the book around and held it in front of Jayson. "Right there," he said, pointing to a place on the page. "Verse four."

Jayson read it silently. *And when ye shall receive these things, I would exhort you that ye would ask God, the Eternal Father, in the name of Christ, if these things are not true; and if ye shall ask with a sincere heart, with real intent, having faith in Christ, he will manifest the truth of it unto you by the power of the Holy Ghost.* Verse five read: *And by the power of the Holy Ghost ye may know the truth of all things.* He felt so intrigued that he turned the page and read verse six. *And whatsoever thing is good is just and true; wherefore, nothing that is good denieth the Christ, but acknowledgeth that he is.*

"Wow," Jayson said again, feeling more intrigued than cynical.

He handed the book back to Trevin, who pushed it back toward Jayson and said, "You can read it if you want to."

"That's okay," Jayson said. "I don't want to take yours. You just keep reading and maybe we'll talk some more later."

"Okay," Trevin said, and Jayson left the room, but not without glancing at the portrait of Christ on his way out.

* * *

Elizabeth was cleaning out the fridge when she heard Trevin say, "You know those extra Books of Mormon we got to give other people?"

"Yes," she said absently.

"Is it okay if I take one to give to somebody?"

Elizabeth peered around the fridge door and looked at him. "Well, of course it is."

"Should I put my picture and my testimony in it like they told us to do in Primary?"

"If that's what you want to do, I think that would be a great idea. Who is it for?"

"A friend," Trevin said and hurried away. Elizabeth smiled to herself, imagining one of his schoolmates going home with a Book of Mormon. She hoped that whoever he was, his parents wouldn't be offended. Trevin's genuine desire to share his beliefs was deeply touching.

Elizabeth considered it an interesting coincidence that the very same day Macy asked if they could talk privately. They went to Elizabeth's bedroom where Macy immediately started to cry, telling

Elizabeth that she'd grown to care for Aaron very much, but his convictions about the gospel were very clear, and Macy didn't know if she could ever make it a part of her life. Elizabeth felt certain it would be best to remain neutral on that issue. She assured Macy that with the gospel, *and* with her growing relationship with Aaron, she needed to take her time, use caution, and follow her heart. The answer soothed Macy, and Elizabeth couldn't help hoping that she might gradually come to accept the gospel into her life. For now, she could only be patient and supportive. She didn't want Macy's father to think that she was pushing religion on his only child.

The following morning they all went to church as usual. Aaron came with them, holding Macy's hand. Occasionally Macy asked Elizabeth a question about one gospel principle or another, and Elizabeth wondered if she might be more receptive to the gospel than her father. Dating a prospective missionary couldn't hurt in that regard. She was grateful for Jayson's ongoing desire to attend church with the family, and to be a part of family home evening and family prayer. But beyond that, religion was never discussed between them. She felt sure his desire to attend church was genuine, but rather than searching out the denomination he'd grown up with, he was showing respect to her family by following their lead. She didn't dare admit, even to herself, how deeply she wanted him to share and understand her beliefs. But she feared he never would, and she wasn't willing to get her hopes up on that count. Still, he was doing well. He was obviously happy, and she was happy to have him around—and coming to church with her, which was something Robert had never done. In truth, Jayson filled the hole in her life that had been left by Robert's absence so thoroughly that she felt terrified to think of him ever leaving. But in that respect too, she had trouble admitting—even to herself— the reasons.

* * *

Sunday night Jayson turned down the covers on his bed and was surprised to find a Book of Mormon on his pillow. At first he thought it was Trevin's, but as he picked it up he realized this had a soft cover, and Trevin's had been hardbound. He chuckled softly and opened the cover, wondering if he really wanted to take the time to read it. Not that he had anything terribly important to do with his time, but still . . .

Jayson's heart quickened a little as he realized Trevin had glued a picture of himself inside the front cover, and below it he had written in barely legible cursive, *Dear Jayson. I know this book is true and I know that Jesus is real and He loves us. Sincerely, Trevin Aragon.*

Jayson absorbed the tender words of a child, bearing a simple conviction that spoke to Jayson's heart. He climbed into bed and propped himself against a stack of pillows, and he began to read. He approached the book with a certain amount of skepticism, but felt determined to read it, if only so he could tell Trevin that he had. He wondered if Elizabeth knew about Trevin's gift; if she did, she hadn't said anything, and that was probably just as well.

* * *

On Wednesday morning the phone rang early. Elizabeth answered it in her bedroom. It was Aaron calling for Macy. She took the cordless phone to Macy's bathroom, where she was putting on her makeup for school. A few minutes later Macy found Elizabeth in the kitchen. Full of excitement, she announced that Aaron had received his mission call, and his mother had invited their family over at five o'clock to be there when he opened it. She then ran downstairs to tell her father.

Jayson laughed to see Macy's excitement. He would have thought she'd be depressed to think of her boyfriend leaving for two years. After Macy and Trevin were off to school, and Will was busy working on taxes, Jayson said to Elizabeth, "If this mission call thing came in the mail, why did he call her early this morning?"

"Oh, our local post office doesn't deliver them with the regular mail. They call early and have the missionary come and pick it up."

"Wow. It's a pretty big deal."

"Yes, it seems to be. You know there are more than sixty thousand missionaries out right now."

"Sixty thousand?" he echoed with a gasp. "Are you kidding?"

"No, I'm not kidding."

"That's incredible."

"Yes, it is," she said and left the room to pursue her current housecleaning endeavors.

At five o'clock, Jayson arrived at Aaron's home with Macy, Elizabeth, and Trevin. Will was busy, and Addie was playing with a friend. Jayson found Aaron's home to be filled with the evidence of many children and a busy mother, but it had a warmth and coziness that couldn't be denied. When he met Aaron's mother, she actually hugged him, expressing what a wonderful girl Macy was and how they had enjoyed the time she'd spent in their home. As everyone gathered around to watch Aaron open the large, white envelope, Jayson couldn't help noting the glow of anticipation about him. He glanced at Trevin and found his eyes wide and eager. Aaron opened the envelope, pulled out a flat piece of paper, scanned it with his eyes and laughed, keeping everyone in suspense. He finally said, "I'm going to Mexico." His mother cried, but they were happy tears. Aaron's brothers and sisters jumped up and down. When the excitement died down a little, Aaron's mother said, "You know, I intended to put some dinner together for everyone, but it just didn't happen. But if you don't mind sticking around for a while, I could throw something together."

"You know what?" Jayson said. "I have been craving pizza, but Elizabeth couldn't seem to fit it into the menu. How about if we order pizza? It's on me." This made the kids almost as excited as the mission call. Aaron's mother said that would be great, and they had some time to visit while they waited for the pizza to be delivered. While they were speculating on Aaron's mission and looking at a map to see the exact area where he would serve, Jayson was imagining the tourist beaches he'd visited more than once. But it became evident that Aaron would be far from the cities, in poverty-stricken villages. Aaron's mother knew of a boy who had served in the same area who had endured horrible living conditions. The apartment they had lived in, if it could be called that, was tiny and had a concrete floor, but they couldn't walk on the floor in bare feet because of the potential bacteria. The shower consisted of a pipe coming out of a concrete wall, with only cold water. Jayson watched Aaron and his obvious enthusiasm and wondered over the source of his conviction in facing such an adventure. Later he posed the question to Elizabeth. She simply said, "There's only one reason they do it. They go to share what they know about Jesus Christ. Simple as that."

While he was letting that sink in, he noticed her grimace slightly. "Are you okay?"

"Yes, I'm fine," she said. "It's just . . . a feminine thing."

"Oh, that," he said and went to his room. He pondered what she had said about missionaries as he stayed up late that night reading in the book Trevin had given him. The following day when Macy came home from school, she said, "Dad, can I talk to you?"

"Sure. What is it?" he asked as she sat beside him.

"Aaron told me last night his mother was really worried about the money for his mission. He's saved some, but he actually uses some of his income to help the kids get things they need. His mother has always had the faith that when the time came, somehow they would manage, but now that it's actually here, she has no idea where they'll come up with the money. He says the Church will help pay for it, but that money has to come from donations, and he doesn't know if the ward has enough to back him, since there are several missionaries out right now, and some of them are getting help from the ward. It costs four hundred dollars every month for the whole time he's out, and that money is supposed to come from the family. And it's going to cost between two and three thousand to get what he needs to go. He says that he's counting on a miracle, and that's what he told his mother." Macy got tears in her eyes and asked, "Dad, he doesn't know about . . . your career . . . and the money. Can you be that miracle? No one would ever have to know it was you."

"It would be an honor, baby," he said, and she laughed and hugged him.

"Okay, but . . . it's just between us, right?"

"Of course," he said. "I'll give some money to the bishop and let him take care of it."

Jayson went to the bishop's home that evening and spoke to him. Even though Aaron was in another ward, this bishop could see that the money got to the right place. Jayson wrote out a check large enough to cover not only the mission expenses, but some extra to be given to Aaron's mother to help the family get by without the household contributions Aaron was making from his own income.

A few days later Macy reported that Aaron had told her of the miraculous anonymous donation. She told Jayson privately of the joy she felt in knowing what she knew. She thanked him profusely, and Jayson felt a warmth in his heart that no words could describe. And for no apparent reason he felt compelled to get out his guitar. Holding it felt strange—and strangely familiar. Alone in his room he started picking out some familiar songs, amazed at how well his left hand was actually doing on the frets. Elizabeth found him at it and gave him a smile that lit her face.

"It's about time," she said, and he agreed. But he still couldn't come up with anything new. It felt all dried up inside of him. Instead of stewing over his inability to write music, he stayed up late reading the Book of Mormon.

The following day, Jayson was sitting on the couch in the living room with his guitar, while Elizabeth sat close by. He noticed she looked pale and asked if she was okay. Again, she said it was feminine, and she lightly told him to mind his business. Trevin came in from school and dropped his backpack like a rock and was immediately next to Jayson, his face full of fascination and eager expectation. He drilled Jayson with questions, and Jayson exchanged an amazed glance with Elizabeth. Jayson showed Trevin a couple of simple chords, then let him hold the guitar and try it. After an hour of impromptu guitar lesson, Elizabeth insisted that Trevin do his chores and his homework.

"Can I play it some more later?" Trevin asked.

"If you get everything done that you're supposed to do," Jayson said.

While Trevin was busy with his homework, Jayson called Drew, glad to find him available with enough time on his hands to follow through on a rather complicated favor.

For another hour before bedtime, Jayson showed Trevin some things on the guitar while Elizabeth looked on with hope shining in her eyes. After Trevin had gone to bed, she said to Jayson, "I can't believe it. He's not shown that much enthusiasm over *anything* for so long that I can't even remember when he did. If I'd had any idea he had that much interest, I would have gotten him a guitar a long time ago."

"I remember him talking to me about it when he was pretty young."

"Yes," she said, "but other things got in the way, and he lost interest, and it hasn't come up for years. Maybe I should consider getting him one," she said.

"Maybe."

"Would you help me pick out the right thing?" she asked. "You do know guitars."

"A little," he said and chuckled.

The following day Trevin was too busy with homework and other activities to spend any time with the guitar. The next day when he came home from school, there were two large boxes sitting in the living room.

"What's that?" Trevin asked his mother.

"I don't know. They came Federal Express for Jayson. He said he'd open them later."

Jayson overheard the exchange from where he was reading a magazine at the kitchen table, and he smiled to himself. At dinner Trevin said to Jayson, "I got my homework done early. Can we play the guitar?"

"Sure," Jayson said, "as soon as the dishes are washed. And I need to get those packages opened and taken care of. I'm sure your mother doesn't want those ugly boxes in her living room any longer."

"Do we get to see what's in them?" Will asked. "I'm assuming it's not more of your clothes or something, or you wouldn't have spent that much on shipping."

"Not likely," Jayson chuckled. "Of course you can see. I think you might find it interesting."

The entire family gathered around, except for Macy who was out, while Jayson took a box cutter and carefully opened the first box, which was nearly as long as the couch where Elizabeth was sitting beside her father. The children knelt on the floor. The top of the box came open, and the children peered in while Jayson dug through masses of Styrofoam peanuts. "You're cleaning that stuff up," Elizabeth said, and he chuckled.

"Of course," he said, then laughed as he'd apparently found what he was looking for. He lifted a hard-sided guitar case out of a shower of white peanuts that mostly fell back into the box. It took only a few seconds for Elizabeth to realize why it looked so familiar. Some very distinctive decals on the side of the case struck her memory, and she gasped, at the same time reaching for her father's hand. He squeezed hers tightly, and she knew that he'd figured it out as well.

Jayson set the case on the floor, and Trevin's eyes lit up as he apparently realized it was a guitar case. Jayson looked directly at the child and asked, "Do you know about your Uncle Derek?"

Trevin nodded. "He died before I was born; even before Mom and Dad got married."

"Yes, he did," Jayson said. "Did you know he was my very best friend?" Trevin shook his head, his eyes showing curiosity and intrigue. "We used to play music together. Did you know he played the guitar?"

"He did?" Trevin said. Elizabeth knew he'd been told, but apparently it had gone over his head at the time.

"When he died, your grandfather gave me his guitars." Jayson opened the case to reveal a well-preserved electric guitar, and Trevin gasped. "This one is my favorite," Jayson said, lifting the guitar out as if it were made of porcelain. "I take it out once in a while, just to hold it and remember Derek. It's a high-quality guitar. Your grandfather bought it for him, and he gave him one of the best. It's been stored properly and taken care of so it still works almost like new. It will need some new strings." He set it into Trevin's hands, while the boy's eyes widened and his mouth fell open with wonder. Jayson's voice revealed a subtle quavering as he added, "Now it's yours."

Elizabeth couldn't hold back tears as the wonder in her son's face turned to stunned amazement. He looked at Elizabeth as if to get her permission to accept the gift. She nodded and watched Trevin's eyes take in the guitar in his hands, then he set it gently back into the case and threw his arms around Jayson's neck. Jayson laughed and hugged him tightly. "Thank you," Trevin said without letting go.

"You're welcome," Jayson said and took the boy's shoulders into his hands, looking into his eyes. "Now, you need to promise me something. Derek wouldn't want his guitar to be sitting around collecting dust. If you're going to own something that meant so much to him, you need to promise me that you will play it. It doesn't matter if you play it onstage or at home, for other people, or just your family. The important thing is that you use it, and that whatever you do with it brings happiness to you and those you love. Do you understand what I mean?" Trevin nodded firmly. "If you get older and decide that you really don't like playing the guitars and you don't use them, then you need to give them to somebody who will enjoy them. Do you understand?"

Trevin nodded again and said, "I understand. Will you teach me?"

"For as long as I'm staying here, I will teach you as much as you're willing to learn and practice."

Elizabeth was still too overcome with emotion to point out that Jayson had said *guitars.* Was his using the plural form an oversight, or . . . The thought had barely occurred to her when Jayson reached into the sea of Styrofoam and lifted out the case for Derek's acoustic guitar, saying with a laugh, "If you're going to learn to play well, you're going to need this one, too."

Trevin squealed with delight, and Jayson laughed again. Will put his arm around Elizabeth. Addie was more interested in the little white peanuts. Jayson opened the case to reveal the beautiful acoustic guitar that Derek had owned, and Trevin seemed even more pleased than he was with the electric one. "Are you sure you want to give them both away?" Will asked.

"I still have the bass guitar in LA," Jayson said. "That's my favorite; that's the one he was gifted with." He smiled at Trevin. "This is where these belong."

"What's in the other box?" Addie asked, as if she hoped it was more of these little white things she could play in.

"Yes, what?" Will asked.

"Well, let's see if Drew got it right," he said, cutting the box open. Inside was an amplifier for the electric guitar, several cords, a foot switch, and two of Derek's guitar stands. "Now, these are yours, too," Jayson said to Trevin. "I'm going to teach you how to take care of all this stuff, but your mother is in charge of noise control. See this?" He pointed to a spot on the amp and nodded toward Elizabeth. "That is a headphone jack."

"But then we can't hear what he's doing," Will said, practically beaming.

"At first that might be good," Jayson said with a chuckle. He added to Trevin, "Now go to my room and get the sack off my bed and bring it here."

He hurried away, and Jayson picked up Addie. He twirled her around then put her, giggling, into the box filled with Styrofoam. "I think I'll send you to my brother in California. He could use a little girl." She laughed and started throwing peanuts at him. "On second thought," he said, picking her up again, "I think we'll keep you here. It would be way too boring without you." He tickled her and transferred her to her grandfather just as Trevin returned with the sack. Inside were packages of new guitar strings and several picks.

For more than an hour Elizabeth and Will sat on the couch and watched Jayson gently teaching Trevin how to string the guitars and to care for them properly. Trevin's eager interest was as touching as Jayson's tender tutelage. Addie was kept perfectly busy with the peanuts. When the guitars were ready to go, Trevin said to Jayson, "Will you play something on the electric one?"

Jayson chuckled, feeling suddenly tense. "It's been a while, kid. And the electric by itself doesn't necessarily sound like much of a song."

"Please," Trevin said.

"Please," Will echoed in the same tone of voice, and Elizabeth laughed.

"I think my father is longing for the good ol' days," Elizabeth said.

"I'm afraid I can't duplicate that," Jayson said.

"Just play something," Elizabeth said, "and stop being such a baby. We're not expecting it to be perfect. Just play it. Surely you can pull off the guitar for one of those number-one hits as easy as breathing."

"Okay, fine," Jayson said and put the strap over his head, settling the guitar into place.

"And you have to sing," Elizabeth said, and Jayson scowled at her.

Jayson set the volume level fairly low, since he didn't have drums he needed to match. He did a couple of test chords and heard himself laugh. As he started to play, he laughed again and realized Elizabeth was right. He could play "Predator" as easily as breathing. And just as easily the lyrics soared out of his mouth. The effect of playing in the house, with Will and Elizabeth sitting there, took him back in time so distinctly that he almost felt like crying. When he'd finished, Will and Elizabeth applauded enthusiastically. Addie jumped up and down. Trevin just sat on the floor with his mouth hanging open. Jayson then put the guitar over Trevin's shoulder and adjusted the strap. He chuckled as he said to Elizabeth, "I was actually about this size when I got my first guitar, and it fit about like this."

"I would have liked to see that," she said.

Trevin tried a few chords with the volume even lower. He almost seemed afraid at first of the noise it made, but within minutes he became more comfortable with it. Elizabeth left the room, then came back about ten minutes later, saying, "Trevin, come here. I want to show you something." As they left the room together, she looked over her shoulder toward her father and Jayson. "You can come too, if you want."

Will stood and followed her, and Jayson followed him. But he had a suspicious feeling that he wasn't going to like it. He found Elizabeth on the couch in the family room, the remote control in her hand. Just as he entered the room, he heard from the television the announcer of the Grammy awards, saying, "This year's hottest band, Gray Wolf." Then applause. The song he'd just been playing filled the television screen and the room, and there he was, front and center, dressed in black, performing with all the energy of his soul while the audience went wild. And there was Drew. Oh, how he missed playing with Drew! But his heart dropped when he saw close-ups of Barry and Rudy—both dead from the result of some very nasty habits. The camera focused on his own face again, followed by a close-up of his fingers on the guitar, then his face again. It felt like a dream, and at the moment, the memory felt more like a nightmare, even though he wasn't certain why. He felt tempted to grab the remote and turn the stupid thing off, but Trevin was mesmerized, and Will and Elizabeth appeared to be enjoying themselves. So he just left the room and hurried up the stairs, while the sound of his own recorded voice grew faint in the distance.

Elizabeth saw Jayson leave the room. She exchanged a concerned glance with her father and handed him the remote before she hurried up the stairs after him. It took her a minute to find him, standing on the deck, huddled in his black leather coat. She grabbed her own coat and stepped outside, closing the door softly behind her.

"You okay?" she asked, and he glanced briefly over his shoulder. He didn't answer, and she added, "I'm sorry if that—"

"No, it's okay. It's just . . . weird. Too many memories all at once, I guess. Playing in the living room like that, I just . . . missed Derek so badly it hurt. And then . . . Rudy and Barry . . . and even Drew. I miss playing with Drew." His voice broke. "I thought I had come to terms with all of that. I thought I'd dealt with it."

"You *have* come to terms with it, Jayson. That doesn't mean you won't have moments of longing, or even grief. Every once in a while I think of Bradley . . . or Robert . . . and I just sit down and bawl my eyes out. I get it out of my system and keep going. I've come to terms with their deaths, but that doesn't mean I don't miss them."

Jayson turned to look at her as he found consolation in her words. He sighed loudly and said, "How do you always manage to say the right thing at the right time?"

"Just lucky, I guess," she said, pushing her arms around him.

"No, I think it's more than that," he said, pressing a kiss into her hair.

She looked up at him and said, "What you did for Trevin today was priceless."

"It's not a big deal," he said. "It's what Derek would have wanted. Maybe it's just the way it was meant to be."

"How do you know it's what Derek would have wanted?"

"I just know," he said, and she smiled.

CHAPTER 7

While spring settled over Utah, Jayson spent some time every afternoon with Trevin and the guitars. It became a pleasant habit over the next few weeks, and along with that, Jayson actually found himself looking forward to bedtime, when he could sit and read for a couple of hours or more without anybody knowing. The further he got into the Book of Mormon, the less cynical he felt. He began to wonder if it *might* actually be true, but then he thought of Joseph Smith claiming to have seen angels—even God—face-to-face, and Jayson just couldn't swallow it. Still, he continued to read, and when he reached the part where the resurrected Christ appeared to the people on the American continent, he actually wept. If nothing else, it certainly was a great story.

Lying in bed that night the images he'd read about wouldn't leave his mind, and he found himself praying silently, asking God if what he'd read could really be true. He was surprised to realize that he *wanted* it to be true. He drifted to sleep and didn't give the matter much thought until the following evening when he sat down to read again, and then he just became immersed in the unfolding drama, interlaced with powerful doctrine—all completely centering around Jesus Christ. He wondered where on earth the rumor began that Mormons were not Christian. The very idea seemed ludicrous, knowing what he knew now.

The following morning, Aaron and Macy were hanging out at the house, since it was Saturday. Aaron had actually spent very little time there, since he was often busy working or at his own house helping with his siblings while his mother worked. While Will was gone to an appointment, everyone else was sitting in the basement, talking and laughing, when Trevin opened the door to his room to get something from the family room, and the music he was listening to suddenly became very loud. It just happened to be Gray Wolf. Jayson hollered facetiously, "Turn it down, kid."

"Oh, I love this song!" Aaron said, and everyone else chuckled.

With mock anger Jayson added to Trevin, "How many times do I have to tell you not to listen to that garbage? Don't you know rock music will fry your brain?"

"Oh, that's pretty funny," Trevin said with a little laugh. But at least he was laughing.

"I'm serious!" Jayson said, then he couldn't hold back a burst of laughter, which was helped along by Elizabeth's comical glare. Trevin laughed again and went back into his room and closed the door, but they could still hear the music.

"He *is* serious," Elizabeth said. "I was listening to this in the car once, and he took it out and threw it in the backseat."

"I was in a bad mood," he said.

"You threw it?" Macy asked, astonished.

"I gave her another one," he said.

"I should hope," Aaron said. "If you ask me, this is one of the best CDs ever made. And it didn't have any words on it that my mother wouldn't let me listen to."

"Jayson's mother wouldn't let him use those kind of words," Elizabeth said.

It became evident that Aaron didn't get the connection when he added with enthusiasm, "It's so cool that you like this CD. I haven't heard it for a while, but I come back to it regularly. I actually saw these guys in concert when they came to Salt Lake once. It was years ago; I was just a kid. My mom actually took me. She likes this stuff, too."

Jayson exchanged a discreetly amazed glance with Elizabeth, then Macy, who shrugged her shoulders. Aaron apparently missed the silent communication as he turned to Macy and asked, "Do you like this?"

"Oh, I love it! I pretended not to when my dad and I were having a generation gap, but I got over it."

Aaron chuckled and said to Jayson, "Then I assume you must like it . . . except when you're in a bad mood."

"It's not my listening preference," Jayson said, suddenly loving this conversation. Elizabeth's smile made it evident she was loving it, too. He said to Macy, "You pretended not to?"

She just shrugged again and laughed softly. Aaron looked at her, then at Jayson. "Did I miss something?" he asked, finally picking up on the humorous undercurrent.

"I'm afraid so," Elizabeth said. "I guess we just assumed that Macy would have told you her family secrets."

"I didn't tell him," Macy said.

"What?" Jayson asked again with mock anger. "First you pretend not to like it, then you're embarrassed to admit to the truth?"

"The last time I tried to tell somebody, you put your hand over my mouth and told them I was delirious."

Jayson laughed. "So I did. But that was just about my playing the piano. But after I played at church, everybody knew anyway."

"You play the piano?" Aaron asked.

"What do the two of you talk about?" Elizabeth asked.

"We talk a lot about the gospel," Aaron said matter-of-factly. Elizabeth wasn't at all surprised by the statement, since Macy had confided as much to her. But Macy glanced cautiously at her father, as if he might be surprised—or disapproving.

Jayson showed no reaction, and Elizabeth added, "Has she not told you her father was giving her lessons?"

"She told me she was taking lessons, but she didn't mention the family connection." Aaron looked at each of them and said, "Okay, what is it? I'm starting to feel really stupid here."

"He's your boyfriend, Macy," Elizabeth said. "I think you're going to have to break it to him."

"And if he doesn't want anything to do with us after you tell him, it's not my problem," Jayson said.

"Aaron," Macy said as if she were about to deliver bad news, "I'm afraid I must confess . . ." she giggled, ". . . that my father . . . is a rock star."

"Was," Jayson corrected.

Aaron looked at her. He looked at Jayson. He looked at her again. His eyes widened, and one word came out of his mouth. "*Wolfe!*" He laughed, then added, "You're Macy Wolfe, and . . ." He looked at Jayson again. "And you're . . . Gray Wolf. "

"Guilty," Jayson said, and Aaron laughed again.

They talked about the ironies, and he asked many questions, but Jayson was relieved to see that he didn't behave any differently toward him, or Macy.

A while later Macy said to her father, "Hey, Dad, if you'll foot the bill, we'll take Trevin and Addie to that new Disney movie they've been begging to see."

"Oh, that would be wonderful," Elizabeth said. "Frankly, I have no desire to sit through talking animals."

Jayson gladly handed over the money, and they all left to go to the movies. A few minutes later Elizabeth said, "I'm going to lie down. I'm not feeling well."

"Okay, what's up?" he asked.

"It's feminine," she said, moving toward her bedroom.

"I thought feminine things were maybe one week out of the month; you don't feel well most of the time lately."

"Okay, so it's not normal. I admit it."

"What do you mean by that?" he asked, a little panicked.

Elizabeth overcame her embarrassment enough to say, "I've been having irregular bleeding and cramping. I'll get a doctor's appointment next week. I promise. Okay?"

"Maybe you should do it sooner."

"Today is Saturday, Jayson. I'm going to lie down."

Jayson didn't argue, but he had to force himself not to push it. He went to the piano to try to distract himself. Fewer than twenty minutes later his cell phone rang, and he pulled it off his belt to look at the caller ID, wondering if it was Drew. But it was the number for the house he was sitting in. He answered and heard Elizabeth say, "I need you, Jayson. Something's wrong."

Jayson didn't even turn off the phone before he ran down the hall into her room. He found her sitting on the floor, leaning against the bed, the phone in her hand. The khaki-colored pants she was wearing were soaked with blood almost to her knees.

"What happened?" he muttered and knelt beside her. She was obviously in pain and didn't answer. He grabbed the phone from her, dialing 911.

Once he'd made the call, she said, "I'm scared, Jayson."

"Well, you're not the only one," he admitted.

"Will you call the bishop? His number's on the ward list. I feel like we need to call him."

Jayson ran to find the number. He dialed it on the cordless phone and returned to find her curled up on the floor, her pain more evident. A woman answered, and when he asked for the bishop, she said he was at the hospital with one of his counselors, visiting a ward member. Jayson told her the situation and she said she would try to locate him and see if he could meet them at the hospital. He'd barely ended the call when the ambulance arrived. He was relieved when they let him stay with her for the brief trip to the hospital, and then as they went into the emergency room. When a medical team gathered around Elizabeth, it was obvious they thought Jayson was her husband. When they began removing clothes, he turned his back and prayed with everything inside of him that she would be all right. A doctor began to speak to him, and he was relieved to see that Elizabeth was covered.

"We're going to have to do a hysterectomy, and now. She's bleeding to death."

"No!" Elizabeth screamed and reached for Jayson's hand. The doctor ignored her and left the room, apparently to prepare for the surgery. "You can't let them do it," she said to Jayson. "Promise me."

"You're bleeding to death," he argued. "I'm not going to let you die."

She looked into his eyes with an intensity that he'd rarely seen, saying with conviction, "You can't let them do it. I'm supposed to have another baby, Jayson. I know it beyond any doubt. You can't let them do it."

Jayson wondered what their options were. He wanted to point out the obvious, that she wasn't even married, and she was in her late thirties, anyway. "Please, Jayson," she muttered, and he could see her weakening, getting close to losing consciousness.

"I'm not going to let you die," he said and realized he was crying.

The door came open, and the bishop and one of his counselors entered the room. "Oh, Bishop," Elizabeth said with a weak voice. "I need a blessing."

Jayson gave them a thirty-second explanation, then watched as these two men put their hands on Elizabeth's head. The bishop closed his eyes and said Elizabeth's full name, then he stated firmly, "By the power of the holy priesthood and in the name of Jesus Christ we command the bleeding to stop. We promise you that your body will heal from this ailment, and you will yet bring forth children into this world."

Jayson wasn't sure if he felt skeptical or amazed. Or if one merged into the other as he witnessed the miracle. The prayer ended. A medical team rushed into the room to prep her for surgery with the doctor giving frantic orders. Elizabeth came more fully awake and said with serenity, "That won't be necessary." She insisted that the doctor check her once more, and he declared with amazement that the bleeding had completely stopped.

"I've never seen anything like it," he said. He gave orders for her to be closely watched, and for some tests to be done.

Within minutes of the trauma, Jayson found himself completely alone with Elizabeth, trying to accept what he'd just witnessed. He'd sat through church meetings where the power of the priesthood had been discussed, but he'd only listened with half an ear, allowing it to go over his head, certain it was just some hokey nonsense. But how could he question what he had just seen with his own eyes?

Elizabeth turned to look at Jayson, noting that he looked dazed. "Everything's going to be alright," she said, reaching for his hand.

Jayson wanted to take her in his arms and bawl like a baby as he realized how close he'd just come to losing her. But he felt so thoroughly stunned that he could only say, "So it would seem."

Elizabeth absorbed the shock in his expression and wondered if he was tallying what had just happened as coincidence and happenstance. She wanted to point out that they'd just been given a miracle, but she felt certain it was obvious. If he couldn't see the evidence of a miracle, there was nothing she could say to convince him otherwise.

By the time Jayson was able to get hold of Will, everyone else had returned from the movie, and they were waiting for the results of the tests. Before Elizabeth came home from the hospital a few days later, a benign tumor had been removed from the inside of her uterus. She'd been given a blood transfusion, and beyond being weak and a little sore from the simple procedure, she felt fine.

The reality of the miracle remained prominent in Jayson's mind. He couldn't help wondering what he might have done if he'd lost Elizabeth. And beyond that, he couldn't help thinking that with the way he felt about her, and his deepest hope that they might yet share their lives completely, that the implication of her having more children was very personal for him.

A week beyond the emergency, Jayson was in the basement sprawled on the couch, toying with his guitar, when Aaron came down the stairs—without Macy. Jayson had never seen him without her.

"Hey, kid," he said, sitting up. "What's going on?"

"Elizabeth told me you were down here. Macy's still shopping, apparently. I was wondering if I could talk to you."

"Sure," Jayson said, setting the guitar aside. "Have a seat."

Aaron sat down at the other end of the same couch, looking a bit nervous. "Well," he said, "you know I'll be leaving in a couple of months for two years."

"Yes, I know."

"And I just wanted you to know that . . . I care very much for Macy. She's amazing, you know."

"Yes, I know," Jayson said with a little laugh.

"I don't know if it could ever work out between us, permanently I mean. I'd like to think so, but I've told her that I don't want her to wait for me. I mean . . . she says she'll write to me, and that'll be great, and if she's still around when I get back, then we'll see what happens. But two years is a long time, and . . . I want her to date other guys. I want her to enjoy this time of her life and not be thinking too much about me. And I guess I just wanted you to know that. I wanted you to know that I've told her that, so you can help encourage her from this end."

Jayson looked at this young man and felt a deepening respect for him. He truly hoped that something would work out between them permanently. It could be a good thing, but as Aaron had just pointed out, two years was a long time. Jayson couldn't help thinking of his own impatience at that age to marry Elizabeth and not be separated from her at all. He wondered now if he'd been more patient and less desperate whether things might have worked out differently between them.

"I appreciate your insight, Aaron," Jayson said. "I'll certainly do my best to help her keep perspective from this end."

Aaron smiled. "Thanks. I knew you would. I just wanted you to know where things stand between us." He cleared his throat and looked nervous again. "There's something else I need to say, and I'm hoping you won't be offended."

"I'm listening."

"I really have no idea how you feel about the Church. I know you've been going to church and stuff, but . . . Macy said you'd told her you respected our beliefs, but you would probably never embrace them. And that's okay."

Jayson had to admit that pretty well described how he felt—or at least how he'd felt not so long ago. Now he wasn't entirely sure how he felt. He was surprised when Aaron added, "Macy and I have talked about it a lot, but I think she might be pretty much in agreement with you on that. And that's okay, too. As much as the gospel means to me, I would never want anyone—especially someone I care for—to become a part of it just for my sake. If a person's conversion isn't complete and for the right reasons, it will never work. I don't want Macy to join the Church for me; that's what I'm trying to say. However—I've told her, and I think you should know—I made a commitment a long time ago that I would be married in the temple, or not at all."

"In other words, if Macy *doesn't* join the Church, you won't be marrying *her.*"

Aaron nodded. "That's what I mean. And like I told Macy, it's not a matter of trying to exclude someone or . . . being prejudiced. It's just a matter of personal conviction."

Jayson had to admit, "I understand, Aaron. I really do. And I respect your conviction. I also agree with you. I wouldn't want Macy to do *anything* just for you, or for any other guy. She needs to make her choices for the right reasons. I'm glad you're willing to be honest with her—and with me."

Aaron let out a deep sigh. "Okay, well . . . I guess that's all, really. I'm glad you're not angry with me."

"Did you think I would be?" Jayson asked with a little chuckle.

"I guess I just . . . don't know you well enough to know whether or not you would be offended by my convictions."

"You're a good kid, Aaron. When I was your age I was married and had a baby on the way. I certainly don't regret Macy's coming into this world when she did, but I admire what you're doing."

"Thank you," Aaron said, then he looked deeply thoughtful, as if something had just occurred to him. He looked up at Jayson, his eyes wide.

"Is something wrong?" Jayson asked.

"It was you," he said in little more than a whisper.

"I'm sorry; you've lost me."

"It was you . . . that gave us the money for the mission."

Jayson tried to appear innocent, but he was taken so off guard that he feared his eyes had betrayed him before he had a chance to look away. When he said nothing, Aaron added, "I honestly had no idea who it could have been. At the time I didn't know about . . . your career, and the money, but . . . it couldn't have been anybody else. Nobody I know has that kind of money . . . except for you."

"Don't be so sure," Jayson said. "You never know what people might be hiding in their bank accounts. If I *had* given you the money for your mission, Aaron, I would want you to know that whatever hands the money might have gone through, it was God's money to begin with, and it came from Him. He gave me this gift of music, and while I worked hard to bring it to its fruition, I didn't necessarily work any harder at my profession than a lot of people work; yet some always struggle financially. I've been very blessed, and I'm only too glad to share what I have for a good cause." He smiled and added, "Supporting somebody like you on a mission is a great idea. I wish I had thought of it first."

Aaron smiled back, and the subject was dropped when Aaron pointed at the guitar. "So, I understand you're pretty good on that thing."

"I have my moments," Jayson said.

"You know . . . I still have trouble believing you're the guy responsible for all that great music. And I actually saw you in concert. I hope it's not obnoxious of me to say that you really were great."

"No, that's not obnoxious. I certainly had my day."

"But surely there are still great things in that head of yours. I mean . . . what an amazing gift you have!"

Jayson couldn't respond. While he wanted to believe there was still a future for his gift, that there might yet be songs unwritten inside of him somewhere, at the moment it just didn't seem possible.

Aaron went on to say, "Which reminds me . . . there's something else I'd like to tell you. I wasn't going to tell you this, but . . . now I feel like I should."

"Okay," Jayson said, intrigued.

"Well . . . after I found out who you were, I dug out those old CDs." He chuckled. "I admit it kind of blew my mind to see your face in those pictures that had been there all along. Anyway, I listened to them for the first time in a while, and I remembered something that had happened a few years ago. I even wrote in my journal about it. You see, in one of your songs you said that nothing lasts forever."

Jayson's heart quickened as he recalled Elizabeth once referring to the same phrase. He'd completely forgotten about that conversation until now. He expected Aaron to tell him what Elizabeth had, that there *was* a forever. He'd been to church enough to know that Mormons believed that through ordinances performed in their temples, marriages and families could be bound together beyond this earth life. Jayson had figured it was mostly something they believed in order to cope with death. But that didn't necessarily mean it was true.

There was something in Aaron's eyes that caught Jayson's attention as he went on to say, "At the time, I was in a pretty cynical stage. You know, all full of teenage hormones, questioning everything I'd been taught, thinking I knew everything. And when I heard that phrase, I actually thought that I felt sorry for anyone who believed there was no forever. And that's when I realized that I *did* believe it; more than that, I knew it was true. And I decided in that moment that I *would* go on a mission when the time came, if only to have the opportunity to find people who didn't know that truth. So, in a way I guess you could say that your music was one of the keys that brought me to this point in my life."

Jayson swallowed an unexpected rise of emotion and forced a chuckle, attempting to keep the conversation light. "What you're trying to tell me is that you felt sorry for the ignorant soul who wrote that song."

Aaron chuckled as well. "Yeah, I guess I did. But now you know there *is* a forever. So I can stop feeling sorry for you. I'll go to Mexico instead and—"

"Oh, there you are," Macy said, coming down the stairs. "Hi, Dad," she said, kissing him on the cheek. Then she did the same to Aaron. "What have you two been doing?"

"Just chatting," Jayson said.

They quickly excused themselves in order to get to a movie, but Jayson stayed as he was, lost in deep thought for a long while. Tidbits of the conversation stayed with him over the next few days, swirling around in his mind like floating pieces of a jigsaw puzzle that had nowhere to fit into his established way of thinking. He felt even more zealous about reading the Book of Mormon, and he was still preoccupied with thoughts of forever when he came across the scripture that Trevin had told him to read. And he was startled to realize that it was in the very last chapter of the book. The index of the book took a significant amount of pages, and Jayson had assumed he had that much more to read. He felt intensely disappointed to come to the end. He nearly went back to the beginning to start over, but he felt compelled to read that last chapter again, the one Trevin had shared with him. He felt deeply touched by Moroni's challenge and promise contained in that verse, but it wasn't until verse eighteen of that same chapter that he felt tears gather in his eyes, without knowing why.

He read that verse again, slowly. *And I would exhort you, my beloved brethren, that ye remember that every good gift cometh of*

Christ. A subtle warmth tingled in his chest, and the moment he stopped to take notice of it, the heat began to build. He gasped from its sudden intensity, pressing a hand over his heart only to feel the warmth filter through every nerve of his body, culminating in hot tears that coursed down his face. In the breadth of a heartbeat everything changed. *Everything!* In an instant he gained a perfect understanding of his life, his purpose, and the reality that everything he had been reading was true. It was *true!* He knew it beyond any breath of a doubt. *It was true!* And everything that it was based upon was true. It was *all* true. He couldn't believe it! But he *did* believe it! All of it.

Jayson was grateful to know that everyone else was sleeping soundly as he crept quietly up the stairs. He went first to the living room and flipped on the light. There above the piano was the image of the Son of God, staring back at him, seeming to echo all that Jayson had felt. He stood there for several minutes, just gazing at the image, pondering what it meant. Then he turned off the light and carefully moved to the family room and flipped on that light. He sat on the floor in front of the bookshelf, desperately hungry for more truth, more evidence. Instinctively he reached for a big black book titled, *Mormon Doctrine.* He thumbed through it for a few minutes, then took it back to his room with him, hoping Elizabeth wouldn't notice it was missing. A part of him wanted to go knock on her door and tell her right now what he'd just learned. But something deeper wanted some time to let it settle in, to become more educated on what he had discovered.

While days passed and Jayson continued studying vigorously, he often took the opportunity to visit with Bert and Ethel, gratified to learn that they were lifelong members of the Church, and they had each served missions in their youth. He learned too that as an older couple they had served three different missions. He was able to ask them some questions, and their answers helped verify all that he was learning.

In spite of the conviction he felt about the truth of what he was learning, he kept expecting to hear answers to his questions that would bother him or make him angry. He kept thinking he might hear something that would discredit what he'd felt. But his conviction only deepened as everything he learned made complete sense. He thought of how he had always instinctively believed in God, but there had always been so much in the religion he'd grown up with that hadn't felt right, or was, at the very least, incomplete. Now he had learned the reality of personal revelation, that by the power of the Holy Ghost he could get the answers for himself and not have to take anyone else's word for it. When it struck him that there was a living prophet on the earth today, he was amazed to realize that he knew this man wasn't the hoax that Jayson had initially believed him to be. He was real. And Jayson knew it. But he asked Bert why there was a need for a prophet, if each person could receive their own revelation. He answered simply that each person can receive answers only for himself, perhaps related to a Church calling, and for those in his steward-ship, such as family members. Only the prophet can receive reve-lation for the Church as a whole.

That answer settled in with every other answer he received until Jayson knew there was only one possible path his life could take. He just wasn't quite sure how to go about it. He wondered why he felt so hesitant to share what he felt with Elizabeth. He came to the conclusion that with the present state of their rela-tionship, he didn't want her to think that his interest in the Church was merely to impress her, or to soften her toward making a future with him. His feelings about the Church needed to be completely independent of his relationship with Elizabeth. But he loved her, and she was the reason he'd become exposed to the gospel. It was impossible to completely separate the two. He finally decided that they needed to talk; the air needed to be cleared between them. But there were other things that needed to be discussed before he could feel comfortable sharing what he'd come to discover.

Jayson woke late, as he often did when he stayed up late reading. He found Elizabeth in the kitchen. She glanced at him and said, "There's some hot water on the stove if you want some cocoa."

"Thanks," he said. He'd given up coffee in rehab when he'd realized that even caffeine could be an addictive substance.

"You okay?" she asked a little too severely.

"I'm fine, why?"

"I've just noticed that you're sleeping awfully late these days, and you're tired a lot."

Jayson felt mildly alarmed. He wasn't ready to tell her his reasons for often reading half the night, but he knew why she was asking. When he didn't respond she added, "Forgive me, Jayson. I'm not trying to be presumptuous or accusing, but they told us very plainly that, as your family, we should take notice of any change of habits, or signs that you might be . . ."

"Taking drugs?" he provided when she hesitated. He wished it hadn't come out sounding so defensive. He softened his voice and said with sincerity, "I appreciate your concern, Elizabeth. It's nice to have someone looking out for me. Truthfully, it just takes me a long time to fall asleep most nights. When I got so used to taking drugs to make me sleep, it can be hard sometimes to sleep without them. I've been reading some. Anyway, that's all. Just not getting as much sleep as I should. It's nothing to be concerned about, but thanks for noticing."

Elizabeth smiled. "Just don't forget that somebody loves you enough to notice."

He smiled back and put some bread in the toaster.

After supper that evening, he found her sitting on the deck, wrapped in a big sweater. He grabbed a jacket and sat beside her, saying, "I remembered something you brought up when I was in rehab. You said you would tell me about it some other time. And you never did."

"What's that?" she asked.

"You haven't told me about forever."

Elizabeth was so surprised she hardly knew what to say. It took her a moment to even recall the conversation he was referring to. She finally said, "You've been going to church for weeks now. Surely you've heard about that."

"Truthfully, I wasn't always paying attention. I've heard a little, but I want you to tell me."

"Well," she shrugged, "it's very simple, really. Through the ordinances done in the temple, marriage can be eternal, and families can be forever. When people are sealed together, then the bonds go beyond death."

Jayson leaned back and absorbed what she was saying. He considered what he'd first assumed when he'd heard the principle: that Mormons had created this illusion to give themselves comfort. Perhaps all the death he'd been close to had added to his cynicism. But hearing these words come through her lips now, knowing what he knew, he wanted to take her in his arms and beg her to be his—forever.

"So, how does that apply to people who have already died?" he asked while the deaths of Derek and his mother came most prominently to mind. Again, he knew the answer, but he wanted to hear her explain it to him.

"Those ordinances are performed by proxy," she said, seeming nervous.

"You seem uncomfortable talking about this with me," he said.

"I am, to be quite honest."

"Why?"

"These things are sacred to me, Jayson. I don't want tension between us as a result of discussing things that we disagree on. It's like . . . well, let's say I've discovered how wonderful a warm chocolate chip cookie is, and you've never tasted one. I think it's heavenly and I would love to share the experience with you, but you adamantly declare that you don't want to taste it. I can't make you taste it. And if you taste it with a determination not to like it, you probably wouldn't like it anyway. And then we'd just end up arguing over whether or not a warm cookie is worth eating."

Jayson had to admit, "That's a very good analogy. So . . . you'll hoard all the cookies to yourself and let me starve."

"I'm sure you could get cookies of your own if you wanted to," she said.

"Touché," Jayson said. Knowing what he knew, he couldn't keep from chuckling. "I'm sure I could." His voice sobered, and he asked, "And what about Robert?"

"What *about* Robert?"

Jayson watched her closely, realizing the answer to this question could be difficult for him to swallow. Her husband was gone, but if work could be done by proxy, he just had to know . . . "Will you be with him forever?"

He was surprised at how quickly she said, "No. I loved him very much. He was a good man. But he had the opportunity laid before him to take hold of the gospel. I wanted him to go to the temple with me so we could be together forever. He chose not to take that path. I know that missionary work takes place on the other side of the veil. He may yet have another opportunity. But he will not be my eternal companion."

Jayson felt deeply relieved to hear her say that. He wondered now if part of her hesitance in getting involved with him was for that very reason. If she wanted an eternal companion, with the same conviction that Aaron had expressed, and he'd blatantly told her he would not convert to her religion, then she would naturally be put off. But knowing what he knew now, he felt a hope like he'd not felt since she'd dumped him when they were eighteen.

"And what about Bradley?" he asked.

"Bradley deeply loved the gospel," she said. "He eagerly joined the Church of his own free will. He talked often about serving a mission, of going to the temple." She got teary as she added, "When the time is right, his temple ordinances will be done by proxy. I will be with my son again. I see my separation from him as yours was from Macy. She was gone; you had no contact. But it was temporary. You're together again. And that's how it will be with Bradley."

Jayson felt deeply touched by the analogy, and by her conviction. Knowing what he knew, he realized he loved her more than ever. In looking at the big picture, he knew the Spirit had guided him to the knowledge of things that made sense of so much of his life—and hers—in a way it never had before. But he knew this was not the time to tell her. He couldn't explain why, but he felt compelled to give the matter some time.

Elizabeth took a long look at Jayson, wondering over the source of his interest in such things. She ached to share the full depth of all she knew with him, but conversations of the past that had ended badly prompted her to hold back—at least for now. But she wondered if a time would ever come when she could tell him how her desire for him to know what she knew sometimes ached in her. When the gospel had brought her such joy, such peace, how could she not want to share that with him?

Jayson looked around himself and took a deep breath before he said, "I love it here, Elizabeth. I love the people, the change of seasons—even the snow. And I love the mountains. There's just such an incredible . . . feeling here."

Going with her own train of thought, Elizabeth said, "Maybe it isn't the mountains."

He smiled and said, "Oh, I know what it is." She looked down, and Jayson felt sure she was thinking that he meant it was her. She certainly had a lot to do with it, but that wasn't the crux of what he loved here. He'd save that conversation for another time.

With her curiosity sparked, Elizabeth was both relieved and disappointed when he changed the subject by saying, "You know, Lady, we have a lot of history together."

"We certainly do."

"There's little that's happened in my adult life that hasn't involved you. And . . . I was thinking that . . . well, how do I explain this?" He was quiet for a minute as if he were trying to find the right words. "I've gone through some pretty drastic changes since I came here last fall—emotionally, spiritually. And I've been thinking about some of the issues of the past and . . . I know we talked through some things while I was in rehab, but I wonder if there aren't some things that still need to be said." She looked at him almost sharply, and he added, "There are things about my marriage to Debbie that I've never told anyone, and I suspect there are things about your marriage to Robert that fall in the same category." She looked away, and he knew that was true, but he clarified, "I'm not expecting you to tell me anything you don't want to tell me. But there are some things I think I need to tell you about my relationship with Debbie. I really don't like to talk about her, but she came between us—and I'm the one who put her there. When I married her, I convinced myself that it wasn't a rebound from you. But looking back, I know that it was. I was in denial, stuffing things into that ugly box. And I must have believed that getting married would solve all my problems. I loved her. I really did. And she loved me. We had some very good times. I don't know what changed her; it doesn't matter. I do know, looking back, that there were signs of problems from the start. There were things that concerned me, things that frustrated me, even hurt me. But when you're married and you share a child with someone, you do your best to look past those things and make the most of what you've got."

"Like what?" she asked. "If you don't mind telling me, of course."

"I don't mind," he said. "In fact, I *need* to tell you . . . if only so I know there are no secrets between us. You are, after all, my best friend." She smiled, and he continued. "One of the things that bothered me most was the way she would talk about my achieving stardom as if it would change everything. When we were poor and had nothing, I remember telling her a number of times that I longed for the financial security, but I didn't expect success to make me happy; I was already happy. And I didn't want it to change our values or the way we felt about each other. I remember feeling uneasy when she made no comment on that, as if she didn't agree with me. I can see now that what she wanted from my success was very different from what I wanted. I've had to wonder if part of her commitment to me didn't come from her belief that I would achieve great success; and that lifestyle intrigued her greatly. Still, I didn't have a problem with giving her a fair settlement in the divorce. She'd worked hard to support me through those tough years. She earned what she got in that respect."

"But all she ended up with in the end was money."

"And lots of friends in the rock industry. It doesn't matter anymore, and truthfully, the thing she did that hurt me the most happened long before the divorce."

"What?" Elizabeth asked, wondering what might have happened that she'd heard nothing about.

Jayson sighed deeply and leaned back. "Having Macy was one of the greatest things that ever happened to me. I wanted more kids, and she knew it. I came home from one of those early tour stretches when I was just a hired musician to find out that she had gotten her tubes tied to prevent her from ever getting pregnant again."

Elizabeth gasped. "Did she . . . talk to you about it?"

"Not a word," he said, "until it was over. She said she was never going through that again, and she didn't want any more children. I was devastated. Not only the loss I felt in knowing there wouldn't be more children, but . . . I felt so betrayed—that she would do something like that without even discussing it with me, with no apparent thought or concern as to what that meant to me. If she'd had some serious medical problem or something, it would have been different. But it was pure selfishness. Knowing what some women go through to have babies, I know she didn't have it that bad. She just didn't want it cramping her lifestyle; she didn't want to lose her figure. I think I knew then that our marriage wouldn't last. But still, I tried to overlook it. I tried to be a good husband."

"And I'm sure you were."

He chuckled without humor. "I'm not so sure, but I did try. It doesn't matter anymore. Anyway, I just wanted you to know that. We can't change the past, but . . . the past is what got us where we are. So now I've said it, and I can stop thinking that I should."

He leaned his forearms on his thighs and sighed. Elizabeth thought about what he'd said, and she knew there was wisdom in this conversation. She'd always wondered if his marrying Debbie so quickly had been a rebound from her own rejection of him. Now he'd admitted that it was. It couldn't be changed, but somehow knowing made a difference. It brought up other points that she wasn't ready to discuss with him yet, but there were other things that she'd wanted to tell him for a long time. Perhaps now that he'd opened the door for such discussion, she could find the courage to walk through it.

"There is something I should tell you, as well," she said, and Jayson looked over his shoulder at her. "Something I've often thought you should know, but . . . it was hard to talk about."

He sat up straight and turned more toward her. "I'm listening."

Elizabeth took a deep breath and looked down. "I'm sure you remember the conversation we had about . . . the problems in my marriage."

"I remember," he said.

"And you know that after our conversation, I did make some progress with Robert. We went to some counseling. And things got better. They were far from ideal, but they were better."

"Okay, I knew all of that," he said, looking out over the yard, covered in darkness.

"Yes, but . . . I don't think you knew that you became an issue in our marriage."

Jayson turned slowly to look at her. "No, I didn't know that."

Elizabeth again took a deep, sustaining breath. "When I sat Robert down to express to him my frustration and hurt with the lack of affection in our marriage, he . . . uh . . . well . . ."

"Just say it."

"It's hard to talk about."

"Would that be because we're talking about sex?" he asked, and she glared at him. "We're grownups, Elizabeth. Just say it."

"Fine. He wanted to know why—if I had been a virgin when he married me—I knew so much about certain . . . aspects of intimacy that had never taken place between the two of us." Jayson's nerves bristled as the implication sunk in even before she added, "So I told him. He knew you and I had dated in high school, but he'd always taken quite literally the theory that you were like a brother to me, that you had replaced Derek as a brother in my life. And in many ways that's true. But that didn't erase what had happened between us. It's simply a fact. As you said, the past is what got us where we are. Still, I want to make it clear that in spite of the problems in my marriage, I was not caught up in romantic thoughts of you."

"But apparently Robert wasn't happy to learn the truth about what happened between us when we were dating."

"No, he was not happy at all. Mind you, he didn't get angry. But he was upset. And I had to admit that if it was the other way around, I probably would have been upset too. If I'd found out the woman my husband talked to regularly, and even spent time with occasionally, was someone he'd once been intimate with to a certain degree, I probably *would* have been angry. Of course, he had to wonder if something romantic had been going on all along. I told him the truth, that nothing romantic had *ever* occurred between us following our marriages. Except for the one time that I almost kissed you . . . and how you stopped me . . . and what we talked about . . . and my reasons for feeling so deprived in my marriage."

Jayson felt a little unsettled by the comment, for more reasons than one. He said with sarcasm, "Oh, I bet that went over real well."

Elizabeth looked directly at him and said, "That was when he started to cry. And that was the first time I had ever seen him cry. That was the point where he was able to understand the damage his lack of affection was doing. That was when he regretted not doing something about the problem sooner."

A thought occurred to Jayson, and he had to say, "I spent time in your home after that, Elizabeth. He never behaved any differently toward me than he had before that. He was always perfectly kind and gracious; I never sensed any tension. I had no idea he knew all of that."

"I know," she said. "And his attitude toward you was completely genuine. He wasn't phony, Jayson. He had a deep respect for you. How could he not when he knew that I had nearly thrown myself into your arms, thoroughly starved for love and affection? But you had stopped it before it got started, and you had insisted that I go home to my husband and work out my problems with him. He also knew that it was *you* who had stopped it from going all the way on the beach. Once he got past the shock of realizing all that had transpired between you and me, he was deeply grateful for your integrity, for your respect for me—and him. He genuinely liked you, Jayson."

Jayson swallowed carefully. "Well, I liked him too. But I don't know that I was nearly so noble as you led him to believe."

"I told him the truth, Jayson. And you know as well as I do that what happened between us was far more my doing than yours. You tried to stop it more than once, as I recall. I think I somehow believed that sharing such an experience with you would have made up for every other hurt and loss in my life. Of course, we both know that when you get past the passionate moment, such beliefs are only an illusion."

"I don't know," he said. "Personally, I think that with the right person, within marriage, such passionate moments could make up for a lot of the hurt in this life." Their eyes met, and his heart quickened, but he hurried to clarify, "Not in and of itself, of course. But with other important elements in place, it could be . . . incredible."

Elizabeth absorbed what he was saying, and an apparent deeper meaning seemed to come through his eyes, and she feared he could hear her heart pounding. She was relieved when he looked away and said, "So, apparently you and Robert came to terms with all of that."

"We did," she said. "Things got better between us, and he remained supportive of my friendship with you. He told me he appreciated my honesty, and I promised to *always* be completely honest with him. We agreed that I would never be alone with you again. He realized that if he had gone to dinner with us that night as we'd invited him to, I never would have been in a position to be tempted to kiss you—even though I didn't. But we also agreed that maybe it was better that something happened to bring the problems to the surface where they could be faced. When I joined the Church, I . . . well . . ." She seemed nervous again. "You see . . . when a person is baptized, it's like being reborn, and it's important to put everything in order before that happens. I talked with the bishop about my past *sins,* if you will, and everything was officially—and spiritually—put behind me. I wondered at the time if I should have talked to you about it, but your mother had just died, and the time just didn't seem right."

Elizabeth looked into his eyes, wondering what felt different between them that made the time right now. Whatever it was, she liked it, but at the same time it was almost frightening. Almost.

CHAPTER 8

Jayson and Elizabeth sat together in silence for several minutes while it became evident there was nothing more either of them felt the need to say—at least for the time being. Elizabeth found her mind attempting to analyze her present feelings for Jayson, and where exactly she stood. She felt unsettled by her own train of thought, and was startled to hear him break the silence by saying, "So, have you like . . . gone out on any dates or anything since Robert died?"

"Not really, no."

"Not really?"

"Well, I went to some single adult things—church things. A couple of dances, and some firesides, but—"

"What's that?" he asked.

"It's just like an evening meeting; usually on a Sunday. They have a speaker and some refreshments."

"So, you didn't meet anybody exciting?"

"Not even close, and, well . . . I don't think I was ready anyway. What about you?"

"What *about* me?"

"Have you dated . . . since the divorce?"

"Yes, actually. I had people trying to line me up all over the place."

"You never told me you were dating."

He chuckled. "I never went out with any woman more than once; there was nothing worth repeating, I can assure you." He cleared his throat and added, "So . . . do you think you might be ready . . . to start dating? I mean . . . you have adjusted to Robert's death for the most part, haven't you?"

"I've come to terms with it, yes," she said, wondering what he might be getting at. "Many good things have come from his death; I can see that now."

"Like what?" he asked.

"Well . . . I'm very grateful to have my father with me. I don't think he would have made the move if I'd had a husband living in my home. But I love having him here. He's told me how grateful he is to be here with us, and his being here prompted him to join the Church, and he's grateful for that, too." Jayson smiled, and she went on. "Speaking of dating, he really likes Marilyn. I think it might come to something."

"Really?" Jayson said with a little laugh. "By something you mean . . . he might marry her?"

"He's mentioned it to me, but don't say anything. I think it's a secret."

"My lips are sealed. But . . . he'd be moving out if he did that."

"Yes, but . . . Marilyn's home is paid for, and she only lives half a mile away."

"Good point." He laughed softly. "That's pretty cool. It's about time he found someone. I hope it works out."

"Yes, I hope so too. I really like Marilyn."

Another stretch of silence ensued before Jayson said, "So what else good came from Robert's death?"

"Well, I think I'm a stronger person because of it. I never would have chosen to lose him—or Bradley—that way, but there has been a great deal of growth for me—spiritually and emotionally."

"I can see that," he said.

Not wanting to get into that, she added, "And did you know he was an organ donor?"

"No, I didn't know that."

"Because of the way he died, they were able to help three different people. One of them had been on the brink of death and would have died within the week. He is now doing well and living a normal life."

"Wow. That's amazing."

"Yes, it is," she said. "Good things often come out of adversity. There's evidence of that all around us."

"Yes, there certainly is," he said.

Elizabeth impulsively took his hand, wishing she could read his mind. They'd been living under the same roof for several months since he'd finished his drug rehab, but they'd not shared thoughts that were so deeply personal since the counseling sessions they'd endured together there. Silently recounting all they had discussed tonight, she wondered what might be going on inside of his head and heart. Their conversation turned to small talk and soon dissolved, but long after she went to bed, Elizabeth stared at the ceiling, pondering all that had been said—and how it made her feel. She hardly slept at all, consumed as she was with feelings too intense to ignore, and a confusion that brought back difficult memories and left her terribly uneasy.

The following morning she was relieved to have Jayson leave to do some errands and to visit Bert and Ethel. She loved the way he'd come to care for the elderly couple and how he checked up on them regularly. While Addie was at preschool, she took advantage of being alone with her father, hoping he could give her some much-needed advice.

"Hey, Dad," she said, coming into his office, "I know tax day is looming right around the corner, but I could really use my dad, if you have a few minutes."

"I'm never too busy for you," he said, turning away from the computer. "What's up, precious?"

"Well, to put it bluntly, I'm falling in love with Jayson."

Will smiled. "You've always loved Jayson."

"Yes, but . . . it's gone through many phases. And now, I'm falling in love with him . . . all over again. He is so . . . incredible. I love everything about him."

Will chuckled and leaned back in his chair. "And there's a problem with that? If you ask me, you should have married him twenty years ago."

Elizabeth looked down abruptly, not wanting to discuss the heartache she felt over that very thing. Instead she focused on the present. "He's a good man, Dad."

"One of the best I've ever known," Will said. "I'm still waiting to hear the problem."

Tears came as Elizabeth admitted, "I want to marry a man who will share the gospel with me. I could never blame Robert for not wanting anything to do with it; I joined the Church after we were married. I was the one who had changed; I couldn't expect him to change with me. But this is different. I don't want to keep going to the temple alone. I don't just want a husband; I want an eternal companion. I want it to last forever. But you know where he stands. He's made it clear he respects our beliefs, but he has no intention of ever joining the Church."

"It's been quite a while since he said anything to that effect," Will said. "His heart may soften yet, if it hasn't already."

"But . . . can I commit myself to him on the hope that . . . maybe one day . . ."

"Listen to me, girl," Will said gently, "this is a decision only you can make, but you have the gift of the Holy Ghost to help you make it. You don't know the outcome, or what's really going on in Jayson's heart. But God knows, and through the Holy Ghost He can let you know the course to take. You need to add it all up in your head, and then weigh that with what you feel in your heart, and make a decision, and God will let you know if it's right. And since you seem to be asking my opinion, I'm going to give it to you. If you start making a list of the qualities you want in a husband and father, you're going to find Jayson measuring extremely high on that list. The history you share, the friendship that has endured over the years—those are huge bonuses. And he goes to church with you; something Robert never did. And there's something else he's got that Robert never had."

"What's that?"

Will leaned closer and said firmly, "Jayson has a deep testimony of Christ, Elizabeth. He's a Christian through and through. Any man with that much conviction, who is willing to support you in your beliefs, cannot be a bad choice. As far as his actually joining the Church and going to the temple with you . . . only time will tell for certain, but I believe he will."

"You really think so?" Elizabeth asked, feeling something come to light inside of her. She'd been so thoroughly convinced that he never would, that the very idea had trouble settling.

Will shrugged. "Of course I can't say for certain. But as I said, God knows. He can tell you what you need to do. As I see it, He's already paved a very clear path. You just need the courage to take the next step."

Elizabeth deeply pondered her father's words, and her own feelings. She fasted for the next twenty-four hours, and was grateful that Jayson knew it was something she did on occasion, so he didn't seem to pay much attention to her going without meals. Praying for a specific answer, Elizabeth felt mildly discouraged when she came to the end of her fast and still found herself logically weighing matters back and forth in her mind. She could assess that there were many good reasons to pursue a future with Jayson, but until her heart could agree, she could never press forward.

Two days later Elizabeth was cleaning up after supper when she heard a ruckus of laughter coming from the living room. She picked up a towel and dried her hands as she ambled toward the sound to investigate. She leaned her shoulder against the wall and smiled to see Trevin and Addie engaged in a ferocious tickling match with Jayson. Just to hear Trevin laugh that way seemed like a miracle. The children broke free and ran past her, challenging Jayson to catch them. As he jumped to his feet, he saw her there and was startled. He laughed and accused her of sneaking up on him. And that's when it happened. She didn't hear a voice or see any visible change take place in her surroundings, or in Jayson. But everything was different. She'd never seen him that way before. There he stood, as familiar to her as the sun and the sky. But now she saw something more than her high school sweetheart and her dearest friend. It was as if she could see her life from beginning to end in his eyes; she could see forever. Her heart swelled, and tears gathered in her eyes as a tiny moment stretched out with a hundred thoughts at once.

"Is something wrong?" Jayson asked, startling her from a daze.

"No," she said quickly and let out an awkward chuckle. "I'm fine. In fact . . . I'm really good."

"That's good," he said while his eyes questioned her regarding the reasons.

Just when she thought she could gracefully leave the room and be alone to absorb what she'd just learned, tears spilled down her face, and Jayson's concern visibly deepened. "What is it?" he asked, wiping at her tears with his fingers.

She looked up into his eyes, wondering if he could sense the changes taking place in her. She wanted to babble a lengthy explanation, or throw herself into his arms and pledge her heart forever. But all she could do was lift a hand to his face and mutter, "Oh, Jayson."

"What?" he chuckled, baffled but apparently less concerned.

"It's just . . . nice to have you here; that's all. I'm grateful . . . that you're here."

"I'm grateful too, but . . ." Before he could finish, Elizabeth hurried away, fearing she *would* babble her feelings otherwise. And the moment just wasn't right. She needed to adjust her own thinking first.

Alone in her room, Elizabeth cried for several minutes. But her tears were only tears of joy and peace. She'd received her answer, more clearly than she'd even expected. She knew now the course that God wanted her to take, and she knelt beside her bed to offer her gratitude, and to ask for guidance in putting the pieces together.

When she saw Jayson a while later in the kitchen, he said nothing about the awkward moment they'd shared, and she figured he had taken it at face value—just as she'd told him, a moment of gratitude that had made her emotional. She was relieved not to have it come up, but knew she couldn't keep these feelings to herself for long.

Later that night, Elizabeth stared at the ceiling and pondered all she was feeling. She could look back over her life and see that she'd been given the answer over and over, line upon line. While she knew there was still at least one unresolved issue between them, she knew beyond any doubt that she needed to commit herself—heart and soul—to this man she had loved for more than half her life. The problem was how to let him know. She felt relatively certain that he was holding back out of respect for her feelings on the matter, and he likely wouldn't press the issue of any romance between them until she gave him some indication that she was ready—and interested.

Praying that she would know what to say—and how and when to say it—she allowed the idea to fully sink into her, realizing she felt happier than she'd felt in years—if ever. She came to the conclusion that perhaps she just needed to start out by asking him out on a date.

* * *

Jayson was astounded to wake up on a beautiful morning in the middle of April with the thought prominently in his mind that he needed to tell Elizabeth about the changes within himself. He wondered what had made the difference. Yesterday it hadn't felt right; today it did. But he didn't question the guidance of the Spirit; he just made up his mind to act on it.

After he'd showered, he was pleasantly surprised to discover that Addie was at preschool and Will had gone somewhere with Marilyn. Having gotten past the tax deadline, he was making up for his recent neglect. Trevin and Macy were in school, as usual. Jayson found Elizabeth in the kitchen, apparently getting ready to bake something.

"Elizabeth," he said, sitting on one of the chairs next to the table.

"Yeah," she said absently with her head buried in one of the cabinets, searching for something.

"Can we talk?"

"Sure," she said. "There's something I need to talk to you about, too." Elizabeth heard herself say the words and almost wondered where they'd come from. Was she ready to tell him how she was feeling? Maybe not. But she could take the first step.

"Okay, well . . . maybe you should go first," Jayson said.

"No, that's okay," she insisted. "You go first."

Feeling suddenly nervous, he considered waiting until another time, but with no one else at home, he knew he wouldn't get a better opportunity than this. "There's something I need to tell you."

The severity of his tone made Elizabeth abandon her task and turn to face him. "What is it? Is something wrong?"

"No," he said. "I just . . . need to tell you something . . . about me."

She saw his expression become even more sober. "What is it, Jayson? You know you can talk to me about anything."

"Yes, I know," he said, meeting her eyes. "I can't begin to tell you what living in your home has done for me—for my life."

"It's been a pleasure to have you here," she said, wondering if this was leading into his telling her that it was time he moved on. She felt something knot in her stomach at the very idea. Would he tell her that even though Macy needed to stay and finish school, he needed to go? She sat down across the table from him and looked at him expectantly, waiting for him to get to the point.

"Elizabeth," he said, and she realized he was nervous, "I want to be baptized. I want to join the Church."

Elizabeth heard herself gasp. She pressed a hand over her heart as if to quell its sudden quickening. She couldn't believe what she was hearing. Certain this couldn't be as it seemed, she wondered over his motives. "Why?" she asked and watched his eyes closely.

"Why?" he echoed with a tense chuckle. "Good heavens, Elizabeth. Why would I be foolish enough *not* to take hold of an opportunity so . . . incredible? Because it has answered every unanswered question; because it has given me peace over things that I thought would forever torment me. It has come to mean more to me than anything else this life has ever given me." His eyes tightened on her, and she felt breathless from the conviction she saw there as he added firmly, "I know it's true, Elizabeth, that's why."

Elizabeth could only stare at him while her thoughts attempted to catch up with what she'd just heard him say. Everything she'd convinced herself of regarding his attitudes and feelings had obviously been way off base. And with one realization came another. She had convinced herself that even with the firm decision to be willing to commit her life to Jayson, she'd had no reason to believe that he would ever embrace her beliefs. But now everything had changed. *Everything.* While her thoughts attempted to settle with this new revelation, she was vaguely aware of him watching her, waiting for a reaction. But she only became aware of the raw vulnerability in his eyes when he muttered, "Say something, for the love of heaven. You're scaring me."

"No need for that," she said, smiling at him. "I'm just . . . stunned. I . . . I had . . . no idea. I was under the impression that you were just . . ." She shook her head. "How did you come to this, Jayson?"

"I've been reading, studying, praying."

"When have you been reading? I haven't seen you reading."

"At night," he said, and his reasons for often sleeping late or being tired suddenly made sense. "I'd go to bed and read, and I just couldn't sleep."

"*What* have you been reading?" she asked.

"Well . . . the Book of Mormon, of course."

"You read it?"

"I did. Trevin gave it to me," he said, and she let out a little laugh of disbelief. "I read it twice, actually. It's incredible, Elizabeth."

"Yes, I know," she said breathlessly. "What else did you read?"

"Well, the Doctrine and Covenants, and *Mormon Doctrine,* and—"

"*All* of it?"

"Well . . . yes. Is that a problem?"

"Of course it's not a problem. It's just . . . a really big book."

"It's so amazing, though," he said, his eyes filled with an excited fervor that exceeded even his most passionate moments of creating and performing music.

Jayson felt a deep excitement overtake him as he told Elizabeth about the journey he'd taken that had led to this discovery. He told her about his conversations with Trevin, and Aaron, and with Bert and Ethel. And with tears he couldn't possibly hold back, he told her about the personal witness he'd received that everything he'd learned was true.

"And almost in the same moment," he said intently, "I knew beyond any doubt that . . ." He laughed with pure joy as it came back to him all over again. "Oh, Elizabeth, I had this over-whelming realization that this gift of music in me truly does come through the light of Christ and . . . well, I always believed it came from God, but now I *know.* And I know that my gift has a very distinct purpose. I don't know what it is yet, but I know that eventually I *will* know."

When Jayson apparently had nothing more to say, Elizabeth forced herself beyond the stunned disbelief she was feeling. She stood up and walked around the table and he stood to face her. A rush of emotion bubbled out of her as she wrapped him in her arms. She laughed and cried, then finally took his face into her hands, saying through her tears, "I'm just so . . . happy."

Jayson laughed and lifted her off the ground with his arms tightly around her. "Well, that makes two of us." He set her down and said, "Now . . . what did you need to talk to me about?"

It took Elizabeth a moment to remember. "Oh," she said with a bright smile, "you know when we were talking about dating."

"Yes," he drawled, wondering if she would tell him she was going out with some other guy. The thought made him a little sick.

"Well . . . I've been thinking about that and . . . I was wondering if I could talk you into taking me on a date." He sucked in his breath, and she added, "You can afford it, can't you?"

Jayson felt the happiness inside of him magnify tenfold. The inexplicable peace and happiness he'd found of late meant all the more to him with the prospect of having Elizabeth in his life, permanently. He knew her well enough to know that officially going on a date was a declaration that she was ready—and open— for the possibility of their relationship going forward. And she'd obviously had it in mind before he'd told her about his change of heart.

"I can afford it," he said with a little laugh. "I'll take you anywhere you want to go."

"The Caribbean?" she asked, and he chuckled.

"Maybe we should save that for our second or third date."

"Okay," she said, but there was something in her eyes that made him believe she had every intention of going to the Caribbean with him. And that was more than alright with him.

That afternoon Macy called Jayson from school and said she needed to talk to him. She assured him it was nothing to be concerned about, but she sounded upset and asked if he'd call and excuse her from her last class so she could come home. He called the office to check her out of school, and ten minutes later she showed up. Aaron was with her. Jayson was sitting in the living room with Elizabeth when they came in. Elizabeth stood up and said, "I'll leave you to—"

"No, please stay," Macy said, and Jayson wondered if that meant his daughter was hoping Elizabeth might buffer his emotion—or his anger.

"Okay," Elizabeth said, and the four of them sat down. Jayson didn't know why, but he was suddenly reminded of the day he and Elizabeth had told her father about their morality problem. Macy had survived rape and teenage pregnancy. He wondered what would bring her to him with such sobriety.

"I'm listening," Jayson said, unable to bear the suspense.

"Uh . . . Dad," she said and looked at Aaron for support before she faced Jayson, visibly nervous. "You've told me that . . . there's a great deal about the Church that you don't believe and—"

"Before you go any further," Jayson said, surprised at the course she'd begun on, "I think I need to clarify that—"

"No, Dad. Just let me say what I need to say." She got emotional. "I just need to say it, and then we'll talk. Okay?"

"Okay," he said, wondering where this could possibly be leading.

"Dad," she said, lifting her chin courageously, "I want to be baptized; I want to become a Mormon."

Jayson reached for Elizabeth's hand and felt her squeeze so hard that it hurt. He was attempting to articulate a response when she hurried on. "Now, before you say anything, I just have to make it clear that I'm not doing this for Aaron. I'm not doing it for anybody but me. I've been studying and praying, and I know it's true, Dad. And I don't expect you to agree with me. I'm eighteen now, and I don't need your permission, but I do want your blessing. Even if you don't agree with me, I hope you'll be happy for me."

Jayson couldn't hold back the tears, and when he saw Elizabeth crying too, he really lost it. Seeing Aaron's stunned expression, he attempted to offer some explanation, but he couldn't even talk.

"Dad, what's wrong?" Macy demanded, sounding panicked.

He shook his head to try to indicate that nothing was wrong, but she seemed concerned. He was relieved when she said to Aaron, "My dad's got a high water table. Crying easily runs in the family."

Jayson finally managed to say to Elizabeth, "You tell her. I can't say it without . . . losing it all over again."

"Macy, honey," Elizabeth said, wiping her own tears, "just today your dad told me that—"

"What's wrong?" Macy demanded. "Oh, Dad! Please don't tell me you have cancer or something. I just can't—"

"Macy," Aaron said, "maybe you should let Elizabeth finish before you get upset."

"Sorry," Macy said, and Jayson chuckled through his tears. It seemed his daughter was as presumptuous as he was.

"Macy," Elizabeth said, "your dad told me this morning that . . ." She actually laughed. "You're not going to believe this."

"What?" Macy demanded.

"Your dad wants to be baptized."

Macy looked at her father, who was still crying. He nodded firmly. She burst into fresh tears as they both stood in the same moment and met with a firm embrace. While they held each other and cried, Elizabeth looked at Aaron and said, "It's a miracle."

"I'd say," Aaron said with a brilliant grin on his face, and a sparkle of tears in his own eyes.

While Jayson held his daughter close and attempted to absorb this miraculous turn of events, he looked up to see the portrait of Christ hanging above the piano. And he knew—he *knew*—that God's hand had been in his life, leading him to this end, long before he'd ever met Elizabeth, long before he'd ever faced grief, or death, or debilitating loneliness. God had been with him every step of the way, leading him, guiding him, luring him along. He recalled once telling God in silent prayer that if He would bring Macy home, Jayson would give the rest of his life to God. And Jayson was more than willing to do it. He'd never comprehended that such happiness was possible.

Not only that, he had a date with Elizabeth.

* * *

Jayson sat with his arm around his daughter, talking for more than two hours about the separate experiences that had brought them to the same end, and miraculously at the same time. Aaron had to leave, and Elizabeth had things she needed to do, but Jayson was grateful for this time alone with his little girl. She was all grown up and they had come to share something more incredible than he could have ever imagined possible. He counted the months he'd been staying in Utah, trying to comprehend the rock-bottom, suicidal state he'd been in prior to coming here. The contrast was beyond his own comprehension.

Will came home and went straight to the kitchen to cook supper. Jayson found him there and said, "Guess what, Dad?"

"What?" he asked, tossing him a smile.

"Elizabeth and I are going on a date."

"Really?" Will chuckled. "I only have one thing to say."

"What's that?"

"It's about time," he said, and they both laughed.

"Guess what else?" Jayson said, leaning against the counter where Will was chopping vegetables for a stir-fry.

"What?" Will asked with a smirk.

Jayson lowered his voice and said, "I'm going to become a Mormon."

Will stopped what he was doing. He looked at Jayson as if to make certain he wasn't joking. He set down the knife and wrapped

Jayson in one of those tight, fatherly embraces that Jayson knew so well. "Little in life could make me happier than that," Will said with the glisten of tears showing in his eyes.

"What *could* make you happier?" Jayson asked.

Will smirked and whispered, "Well, it would be nice if you'd make yourself a part of the family—officially."

Jayson smiled and said, "I'm working on it."

While Will cooked, Jayson shared, once again, the story of his personal conversion. And when Will heard about Macy's announcement, he laughed out loud, as if he just had too much joy to hold inside.

That very evening the local full-time elders came to the house. Elizabeth had called them, and they'd had no appointments set for the evening. Elder Kincaide was from upstate New York, and Elder Ward was from Australia, and they'd both been called to serve full-time missions in Utah. They listened eagerly as Jayson and Macy each expressed their desire to be baptized, and bore testimony of what they knew was true. They set some appointments to meet together and see that they were well prepared, then they asked if they would like to set a date for the baptism.

"May eighteenth," Jayson said.

Elizabeth looked at him. "That's the day Derek was killed."

"Exactly," Jayson said. "Exactly twenty years ago. That was the day my life started spiraling downward. This will be the day I start a new life."

As Jayson lay in bed that night, contemplating the events of this day, he felt the anniversary of Derek's death was especially appropriate. Drastic changes had occurred then too, in a very short time. In the years since, Jayson had been blessed with so much— but he had lost so much. And now all he had lost was being restored in ways he never would have comprehended.

The following day, Elizabeth was extremely busy, but every once in a while he'd cross her path in the house and she'd just look at him and let out a delighted little laugh. He knew just how she felt, but it was touching to see that this step for him was bringing her such joy.

When Macy came home from school, he took her with him to the mall where she helped him pick out a dark, double-breasted suit. He'd never actually owned a suit. A couple of tuxes, yes, but not a suit. He told Macy if he was going to be a Mormon, he should have a suit. By paying a little extra they were able to have the minor alterations taken care of within a couple of hours, so they went shopping to fill the time and bought Macy a new dress and shoes. And Jayson also purchased a couple of white shirts and some ties, and new shoes as well.

When they got back to the house, Jayson hurried to get changed for his date. He arrived in the dining room at 6:25 to find everyone there, even Aaron. They made a big fuss over how nice he looked in the suit. He simply said, "Well, I did tell her to dress up. It's our first date." Everyone laughed, and he added, "Okay, well . . . it's our first date in nearly twenty years."

Elizabeth entered the room wearing a red silky dress that hung to her knees—and red high-heeled shoes. She looked absolutely gorgeous, and Jayson couldn't keep from staring. But then he realized she was staring at him, too.

"Wow," they both said at the same time, then they laughed—and so did everyone else.

"Okay, let's get out of here," Jayson said and took her arm, urging her to the garage. Opening the car door for her, he said, "Those shoes make you awfully tall, but we won't be sharing a microphone."

"No, but I have my reasons," she said. "I did buy them specifically for this date."

"Really?" he said and got in the car. "So what are the reasons?" he asked, backing out of the garage.

"Maybe I'll tell you later."

Jayson took her to one of the finest restaurants in the valley, where they ate very slowly, talking and laughing as if they'd not seen each other in months. They kept talking long after they'd finished the dessert they shared, and the restaurant became almost completely empty. When a lull finally came in the conversation, Jayson looked at her across the table and impulsively said, "Dance with me."

She glanced around and laughed softly, "I don't think this is one of those dancing places. And the music's too soft to even hear it."

"I don't care," he said. A server walked by, and Jayson said, "Excuse me. Do you have any rules here against dancing?"

Elizabeth put a hand over her mouth to keep from laughing out loud as the woman said, "As long as you keep it quiet and don't swing from the light fixtures, we're okay with that."

"Thank you," Jayson said as he stood and took Elizabeth's hand. She laughed as she came to her feet, and he immediately moved her into a simple dance step, softly singing the song, "Harmony." The words brought back so many memories that Elizabeth didn't know whether to laugh or cry. Between verses he did an elaborate turn and lowered her back over his arm. They both laughed as he resumed their simple step, then he went on singing. Following more elaborate turns that made her giggle, he finished the song while looking deeply into her eyes as he sang. When the dance was apparently done, they were surprised to hear some applause and turned to see three servers watching them.

"And you'll be wanting a tip too, I suppose," Jayson said lightly.

"Oh, no. The entertainment was great," one of them said.

Jayson left a generous tip, and they went out to the car. He drove to the Mount Timpanogos Temple, and they walked arm-in-arm to the east side where they sat and talked for another hour. Still, throughout the course of the evening nothing romantic came up; there were no references to sharing a future beyond what they already shared. When they got out of the car in the garage, Elizabeth took his hand and said, "We have a problem."

"What's that?" he asked as they walked into the house to find it silent and dark except for the little light above the stove.

"Well . . ." she said, taking his other hand and turning to face him, "when we were dating in high school, I always looked forward to that kiss on the doorstep. But we live in the same house."

Jayson smiled. "If you want me to kiss you, all you have to do is say so. You don't have to hint around."

She eased subtly closer and lifted her lips toward his. When they were almost touching she said, "Kiss me, Jayson."

"I thought you'd never ask," he said and pressed his lips to hers.

Following a lengthy kiss, Elizabeth murmured, "If you wanted to kiss me, all you had to do was say so. Better yet," she pressed a hand into his hair, "just do it."

"Stop talking," he said and kissed her again, "and let me kiss you." And again.

"I think we'd better go to bed," she said, and he drew back in mock astonishment. She giggled and added, "I mean . . . you'd better go to bed in your bed, and I'd better go to bed in mine."

"You scared me there for a minute," he said, not at all serious. "I have to be a good boy, you know. I'm going to be a Mormon."

"You were always a good boy," she said, touching his face.

"Not always," he said almost sadly.

"We made a mistake; we made it together. That was a long time ago."

"Yes, it was," he said and kissed her again.

"By the way," she said, "this is why I wore these shoes."

"Why?"

"So you wouldn't have to bend over so far to kiss me."

Jayson chuckled and kissed her once more, then he sent her to her room, and he went to the basement wondering how he might go about proposing.

Elizabeth lay awake pondering the path her life was taking. The changes Jayson had made left her happier than she'd ever thought possible, and it seemed inevitable that they would eventually be together in every respect. Her thoughts kept her awake far into the night, but as the clock ticked on, the darkness deepened around her. Thoughts that had begun with perfect peace and happiness merged into an uneasiness that she couldn't shake off. She'd endured counseling with Jayson, and they had shared many long, deep conversations. But there was one issue that had never been addressed, one point on which she had never had the courage to come clean. And as her thoughts roiled with it, she felt suddenly unworthy of Jayson's love, thoroughly afraid. By morning, with practically no sleep behind her, Elizabeth knew she had to come clean now, or she would never be able to move forward in her relationship with him. She just wasn't exactly sure how to go about it.

* * *

Jayson woke up feeling like the happiest man alive. He was in the kitchen early and helped Will get Trevin and Macy off to school. He was putting frozen waffles in the toaster for Addie when Elizabeth came into the kitchen, wearing flannel pajamas, looking awful.

"Good morning, gorgeous," Jayson said brightly.

"Eat a rock, Jayson," she said. He was grateful to have Will in the kitchen. The comical glance he gave Jayson helped him take her attitude in stride.

"I would," he said, "but then you'd have to take me to the dentist."

While she was pouring herself a glass of orange juice, he said softly, "You really are beautiful, you know—even in your pajamas."

Elizabeth glared at him and said, "I don't know if you've noticed, but I'm not a size ten like I used to be; or actually I was an eight when I first met you, I believe."

"You were sixteen years old," Jayson said while he wondered where this was coming from. Was this the same woman he'd been kissing not so many hours ago?

"Yes, and so were you. And you've hardly changed, except for getting . . . better looking all the time. Me, I've just given birth a few times and filled out to a well-rounded size fourteen and—"

"Oh," he said with mock astonishment, "let's call *The Enquirer.* How scandalous of you, Mrs. Aragon, to actually be shaped like a woman instead of a child." He lowered his voice and tightened his eyes on her. "When I stepped off that plane and saw you last fall, you took my breath away. You are the most beautiful woman I have ever known—and you become more beautiful every year."

She started to cry, and Jayson got another comical glance from Will before he left the room. Addie was eating her waffle, oblivious to anything but the amount of syrup on her plate. Jayson put his arms around Elizabeth, relieved that she didn't resist. "What is this?" he asked softly. "PMS maybe?"

"I don't know," she sniffled. "Maybe. I just . . . didn't sleep."

"Why not?"

"A lot on my mind, I guess."

"Anything you want to talk about?"

"No, but . . . we probably should anyway."

"Oh, I see," he said, realizing that something was bothering her—and it had to do with him. "So, when should we have this conversation that we should probably have—even though you don't want to?"

"I don't know," she said. "Later. I'm going to take a bath."

"Take your time," he said, watching her leave the room. "Addie and I will just . . . watch public television, or something."

He turned to look at Addie who said, "Mommy's in a bad mood."

"Yes, she is," Jayson said. "What should we do while Mommy takes a bath?"

"We could color pictures."

"That's exactly what I was thinking," Jayson said. "We could color pictures."

During the course of the day, Elizabeth's mood didn't improve. She stuck mostly to her room while Jayson did his best to keep everything under control. He'd become so comfortable with the children that it was easy to think of officially becoming their stepfather. He hoped that whatever might be weighing on Elizabeth wouldn't bring such hopes crashing down around him. If she told him she couldn't marry him now, would he be able to cope? He knew he'd survive somehow. But in the deepest part of his soul, he believed they were supposed to be together.

CHAPTER 9

After supper was over, homework done, and the kids in bed, Jayson realized he'd not seen Elizabeth since they'd actually eaten at the same table. He debated whether or not to just go to bed, but he ended up on the deck, wondering what might be wrong and whether or not he should go hunt her down and demand that she talk to him—or if he should leave her alone and go to bed.

He felt genuinely surprised when she came out of the door from her bedroom, wrapped in a lightweight blanket. "Mind if I join you?" she asked.

"Of course not," he said, and she sat beside him.

"I apologize for my foul mood. It probably is PMS. The problem comes when something hard hits you and you *do* have PMS. I read an article once about coping with PMS, and it said to manage your life around it. Don't plan big things or deal with stressful situations during that week of your cycle. So, I came to the conclusion that I should be able to move Thanksgiving dinner, and Christmas Eve, and all my children's activities around my cycles."

Jayson chuckled and said, "Good plan." She said nothing for a few minutes, and he asked, "So what hard thing hit you, Elizabeth? It wouldn't have anything to do with our little outing last night, would it?"

"Last night was wonderful," she said. "It was perfect."

"But?" he pressed.

"I guess I just . . . got thinking about . . . where you and I began, and how we got where we are. I know we can't go back and change it. And we really wouldn't want to. I mean . . . we can't regret our children being who and what they are, but . . . there are some things I look back on, and I think I really blew it."

"That's all in the past, Lady. Whatever you did or didn't do, you did the best you could."

"But what if I *didn't* do the best I could? What if I could have done better? What if I should have done something different?"

"I'm not sure what exactly you're referring to, but isn't that what the Atonement is all about? It makes up the difference for those mistakes, those weaknesses, for that gap between what we did and what we should have done. So, you made some mistakes. We all do. The Atonement still applies."

"But what if . . . they're life-altering mistakes? What if those mistakes affected other people's lives and caused them great grief?"

Jayson looked at her and sensed she was trying to tell him something deeply personal and significant, but he wasn't getting it. "So, what if you did? It's in the past. You can't change the past. You come clean and start over."

Elizabeth's heart started to pound. She knew she would never be able to go any further in her life—or her relationship with him—if she didn't do just that: come clean. She drew courage and looked into his eyes. "Okay then," she said, her voice quavering, "I'm coming clean."

Jayson looked into her eyes and felt his heart quicken before he fully perceived the implication. All of her concern, her emotion, her heartache, her regret . . . had something to do with him. While a formless dread tightened inside him, silence persisted, creating a painful anticipation. Hoping to break the tension, he said, "I'm listening."

Elizabeth closed her eyes and turned her face away, unable to look at him as she forced the words out. "I lied to you, Jayson. When I was baptized, I really believed I had put everything in order, that I had put all of those past things to rest. I didn't even think about this at the time. Then one day it just . . . popped into my head, and I knew I had to tell you the truth. But I just haven't been able to bring myself to do it. The bottom line is that I lied to you. At the time I convinced myself that it would be better for both of us, that I was doing you a favor. But deep inside I knew then—as I have come to know more with every passing year—that I was only kidding myself. I was scared, plain and simple. And I was wrong. And when I see the grief you've been through, I can't help wondering how different it might have been if I'd had the courage to say what was in my heart, and not cower from it in fear."

Her tears started to flow while Jayson felt his own breathing become shallow. He began to suspect where this might be headed, but he still couldn't fathom the reality of what she might say. She sniffled loudly and wiped at her face, but still she wouldn't look at him as she went on. "When things started falling apart between you and Debbie, and I saw how horribly she was treating you, I just . . . I just . . ."

"Get to the point," he said with mild anger. "How exactly did you lie to me?" She hesitated, and he took hold of her chin, turning her face toward him, but she kept her eyes squeezed shut. "Look at me and tell me," he insisted.

Elizabeth forced her eyes open, seeing more sorrow than anger in his expression. "That day . . . on the beach . . . after Derek was killed," she said and saw the muscles in his face tighten; he knew what she was talking about, and she wondered if he knew what was coming. She swallowed hard and forced the words out. "I told you I didn't love you . . . enough, that I could never feel for you the way you felt for me."

While Jayson had suspected her confession would have roots in her feelings for him, he wasn't prepared for the way his insides knotted up hearing it spoken. He thought of how his instincts had screamed at the time that their being apart was all wrong. An unfathomable anger tightened around his heart. He barely managed a steady voice as he asked, "And the truth would be?"

Elizabeth sobbed and squeezed her eyes closed. She attempted to turn away, but he held tightly to her chin. "I loved you so much that it hurt," she muttered and sobbed again. "And it scared me senseless. I never stopped loving you, Jayson. And I never will. I want to be with you forever."

Jayson heard his own breathing become audible, shallow, and raspy. He erupted to his feet as if his insides might explode otherwise. Then he became light-headed and quickly took a few steps, taking hold of the rail with both hands. He lowered his head in an effort to gain his equilibrium and heard himself groan.

"I'm so sorry, Jayson," he heard her mutter somewhere on the brim of his consciousness. "Never in a million years would I have dreamed that . . ."

"That what?" he snarled without lifting his head, fearing he'd pass out if he did. "That you'd have to face me with the truth nearly twenty years later? How can I trust *anything* if I can't trust you?"

"It was one lie, Jayson. I've never been anything but completely honest with you otherwise."

"Other than pretending all these years that what you felt for me wasn't some . . . farce . . . some sick joke or—"

"That's not fair, Jayson." She jumped to her feet the same moment he raised his head and turned to face her. "Don't go twisting everything else out of proportion because of one little lie."

"Little?" He gave a scoffing laugh. "My heart was bleeding all over the ground, and you couldn't find the courage to tell me that yours was bleeding too? One *little* lie that triggered a series of events in both our lives that . . . that . . ." Jayson couldn't finish the sentence. He felt suddenly so overwrought with confusion that he almost felt dizzy again. He looked at Elizabeth, and his confusion deepened. Unable to speak, he rushed into the house, grabbed his keys, and had his car in gear before the garage door was up.

Elizabeth heard his car squeal out of the driveway, and she sank onto the bench again, sobbing into her hands. She was grateful her father and the children were all in bed; she wouldn't want to explain to them, or anyone else, the horror that was unfolding. Maybe she would have been better off just keeping it to herself.

Jayson drove up American Fork Canyon, pulled the car into a turnout and got out, slamming the door. He could hear water running and knew the river was nearby. He paced and pondered and cursed under his breath, then he finally dropped to his knees, where he prayed—and cried. And while he prayed, the last twenty years marched through his mind. He thought of the immeasurable grief he'd felt in leaving Elizabeth behind, and each step he'd taken since then that had only piled more grief into his life. He wondered what his life might have been like if he'd married Elizabeth. She never would have cheated on him the way Debbie had, never would have allowed horrors to happen to his daughter that had driven her from home. Then he thought of Elizabeth, the life she had found, the good things that had come out of her marriage—her beautiful children. He thought of Macy, her strength and wisdom and how gracefully she had risen above her struggles. He realized that any other course might have eliminated some of the bad things, but it also would have altered all of the good things. As he prayed for nearly an hour, his mind was opened to a broader understanding; he realized that their lives were—and always had been—in God's hands.

Driving back to the house, he marveled at how pieces of memories came together with clarity in his mind. By the time he pulled into the garage, he felt completely at peace. He only hoped he could convey that peace to Elizabeth, that she would forgive him for his anger. He found the house dark and quiet, but he wasn't surprised to peer out the window and see Elizabeth standing on the deck, still wrapped in a blanket, leaning against the rail.

Elizabeth turned abruptly when she heard the door open. In the glow of a partial moon she saw Jayson step outside and close the door. He leaned against it, and she turned back to look out into the darkness, terrified of what other accusations he might throw at her. And maybe he was right. She sensed him stepping toward her, but she was still startled to hear him say her name in a whisper, close to her ear. "Forgive me," he added, and she squeezed her eyes closed.

"You're not the one who lied, Jayson," she said in a hoarse voice that made it evident she'd been crying long and hard. "It is I who must beg your forgiveness."

"Done," he said, and she looked over her shoulder to see his face. His sincerity was evident, but there was something else, something in his eyes that made her heart quicken. She looked back at the view, attempting to catch her breath. Her breathing sharpened when she felt his hands on her shoulders, with a warmth in his touch that penetrated through the blanket, a tenderness that didn't ring true with his previous mood. "Forgive me for my anger, Elizabeth," he said softly, close to her ear, sending a wave of goose bumps down her arms.

"Your anger is understandable."

"Perhaps, but . . . not appropriate. I've been thinking and . . . praying, very hard. There's a great deal I want to say, so . . . bear with me. You see . . . I can look back over my life and realize there were many times when God was guiding me . . . through my thoughts and feelings. Now I have learned to understand how that works, and how to recognize it for what it is. Elizabeth, there is something very important that you're forgetting."

"What?" she asked, turning to look at him.

"You told me then that you knew in your heart it was what you had to do."

"But I was . . . scared."

"And maybe for good reason. The point is that—"

"No, wait," she said. "There's something else I have to tell you."

"Okay," he drawled.

"I quickly regretted it, Jayson. It didn't take me long, once I got to Boston, to realize how I loved you, how I needed you. I tried and tried to call you." Jayson took a deep breath as he realized where this was headed. "When you finally called me . . . I was ready to tell you that I'd made a mistake, but . . ."

"I was married," he said and had to sit down.

"Yes, you were married," she said. "I had expected you to maybe tell me you were dating someone, or engaged, and . . . I was ready to beg you not to go through with it. But . . . you were married." Tears came as she admitted, "I gained a perfect empathy for the pain I had put you through. Of course you know that gradually I came to terms with it. And you know the rest of the story. There. Now I've said it. I've come clean with you. I only hope that you can forgive me for . . ."

"There's nothing to forgive," Jayson said, realizing that this new revelation didn't change what he had come to realize through his drive into the canyon and back. "I'm truly sorry for the pain I put you through. And I know you feel the same. But what you need to understand is that it was all necessary, Elizabeth. Whatever decisions we made, however immature or afraid or stupid we may have been, God knew what those decisions would be. He knew us, our personalities, our circumstances, and He knew the paths we would follow. It was all meant to be, Lady. It was all necessary. I believe that at some level you felt compelled to do what you did because it was what we both needed in order to bring us to this day. If we hadn't been as close as we were, we would not have remained close through all these years. But our separate paths were necessary, Elizabeth. Would we have found the gospel if you had married me and we had settled in LA? Would our marriage have survived the fame and the concert tours? Maybe. Maybe not. I know you had very strong feelings about what you wanted your life to be like, and you made that happen. You created a world that gave me sanctuary when I was dying—literally—in the pit I'd made of my life. There was so much about the life I lived in LA that I never told you about. I was too humiliated, too embarrassed to admit how bad it really was.

"Through those years of struggling to make something of myself, we lived in the most horrible, dumpy apartments you could ever imagine. No, maybe you couldn't. I worked changing oil and waiting tables when I had sworn I would never work doing anything but music. I had to grovel to try and get any respect at all in the music business. And there were times when I got so depressed and angry that Debbie didn't even want to be in the same room with me. Then overnight everything changed. And then it was an entirely different kind of horrible. The PR stuff was so phony, so full of garbage. My wife was being propositioned very crudely by people we had to associate with who were drunk or stoned. I can't even begin to tell you how upset and disgusted I felt through so much of what we had to do." He looked at her hard and added firmly, "There were a thousand times when I thought, 'I am so grateful Elizabeth isn't being subjected to this.' You deserved better, and you got it. And you were there to save me when I needed saving. You did what you had to do. And so did I. And now, there's only one thing that really matters. You see, I was so angry that I completely missed the most important thing you said earlier; something that puts everything else into perfect perspective." Jayson stood and took her shoulders into his hands, saying softly, "You told me that you love me, that you've always loved me, that you always will. You said that you want to be with me forever." She felt his sigh caress her skin. "Just tell me you mean it, Elizabeth; tell me it's true. If you love me that much, then nothing else matters."

Elizabeth let out a one-syllable laugh that turned to a sob. "I love you, Jayson," she muttered, and the same sound came out of his own mouth. "I want to be with you forever."

"Nothing else matters," he said, taking her face into his hands.

In spite of all he had told her, she still said, "How can you say that when so much has—"

"Shhh," he whispered and pressed a thumb over her lips. "It needed to be this way, Lady."

"Oh, you really mean it."

"I do."

"Tell me again."

"We needed these experiences. How can we regret the existence of our beautiful children? How can we wish away all the good we've had in our lives while we're wishing that the bad never happened? We can't go back and change it, but even if we could, would we really want to? We have no way of knowing what other struggles we might have endured if our lives had taken different paths. Maybe it would have been worse. But most importantly— my lady—oh, most importantly, I wonder if we would have found, or would have been able to accept, the gospel into our lives. We're here now, Elizabeth. We have the gospel. We have each other. You love me and I love you, and nothing else matters."

Elizabeth heard herself sob just before she heard rain beginning to fall on the roof above them.

"It's raining," she said, as if he might not have noticed.

"So it is," he said and took her hand, leading her into the house and down the stairs, out the door beneath the deck and onto the back lawn, illuminated by the light from the porch. "Do you remember the first time you told me that you loved me?" he asked as the rain fell over them.

"I remember," she said. "We were standing in the rain in the backyard. And it was the first time you kissed me. Kiss me now," she added and closed her eyes, clutching onto his shoulders, feeling the rain bathe over her. She whimpered when their lips met, feeling such perfect, uncontainable joy in the sensation. His kiss was meek but full of promise. He eased back to look into her eyes, and she found tears on his face.

"You're crying," she said, wiping his tears away.

"So are you," he said with a little laugh, doing the same.

He kissed her again, and the years fled. They were young again, innocent and naive, just sharing the first budding awareness of love. The passion that crept into their lengthy kiss felt eerily familiar to Elizabeth, and comfortingly warm. He kissed her over and over, holding her impossibly closer, as if he could saturate himself with her enough to compensate for the years that had kept them apart. He finally pulled his lips from hers as if the separation was necessary but painful, then he pressed his brow to hers and let out a contented sigh. "Oh, how I love you," he murmured.

Elizabeth laughed softly. "That's just what I was going to say."

"Say it."

"Oh, how I love you!"

Jayson laughed softly and looked into her eyes. He hardly thought about the words he wanted to say before they rolled off his tongue. "Will you marry me?" he asked, and her eyes widened.

He felt nervous for only a moment before a smile spread over her face and she said firmly, "Yes, I will."

Jayson laughed and hugged her tightly, lifting her feet off the ground as he twirled around. She laughed with him, and they both fell on the ground from dizziness. Jayson helped her up, then kissed her before he commented, "Your hair is curly." He pressed his hands through it. "I love it when it's curly."

"And your hair is longer than mine," she said, pressing her hand down the length of his ponytail.

"Not for long," he said firmly.

She looked astonished. "You're not going to cut it off?"

"Before I'm baptized, I am."

"You can be a good Mormon with a ponytail."

"I'm sure I can, and most of the people around here have been very accepting of me in spite of my rebel appearance. But in this, I'm done being a nonconformist. I'm ready for a change."

"I love you, Jayson Wolfe."

He laughed and hugged her tightly. "I love you too."

"So when do you want to get married?"

He laughed again, so thoroughly happy he could hardly believe it. "Well . . . as soon as I'm baptized we can—"

"No, before," she said. "Unless there's some reason you want to wait."

"Not specifically, no," he said, attempting to absorb her enthusiasm.

"As I see it," she said, "we're already living under the same roof. It doesn't have to be a big production. There's nobody we'd want there that we can't invite over the phone."

"Okay, I can agree with that."

"So, how about a week from Saturday?" she asked, and he laughed again. "I'm serious!" she insisted. "That would give us time for an adequate honeymoon, and we can be back for the baptism."

"You won't get any arguments from me," he said. "I'm just wondering . . . why the rush?"

She laughed softly and said, "It's not going to be easy staying chaste living in the same house with you, now that we're officially engaged."

Jayson chuckled and had to admit, "Okay, I can agree with that too."

"Although, I shouldn't be at all worried. I'm absolutely certain that you're a perfect gentleman—and very disciplined."

Jayson just smiled and kissed her.

* * *

Again Elizabeth had trouble sleeping. She was so thoroughly filled with happiness that she felt like a giddy teenager. She finally got up and went to the kitchen in search of something to help her sleep. And as she often did when she got up in the night, she felt compelled to peek in on her children. She went upstairs and peered carefully into Addie and Macy's rooms, then she went to the basement to Trevin's room and peered in to see evidence of him breathing softly in his sleep, just as the girls had been. She pressed a kiss to his forehead and crept quietly out. And that's when she

heard the picking of an acoustic guitar. Moving closer to the door
of Jayson's room, she heard him picking out something, and then
silence. Then more picking; the same thing over and over. *He was
composing music!* She wondered if she should bother him, but she
couldn't resist an opportunity to see him this way. She nearly
knocked but decided that might ruin the effect. She carefully and
quietly opened the door just enough to see him wearing the usual
plaid flannel pajama pants and a T-shirt, sitting on the edge of a
rumpled bed. Relieved that he'd not noticed her, she watched in
awe as he picked out a series of chords, humming sporadically as
he did, then he scribbled notes in a music notebook at his side. He
put the pencil in his teeth and picked it out again. But most
impressionable was the light in his eyes, a sparkle akin to what
she'd seen there when he'd told her of his burning testimony.
Elizabeth felt moved to tears to see the reality of this awakening in
him, to see evidence of the gifted musician at work, and to think
that the love blossoming between them might have something to
do with what was coming back to life in him.

When she wiped the tears from her face, Jayson caught the
movement and looked up, startled. "How long have you been
there?"

"Sorry," she muttered, "I couldn't sleep and I . . . checked on
Trevin and heard you. I . . . was just . . . overcome with watching a
genius at work."

"I'm sorry if I disturbed you," he said, feeling like he was lying.
He was so glad to see her he could hardly stand it.

"Oh, no," she said. "I couldn't sleep. I was on my way to the
kitchen. I didn't even hear you until I walked past your room, but
. . . I'm glad I did."

"Me too," he admitted with a smile. "Come here. Listen to
this." He cleared his throat, picked out the beginning, then sang
softly, *"You stood tonight . . . beneath the light of heaven's narrow
moon. And on your face . . . I saw a trace of a love that waned too
soon.* This is the chorus," he said with a little smirk, then he gave

up on the guitar and just sang. *"When love bleeds red, the words you said pierced me to my core. When all is said and done, the battles fought, the victories won, what could I do more . . . to show you that I love you? Oh, how I love you!"* He smiled and leaned over the guitar to kiss her before he said, "Okay, the second verse is my favorite." He gave himself a chord, then sang, *"A trace of love gleamed in your tears and trickled down your face. A glimmer of the love we shared in another time and place. I reached for you, you reached for me, and the glow burst into flame. My lips met yours, your tears met mine, and I knew that we could have it all again."*

"It's beautiful," Elizabeth said, wiping new tears from her face. "Sing the chorus again."

Holding her hand, he sang while looking into her eyes, *"When love bleeds red, the words you said pierced me to my core. When all is said and done, the battles fought, the victories won, what could I do more to show you that I love you? Oh, how I love you!"* The final note merged into a kiss as he leaned closer to her.

"Oh, how I love *you,"* she whispered and kissed him again. "And I think I'd better go upstairs and get some sleep."

"Good plan," he said and watched her walk away. She smiled before she closed the door behind her. "Thank you, God," he whispered and set the guitar aside, figuring he could use some sleep himself.

The following morning Elizabeth appeared for breakfast with her hair curly—and it stayed that way. She was a completely different woman from the one who had shown up twenty-four hours earlier, looking as if her world had ended. When the children were all in school, Jayson took Elizabeth's hand and took her to find Will, who was sitting behind his desk with a book.

"Hi, Dad," Jayson said. "Can we talk?"

"Sure," Will said, looking more suspicious than concerned. "What's up?"

"I have a question for you."

"Okay, shoot."

"Is it all right with you if I marry your daughter?"

Will let out a boisterous laugh then said, "You're a big boy. You don't need my permission."

"Your opinion, then," Jayson said.

"I think it's about time," Will said and laughed again.

Jayson smiled at Elizabeth and kissed her hand. "I knew the first time I laid eyes on her that we were meant to be together forever. I just didn't know it would take more than twenty years to make it happen."

"Some miracles just take a little more work and time than others," Elizabeth said.

"So, when is this grand event?" Will asked.

"A week from Saturday," Elizabeth said. "And then we were hoping you'd be willing to watch the children while we leave town for a week or so."

"It would be a pleasure," Will said.

Jayson couldn't take his eyes off Elizabeth, and he felt compelled to say, "Isn't she beautiful, William?"

"She certainly is, and you are the luckiest man alive."

"Blessed," Jayson corrected. "I am extremely blessed."

While Elizabeth made some phone calls, Jayson worked on the song he'd started in the middle of the night. To be writing music again was the icing on a beautiful, perfect cake. He picked up Addie from preschool and kept track of her while Elizabeth was busy. Before Trevin and Macy came home from school, Elizabeth announced that she had arranged to use the church building, where they would be married in the Relief Society room, and then have a meal in the multipurpose room. The food had been ordered from a caterer, and some ladies in the ward would be serving it. They needed to go order a cake, some flowers, rings, and announcements that would be sent out *after* the wedding, just to let people know they were married. She'd even spoken to the bishop, and he had eagerly agreed to perform the ceremony; he'd set up an appointment to meet with the two of them in the meantime.

"So, tomorrow we're going to do all of that other stuff and call it good," Elizabeth said.

"You are as efficient as you are amazing," Jayson said and kissed her.

When Macy and Trevin came home, Jayson told them they were having an impromptu family council. Will and Addie joined them, and they all looked expectantly at Jayson. Macy took visible notice of the way he was holding Elizabeth's hand.

"So, here's the deal," Jayson said. "We are all going to be an official family." Macy let out a squeal of excitement before he added, "Elizabeth and I are getting married."

He watched Trevin and Addie closely, wondering what their reaction might be. Trevin's face lit up, and he asked, "Does that mean you're going to live here forever?"

"That's what it means," Jayson said, and Trevin stood up and hugged him tightly.

Addie asked, "Are you going to be my daddy now?"

"Well, I'm going to be your mommy's husband. It's up to you if you want me to be your daddy."

She looked at her mother and asked, "Can he be my daddy now?"

"Yes, he can if that's what you want."

"Okay," she said and ran off to play. The fact that Jayson had lived for several months in the same home with Elizabeth's children would obviously make the transition easy.

Macy stood up and hugged her father, then Elizabeth, saying, "I couldn't ask for a better mother." Elizabeth got a little teary and hugged her again.

They talked over their plans, then Jayson decided they should all go out to dinner to celebrate. They were going to be a family, and with time, they would be an eternal family. There was no greater cause for celebration than that.

A while after they returned home, Elizabeth was busy helping Addie in her room with something. Apparently Addie was in a foul mood and not very happy about picking up her toys and getting ready for bed. The phone rang, and Jayson picked it up.

"Hello," he said.

"Who is this?" a woman asked, and he didn't even have to wonder who it was. He hadn't heard her cynical voice for twenty years, but he knew it was Elizabeth's mother.

"I live here," he said. "Who is this?"

"Maybe I have the wrong number."

"Depends on who you want to talk to," he said.

"I'm looking for Elizabeth Aragon." She spoke like an attorney.

"Mrs. Aragon is dealing with her daughter's tantrum. May I take a message?"

"Who is this?" she asked again.

"Who's asking?" he countered.

Indignantly she said, "This is Elizabeth's mother, and I think I have a right to know if my daughter has a man living in her home."

"Why, hello, Meredith," he said with false diplomacy. "It's been a long time. This is Jayson Wolfe."

"Jayson," she said with an equally dramatic change in her voice, "how long has it been?"

"Twenty years," he said gravely. "At the funeral."

"So it was," she said as if they'd been the best of friends. He understood the source of her positive zeal when she added, "I've heard great things about you and your career. You really took the world by storm."

Jayson just grunted, then asked, "What is it I can do for you?"

As if her mind had gone back to the beginning of the conversation, she asked with more pleasure than disgust, "You're living with my daughter?"

"We're sharing a kitchen, but we have separate bedrooms," he said.

"I wouldn't have expected anything less," she said when he clearly knew that she already had.

Beginning to feel angry, Jayson was relieved to see Elizabeth coming down the stairs. "Oh, here's your daughter," Jayson said and abruptly pushed the phone toward her. "Your mother is as charming as ever," Jayson whispered with his hand over the mouthpiece.

Elizabeth scowled, then forced a polite voice as she said into the phone, "Hello, Mother. You must have gotten my message."

Jayson attempted to leave, but Elizabeth caught his arm and urged herself close to him. She put her hand over the mouthpiece while her mother was apparently rambling about something. Elizabeth kissed Jayson, then quickly said into the phone, "Okay, well . . . I just wanted to let you know that I'm getting married." A moment later she said, "Yes, I'm marrying Jayson."

Jayson listened to her side of the conversation while she told her mother when and where the wedding would take place, and that it would be a simple affair and they were requesting no gifts. He then realized that Meredith was talking a great deal while Elizabeth was growing irritated—then angry. The only clue he got to what she was saying was when Elizabeth said, "I'll certainly take note of your advice, Mother. I need to go. I understand if you can't make it; it's not a big deal. I'll be in touch."

She ended the call, then pushed her arms around Jayson, saying, "Tell me why it still hurts when she treats me that way."

"Because she's your mother, and you can't help hoping that you might one day get some validation and acceptance. I think that's why I cried when my father died." He paused and added, "What did she say?"

"Her take on the situation—given that I've only talked to her once since Robert's funeral and she has no idea what's going on in my life—is that it's convenient that I could get you to marry me now, since the millions you must have in the bank will leave me set for life. She said she hoped you hadn't been an idiot and spent it all, and she told me not to sign any prenuptial agreements that would exclude my rights to the money in case it didn't work out."

Jayson held her more tightly and murmured, "I told you a long time ago that I would give you all of my money. You don't have to marry me to be set for life."

Elizabeth tightened her arms around him and sighed. "Why does she assume that I'm the way she is?"

"Because she's too blinded by her own misery to see what an incredible person you are," he said.

Elizabeth looked into his eyes. "I love you, Jayson Wolfe."

He smiled. "I love you too . . . and in not very many days, you're going to be *Mrs.* Wolfe."

"How delightful," Elizabeth said, and the sorrow dissipated from her eyes just before he kissed her.

With the house quiet, Jayson knew he needed to make a few phone calls of his own. There were only a handful of people that he cared to invite to his wedding, and the most important of those was Drew. He didn't answer his cell phone, but Jayson left a message, and he called back a little after ten.

"Hey, Bro," Jayson said after they'd exchanged typical greetings. "Would you be up to a quick trip to Utah? I'll even buy the ticket."

"I think I can afford the ticket. What's up?"

"I just really need you here . . . a week from Saturday. You don't have to stay long."

"What exactly is it you need?" Drew asked, sounding suspicious, perhaps even concerned. "More counseling?"

"No," Jayson laughed. "Thankfully, no. I need you to be my best man."

"Are you kidding?" Drew said and laughed. "You're getting *married?*" Jayson heard him say to someone else, "My brother's getting married." Into the phone he added, "Do I know the bride?"

"You do," Jayson said, and Drew laughed loudly.

"It wouldn't be the woman you've been living with, would it?"

"Whoa," Jayson said. "I don't I like the way that sounded, especially if somebody else heard that. I can assure you we've been perfectly chaste."

"Okay, the woman you have been staying with; no sleeping together."

"That's better. And yes, it would be that woman. Like I told Will, I knew I was supposed to marry her the first time I saw her, but I didn't think it would take more than twenty years."

"Well, that's wonderful," Drew said. "I'm truly happy for you."

"So, when are *you* going to take the plunge, little brother?" Jayson asked.

"Actually," he said, "I don't think I'll be far behind you."

"Are you kidding?" Jayson said and laughed.

They talked for nearly an hour, catching up mostly on their love lives. Drew had been dating a woman named Valerie for a few months, and they were talking about marriage. Nothing was official yet. He agreed to be at the wedding, and he would be bringing Valerie along. Jayson and Elizabeth spent the following day picking out and ordering all they needed for the wedding. And they had some pictures taken—with Elizabeth's hair left curly. He kept touching it, loving the way just the feel of it took him back in time. Jayson was amazed to realize that everything was planned and under control, and they'd only been engaged a couple of days.

After school, Elizabeth took Macy, Trevin, and Addie shopping for new clothes for the wedding, and they helped her pick out a wedding dress. She'd told Jayson she just wanted to wear a simple white dress, but he'd insisted that it would be a *wedding* dress, full and long and memorable. He'd imagined marrying her many years ago, and he wanted her in the right kind of dress. Elizabeth found what she thought was perfect, and Macy and Addie agreed. Trevin was terribly bored.

After the shopping, she walked into the kitchen and announced to her father that they were completely ready to get married.

"And what about a honeymoon?" Will asked.

"Oh, that's taken care of, too," Jayson said, and Elizabeth looked at him in astonishment.

"Well," he shrugged, "you did say you wanted to go to the Caribbean for our second or third date, so . . ." He couldn't finish due to Elizabeth jumping—literally—into his arms, laughing like a child. He laughed with her. "There was a cancellation so I got us booked on a cruise." She laughed louder, and he twirled her around, certain that life could be no better than this.

During the following week, however, Jayson began to understand the concept that there was opposition in all things. He'd learned the principle that Satan would work very hard to prevent good things from happening, but he quickly discovered the reality of that concept. It started with Trevin having a scooter accident and breaking his leg. Then everyone *but* Trevin got the flu. It started with Addie and went through everyone in the house. Thankfully it was just the twenty-four-hour kind, but it was nasty while it lasted. Mozie was attacked by another dog that came into the yard, and he needed several stitches. The computer crashed just before Macy was ready to print a huge report she'd been working on. Two of their three vehicles needed major repairs, and Aaron and Macy were in a minor car accident that left Aaron's car relatively useless—but Aaron and Macy escaped with insignificant injuries, and they were all grateful. Jayson broke a glass and stepped on a piece before he could get to the broom. He needed six stitches in the bottom of his foot. And that was only during the course of a week. Then the caterer canceled, and Elizabeth had trouble finding another one on such short notice, but she finally did. Still, in spite of their challenges, Jayson never lost sight of the reality that he would soon be married to the love of his life, his sweet Elizabeth. It was a dream come true. He wasn't naive enough to believe that life would be perfect, but they would be living it together, and they would have the gospel. He'd never dreamed he could be so happy.

Drew flew into Salt Lake City the night before the wedding. Jayson and Elizabeth met him and Valerie at the airport, and they all went out to dinner. Jayson really liked Valerie, and he liked the way she brought out the best in Drew.

When Drew asked exactly where they were getting married, the conversation led naturally into religion. He was surprised to learn that Elizabeth had become a Mormon, and that a Mormon bishop would be performing the marriage. Jayson was proud of the way she bore simple testimony of her beliefs, and how she gently explained to Drew that although his father had technically been a Mormon, the lifestyle he had chosen had little to do with what the religion fully entailed.

"Wow," Drew said, "I guess that shows how uneducated I am on such things."

"Yes, well . . . I was, too," Jayson said. "But it really is quite remarkable."

Drew looked closely at Jayson, seeming to sense something deeper in the statement. He asked, "Are you trying to tell me something?"

"Only if you're interested."

"I'm listening."

"Macy and I are both going to be baptized into the Church . . . on May eighteenth."

Drew looked a little stunned. "You're serious."

"I am," Jayson said.

"Wow," Drew said again. "Well, if it's something you believe in, then you should do it." He paused and added, "That's the date Derek was killed."

"It's been twenty years," Jayson said.

"Really? Has it been that long?" Drew asked, and the conversation moved into nostalgia.

After dinner, Drew and Valerie came back to the house with them. Will was as glad to see Drew as Drew was to see him. Macy and Aaron showed up to find the entire family gathered in the living room. Drew stood and hugged Macy tightly, saying with obvious pleasure, "Oh, it's so good to see you! You're all grown up."

"She'll always be my little girl," Jayson said.

Macy stuck her tongue out at him, making him laugh, then she introduced Drew to Aaron. They all visited for a long while before Will said, "Something's missing, you know. We need music."

"The stereo is right over there," Jayson said, and Will playfully slapped his shoulder.

"You know very well what I mean," Will said. They were still teasing back and forth when Macy appeared with Jayson's guitar, although no one had noticed her leaving.

"Come on, Dad," she said. "You've never actually played for Aaron beyond a little messing around here and there."

"I did too," Jayson said with mock defensiveness. "I played for him at that concert back in—"

"Me and twenty thousand other people," Aaron said.

"Oh, I guess I played for him, too," Drew said, and Aaron looked astonished.

"Oh!" Aaron said. "Your brother. The drummer. I get it now."

"Aaron's a little slow," Will said, "but we love him anyway."

"Play a song, Dad, or we will tie your bedroom door closed tomorrow, and you won't be able to get married."

"Oh!" Jayson pretended to be terrified. "Fine, you scared me into it." He pointed at Drew. "But I'd bet my right hand that little brother there has some sticks and a pad in this luggage. We may not have a drum set, but I bet he could plunk out a little rhythm for me."

"I bet he could," Valerie said and left the room, coming back a few minutes later with the sticks and a practice pad.

Elizabeth felt deeply gratified to watch Drew and Jayson playing and jamming, talking and joking. And she loved the way the children joined in the laughter, watching with awe these great musicians sitting cross-legged on the living room floor.

When the music had died down, Drew said, "That's a beautiful piano. Your piano at home is awfully dusty."

"Don't you have a cleaning lady come in?"

"Yes, but . . . it's dusty, figuratively speaking." He smirked at Jayson and said, "How long has it been since you've played the song?"

Jayson knew what he meant and chuckled dubiously. "Far too long. I don't know if I can even remember it. I'm certainly not going to play it now."

Everyone in the room groaned and pleaded, including those who had no idea what they were talking about. "Oh, that song is like breathing," Elizabeth said. "You don't have to do it perfectly. Just do it." In a simpering voice she added, "You wouldn't want to be sleeping on the couch tomorrow night."

Jayson laughed. "Will there *be* a couch in that hotel room?"

"Not likely; but there will be a floor," she said, feigning anger.

"Very well," Jayson said with a loud sigh. He stood up and handed the guitar to Trevin for safekeeping. "But this is considered a practice run. I haven't played it since before I hurt my hand, and that was more than a year ago."

"Still," Drew said, "Elizabeth's right. It's got to be like breathing. You've played that song a thousand times."

"That's easy for you to say," Jayson said to his brother, "when it's impossible for you to play with me. Why don't people keep drum sets in their living rooms as a standard?"

"*I* do," Drew said, and they all laughed.

Jayson sat at the bench and focused his mind on the keys, the memory of the song that was filed away somewhere in his mind, and the irony of what this song had meant throughout the course of his life. The greatest irony was that now it could only have a joyful, triumphant meaning. He put his hands on the keys and began, surprised at how easily those first few bars flowed through him, sad and sweet. He closed his eyes and moved into the fluid building of momentum and realized Elizabeth had been right. It *was* like breathing. And then it surged into the power and complexity of his favorite part and flowed on from there. When he'd finished and pulled his hands away, the room erupted with loud cheers and applause. He found Elizabeth on the bench beside him, kissing him, which provoked whistles and more applause. He heard Macy say to Aaron, "That's my dad."

Aaron just said, "Wow!"

They finally made the kids go to bed at midnight, and Jayson let Drew and Valerie borrow his car to go to the nearby hotel where they had rooms reserved. The house was quiet when Jayson said goodnight to Elizabeth at the top of the stairs.

"You know, Jayson," she said, "there's something we haven't talked about that maybe we should."

"What? You think I'll change my mind if I don't hear what you have to say?

She smiled. "No, but . . . well, I think you should know that I never had trouble getting pregnant. Considering the challenges in my previous marriage, the fact that I had three children is a miracle."

"Are you getting to a point?" he asked with a smirk.

"Well," she put her hands on his chest, "we *are* getting married tomorrow."

"Later today, you mean," he said, glancing at his watch.

"Yes, later today."

"And if we're married, I assume you'll be wanting to . . . you know."

"Are you talking about sex?" he asked, and she laughed softly.

"Yes, I am," she said. "And I might get pregnant."

"Oh, I hope so!" he said, and she laughed again.

"So, I take it you're all right with that."

More seriously he said, "I've wanted another baby since Macy was a year old. I'm more than all right with that." He wrapped his arms around her and added, "Which reminds me, you never told me how it was that you knew you were going to have another baby. When you were in the hospital bleeding to death, you seemed pretty certain."

"After Addie was born, I just felt very strongly that she wasn't the last. When Robert was killed, that was one of many things that I struggled with. I can only say that one night while I was praying, the Spirit let me know beyond any doubt that I would have another child."

"The blessing you were given in the hospital said *children*. Do you think there could be more than one?"

"It's possible," she said. "I guess we'll see how my body handles giving birth at this age."

Jayson absorbed the full depth of this conversation and felt suddenly overwhelmed and humbled beyond description. He pressed a hand over her face and into her hair. "I love you, Elizabeth. I love you with all my heart and soul."

"You're talking like a songwriter," she said.

"You make me *feel* like a songwriter."

"There you go again."

"Shut up and kiss me," he said. And she did.

CHAPTER 10

Jayson came awake abruptly in the darkest part of the night, chilled from his own sweat, breathing loudly while the beat of his heart overpowered the sound. It took him a full minute to recall the dream that had caused such a reaction, then he groaned and rolled his face into the pillow, as if it could protect him from the sudden, undeniable fear he felt.

For more than an hour, Jayson hovered in his dark room, unable to close his eyes, unable to hold still. He paced while he prayed, then he tried to rest but only tossed and turned, so he paced some more. Finally he dropped to his knees beside the bed and recounted his dream—and the reasons he had for finding it so disturbing. He didn't have any trouble believing that his prayer was being heard, and he knew that the listening ear was already well aware of his dilemma. Nevertheless, he poured out his every fear and concern. And then he waited and listened. He crawled back into bed while he was still listening. The absence of tossing and turning didn't occur to him until he was almost asleep, and his next awareness was the room becoming filled with early-morning light. He silently recounted the night's events and his present state of mind. He felt more calm, and definitely comforted. But one unsettling thought still lingered, and he jumped to his feet and went upstairs, not bothering to change from the pajama pants and T-shirt he'd slept in. The house was quiet, with no sign of daily life yet visible. He hesitated in the hallway, wondering if he should wake her, or just wait. The need he felt to talk to Elizabeth was undeniable, but this would be a big day for both of them. He didn't want to interrupt her precious sleep.

Jayson was still standing in the hall silently debating his options when Elizabeth's bedroom door came open, startling him. When he gasped, it startled her. She let out a whispery scream, then laughed even while she scowled at him. "What *are* you doing?" she whispered.

Jayson took her arm and guided her to the living room where they could talk without being overheard or disturbing any sleeping children.

"What is it?" she asked, sitting beside him. "What's wrong?"

Jayson registered the concern in her eyes, then just hugged her. She hugged him back, then chuckled softly when he wouldn't let go. "Jayson?" she said close to his ear. "Is something wrong?"

He took hold of her shoulders and looked at her straightly. "Just . . . tell me everything is going to be okay."

"Everything?" she asked, not certain what he meant.

"You and me. Us. The life we're making together."

Elizabeth attempted to read between the lines, wondering what might be the source of his distress. She finally just asked. "What's happened to upset you, Jayson? You and I both know that every-thing is as good as it can possibly be—for both of us. This is the right decision at the right time."

He let out a sigh so weighty that she saw him slump with the exhale of breath. "Maybe I just needed to hear you say it."

"Tell me what's going on," she insisted.

"I just . . . had a dream, a terrible dream. It was like when you'd left me all those years ago, only it was us . . . now . . . the way we are now. And when I woke up, I just couldn't shake this feeling of . . . dread." She saw tears in his eyes. "If you left me now . . . I don't know if I could survive it."

Elizabeth touched his face with tenderness. "Jayson," she whis-pered, "all of that is in the past. And you and I both know that you *could* survive if I left you; you could!" His eyes narrowed, and she hurried to add, "But I'm not going to. I love you, Jayson, with all of my heart. And we are going to be together forever."

Jayson inhaled a long, slow breath, taking in her words with careful deliberation. A sweet spirit surrounded them as what she'd said merged with what he already knew, and his fears subsided entirely, as a perfect sense of peace settled over him.

"I just needed to hear you say it," he said again and gave her another long, tight hug. "Come on," he said, standing up with her hand in his. "Let's get some breakfast. We've got a big day ahead."

"So we do," she said with a little laugh and followed him to the kitchen.

* * *

Jayson stood in the hallway of the church building while Macy pinned the boutonniere of white roses on the lapel of his suit coat. On the other lapel he wore the little guitar pin that had once been Derek's. He momentarily recalled the nightmare that had upset him not so many hours ago, and the peace that had followed when he'd turned to prayer. He knew, as Elizabeth had assured him, that this was the right decision at the right time. Macy smoothed the front of his tie and buttoned the jacket. "You look sharp, Dad."

"You look pretty good yourself," he said with a smile.

"Are you ready?" she asked.

"More ready than you could possibly imagine."

"You've loved her your whole life."

"Well, a good percentage of it, yes."

Macy's eyes became somber as she asked, "Do you regret marrying Mom?"

"No," he said, quickly and firmly. "I could never regret any part of my life that made you who and what you are—even the tough things. It had to be this way, baby. We are who we were destined to become; we are where we were destined to be."

Macy smiled and said, "That sounded like something from a song."

Jayson chuckled. "So it did."

"Okay, well . . . I'm going to go help the bride. I'll see you in a few minutes."

Jayson stepped into the room where he would be married and hovered near one of the two doors that led into it. The decor was in soft greens. It was a simple room, with the chairs arranged neatly and mostly filled with the limited guests they'd invited. Thankfully, Elizabeth's mother was absent. The decorations for the wedding were minimal. A white lattice archway covered with silk ivy stood between two tall, silk ivy plants. Near the door on a little table with the guest book were two framed pictures of him and Elizabeth: one that had been taken last week, and the other that had been taken at prom, their senior year of high school. Everything was simple but beautiful, just the way his life had become. He was surprised to see Elizabeth appear in the other doorway, and seeing her took his breath away. Her curly hair was arranged high on her head, with white roses woven into it. She wore pearl earrings, and the white satin gown flowed over and around her like a piece of heaven. Their eyes met, and they exchanged a smile that spoke volumes of all they were feeling.

The bishop announced that they were ready to begin. There was no pomp or pageantry. Jayson simply took her hand and led her to the front of the room, where vows and a binding kiss were exchanged. Drew and Macy each handed over the matching gold wedding bands. Jayson's mind wandered to his yearning for the day when they would be able to go to the temple together and have their marriage sealed for time and all eternity. But for now, the moment was perfect.

When the ceremony was done, Elizabeth was surprised to hear the bishop announce that Jayson would be taking a few minutes to give his bride a wedding gift. He took her hand and escorted her to a strategically placed chair, and he sat directly facing her. Then

Drew appeared with Jayson's guitar and gave it to him. Elizabeth already felt emotional, realizing what this meant.

"I wrote this three days ago," he said as he began picking out an intricate strain. He looked directly into her eyes as he sang with all the crooning tenderness that she would have expected from a love song: *"I've heard it said that true romance only comes once in a lifetime. And for fools who miss their chance, fools who pay the fiddler but miss the dance, they'll spend their days with only memories to keep them warm. But memories grow faint with time, and the years become a stale companion, and with each passing day I only missed you more. But I'm a man who believes in miracles, and lady you're the one . . . who turned around and took my hand and said, 'We've paid the price. The fiddler's tired, the band's expired, but we still have time to dance.' I'm a man who knows beyond a doubt that God smiles on fools like me. I'm a man who got a second chance."*

He closed his eyes and played a delicately intricate bridge, then he looked at her again and sang, *"You are my music, you are my song. You are the right that counteracts my every wrong. You are the rhythm in my heartbeat, you are the breath beneath my voice. You are the light dispelling dark in every choice."* And then the chorus again, with even more intensity than the first time. *"Yes, I'm a man who believes in miracles, and lady you're the one . . . who turned around and took my hand and said, 'We've paid the price. The fiddler's tired, the band's expired, but we still have time to dance.' I'm a man who knows beyond a doubt that God smiles on fools like me. I'm a man who got a second chance."*

Elizabeth tried to hold her tears back, but when tears leaked from Jayson's eyes, she just couldn't do it. He finished the song, and no one in the room made a sound, as if they were all caught up in the spell Jayson had woven with his music. He stood at the same moment Elizabeth did, and they wrapped their arms around each other while he held the guitar behind her back, pressing her close with his other hand. Drew took the guitar from him, and he held her more tightly.

The remainder of the wedding festivities was filled with laughter and celebration. They gathered with all of their guests to share a lovely meal, and they even danced. Then Elizabeth announced that she had a gift for Jayson.

"Mind you, it's not as creative as his," she said, "but . . . it does have meaning."

Drew carried a very large, nearly flat package into the room, and Jayson said, "We're keeping you busy, little brother."

Jayson felt certain it was something to hang on the wall, just by its shape and size. He pulled the silver paper away and caught his breath. It was a copy of a painting, beautifully framed. The high-quality print depicted a woman in a long dress, with an old-fashioned feel to her attire. A man, wearing a tuxedo, had a violin in his hand, and he was standing beside a piano. He was kissing the woman, and his arm was around her waist, holding her in a passionate embrace, as if he had just lifted her off of the piano stool. Jayson took it in with incredible wonder, then met Elizabeth's eyes and knew well that the painting stirred the same memories for her as it did for him. How could he ever forget playing that song with her, and the warm spirit that had surrounded them, and the divine kiss they had shared? It was as if heaven had swirled around them, luring them toward their destiny to be together. It had been a perfect oasis of romance with only friendship leading into and beyond it. And the painting in front of him had somehow captured the moment perfectly, even though he felt certain it had been originally painted a very long time ago.

"Hey," Drew said as Jayson turned it around for everyone to see, "I didn't know you played the violin, little brother."

"He doesn't," Elizabeth said, "but I hear violins in my head when he kisses me. They got the kiss right."

"Yes, they certainly got the kiss right," Jayson said, and Elizabeth kissed him. "Thank you," he said more quietly. "I love it; it's perfect."

"I thought so. We'll hang it in the bedroom."

He smiled and kissed her again.

A short while later they were on the freeway, with *Just Married* written across the back window of the car. Will would be taking Drew and Valerie to the airport while Macy stayed with the children, and beyond that, Jayson didn't care what they did—as long as they stayed safe. He looked over at Elizabeth, drowning in white except for her face and hands. She'd never looked more beautiful. He took her hand and kissed it, marveling at how his every dream was coming true—and some he'd never even thought to dream.

Arriving at the hotel in downtown Salt Lake City, Jayson got their overnight bags out of the trunk, leaving there the luggage they would take with them on the cruise. He left the car with a valet, and he thoroughly enjoyed the glances and smiles they got as they checked in and went to their room, wearing wedding attire. At the door to their room, Jayson set the bags inside, then carried Elizabeth, laughing, over the threshold. He set her carefully on her feet, took her face into his hands, and kissed her in a way he'd never dared since that night on the beach when such a kiss had pressed them beyond a threshold that neither of them had been ready to cross. They'd certainly shared passionate kisses since, but not like this! Jayson eased her fully into his arms, holding nothing back, as if his kiss alone could fully express the love he felt for her, and the joy he found in knowing she was his, he was hers, and all was right between them.

* * *

Elizabeth thoroughly enjoyed every minute of her honeymoon. The Caribbean was more beautiful than she ever could have believed from pictures she'd seen, and being there with Jayson made it feel like heaven on earth. She was pleased to see him often jotting things in a notebook he'd brought along. His creative mind was churning with new songs, and she greatly looked forward to seeing what might evolve from his inspiration.

On the flight home, as he was frantically scribbling lyrics, she said, "You're getting quite a collection. What are you going to do with all this new music?"

He shrugged. "Whatever God wants me to do."

Upon returning home, they quickly settled into a familiar routine, except that Jayson was now sharing the master bedroom with Elizabeth. He felt more comfortable in taking an active role in helping with the children, and he couldn't help being pleased when they took to calling him Dad. Trevin had graduated from crutches to a walking leg brace and was managing rather well.

As the day of the baptism drew near, Jayson felt an excitement not unlike the excitement he'd felt when he married Elizabeth. This too was a glorious and wonderful step in his life. The combination had given him boundless happiness.

The night prior to the baptism, Jayson had trouble sleeping. His mind wandered through many varied thoughts and finally came to rest on the question Elizabeth had recently posed to him. *What are you going to do with all this new music?* With the changes in his life, he couldn't imagine doing anything with it that wasn't of a spiritual nature. He'd devoted his life to doing whatever God wanted him to do, and logically, it just seemed obvious that his gift of music should be used for spiritual matters. Much of what he'd been writing lately had stemmed from his feelings about the gospel and his love of the Savior. While he was lying there, an idea came to his mind with clarity. He clearly envisioned making a CD for an LDS audience with some originals that he was working on, and a few of his own arrangements of his favorite hymns. Elizabeth could play some flute and violin. He could put down separate tracks and play both the piano and the guitar. He also thought of how much he would enjoy doing a Christmas CD using the same formula. He could do his own recording at his own pace, and this type of audience wouldn't require world tours to promote the product. While his mind churned with the possibilities, he became so excited that he had to wake Elizabeth and share it with her. Once she could focus on him clearly, her enthusiasm for the idea was evident.

After breakfast, Elizabeth said, "There's something I want to show you."

"Okay," he said and followed her into the garage.

She hesitated and said, "I've wanted to show you this for a long time, but I realized that it might be better to wait until you were ready."

"Okay," he drawled, almost feeling nervous.

"Truthfully, this idea wouldn't have had much substance if your being here was only temporary. But now that I know you're staying . . . forever . . ." she smiled and kissed him, "I can tell you what I've been thinking."

She leaned against the car as if to make herself comfortable for some kind of explanation, but he wondered what she intended to show him once she'd said what she wanted to say.

"When we were looking for a home, there were many reasons why I liked this one. But the most important is that it just felt right. Of course, I didn't understand then how God can guide our lives, but I've always tried to listen to my instincts. I knew that where we chose to live could have a huge impact on so many different facets of life. So what I'm going to show you was not the foremost reason for choosing this house, but when I saw it, I remember having a vivid image appear in my mind that really seemed to have no relevance, but it was . . . comforting, somehow. After Robert died, and I understood the workings of the Spirit, it crossed my mind a couple of times that what I'd envisioned might actually have some meaning beyond nostalgia or wishful thinking. When I realized that you and I were going to be together permanently, I knew that I really had been guided; I'd been shown the possibility of something that could actually come to pass. But I wanted to share it with you when you were ready."

"And what suddenly made me ready?" he asked, thoroughly intrigued and completely baffled.

"If you're going to start laying down tracks, you're going to need a place to do it." He watched her move a box from the top of a stack of four. She handed it to him, and he set it down. She moved another, and he realized the stack of boxes was blocking a door—a door he'd never even realized was there. The implication began to sink in before she pulled open the door and flipped on a light. He stepped in behind her and gasped. "Surely you've noticed," she said, "that from the outside the garage was twice as deep as it needed to be to park the vehicles."

"Actually, I didn't even think about it," he said breathlessly as he walked into the center of the room and turned in a full circle, imagining the possibilities. It was the size of a three-car garage, and completely empty.

"A retired couple built this home," Elizabeth explained. "The gentleman was a carpenter. This was built as a woodworking shop. He died a couple of years after the home was built, and his wife sold the home—to us. I would bet that some relatively simple construction could create a fairly adequate recording studio with decent acoustics." Jayson let out a breathy laugh, and she added, "And there's plenty of room for a piano, as well as everything else you'd need."

"I do believe you're right," he said, looking around himself again. Then he looked directly at her, recalling where this conversation had begun. "What *did* you see in your mind the first time you saw this room?"

"What I just told you. A recording studio; the piano. Wood floor; soundproof walls."

Jayson smiled, then he laughed. He hugged Elizabeth tightly and lifted her feet off the floor. "It would seem I have stumbled onto my destiny."

"Not stumbled," she said. "You took many difficult, grueling steps to get here. And this evening you're going to be baptized."

"So I am," he said and laughed again.

A short while later Jayson came to Elizabeth with a couple of elastics in his hand and a pair of scissors. "I need your help," he said.

"What?"

He pointed to the back of his head. "I want you to braid it, and then cut it off. I have an appointment for a haircut in half an hour, and they can even it up."

"You're serious," Elizabeth said.

"Of course I'm serious." He kissed her quickly. "It's time for the new me to emerge."

"I hope he's not too different from the old one."

"Just a clean-cut Mormon boy," he said and sat down. Elizabeth carefully smoothed his hair and put an elastic tightly around the top of the ponytail, but not too close to his head. She braided the hair and put another elastic tightly at the bottom. "Okay, here goes," she said and couldn't hold back a little laugh. "I can't believe I'm doing this." She pulled back. "I don't know if I can."

"Oh, just do it. It's only hair. Just cut it off and get it over with, or I'll be late for my appointment."

"Okay, fine," she said and just quickly did it. "There. It's done," she said.

Jayson reached a hand back to feel the absence of hair that had been there for more than two decades. He laughed softly, then looked at the braid in Elizabeth's hands. "Maybe you'd better keep it," he said. "Someday you can tell our grandchildren what a rebel I was."

Jayson left to get his haircut, and Elizabeth went to her room where she wrapped the braid in white tissue and set it on the dresser near the jewelry box Jayson had given her in high school. As the music box began to play, the irony of all they had shared rushed over her, and she sat on the edge of the bed and cried. She could feel nothing but joy in the present state of their lives, but perhaps there was residual grief that she'd never been able to be free of. She was still sitting there when Jayson came home.

"Whatever is wrong?" he asked, coming into the room.

Elizabeth said nothing. She just opened the drawer, and the music box began to play. Softly she sang along with the tinkling notes. He held her tightly while she said, "Every once in a while I'd listen to it and cry, wondering what had gone wrong. Now I know that it was all right all along; we just didn't understand what needed to happen." She looked into his eyes. "We've finally found the place for us, Jayson." He smiled, and she added, "Your hair looks really great."

He reached a hand behind his head and chuckled. "It could take some getting used to."

"But it really doesn't look much different in the front." She touched the shorter hair on top of his head. "You look adorable, as always." Noticing something else that was different, she tilted his face to get a better look at his ear. "It's gone," she said.

"No, it's right here," he said, pulling the little silver earring from his pocket. "I'm going to give it to Macy."

"What a good idea," she said, picking up the little ring to hold it fondly for a moment before she set it back in his hand. "And I think we'd do well to be getting ready. We don't want to be late."

Jayson glanced at the clock and felt butterflies. "No, we certainly don't."

Jayson hurried to Macy's room where she was just pulling a dress out of the closet. "Hey, baby," he said, and she smiled. "I have something for you. It's a little . . . souvenir. Hold out your hand and close your eyes."

She did so, and he placed the earring in her palm. She opened her eyes and looked at it, then she looked at his ear and touched it. "Wow," she said. "I've never seen you without it."

"Well, I want you to have it. I don't know why, really. I just do."

She smiled. "Thank you. I will treasure it always."

"So, do you like the new me?" he asked, turning around.

"Oh, my gosh!" she said and touched his hair. "I can't believe it." She laughed. "That is so weird."

"Thank you very much," he said with sarcasm.

"I like it, actually," she said. "But it could take some getting used to."

Jayson looked at her and sighed. "We'd better get ready." He took her hand. "This is a big day for us."

She smiled, then threw her arms around him. "I love you, Dad. I never could have asked for a better father."

He hugged her tightly, saying, "You are so precious to me." He looked into her eyes. "And little could mean more to me than our doing this together."

"I know exactly what you mean," she said, and he left her to get ready.

* * *

Elizabeth drove to the church with Addie and Trevin, since the others had gone ahead, needing to be there early. They sat in the room where the doors to the baptismal font had been opened and the font had been filled. While a sister in the ward played some soft prelude music on the piano, Elizabeth contemplated the miracle taking place this day. Her love for Jayson—and for the gospel—swelled inside of her to the point of pressing her to tears. She might have been able to hold them back, but then she looked up to see Jayson enter the room, dressed entirely in white. She stood when their eyes met, and she moved to embrace him.

"Tears?" he asked, wiping them away.

"Happy tears," she said. "White suits you well."

"Yeah," he chuckled, "I like it."

The meeting was soon underway, and Elizabeth felt that it couldn't have been more perfect. Aaron baptized Macy, and then Will baptized Jayson. When he came up out of the water, it occurred to Elizabeth out of nowhere that Derek was present. She watched Jayson and her father embrace while the thought settled in with such verity that she was overcome with chills and tears. Before

Jayson moved out of the font, he looked up to meet her eyes, and she saw tears on his face as well. Waiting for Jayson and Macy to change into dry clothes, Elizabeth pondered what she'd felt, and she knew beyond any doubt that her brother's spirit had been close beside her. She felt awestruck at the miracle, and even more so when Jayson appeared, wearing his suit and tie, his wet hair combed back off his face. She was trying to absorb the distinctive glow about him when he whispered close to her ear, "Derek was here."

She met his eyes and smiled, saying, "I know." They shared a long gaze while no words were necessary to fully understand all they were feeling but could never say. Jayson was simply grateful that he'd been given this second chance at life, and the knowledge that the losses he'd experienced were not necessarily permanent.

The very next Sunday, the bishop asked Jayson if he would serve as the Primary pianist. He eagerly agreed, and Elizabeth gave him her Primary songbook so that he could become familiar with the songs, and become more accustomed to playing impromptu by sight reading.

The following week they were preparing for Macy's graduation. A week after that, Aaron would be going into the Missionary Training Center, and they wouldn't see him for two years. But Macy had registered for some classes at Utah Valley University that would begin right away. She felt certain that staying busy would be the best way to adjust to being without him.

The morning of graduation, Macy left to go to the high school to take care of something. Trevin was in school for half a day, and Will had taken Addie to the grocery store. The doorbell rang while Elizabeth was putting cookies out on a pan as the others were baking in the oven.

"I'll get it," Jayson said and pulled the door open, wishing he hadn't.

"Jayson!" Debbie squealed with delight and threw her arms around him. "I do have the right house!" He stepped back. "Oh, it's so good to see you. You look great. How are you?"

"I'm fine," he said. "How are you?"

"I'm great," she said with a little too much jubilance, and he closed the door.

"Forgive my surprise, but . . . what are you doing here?"

"Is our daughter not graduating from high school today?"

"Uh . . . yes," he said, realizing now that Macy must have sent her an announcement—and apparently it had included a return address. She'd said nothing, but then she probably hadn't expected her mother to actually show up—at least not without calling first.

"So, I'm here for the big event. I apologize for dropping in like this, but I wanted to surprise Macy."

"Well, she's . . . on an errand," he said, not wanting to invite her to sit down, but knowing he needed to.

Elizabeth heard a woman's voice squealing with excitement to see Jayson and tuned her ears to listen to the conversation going on just around the corner. Realizing who this was, she felt a mixture of emotions. She'd never actually met Debbie, and knowing what she knew, she didn't necessarily want to. But she reminded herself to be forgiving—and gracious. She stepped into the little bathroom just off the kitchen and checked her appearance before she moved into the hall. Her first glimpse of Debbie revealed that she was shorter than Elizabeth had realized. She was dressed like a fashion ad in a magazine. Her light green pantsuit was impeccable accessorized with expensive leather pumps and a matching purse, which she wore over her shoulder. She wore way too much jewelry and makeup, and Elizabeth noted the dramatic difference from the pictures she'd seen of this woman during the days of her marriage to Jayson when she had appeared very down-to-earth and conservative.

"Hello," Elizabeth said, and Jayson felt deeply relieved to have her beside him, even though it felt terribly strange to see these two women standing face-to-face.

"Oh, hello," Debbie said, taking Elizabeth in with curious eyes. "You must be Elizabeth."

"That's right," she said, reaching out to take the hand that Debbie offered.

"Debbie Wolfe," she said in a tone that verged on bragging. Jayson bit his tongue to keep from calling her a hypocrite. She used the name freely because it gave her prestige in the social world of rock music, in spite of his retired status. But he felt a little sick thinking how thoroughly she'd defiled his name, and she'd certainly not had any motivation to be loyal to it when she'd been his wife.

"So, we finally meet," Elizabeth said, unable to say it was a pleasure.

"After all these years," Debbie said. "I hope my dropping in like this isn't a problem. I wanted to surprise Macy, but apparently she's not here and—"

"She should be home soon," Elizabeth said. "Why don't you come in and sit down."

"Thank you," Debbie said, and they moved into the living room. "You have a lovely home, Elizabeth."

"Thank you," she said, then the buzzer on the stove rang. "Oh, excuse me just a minute." She hurried out of the room.

Jayson watched Debbie sit down, but he preferred to stand. He was surprised at how he didn't feel angry with her for all the hurt she'd inflicted on Macy—and himself. He found instead that he felt rather sorry for her. The life she lived was pathetic. His own life was incredible, and he was deeply grateful.

Debbie watched Elizabeth leave, then she said quietly, "You've been living here for months, Jayson. The two of you must be a thing now, eh?"

"My reasons for living here initially had nothing to do with my relationship with Elizabeth, beyond her being a good enough friend to open her home to me when I needed a place to go. Her father lives here as well; technically, it was he who invited me to come. We stayed because Macy liked it here and she needed the stability—and the distance from LA. Elizabeth and Will have been very gracious to open their home to us."

Debbie didn't seem interested in discussing Macy's stability. Instead she asked in a whisper, "You're not sleeping with her, are you?"

"Is that any of your business?" he asked, realizing the hand that bore his wedding ring was in his pocket.

"Just curious," she said, sounding defensive.

"Well, as a matter of fact, I *am* sleeping with her."

Debbie's eyes went wide as she said, "I didn't think you had it in you to be . . . promiscuous."

She said it as if being promiscuous might have made him more of a man. He found her statement ironic as he recalled her once telling him that she'd assumed he would be sleeping around, as if that might excuse her doing the same. He couldn't keep from saying, "I *don't* have it in me to sleep around freely. Elizabeth is my wife."

Debbie's eyes widened further. She asked in an astonished whisper, "You got *married?*"

"I did. And you don't have to whisper. It's not a secret."

"Well, I didn't know about it."

"Now you do," he said, not bothering to tell her his reasons for not sending her an announcement. As indifferent as he'd come to feel about Debbie, he'd simply felt no incentive to notify her of *anything*.

Jayson was relieved when Elizabeth returned, even though Debbie's first comment to her was, "So, the two of you finally ended up together. Isn't that quaint?" She said it lightly, but there was something harsh in her eyes.

Jayson felt proud of Elizabeth for the way she smiled and said with no hesitation or apology, "Yes, we finally did. Isn't it wonderful?"

Debbie made a noise to indicate she didn't necessarily agree, despite her forced smile. Elizabeth graciously guided the conversation into some friendly small talk, but watching them together felt a little too weird to Jayson. He was relieved to hear a car pull into the garage, and he hoped it would be Macy. But he heard Addie running into the kitchen and knew she and Will had come back from the grocery store.

"Daddy, Daddy!" she called, running to find him. He was vaguely aware of Debbie's eyes going wide as Addie jumped into arms.

"What is it, precious?" he asked with a little laugh, glad to have his attention turned away from his ex-wife.

"We saw Bert and Ethel at the store, and they said that me and Trevin could come and have a sleepover now that school's out, if it was okay with you and Mommy."

"We'll talk about it later," Jayson said. "It will probably be fine. I just need to talk to them first."

"Okay," she said, then turned to see a stranger.

"Hello," Debbie said, and Addie responded in her typical way when meeting someone new. She buried her head against Jayson's shoulder and said nothing.

"This is Addie," Jayson said.

Addie lifted her head to look at him, able to speak as long as she ignored Debbie. "Grandpa's making tacos for lunch."

"Good," Jayson said. "Maybe we should help Grandpa unload the groceries."

"You're welcome to stay," Elizabeth said to Debbie, coming to her feet. Then to Jayson, "I'll help him. I need to be in the kitchen anyway."

He gave her a subtle glare that only made her smile. She was leaving him to deal with the former Mrs. Wolfe, and she knew very well how badly he didn't want to. He could almost hear her saying, *You're the one who abandoned me and married her. You can deal with her.*

Left alone with Debbie, he started telling her about Macy's plans for college, her friends, her boyfriend.

"She's not getting married, is she?" Debbie asked.

"We wouldn't want her to get married as young as we did," Jayson said firmly. "No, she's not getting married. He's leaving next week for two years."

"Two years? Where's he going?"

"He's going to Mexico to be a missionary."

Debbie looked stunned. "You're kidding. Our daughter's in love with a . . . missionary?"

"Most of the young men around here serve missions when they turn nineteen," he said. "It's really not that strange." Jayson shifted to talking about Aaron's fine qualities, his hobbies, and his goals beyond his mission. He figured that avoiding the subject of religion with Debbie would be wise. Will came into the room to meet Debbie, and she was gracious as she told him how nice it was that he'd always been like a father to Jayson, and it was nice to finally meet him. Will chatted with her until Macy came in. She actually seemed pleased to see her mother, and Jayson was glad to leave them alone to visit.

Lunch wasn't terribly uncomfortable, but Jayson wished that Debbie would leave. They had three hours before they had to go to graduation, and he didn't want to spend the time talking to Debbie. He was relieved when she thanked them for lunch and said she was going back to her room to clean up before the big event. Jayson printed a map off the Internet, detailing how to get from the hotel where she was staying to the Marriott Center in Provo where the graduation ceremonies would take place. He would have preferred not to see Debbie there, but he told her which section they planned to sit in for the best view, and when they arrived she quickly found them. Aaron was sitting with them, and Jayson introduced him to Debbie. He was glad when Aaron sat beside her, seeming pleased with the opportunity to get to know Macy's mother. The ceremony went well, albeit it was rather long. Jayson's mind was drawn back to his own graduation—and Elizabeth's. They had been so strained with grief at the time that the event had held little joy.

When the ceremony was over, Jayson took everyone out to dinner, including Debbie, and Aaron appeared to be enjoying his ongoing conversation with her. Jayson heard little of what they were saying. He leaned over to Elizabeth and said, "Maybe he's practicing his missionary tactics on her. Maybe she'll convert."

"Maybe," Elizabeth said facetiously.

When dinner was over, Macy and Aaron left to go to the graduation dance, and Debbie thanked Jayson and hugged him before she said good-bye to everyone else and left.

"Well, that was weird," Jayson said after she'd walked away.

"I'm glad you're not married to her anymore," Trevin said with mild disgust.

"You and me both," Jayson said and took Elizabeth's hand, grateful he didn't have to live the last twenty years over again.

CHAPTER 11

Sending Aaron off on his mission was more difficult for Jayson than he'd expected. He really was going to miss the kid. Macy struggled with seeing him go, but she handled it with dignity. She didn't whine or complain; she just kept busy, wrote him letters, sent him care packages, and spent time helping Aaron's mother with the kids. Jayson told Aaron's mother straight out that if they ever needed anything, to please say so. He didn't want the family going without. She tearfully thanked him, and he wondered if she suspected, as Aaron had, that the money to support the mission had come from him.

Jayson quickly found a good contractor, and construction began on the studio. He felt impatient but tried not to think too much about it for the time being. He loved playing the piano in Primary. He loved hearing the children sing, and he loved the way he could play a song he'd never heard before and even miss a note or two and it was okay. He continued singing in the ward choir, something he'd started doing with Elizabeth several weeks earlier. And he loved that, as well. One time when the pianist was ill, he filled in. He impressed them so thoroughly that it was suggested he take over that job. But he assured them that the present pianist was doing just fine and he'd rather sing. He felt sure if the Lord wanted him to be the pianist for the choir, the call would come through the bishop, not peer pressure.

Jayson and Elizabeth took Trevin and Addie on a vacation since they were out of school. Macy didn't have much fascination with going to California, and besides that, she was enrolled in school. The four of them flew to LA and stayed in the condo with Drew. They took a couple of excursions to the beach, which was easy since Jayson had left his SUV in the garage. They also went to Disneyland for a couple of days, then Drew and Valerie spent some time with the kids, taking them shopping and to movies while Elizabeth helped Jayson sort through and pack up his belongings. They rented a small U-Haul and loaded up everything he owned that was worth keeping—everything except the piano. While he knew he could sell it and buy a new one in Utah, this was the piano Drew had given him, and they made arrangements to have it moved when the studio was completed.

Jayson drove the U-Haul back to Utah while Elizabeth followed him in the SUV, and the kids took turns riding in each vehicle. They stopped in Las Vegas and stayed a couple of days, searching out the attractions that were family appropriate, then they completed the drive to Utah. They returned home to the announcement that Will and Marilyn were getting married, and Will would be moving in with her after the wedding, which would take place in a few weeks.

"Boy, that's a relief," Jayson said to him. "Now that I've brought home another vehicle, we don't have room for your car in the garage." Will laughed, and this began a running joke about who got to park in the garage. Jayson decided to let Macy keep the car she'd been driving, since she was getting good grades and doing well; she needed transportation regularly, and he didn't want to coordinate his driving schedule with hers.

Jayson felt good about the progress on the studio that had taken place in his absence, but still he felt terribly impatient. He oversaw the construction enough to make certain it was being done the way he wanted it, and he focused his time on putting together the music in his head to a point where he actually *could* record it. He began to feel frustrated when music kept coming into his mind that simply did not fit with his idea of the direction he should be taking. Hearing powerful rhythms and electric guitars in his head, he began to wonder if there was something wrong with him. He fought it boldly, trying to focus more on putting layers to the spiritual songs he had written. But the impulse for rock music screamed so loudly in his mind that he couldn't write anything at all. He finally decided to take the problem to his wife.

"You know the course I'm trying to take with my music, right?"

"Right," she said, folding laundry as she listened.

"It was a good idea, don't you think?"

"An excellent idea; inspired, I'm sure."

"Okay, well . . . then why do you suppose I can't seem to get it to . . . come?"

"Opposition?"

"Maybe. Maybe my brain is just fried from too much rock and roll."

"*Good* rock and roll does not fry *anyone's* brain," she said.

"Well, I think it fried mine. All I can hear in my head is . . . rock and roll."

Elizabeth turned to look at him. "And that's a problem?" He didn't answer. "Are you hearing bad language in this rock and roll? Questionable lyrics?"

"No, of course not, but . . . I'm supposed to use my gift for good, for spiritual purposes."

"You always did use your gift for good, Jayson. Your music was always uplifting and empowering; always inspired. Besides, *all* things are spiritual to God."

"*All* things?" he asked.

"It's in the scriptures. All things are created spiritually before they are created temporally, and all things are spiritual to God." She smiled and added, "Even rock and roll." While he was trying to let that sink in, she went on. "Of course, many things in this world come from the wrong spirit, but you're a good man trying to live a righteous life. You're not going to be inspired with something that isn't good. And all good things come from the light of Christ." She stopped what she was doing and faced him directly. "Is it possible you're getting stupor of thought because it's not the right direction at this time? The spiritual stuff, the Christmas stuff—it's a great idea. But maybe it's an idea whose time has not yet come. Maybe it's something to work toward. Maybe now, at this time in your life, God has something else in mind for you, and you're fighting it instead of listening to it."

Jayson actually heard himself gasp. But he had to say, "I don't want to be in the rock world; I don't want to do world tours and—"

"Jayson," she said as she put her hands on his chest, "you have a gift that is deeply profound. Few people in this world have the potential to make the impact with music that you do. God loves all of His children. Do you think He wants your gifts to be shared with only a select few? Now that you have reached this point in your life, you have even more to give." Her eyes filled with light. "Think for a moment what your music could do if it were ever-so-subtly laced with belief in God, with spiritual concepts. The world is full of music that is subtly laced with evil. We don't need any more of that. What we need is something to compete with all the garbage. And *you* have the ability to do that. Maybe you don't want to go on a world tour, but maybe that's what God wants you to do. And maybe He's giving you the music that will get the world's attention. So, write it, play it, sell it, sing it to the world. Get out there on the stage and be a beacon for everything that's right and good. Prove to the world that music can be loud and fun and full of life without being bad for us or our kids."

Jayson was stunned by what he was hearing, and even more stunned to realize how it was going straight to his heart. He knew she was right. It was as if she'd seen a vision that he had been too blinded to see. Or perhaps too afraid, which prompted him to admit, "It frightens me."

"What? The possibility of success? What?"

"Dealing with the cutthroats and the drugs and the sex; it's like Sodom and Gomorrah out there."

"And you have a testimony of the gospel and your feet firmly planted in its values. You never gave in to that evil before. Why would you now when you have so much more to hold you up? You don't have to stress about making money; you have enough money. If you don't need the money, you can call the shots. You can expect that it will be temporary, and when it's done, you'll know you made a difference, and you will have a family waiting for you at home."

Jayson sighed. "Now, wait a minute. If I'm out touring the world, what are you going to be doing?"

"I'll be baking cookies," she said with a smile, but it was a sad smile.

"Elizabeth, I can't leave you here and—"

"Jayson," she pressed her fingers over his lips, "in the early days of the Church, married men were asked to leave their homes and families and go out into the world and share the gospel. Women were left to tend farms and fight for survival. But they did it because that's what God asked them to do. I am going to be here with every possible comfort, and my father to look out for me. I'm going to fly out to meet you whenever possible, and you'll fly home whenever you can. And you will have a cell phone, and I will have a cell phone, and we will always be only a phone call away." She became teary. "And you will vibrate the music industry with messages of hope and goodwill. You will bear your testimony of God's existence through your music, and people will feel good listening to it without even knowing why. But if they're paying attention, they can figure out why. There will be interviews, and you can have a website, and fans will want to read everything about you, and they will know of your beliefs. And even if the success is short-lived, it will leave a dent in the world." She sighed. "And then you can come home and compose Christmas music."

Jayson took a minute to let all of that sink in, while he held her in his arms and looked into her eyes, as if doing so might help him to better see the vision she had presented to him. "So," he finally asked, "are you saying I should . . . get a band together? Just finding the right people could be—"

"I'm saying that you should write and record everything you can possibly do yourself. This is a Jayson Wolfe project. When you need to hire musicians, you hire them. This is your baby; you call the shots." She smiled and added, "I bet you could do nearly everything yourself in the studio—except the drums. Well, I know you can put down a basic beat, but when you really get into it . . . I know a great drummer that I bet we could talk into working with you. He would probably be thrilled. He hasn't done anything major since that last band broke up. He's keeping a low profile. It's worth a try."

Again Jayson absorbed what she was saying, amazed at how perfectly right it all felt. He could look ahead and see probable challenges, and aspects of the situation he didn't necessarily like. But he could feel in his heart that it was what he needed to do, and he had to find a way to do it.

"So, tell me," he said, "why you get all these visions on my behalf?"

She smiled and touched his face. "Woman's intuition."

"Okay, I can accept that."

"And how long have you had this idea?" he asked as she returned to folding the laundry.

"A while now; I was just waiting until you were ready to hear it."

"Okay." He laughed softly and leaned against the dryer, folding his arms over his chest. "Is there anything else you need to tell me that you're holding out on until I'm ready to hear it?"

Elizabeth couldn't hold back a little laugh. There *was* something she needed to tell him, and he couldn't have given her a more perfect setup. "Just one," she said.

"And how long have you been holding this one in your busy little head?"

"Oh, just a couple of hours. But I wasn't going to hold out too long."

"I'm listening," he said.

She wrapped her arms around his waist and looked up at him, saying in a whisper, "I'm pregnant."

Jayson let out a breathy laugh, then asked, "Really?"

"Really."

He laughed again. "When is it due?"

"I don't know exactly. I just did a home test; I'll go to the doctor soon, but I'm guessing it will be the middle of March."

Jayson felt deliriously happy with the prospect of having a baby. He concluded that nineteen years between children was certainly not the norm, but Trevin and Addie helped fill in the gap.

It quickly became evident that Elizabeth tired easily and felt a little sick in the mornings, but she actually managed rather well. Will and Marilyn's wedding was beautiful—or so Jayson was told. Since Will had passed the waiting period from his baptism, he was able to go to the temple, and he and Marilyn were sealed for eternity. Jayson learned then that Marilyn had been married in the temple previously, and had raised five children with her husband before he left her for another woman. The sealing had been canceled through a difficult process, and Jayson was amazed that anyone would turn their back on such tremendous blessings. Marilyn was an incredible woman, and it was good to see her and Will so happy. Jayson couldn't help thinking of the romance that had once existed between Will and his mother. Her absence in his life still felt wrong, but he focused on the present and felt genuinely happy for Will and Marilyn. Following the temple ceremony, they had a wedding breakfast and a little open house, and Jayson enjoyed being a part of that. But he longed for the waiting period to be over for himself so that he could go to the temple with Elizabeth and know that she was his forever.

After Will had moved in with Marilyn, the household routine took some adjusting. And Jayson often teased Will about how they weren't eating nearly as well. Elizabeth cooked a few times a week, but she was busy and pregnant, and Jayson couldn't do much beyond Hamburger Helper.

When Jayson called Drew to give him the news about the expected arrival, Drew told him that he and Valerie were married. They just went to Vegas and did it quickly, which explained why no one was invited. Jayson was glad that his brother was married and happy, but he didn't envy the Vegas wedding.

As the studio neared completion, Jayson began purchasing the equipment he would need, as well as some new instruments. He often took Trevin with him, and the child dearly enjoyed exploring music stores. Jayson felt compelled to buy a mandolin; it was an instrument he'd always admired and had toyed with the idea of learning to play it. He decided now was as good a time as any. Trevin enjoyed playing with the mandolin, and Jayson found that the boy actually could make some music with it. He had also shown steady improvement with the guitars.

When the studio was completed, Jayson oversaw the next stage of having the recording equipment installed. When that was done and working properly, the room began to fill with instruments— and a spirit that Jayson could literally feel each time he stepped into it. He was reminded of the music room in the basement of Elizabeth's home in Oregon. Only it was better. When the piano finally arrived, it felt complete.

He came home one afternoon to hear his wife say, "The studio's done now."

"I thought it already was."

"Oh, now it's really done. I didn't want to hang anything in the studio; we don't want to mess up the sound. But I put a little decor in the sound booth."

"Really," he said and chuckled, hurrying out to the studio, with Elizabeth following. He entered the sound booth and laughed to see two framed posters, side by side. One was of Gray Wolf, and he was prominently in the foreground. And the other, which he liked much better, was of *A Pack of Wolves,* with him and Elizabeth in the center, standing close together, their faces almost touching as they looked into the camera. Drew was in the picture—and Derek. "Wow," he said. "There's only one problem."

"What?"

"Your red shoes don't show in this picture."

"Too bad," she said and kissed him.

"Thank you," he said. "I love it." He glanced at the Gray Wolf poster and said, "That one's not bad either, but I really love this one."

"The woman who framed them was very impressed, especially when she realized it was me in this picture with you a hundred years ago. But that didn't impress her nearly as much as when I told her I was going to have your baby."

Jayson just laughed and kissed her again.

* * *

Jayson began spending long days in the studio, laying down tracks for a number of different songs. He treated it like a job and left it behind during the evenings and on the weekends so that he could take an active part in family activities. Occasionally he had Elizabeth come in and listen to something. Her genuine enthusiasm and encouragement kept him going. He bought a drum set and played around with it enough that he could put down a basic rhythm, not as a final layer, but just to give him something to follow. When he reached a point where he simply couldn't do it alone, he finally broke down and called his brother. He'd felt hesitant to approach Drew with a request for his help, even though he wasn't certain why. He'd never felt any hard feelings or tension between him and Drew, but their musical separation had been difficult for Jayson. And Jayson felt very strongly that the project he was doing now needed to be a *Jayson Wolfe* project. He needed Drew's help, but he wasn't quite sure how to approach it.

They talked on the phone for more than twenty minutes before Jayson finally said, "Hey, I'm doing a new project."

"Really?" Drew sounded genuinely enthused.

"How does a Jayson Wolfe solo album strike you?"

"I'd say it's about time."

"Really?"

"Really. You're a genius, little brother. I can play the drums. I don't hear music in my head."

"Well, you might be grateful for that," Jayson said. "It can be a curse sometimes. And you *are* a genius on those drums."

"So tell me about it," Drew said, and Jayson told him about the studio, the songs he'd come up with, and how he was going about laying down tracks on his own.

"I only have one real problem."

"What's that?"

"I need a great drummer, Drew—both in the studio and on the road if I can actually sell the thing. It just doesn't seem right without you. The job pays well. Would you consider it?"

"Consider it?" Drew laughed. "Oh, Jayse, nothing could make me happier than to work with you again. I don't need any credit, and you don't even have to pay me. I would *love* to just *do* it. When do we start?"

Jayson had trouble answering, overcome by an unexpected rush of tears. He chuckled through them when Drew said, "Are you having high-water-table problems again?"

"I'm afraid so," Jayson said. "This just . . . means so much to me."

"And to me," Drew said. "Mom would be pleased."

"Yes, she would," Jayson agreed. "And we can start any time. The problem is that the studio is here, and I need to be with my family. But I have a proposition. Will has moved out; he left two good-sized empty rooms in the basement, with a full bathroom, and there's even a partial kitchen down there. How would you and Valerie feel about just staying with us for a couple of months?"

"Well, I can't speak for Valerie, but I think it sounds great."

"Talk it over with your wife and let me know. I'll pay all of your expenses and some salary; I know you don't need it, but it's the principle of the thing."

"I'll talk to her and call you back," Drew said.

Jayson got off the phone and found Elizabeth soaking in a bubble bath. He closed the toilet lid and sat there as she announced, "I'm taking a bubble bath."

"I can see that," he said. "That's why you're all covered with bubbles."

"Well, it's wonderful."

"I'm glad you're enjoying it."

"What's on your mind?" she asked.

"I called Drew," he said, and her brow furrowed. "He's thrilled and can't wait to start. He's going to talk to Valerie about coming to stay for a couple of months."

"Oh, that's wonderful!" she said.

"I hope she's okay with it. I don't think I can do it without him, and I don't want to go to LA—not yet anyway."

"I love you, Jayson Wolfe," she said, "and I'm proud of you."

"I love you too, Elizabeth Wolfe." She smiled, then threw a handful of bubbles at him, making him laugh.

* * *

Drew called the next day to report that Valerie was not only willing, she was eager. The timing was good because she'd recently been laid off from her job and, since Drew wasn't doing much work, they had just decided to take a long vacation.

"Well, this won't be much of a vacation," Jayson said.

"Oh, we'll do that later," Drew said. "Valerie's like me in the respect that she doesn't have much in the way of family. She really enjoyed coming out there for the wedding, and she loved it when you came out here to stay. I think she'd like to get to know Elizabeth better, and spend some time with the kids."

"Well, I guess we're in business, then," Jayson said.

Drew and Valerie arrived a few days later. When Jayson took his brother into the studio, Drew actually got tears in his eyes. "It's like a dream come true. Even though we've had many dreams come true, this is different." He chuckled. "You even have drums," he said. "That's good, because mine wouldn't fit in my suitcase."

"They're the best," Jayson said, "with all the features you like best."

"I can see that," Drew said and sat on the stool. He made a couple of adjustments and picked up the sticks left laying over the snare. He smirked at Jayson and said, "Do you think we could do it?"

"It?"

"You know what I mean. We haven't done it together for years, but I know you can still play it, because you did it not so long ago. What do you think?"

"Let's go for it," Jayson said and sat at the piano.

"You got the mike set up? I think you'd better sing it." Drew smiled and added, "Let's do it for Mom."

Jayson stood up and adjusted the microphone stand and the amplifier. While he was doing a sound test, Elizabeth and Valerie came in. "You're just in time," Drew said.

"What are you doing?" Valerie asked.

Jayson looked at Elizabeth and said, "We're going to play our song for our mother. We figure she'd appreciate having us back together making music. It only seems right to start with this one."

He knew by the way she smiled at him that she understood what this meant to him, even if he could never explain it.

While Drew and Jayson were making some final adjustments, Elizabeth discreetly went into the sound booth, grateful that Jayson had shown her some of the basics so that she could help him occasionally when he just couldn't be two people at once. With everything on FULL RECORD, she locked the studio door and turned on the light that would shine on the other side to indicate that recording was in session. She felt secretly thrilled to think of getting this recorded—if only for their posterity. It didn't matter if they did it perfectly; they'd not practiced together in years. It was the spontaneity of the moment that she hoped to capture. Hearing their typical banter as they got in place, she couldn't help being pleased to know that it would be recorded as well.

"I take it this song has some significance," Valerie whispered.

"Yes, it certainly does. I'll tell you later," Elizabeth said, and they sat down to listen.

Memories washed over Elizabeth as they began with perfect synchronization. *It's like breathing for them,* she thought. They played the song with all the energy and finesse it had always had. Elizabeth enjoyed seeing Valerie's amazement. She'd seen Drew play a great deal, and she'd seen Jayson play part of this song on his own. But there was something about the way they played together that filled the air around them with an almost palpable energy. When their ten-minute song came to an end, Jayson and Drew both flew off their seats with a spontaneous whoop. They did a high-five and laughed like a couple of kids while Elizabeth and Valerie applauded and cheered.

While everything was still being recorded, Elizabeth talked them into doing "Harmony." Jayson actually began the song by saying into the microphone, "This is for you, Mom, although I must admit the song is definitely about my wife. She is my Harmony."

It came out sounding so beautiful that Elizabeth was left freshly in awe of her husband's tremendous talent—and the fact that he was her husband. When they were finished, Elizabeth decided to break the news. "That was incredible, and someday your children will be glad to know that I recorded it."

"What?" they both shrieked.

She laughed and said, "Still recording. And if you so much as touch it, Jayson Wolfe, you'll be sleeping on the couch."

Later when Elizabeth let Macy hear the recording, the last thing they heard was Elizabeth's laughter as Jayson started tickling her. Then Drew had turned off the recording equipment.

"That is so cool," Macy said.

"Okay, it's cool," Jayson admitted, "but we keep it in the family. Those songs are personal. And I'm not paying Elton John any royalties." He smirked and added, "I sent him a thank-you note once; that's all he's going to get."

"You did, really?" Elizabeth said.

"I did, really. I was famous by then, so he actually sent me a note back."

"Cool," Macy said.

Over the next several weeks, Jayson and Drew put in full work days, five days a week, while their wives enjoyed getting to know each other better. On Saturdays they did a variety of activities, usually involving the children. On Sundays the family went to church while Drew and Valerie did their own thing. A few weeks into their stay, Valerie discovered she was pregnant, and they had great fun speculating over the little cousins that would be born within weeks of each other.

School started, and Trevin went into seventh grade while Addie began kindergarten. Macy pressed forward at UVU, and she did volunteer work at a local nursing home. She continued to write to Aaron and kept the family posted on his experiences in Mexico, although Jayson was glad to see her dating and spending time with friends.

The first weekend in October, Elizabeth informed everyone that she and Jayson would be going somewhere Saturday morning early, and they wouldn't be back until late afternoon. She told him he needed to put on his suit but wouldn't give any other explanation.

"But general conference is on TV," Jayson protested. He knew that every six months the Church had a huge conference where the prophet and many other leaders spoke during four different sessions over Saturday and Sunday, and that the conference was broadcast over television, radio, and Internet all over the world. During the last conference, Jayson had watched bits and pieces on television and it had fed his budding testimony. Since his personal conversion, he had been eagerly looking forward to watching every minute, seeing the prophet on TV and hearing what he might say. And now Elizabeth was dragging him away from home.

"I've arranged to have it all videotaped, and you can watch it later," she said. "Come on, let's go."

"So, where are we going?" he asked once they were in the car and she was driving.

"It's a surprise," she said with a little smile.

They drove for about twenty minutes, and she pulled into a Trax train terminal. He'd never ridden the train, but he knew it made several different stops—the last being in the heart of Salt Lake City.

"The train?" he asked while they were standing at the terminal, waiting for the next northbound train to pull in.

"It's not easy getting a parking place downtown this weekend," she said with a smile.

"Downtown?" he echoed.

"There's just the most amazing feeling in the city during conference," she said. "I thought we could go and watch all the Mormons coming and going. They come from all over the world for this, you know."

"So I've heard," he said with a suspicious chuckle.

Jayson enjoyed the train ride with Elizabeth sitting close to him. He was surprised to hear a college-aged girl say to him, "You're going to think I'm crazy, but . . . you look so much like one of my all-time favorite musicians. I mean . . . I used to have posters plastered all over my bedroom. So, I just have to ask . . ." She wrinkled her nose and looked embarrassed. "Are you Jayson Wolfe?"

Before Jayson could answer, Elizabeth turned to him, pretending to be astonished, *"Are* you Jayson Wolfe?" she asked. "That's not possible! A world-famous musician on a train in Utah? I don't believe it. Let me see your driver's license."

Jayson looked at the woman who had posed the question and found her expression amused—and amazed. He winked at her as if to imply that they should humor Elizabeth. Pulling out his wallet he said, "I'll show you mine if you show me yours."

"Fine," Elizabeth said and pulled her wallet out of her purse.

Elizabeth looked at Jayson's driver's license and gasped, "Oh, my gosh. I can't believe it. It's you!" She showed it to the woman sitting across from them, who let out a quiet squeal that made Jayson laugh and drew a certain amount of attention.

"It *is* you," the woman said.

"I'm afraid so," Jayson said and grabbed Elizabeth's wallet to show the young woman *her* license. "And as you can see, this silly woman with me is my wife, *Mrs.* Jayson Wolfe."

"It is so nice to meet you," the young woman said, holding out her hand, and Jayson shook it.

"And it's nice to meet you," he said. "It's nice to know that *somebody* listened to my music."

"Are you kidding? It was incredible. I keep wishing you'd come up with more."

"Well, Gray Wolf is no longer and never will be again, but—"

"But he's doing a solo project," Elizabeth interrupted. "I've heard samples. It's going to be amazing."

"Okay, that's good, Mrs. Wolfe," Jayson said. "I'm sure this young lady doesn't want to hear about—"

"Oh, but I do!" she said. "That's wonderful."

They chatted for a few minutes, then she asked, "So, I have to ask why you're here. I mean, you're all dressed up, going to Salt Lake, right? I wouldn't even dare believe that you might be . . ."

"A Mormon?" Elizabeth suggested, and the young woman nodded sheepishly, as if she feared she might have offended them.

"Actually, I am," Jayson said proudly, liking this vein of the conversation much better. "I was baptized in May."

"Are you *serious?*" she said. "That is the most awesome thing I've ever heard." She shook his hand again, this time more eagerly. "I'm getting married in the Jordan River Temple next month."

"Well, congratulations," Jayson said, and a minute later the young woman got up and left as the train reached the stop where she got off to go to work.

"My driver's license?" Jayson said when she was gone. Elizabeth just laughed.

A short while later they got off the train right next to Temple Square, and Jayson realized he'd not been here since Elizabeth had brought him during a rehab break. He couldn't help pondering the changes in his life since then as they walked hurriedly across the Square.

"Are we in a hurry?" he asked.

"As a matter of fact, we are." She pulled two tickets out of her purse and handed them to Jayson. "It's a big event."

Jayson stopped walking as he looked at the tickets and realized what they were. They were actually going to be sitting in the Conference Center for the first session of general conference.

"How did you get these?" he asked.

"They're distributed to various stakes and wards. They just kind of . . . fell into my hands."

"Is the prophet going to be there?"

"I would assume," she said and hurried him along.

"Wow," he said, almost feeling emotional. Then he did a fair imitation of the young woman on the train. "Oh, my gosh. I can't believe it."

Elizabeth laughed and took his hand.

In the Conference Center, Jayson was mesmerized by the beauty of the place—and the size. It had been built specifically for this purpose, and it held somewhere in the neighborhood of 24,000 people. And every seat had a good view of the pulpit. They were seated long before the meeting was scheduled to start, and he felt an excited anticipation. He was surprised when Elizabeth leaned over to him and said, "The last time I was in a room with this many people—waiting for a great event—it was a Gray Wolf concert.

"I'm sorry," Jayson said.

"Oh, it was incredible! It was one of the highlights of my life."

Nothing more was said, but Jayson couldn't help pondering the irony. Those days of performing on stage to thousands of screaming fans seemed like a dream. The eager expectation he felt now, being in the audience, waiting to see someone he admired, was a remarkable contrast. While the crowds around him buzzed with chatter, his mind wandered again through the changes that had occurred in his life in the last year. Then it struck him that it had been a year ago this month that he had been rock-bottom suicidal. He actually gasped at the thought, finding it impossible to comprehend.

"Is something wrong?" Elizabeth asked.

"I was just thinking," he said, "about where I was a year ago." He gave her a wan smile. "I'm glad I didn't go through with it."

Elizabeth realized what he meant and felt suddenly choked up. She touched his face. "So am I."

A sudden hush fell over the room, and Jayson felt astonished at how such a huge crowd could become so immediately silent. And everyone rose to their feet. As if Elizabeth had read his mind, she whispered close to his ear, "That's him. The prophet just came in."

Jayson took a deep breath and held Elizabeth's hand tightly as he watched the prophet walk to his seat, waving occasionally toward the huge audience. Even from a distance, Jayson could feel an undeniable presence. He could never explain *how* he knew, but he *knew* this man truly was a prophet. He knew it beyond any doubt.

The conference session was so marvelous that the two hours flew by. Feeling an incredible spiritual high, Jayson and Elizabeth walked hand-in-hand back across the street to Temple Square. They encountered several anti-Mormon protesters, which Elizabeth said was typical. *Opposition,* Jayson thought. Satan wouldn't work so hard to oppose something if it weren't right and good. Coming into the Square, they stopped at the North Visitors' Center to see the *Christus.* Jayson found that he was completely speechless. There was absolutely nothing he could say to express how full his heart was. But Elizabeth seemed to understand as evidenced by her own contemplative silence.

They moved with masses of people to a nearby restaurant to get some lunch. But Jayson enjoyed being surrounded by hundreds of people all dressed in church clothes on a Saturday. They all had something wonderful in common, and he realized that Elizabeth had been right. There was an unmistakably unique feeling in the city.

They ate and wandered through the grounds surrounding the Church Office Building and the Main Street Park, then they went into the Joseph Smith Memorial Building. Standing in the lobby, Jayson stood before the huge statue of the Prophet Joseph Smith and saw something completely different than he'd seen on his previous visit. He was surprised to hear Elizabeth say, "You know, what he did has been thoroughly criticized, mocked, and discredited, but do people ever stop to wonder why a man would endure such horrible persecution in order to defend something that wasn't true?"

"Like what?" Jayson asked, realizing that apart from his testimony of what Joseph Smith had done as a prophet, he actually knew very little about the man.

"Well, as I understand it, Joseph and his wife, Emma, never had a home of their own. They were much like gypsies, I think, traveling from one place to another, staying wherever someone was good enough to take them in while Joseph kept to his work. I think such a life must have been difficult for Emma."

Jayson was surprised to hear mention of Emma. He'd heard a great deal about the Prophet, and he'd heard an occasional piece of information about his wife, such as the fact that she'd compiled a hymnbook. But he'd never quite pictured Joseph Smith having a wife and family who had been affected by his afflictions.

Elizabeth went on. "Of course, persecution followed Joseph everywhere he went. It seems he was constantly trying to keep peace with the Lord and press forward, while the Saints were being driven out of their homes, even killed. I cannot imagine how he must have felt to be sitting in prison, knowing that such things were going on. He was beaten by mobs, and he was actually tarred and feathered."

"Good heavens," Jayson said with a gasp.

"They say that the tar wouldn't come off without bringing skin with it." Jayson grimaced at the thought, then Elizabeth added, "And I believe that when the mob dragged him out of his home, the door was left open. The exposure to the cold is what killed their baby."

Jayson gasped again but couldn't speak. Elizabeth concluded her oration, saying, "Joseph and Emma had eleven children; only five of them lived. And in the end, Joseph's testimony was sealed with his blood. He was shot and murdered by an angry mob." She looked up at the statue. "Now why would a man go through such things, when all it would have taken to be free of the persecution would have been to deny what he had seen?"

Jayson let that thought settle into him as his prior prejudice against Mormonism and Joseph Smith seemed difficult to comprehend.

They wandered around a bit more, then rode back on the train during the afternoon conference session when the crowds would be at a minimum. Back at the train terminal as they were getting into the car, Jayson kissed Elizabeth and said, "That was a pretty incredible day. Thank you."

"My pleasure," she said, and he kissed her again.

CHAPTER 12

Jayson began to feel a certain frustration in getting his CD put together. As he listened to material they'd worked hard on, some of it just didn't feel quite right. Drew was patient and willing to keep working with him. He and Valerie both seemed fine with staying on a little longer.

"You know," Drew said one afternoon while they were eating a late lunch in the sound booth, listening to what they'd recorded that morning, "I think we have a missing ingredient." Jayson looked up abruptly, and he added, "The stuff Elizabeth does on the flute and violin is a nice touch, especially on the love songs, but . . ."

"But?" Jayson pressed when he hesitated.

"I just keep thinking of how the two of you sounded singing at Derek's funeral—and Mom's. Your voices harmonize like a match made in heaven."

"Well, I won't argue with that," Jayson said in a calm voice that didn't betray his quickened heart. There were no words to describe how the idea struck him to the very core. Still, he had to say what he knew. "But if I take this on the road and want it to sound the way it does on the radio, I can hire someone to play the flute or violin, but . . . only Elizabeth has Elizabeth's voice. She won't do it."

"Have you asked her?"

Jayson pushed his chair back and stood up, repeating, "She won't do it."

Drew smirked at him as he left the room with the determination to talk to her about it right now. He found her sitting at her sewing machine, mending a pair of Addie's pants.

"I know you," she said with mock astonishment. "You're that famous Jayson Wolfe!"

"Yes, I am," he said, "and I know you! You're that girl who shared a microphone with him on stage, wearing those great red shoes."

Elizabeth gave him a sidelong glance. "No, that girl grew up."

"She has the same voice," he said and sat down close beside her. "Elizabeth," he said intently, and she stopped what she was doing, looking visibly concerned. "I need your voice. You're the missing ingredient."

"Oh, no," she said. "If I record it you'll want me to perform it with you. I'm going to have a baby, Jayson. My place is here."

"Your place is with me, and onstage together we were magic."

"We are magic enough right here at home. You're the performer, Jayson."

"Just . . . record it with me. I need your vocals. My gut tells me that it's the extra something that's missing."

"No, I'm not going to do it," she said so firmly that he realized he actually felt angry with her. They'd hardly had a tense word between them since they'd become engaged. He wasn't sure how to handle it.

"And that's it," he said tersely.

"That's it," she countered.

"What are you afraid of?" he asked.

"Afraid? I'm not afraid! I just know I'm supposed to be home taking care of my family. And if you get my voice on the recording, you're going to want my voice on the stage. You'll want it to sound as close to the recording as possible. I know you. And I'm not going on tour."

"You're terribly stubborn when you want to be," he said. "I would think you'd at least *consider* the possibility."

"What possibility? I'm going to have a baby, Jayson. Are you suggesting we drag the kids all over the world with us on a concert tour with a nanny in tow?"

"Maybe," he said. "Will and Marilyn would make great tour nannies."

Elizabeth stood up and made a disgusted noise. "That's the most ridiculous thing I've ever heard."

"And what if God wanted you to do it?" he asked. She stopped her attempt to leave the room and stared at him, the disgust in her countenance deepening.

"God would want me to be home with my children!"

"Are you sure?" he asked. "God would want us to make our children our highest priority, and see that they are nurtured and cared for properly. He doesn't necessarily dictate that there aren't a number of different ways that can be accomplished. But you've made up your mind without even bothering to ask Him. Going on tour isn't necessarily high on my priority list, but I feel like I'm supposed to do it—and I feel like maybe, just maybe, you're supposed to go with me. I would think you could at least ask."

Jayson left the room and returned to the studio, where Drew again smirked at him. "She told you no, didn't she."

"Yes, but it's not over yet."

"How's that?"

"I told her to ask God," he said, and Drew's eyes widened. They shared a brief conversation on personal revelation, then they listened to the recordings again, analyzing what might be wrong. The more Jayson listened and thought about it, the more he believed that Drew had been inspired. Elizabeth *was* the missing ingredient.

When Jayson went into the house for supper, Valerie was cooking and said that Elizabeth was lying down. He entered the bedroom quietly to find her not sleeping, but sniffling.

"What's wrong?" he asked, alerting her to his presence.

"I'm just tired," she insisted.

"Does fatigue generally come with tears?" he asked, sitting on the edge of the bed.

"Occasionally," she insisted. "I'm pregnant. I have the right to be excessively emotional."

"Okay, I concede that, but given our most recent conversation, I have to assume that your tears have something to do with me." She said nothing, and he asked, "Are you angry with me?"

She hesitated long enough that he felt sure she wanted to say yes. "I'm not angry," she finally said. "I'm just . . . confused, and . . . frustrated. What you're asking just feels so . . . impossible."

"Impossible, or just very much against your preconceived ideas?" he asked. She looked defensive, and he quickly added, "I thought with God nothing was impossible. If you ask God with real intent, Elizabeth, and you can feel confident in knowing He doesn't want you involved directly with this project, I will accept that and let it drop. And I will find another missing ingredient." He leaned over and kissed her brow. "And you will always be the most important person in my life, whether we're onstage together or not."

She put her arms around him and held to him tightly. He kissed her, and she urged him closer. "Whoa," he said when her kiss became intimate, "I don't know if this is a good time for . . . such things." He laughed softly.

"Drew and Valerie will keep everything under control. They'll think we're arguing."

"Okay, you talked me into it," he said and kissed her again.

* * *

Given the time to think about Jayson's request, Elizabeth knew he was right. She couldn't brush it aside without at least asking. She wished that she could fast in order to feel closer to the Spirit, but her pregnancy wouldn't allow it. She did, however, go to the temple. She sat in the celestial room for more than an hour, praying and pondering the situation. She didn't get any definitive answers, but she did leave feeling a distinctive peace. She felt certain that whatever course she took, all would be well. Still, she truly believed that while Jayson's mission was to leave an impression on the world, hers was to be a silent partner at home.

Returning home, Elizabeth was surprised at how tense and irritated she felt. Generally her visits to the temple had the opposite effect. Analyzing her feelings, she realized that her mind felt cloudy and weighed down and just plain confused. After she'd snapped at Addie over something ridiculous, she went to her bedroom and straight to her knees. She asked that her mind be freed of this unsettling tension, and that she would be able to do all that was required of her. She remained on her knees for several minutes, just trying to calm herself down and think clearly. And that's when a memory came into her mind with perfect clarity. She'd not been thinking about her high school days with Jayson, but out of nowhere, she recalled the day that she had walked onto the stage to perform and found a brand-new microphone, with a big red bow tied to it.

Jayson began the show by saying to the audience, "Elizabeth has a new microphone."

"That's pretty cool," Elizabeth said into the mike.

"The bow matches your shoes," Derek said into his mike, and the audience laughed.

"She's pretty cute though," Jayson said to the crowd. "I think I'd still prefer sharing the mike with her. What do you think?"

A cheer went up, and Jayson started the song, although from that day forward he occasionally still shared the mike with her.

The image of her sharing that microphone with Jayson stuck in her mind, even while her mind wandered to the day they had first auditioned at the dance hall in Portland.

Elizabeth walked through the door with the microphones and asked, "Where do you want these?"

"You brought a girl," Joe said. "Is she in the band?"

"She is now," Jayson said as Derek walked past them toward the stage door, carrying an amp.

"That's great. Nothing like a pretty girl to liven up a show."

"Amen," Jayson said and comically lifted his brows toward Elizabeth, who just scowled and walked in the direction where Derek had gone.

In her mind, in an instant, the past merged with the present, and with the future, and she let out a breathless gasp. She was supposed to be onstage with Jayson Wolfe—her husband, her lover, her best friend. Her partner in music.

Elizabeth sat on the floor for nearly an hour, letting the idea settle into her, and attempting to reconcile the fears that she had. She finally knew that she could go no further in her reconciliation without talking to her husband.

Going to the studio, she opened the door to hear him at the piano, plunking out a spirited rhythm that she'd never heard before. It had the feel of rock-and-roll piano at its finest. Drew was drumming along, and thankfully neither of them noticed her. She didn't want to interrupt, and she was actually relieved to have a few more minutes to think through what she needed to tell Jayson.

"Okay," Jayson said into the microphone so Drew could hear him. "Do it again from the top. I think I've got the bridge now."

Drew hit a one-two-three, and they soared through a catchy intro. She sat down to listen. Great dancing music, she thought. Just the kind of thing to rock the radio and bring concert halls to life. But it was obviously a new creation; she'd heard nothing of this one before now. She was wondering if he actually had lyrics, or if that was yet to come, when he belted into the microphone, *"Something's missing in this* cake; *it's tasting* fake *and I can't* take *the pressure any more . . . Something's missing in this* song; *it sounds all* wrong *and all* along *I'm trying to hear the score."* The music changed, and his voice changed pitch as he sprang into the chorus. *"My life is* spent, *my money's* lent, *I've handed over my last red* cent *looking for the missing ingredient . . . My pen is* bent, *and the words I* sent *won't make a* dent *in where I* meant *to find the missing ingredient."* A catchy drum sequence moved into the second verse, while Elizabeth felt delightfully chilled at the sharp, catchy quality of the song. *"Something's missing in my* head; *my thoughts are* dead *and as you* said *this life is such a bore . . . Something's missing in my* heart; *I've played the* part *and for a* start *I'm going on as before."* The chorus was repeated with even more vibrancy, ending with a powerful fusion and a repeating strain. *"So, tell me, baby, where you* went, *when you left me here to pay the* rent *with the need to* vent *for the heart's blood* spent *on searching for the missing ingredient . . . I need the missing ingredient . . . I ache for the missing ingredient . . . My heart's blood is spent on the missing ingredient . . . You are the missing ingredient."*

When the song was done, Elizabeth said, "That was incredible." And they both turned toward her in surprise.

Jayson immediately noticed evidence that she'd been crying and hurried to ask, "What's wrong?"

Drew moved toward the door saying, "I'll just . . . uh . . . go see what Valerie is up to."

After he'd left the room, Jayson repeated, "What's wrong?"

"The song is great; it sounds like a top-ten hit to me."

"We can hope," he said. "Now, what's wrong?"

"You know in the Book of Mormon," she said, "when Nephi says that he was led by the Spirit, not knowing beforehand the things that he should do?"

"Yes, I know," he said.

"So . . . he knew what the Lord wanted him to do, but he didn't know how he was going to accomplish it. And yet he knew that the Lord wouldn't command him to do something without providing a way."

"Yes, I know that, too."

"So," she squeezed her eyes closed, and her voice cracked with emotion, "do you think the same thing applies to . . . a mother going on a concert tour?"

Jayson took a sharp breath as he realized what she was saying. His heart leapt inside of him, while at the same time it ached for her obvious concern. He moved toward her and knelt to face her, taking her hands into his. She looked into his eyes and said, "I'm supposed to be onstage with you, Jayson. I don't know why it's so important, but it is. I have absolutely no idea how to make that work and be a good mother, too. And it scares me."

"We will find a way," he said and put his arms around her. He felt deeply grateful to know that his own feelings weren't off base. His prayers had been answered, and he knew that, just as with Nephi, God would provide a way.

Over the next couple of weeks, Elizabeth spent a fair amount of time in the studio while the kids were at school. Jayson was amazed—and Drew agreed—at how perfectly her backing vocals added a richness to the texture of the music. She truly was the missing ingredient; she always had been.

Finally a day came when Jayson listened through each of the ten songs they'd done and felt good about every one of them. It was hard to see Drew and Valerie go; Jayson had become accustomed to having his brother around, and he'd grown to love Valerie, as he knew the rest of the family had. But they promised to keep in closer touch with each other than they'd done previously, and Jayson knew he would be going to LA for business if he ever hoped to sell what he had just produced. He felt decidedly nervous as he began the arduous process of selling himself to the record industry. He spent a great deal of time on the phone, and made several trips to LA, all with disappointing results. He found that his name was highly respected, and his work was greatly complimented, but no one believed in it enough to represent it. He considered overseeing mass production and distribution on his own, but not only would it be a huge amount of work, he just didn't feel like it was the right course to take.

Christmas came and went, and he decided that he just needed to let the project lie. "Maybe I just needed to *make* the CD," Jayson said to Elizabeth. "Maybe the rest simply wasn't meant to be; maybe it was some kind of test."

"Did you enjoy making the CD?"

"Yes, actually. I did."

"Well, then it has value in that alone. The people who love you will always treasure your music, whether the world does or not."

"I appreciate the theory; really I do. But my gut instinct tells me it's supposed to get out into the world. It has the ability to be inspiring and empowering to a great many people."

Elizabeth smiled at him, grateful to hear how he had captured the vision of his own potential. That alone would ensure his success. "Just give it some time," she said. "If you're stressing over it, then you're not putting faith in the Lord to help make it happen in His time and in His way. If it's meant to be, it will happen." In her heart, she knew it was meant to be.

Around the first of the year, Jayson was surprised to be called into the stake president's office, and Elizabeth was asked to come along. He felt decidedly nervous. This man was the leader over ten wards, but Jayson had never even met him. Once they were seated across from President Stokes, with his large, uncluttered desk between them, Jayson felt *really* nervous. He knew there were certain Church callings that came from this level, but it was his understanding that he'd not been a member long enough to serve in such callings. Or it crossed his mind that perhaps his past endeavors in the rock world might not be appreciated, or perhaps misunderstood. Maybe there was concern over his reputation.

"Brother Wolfe," the president said, "I understand you're a rather talented musician."

"That's the rumor," Jayson said tensely, and the president chuckled.

"Well, I've heard that you've done some rather amazing musical numbers in your ward, along with your wife. And you're enjoying playing for the Primary children?"

"I am," Jayson said firmly. He ignored the previous compliment.

"My son recently drew my attention to the fact that he owns a couple of CDs you were involved with; apparently they did very well."

"Another rumor," Jayson said and felt a little nauseous. Perhaps he would be asked to give up any further efforts in the rock industry because it wasn't seemly for a good Latter-day Saint.

"It's all true, President," Elizabeth said. "They did *very* well."

"I confess that I listened to them," President Stokes said. "I was pleasantly surprised to find nothing offensive. I know they were made before you joined the Church, but apparently you've always had values."

"I always tried to do what was right," Jayson said, feeling some measure of relief but wondering what the point of this might be.

"Brother Wolfe," the president said, leaning his forearms on his desk, "our youth struggle a great deal with the influences of the world. It's hard for them to find people they can look up to and relate to. Later this month we are having a fireside for all of the youth in the stake and their parents. We want it to be highly attended, and we want it to have an impact for good on our youth. As a stake presidency, we are hoping that you would be willing to do that fireside for us."

Jayson shifted in his seat and cleared his throat more loudly than he'd intended. "I'm afraid . . . I don't understand the question . . . exactly."

"Well . . . I was thinking if you could just take an hour or so. Tell the story of your conversion and the challenges that led up to it. I confess I've spoken with your bishop, and he shared a little of your history with me—in confidence, of course. What you share publicly would be up to you. Intersperse your story with a few songs. They can be hymns that you've performed in sacrament meetings, or anything you may have come up with that is spiritually appropriate for a meeting in the chapel. Sister Wolfe could be involved, if you wish."

Jayson met Elizabeth's eyes, wishing she might say something to rescue him. He wanted to tell this man that he could perform rock music in front of thousands of people without any hesitation or fear. But what this man had proposed sounded terrifying. Then he recalled vividly the scripture that stated, *Whether by mine own voice or by the voice of my servants, it is the same.* He knew this man had been called of God to serve in this position, and he was asking Jayson to do something to help the youth in the stake. How could he possibly refuse?

"Frankly, President," he finally said, "the very idea is pretty . . . unsettling. But if you want me to do it, I will do my very best."

President Stokes smiled. "I know you will." He told them the date and time of the meeting, then moved into friendly conversation, asking about their family and their plans for the future. He wished them well in their future musical endeavors, and expressed confidence that their talents would yet bless many lives.

During the weeks preceding the fireside, Jayson explored several different avenues for telling his story, and he worked on a few different versions of hymns that he might perform. He fasted and prayed that he would be guided, and that he could be an instrument in the hands of God to touch the hearts of those who might come to hear him. He started seeing posters advertising his forthcoming speaking engagement, and it was announced in all of the meetings at church. Many people told him they were greatly looking forward to it—and he was dreading it with every fiber of his being.

The day before the scheduled event, Jayson woke up with a song in his head. He hurried to the studio, and with the help of the piano he worked it into something presentable by the end of the day, only taking breaks long enough to eat. He played it for Elizabeth that evening, and with tears in her eyes she told him it was one of the most beautiful things he'd ever done. The following morning he woke up with an analogy of how his story should be presented; an idea he'd never even considered before. But he felt more calm about what he needed to do. It was evident the Spirit was guiding him.

That evening Jayson sat in one of the many seats behind the pulpit, with Elizabeth beside him, her hand in his. He watched as the large chapel filled up completely. They opened the huge accordion doors to the overflow, and that filled up as well. They opened the second set of doors into the gymnasium that was filled with chairs, and that filled up as well.

"The place is packed," he said to Elizabeth.

"You always knew how to bring in the crowds," she said with a little smile, but he didn't think it was funny.

He prayed silently, and impulsively said to Elizabeth, "We're starting with the song."

"I thought you wanted to do that after you—"

"We're starting with the song," he said, and the meeting began.

Following an opening hymn by the congregation and a prayer, Jayson was introduced by a member of the stake Young Men presidency who talked briefly about his discovery that some CDs owned by his college-aged son had been the brainchild of a new member of the stake. He repeated statistics of Jayson's record sales and awards that were startlingly accurate. He finished by saying how privileged they were to have such talent in their presence, and especially because Jayson had found the gospel. He sat down, and Jayson went to the pulpit. He looked out over the audience and told himself this was no different than introducing a song in a concert setting. He began by saying, "Since I'm much more comfortable playing music than speaking, I'm going to start out with a song. I realize Christmas was a month ago, but since Christ should be a part of our lives all the time, I felt it was appropriate. I gained a testimony of the power of the Atonement during the Christmas season, and this song has special meaning for me. My wife, Elizabeth, will join me on the violin."

Jayson moved to the piano, and Elizabeth stood with the violin where they could see each other clearly. He smiled at her and began to play. Within seconds he was completely relaxed as "O Holy Night" flowed through his fingers. The violin came in with perfect grace. The warm spirit that filled the room surrounded Jayson with the confidence that he could get back up there at the pulpit and finish what he'd begun. When the song ended, he stood before the congregation and noticed something he'd missed before. His family was seated on the third row, directly in front of him. He looked at them and began to speak.

"I want to talk to you about Job," he said. "Job was a good and faithful man who had always tried to do what was right, but still, he lost everything. There was a time in my life when I felt very much like Job. I hadn't lost *everything*, but I'd lost a great deal. I want to tell you what I lost, but first I have to tell you what I had in order for you to understand the loss."

Jayson told a brief overview of his childhood, of his alcoholic father, and his amazing mother. He talked about the gift of music and the dreams he had. He told the story of leaving the piano behind, and how he'd been led to a friend who shared his musical gifts, his family, and his home with him. He told of Derek's death, and of the girl he loved who left him soon afterward. Without using Elizabeth's name he spoke of his heartache, his impulsive marriage, his struggle to make it in the music industry. With intermittent humor he talked of the climb to the top and the joy of success, the wife he loved, his beautiful daughter, the ongoing love and support of his mother, and the bond he shared with his brother. With the stage set, Jayson paused, then stated in a grave voice, "The first thing I lost was my wife. I came home in the middle of a tour to surprise her, but she surprised me—with her boyfriend. I learned to cope with that over time. And then the losses began piling up." He talked of the band falling apart, and how eventually his bandmates had died—one of a drug overdose, the other of AIDS. He spoke frankly of the bad choices he'd seen them making long before they each came to their untimely demise. He talked of his brother taking a different path, of his mother's death from cancer, and his sweet daughter being lured into the horror of a world he had subjected his family to, and of how she'd run away at the age of fifteen. With a cracking voice he explained how music had been his one saving grace—and then he had lost the use of his hand.

Elizabeth noticed many people in the audience wiping their eyes as Jayson spoke eloquently of his pain that gradually became buried in the drugs, and of how close he'd come to taking his own life. He told the story of the miracle that had saved him that night, and how he'd gotten on a plane the next day to come and stay with the people who had remained his only true friends throughout the course of his life. He spoke of the influence of the gospel in their home, and the horrors of drug rehab.

"And then," Jayson said, "like Job, all things became restored to me—with added blessings I could have never comprehended." He told how his daughter had come back to him, and he told the story of how he'd come to read the Book of Mormon, and how he'd gained a testimony.

"The same day I finally admitted to Elizabeth that I wanted to be baptized, my daughter came home to tell me that she wanted the same thing." He expressed his incomparable joy in finally marrying his high school sweetheart, his lifelong friend, only a couple of weeks before his baptism, and how sweet his life had been in the months since.

"And now," he said, "I would like to play you a song that I wrote just yesterday. I believe it was given to me specifically to share with you tonight."

Jayson sat at the piano and adjusted the microphone he'd set up previously. He played several bars of the intricate melody before he put his mouth to the mike and sang with reverent fervor, "*Standing on the stair, I saw your image there, looking back at me with eyes of blue that pierced me through and challenged my soul to sing. Frozen there I felt the steps behind me luring me back to caverns filled with dust, memories rotting in rust that threatened to tear my heart in two. But you beckoned me to take a step, just one step, and then you took my hand and led me into the light. Into the light. Into the light. I found the soul in my song, and my song filled my soul when I stepped into the light. Standing on the stair, I felt your Spirit there, filling me with strength and love, trickling from above, that pressed my soul to sing. Moving up, the darkness fell behind me . . . and the doors were open wide, luring me inside . . . into the light. Into the light. I found the soul in my song, and my song filled my soul when I stepped into the light. Into eternal light.*"

Jayson went back to the pulpit and expressed deep gratitude to his beautiful and talented wife, to Will for being a father to him, to Marilyn for making Will so happy, and to all of his children for their love and acceptance. He bore fervent testimony of the truthfulness of the gospel, and of the divinity of Jesus Christ. He finished by saying, "And now I will end by expressing my testimony through song." He sat at the piano and did his own embellished composition of "I Believe in Christ."

The meeting was closed with a prayer, then Jayson stood for more than an hour while people lined up to shake his hand and express their appreciation for his music and for the words he'd spoken that evening that had touched them deeply. President Stokes complimented him profusely and thanked him for his efforts, certain that his message had touched many hearts and been an influence for good. When the crowds finally filtered away, Elizabeth looked at him and said, "I think you've just discovered a new gift, my love. I have a feeling this is the first of many firesides you may end up doing all over the place."

Jayson didn't respond. He had a feeling she might be right, but the idea of his story having that much impact was difficult for him to comprehend.

At home, Elizabeth went straight to bed, exhausted from a big day and being pregnant. Jayson went to Trevin's room, then Addie's, to make certain all was well. Then he found Macy sitting in the living room, looking thoughtful.

"What's up?" he asked, sitting across from her.

"That was pretty powerful stuff," she said. "I've always admired you, but never so much as I did tonight."

"Isn't that stretching it a bit?" he asked lightly, but she looked up at him with huge tears in her eyes.

"I had no idea you had suffered so much," she said.

"My purpose was not to whine or complain," he said firmly.

"I know, and you didn't. You were right. People can't appreciate how far you've come without seeing how bad it was. You told the story beautifully, Dad, but . . ." She became too emotional to speak.

Jayson moved beside her and put his arms around her. "What is it, baby?" he murmured gently.

"I didn't know . . . that you came so close . . . to ending your own life." She clutched onto him tightly. "I'm so grateful you're here, that you didn't do it. I had no idea my absence was causing you such grief on top of everything else."

"It's in the past, Macy," he murmured. "It was all necessary to bring us to where we are. I'm grateful too."

They talked for a long while before she went off to bed, then he slipped into his own room. By the light from the bathroom he sat on the edge of the bed and watched Elizabeth sleeping. He pushed her curls back off her face without disturbing her, and whispered to himself, "Life doesn't get any better than this."

* * *

The following morning, the phone rang right after Trevin and Addie had left to catch the bus. Jayson answered it and heard a deep voice say, "I'm looking for Jayson Wolfe."

"You've got me," he said.

"You don't have an agent," the voice said, and Jayson's heart quickened.

"No. Do I need one?"

"Not if you can give me the answers I need."

The man introduced himself as Rick Langley, and said he'd just been promoted to an executive position with a reputable record company. Trying to clean up the mess that had been left behind by his predecessor, he'd come across a letter and a demo CD that Jayson had sent in months ago.

"And?" Jayson said, his heart now pounding audibly.

"I'm really talking to Jayson Wolfe," Rick chuckled.

"You really are."

"I looked up some old stuff on you," he said. "You are a pretty sensational guy." Jayson noticed he didn't say it in past tense, as most people did. "So, this CD I've got in my hands. You really did this yourself?"

"I had some help from my wife and my brother."

Rick laughed pleasantly. "And you think you could do this stuff on the stage?"

"With the right musicians," Jayson said, "I can make it come alive onstage."

"How fast can you get to LA?" Rick asked.

"Depends on what you want me to do when I get there," Jayson said.

"I've got a slot to fill, Mr. Wolfe, and it needs to be done quickly. I need to have a couple of great songs hit the radio this spring, with a great album to hit the stores. I need a summer tour to back it up. I need it to bring in big money. I think you're the answer to my prayers, Mr. Wolfe. Now, how long will it take you to get here? We've got some paperwork to do."

"So, you're a praying man," Jayson said, keeping the joy out of his voice. "In that case, we might have something to talk about."

Jayson asked some hard questions about what the contract would entail, and made it clear he wasn't going to waste the trip if he wasn't going to get what he wanted. He told Rick he would not work or perform on Sundays, that his family would be with him throughout the bulk of the tour, that his hired musicians would have to be drug-free, and that promiscuity would not be allowed on the tour.

"If you can do all that for me," Jayson said, "then you're the answer to my prayers too."

Rick laughed. "Get a plane ticket. We've got work to do."

Jayson got off the phone and resisted the urge to let out a loud cry of joy. Instead he silently thanked God for a miracle before he went to find Elizabeth.

"Who was on the phone?" she asked casually.

"A guy by the name of Rick. He wants me on the next plane to LA." Elizabeth looked up, her eyes as wide as her mouth. He grinned and added, "He's going to give me everything I asked for, and he's putting a big rush on the production. He's got a slot to fill."

Elizabeth squealed with delight and rushed into his arms. He held her, and they laughed together. It seemed that miracles were in steady supply.

* * *

Jayson was deeply pleased with the contract he got and the way these people were treating him as the CD went into mass production, and marketing plans were discussed. Drew was ecstatic over the deal and eagerly agreed to be the resident drummer no matter when or where the show might go. Jayson enjoyed being able to stay with Drew on his trips back and forth to LA. He was quickly guided to finding a couple of musicians that he liked and felt good about, and they were contracted to do the tour with him. Everything came together so well that he couldn't doubt that God's hand was guiding the process. He found it an interesting twist that part of the downfall of Gray Wolf had been the result of a change in record company executives that had worked against them. In this case, an equivalent change had worked in his favor. Like Job, he was being given back all that he'd lost—and so much more. His family was healthy and happy and doing well, and the baby's arrival was getting closer. Elizabeth felt relatively well and managed to keep the household running smoothly, even with Jayson's frequent business trips. Macy was always eager to help when she was around, which was a great boon to Elizabeth, especially when Elizabeth got a new Church calling as a family history specialist, which required time each week researching genealogical records in the family history library.

Jayson was glad to have everything for the release of the CD well under control a few weeks before the baby was due. He intended to spend every minute possible with Elizabeth during this experience, and he wouldn't even begin doing any promotions until more than a month beyond the due date. The tour was scheduled to begin the first week of June. The hired musicians had been given all they needed to learn their work independently, and group rehearsals would start the beginning of May and take place in Jayson's studio so that Elizabeth could rehearse and be at home and close to the baby. Drew and Valerie would be staying in their home as well, and the other two guys would have hotel suites with kitchenettes that had already been reserved close by. A college-aged girl that lived in the ward had been hired to be in the home during rehearsal hours to help with the baby. The bulk of the tour would take place during the summer months. Macy was taking the summer off from college to go with them and be the tour nanny, although she would only be fully responsible for the baby during the actual performances. There would be separate buses for the family and the band. There would be a couple of stretches where Trevin and Addie would be with them, as well, and the dates and locations had been scheduled so that the family could do some sightseeing and spend time together between performances. Jayson was certain the bus tour would quickly get old for the children, so

Trevin and Addie would be staying with Will and Marilyn for part of the summer, but they wouldn't go more than a couple of weeks at a time without seeing their parents.

The first week of March, Elizabeth went into labor in the middle of the night. Jayson drove her to the hospital, and less than an hour later she gave birth to a perfect baby boy. Jayson's tears wouldn't stop as he absorbed the wonder and his own joy. Derek Jayson Wolfe was officially blessed and given his name by his grandfather. Little Derek filled the home with a new level of joy. The children all dearly loved him and were eager to help and be a part of his care. Jayson and Elizabeth frequently agreed that they'd never been happier.

Derek was a couple of weeks old when the song "Missing Ingredient" hit the radio and leapt into the top forty. The CD hit the stores, and sales quickly exceeded Jayson's expectations. He found it difficult to believe—especially when his life at home was so thoroughly good that he almost didn't care if it sold or not.

They started seeing the cover of the CD in ads all over the place, and posters of it were in music stores everywhere. The cover photo was of Jayson sitting on the top of a black grand piano, dressed in white jeans, a white silky shirt, and a white vest unbuttoned over it. It had been Elizabeth's idea for him to wear the exact outfit he'd worn at the very beginning of his career, except to have it all white, instead of all black. His feet were bare, and he was holding his acoustic guitar, cradling it in one arm. The background behind the piano was all white. The black lettering across the top simply said *Jayson Wolfe,* and at the bottom, *Second Chance.* The title track was the song he had sung to Elizabeth on their wedding day.

In April, Drew and Valerie became the parents of a little girl that they named Leslie after her grandmother. Jayson got the phone call with the good news while he was in charge of Derek, since Elizabeth was at the church doing her family history assignment.

Jayson knew that the following week he would be traveling to New York and LA to do some television promotions. He would only be gone a few days at a time, but he dreaded leaving his family and missing even an hour of his son's new little life. But he'd been truly blessed in being able to spend far more time with the baby than most fathers ever did. And he'd certainly been able to enjoy him a lot more than he had Macy as an infant, when he'd hardly been home at all. Life was good, and he was grateful.

CHAPTER 13

Elizabeth stared at the computer screen in front of her, feeling incredibly frustrated. The avenue she was trying to follow in order to piece together the names of people long dead was getting her nowhere. She felt tired from nighttime feedings and wondered if she should just go home. While she sat with her eyes closed, rubbing her temples, a thought occurred to her that made her gasp.

Jayson had once been prejudiced against the Church because his father was a *Mormon*. For the next hour Elizabeth frantically searched through records of Wolfe family lines, praying in her mind as she did. If any of Jayson's father's close relatives had submitted the typical records, then his father's name should show up somewhere. She couldn't find a Jay Wolfe anywhere and felt deeply frustrated. She phoned Jayson at home to see how the baby was doing, then she asked, "Hey, what's your father's birth date? Do you know it? You did order his gravestone."

"Yes, I know it," he said. "Why?"

"Just checking something out of curiosity," she said.

He told her the date, and she got off the phone to continue her search. Checking through the possible choices again, she was startled to see the name Lawrence J. Wolfe—with the right birth date, and no other personal information. But there was a great deal of information on his family. Going back not very many generations, there was a Jason Wolfe who had been born and baptized in England, married in New York, and endowed in the Nauvoo Temple at a date just prior to the pioneer trek west. Jason's children had received temple ordinances in the Salt Lake Temple. As Elizabeth connected records to the generation that Lawrence J. belonged to, she found that he had three older sisters, and they were all listed as living. The parents of these children were the senior Lawrence J. and Ruth Wolfe. There was a death date for Lawrence, but not for Ruth, although, according to her birth date, she would be pretty old if she were still alive. Chances were that she'd passed away since the records had been updated.

Elizabeth printed out the information she felt was pertinent and went home. Jayson had Derek ready for bed, and Elizabeth set the papers aside to nurse the baby while Jayson went to check on Trevin and Addie and make certain their homework was finished and that they were getting ready for bed. When they were all down for the night, Elizabeth sat next to Jayson on the bed. "Does the name Lawrence Wolfe ring a bell?" she asked.

Jayson felt something prickly go down his spine. "Lawrence is Drew's middle name. Why?"

Elizabeth stood up and got the pedigree chart she'd printed out. She handed it to Jayson and said, "Is it possible that the Lawrence J. Wolfe—with your father's birth date—is your father?"

He looked at her in astonishment, then scanned the paper with frantic eyes. "You'll notice," she said, "that this family has obvious pioneer heritage. Is it possible that it could be *your* family?"

"Good heavens," he said breathlessly, staring at the paper in his hand. She pointed out the name Jason Wolfe and the ordinance dates and locations that told a story. The very idea of having extended family connections—within the Church—left him stunned speechless.

"You know what this means?" Elizabeth said.

"What?"

"You have relatives, Jayson. I bet it wouldn't take much effort on the Internet to find them."

While the idea filled him with great joy, he felt some trepidation. He wasn't fond of his father—at all. Would he really want to know his father's family? If they were all like his father, he'd rather not alert them to his existence. And for all he knew, the birth date and name could be a coincidence. Not likely, he concluded, but possible. He talked his feelings through with Elizabeth, and she encouraged him to take a cautious approach. He went to bed telling himself he'd give it some time and thought, but right after breakfast he was sitting in front of the computer, typing in the name Lawrence Wolfe. So many listings came up that he couldn't possibly know where to begin. He typed in Lawrence J. and Ruth Wolfe and expected to be told there was no listing with that combination. But up it popped, with an address and phone number—in Virginia. He felt suddenly terrified.

"Elizabeth!" he called, almost frozen in the chair.

"What is it?" she asked, sounding a little panicked from his urgency. He just pointed to the computer screen. She read it and gasped, then she clicked PRINT.

"Are you going to call them?" she asked.

"No."

"Would you like me to call them?"

"Yes," he said, "but take it slow. I trust your judgment. I've got some work to do." He went to the studio, and Elizabeth wondered if she should hold off, but once the baby was down for his nap, she felt compelled to just make the call. If Lawrence was already dead, and Ruth likely dead, then the lead might come to nothing, anyway. And then they could stop wondering.

She uttered a prayer, took a deep breath, and dialed the number. A woman answered the phone, and Elizabeth said, "Hi, I don't know if you can help me, but . . . I'm actually looking for a Mrs. Wolfe who was once at this number. I was wondering if you might know how I could locate her."

"That might depend on why you want to know," the woman said, but she said it kindly.

"Well . . . I think we might be related. My name is Elizabeth Wolfe and—"

"Really?" the woman said with enthusiasm. "Are you from the Anthony Wolfe line? He had so many children that we've got cousins of all kinds all over the place."

Elizabeth recognized the name and knew she meant the man they suspected was Jayson's great-grandfather. "Well, actually I married into the line, and the truth is that we've had no family connections, and so we're not certain if my husband fits into this line or not. Ruth Wolfe is a name that might connect us; we found it on some genealogical records, but . . . we don't know much more than that."

"Well," the woman said, sounding excited, "Ruth Wolfe is my mother. My name is Rebecca Burke, and my husband and I recently moved into her home."

Elizabeth looked at the pedigree in her hand. Sure enough, Lawrence J. had an older sister named Rebecca. They quickly established through their conversation that they were both active members of the Church. When Rebecca realized that Elizabeth was a convert, she wanted to hear her conversion story, then she shared with Elizabeth the story of her ancestors who had crossed the plains, and how proud she was of her pioneer heritage. She was especially proud of Jason Wolfe, who had joined the Church in England and had made many sacrifices to cross the plains with his family. It was evident that this man was the family hero. When a lull came in the conversation, Elizabeth was tempted to just ask the question on the tip of her tongue, but she took a more cautious approach. "Would you mind telling me just a little about your family?"

"Not at all," she said. "I'm one of four children. I have two older sisters and a younger brother." She told Elizabeth a great deal about herself and her sisters, Beverly and MaryAnn, what they were doing, how many children they had, and what those children were doing. It was evident that Rebecca loved to talk, but she wasn't telling Elizabeth the information she wanted. Finally there was enough of a break for Elizabeth to say, "And what of your brother?"

Following a lengthy silence, Rebecca said, "My brother left home more than fifty years ago and was never heard from again. We have every reason to believe that he didn't live long after that. He had some . . . challenges."

"Challenges?" Elizabeth echoed, her heart quickening.

"Well . . . he just had one of those spirits that was difficult to reach—or live with. He got into drinking and smoking at a young age, causing all kinds of grief for the family. He never cared for the gospel at all. Then one day, he just . . . up and left. My mother never got over it. She never stopped worrying and wondering, even though we had reason to believe he didn't live long after leaving here."

"What reason is that?"

"Well . . . I don't remember exactly. It's been so long. Maybe it was simply that he never contacted us. How can someone never contact their family?"

"I don't know. Maybe he had his reasons. He obviously had some problems; it's hard to say what his motives might have been."

Rebecca made a thoughtful noise but said nothing more on that point.

"May I ask his name?" Elizabeth asked, while a distinct warmth burned in her chest.

"It was Lawrence," she said, which rang true with the records Elizabeth had seen.

She came right out and said, "I must confess that I found your family pedigree in the Church database. It says Lawrence J. What does the J stand for?"

"It's just a J," Rebecca said. "Our father's name was the same. That's his legal name. Lawrence J. But since my father and brother both had the same name, my brother picked up the nickname Jay. You know, like a Blue Jay."

Elizabeth suddenly felt emotional and couldn't speak. She heard Rebecca say, "Are you still there?"

"I am," Elizabeth said in a voice that cracked.

"Is something wrong?" Rebecca asked.

"No," Elizabeth said with a little chuckle. "I don't know Jay Wolfe, but I know of him."

Rebecca gasped. "Jay Wolfe? You know a Jay Wolfe?"

"Know of him," she said again.

"How old is he?"

"Well, he died about eight years ago, but his birth date is the same as the one on these records."

"I can't believe it," Rebecca said, sounding emotional as well. "Tell me. You must tell me."

"His life was not good, I'm afraid . . . which is reason enough to believe we're talking about the same man. He was an alcoholic in the worst way." She paused and added, "He was my husband's father."

Elizabeth wondered if Rebecca was hyperventilating, given the breathless gasping she was hearing through the phone. She finally managed to say, "He had children?"

"Two sons," Elizabeth said.

"And one of them is your husband?" she asked, obviously teary.

"That's right."

"Okay," Rebecca said more calmly, "it sounds certain, but . . . how can we be sure that my brother and your father-in-law are the same man?"

"Well, we could compare photographs for starters," Elizabeth said, and Rebecca made an excited noise. Elizabeth added, "It's too bad your mother isn't still alive. I think she would—"

"Did I say she wasn't alive?" Rebecca asked with a laugh.

"Well . . . I got that impression. You said you were . . . living in her house and . . ."

"She's in the other room taking a nap," Rebecca said with another laugh, and Elizabeth laughed with her. "We just moved in to look out for her. We sold our own home when we went on our first mission. Mom gets around pretty well, but we just thought this would be a good arrangement."

"Oh, my," Elizabeth said as the thought of Jayson having a grandmother, alive and well, filled her with anticipatory joy.

"So," Rebecca said eagerly, "can I mail you some copies of photographs and—"

"That would be great," Elizabeth said. "But . . . do you have email?"

"I do."

"I have some photos on file that were scanned a long time ago, and I could send them to you right now. If you don't have high-speed Internet, they can take a little more time to download, but—"

"Oh, we have that," Rebecca said, and Elizabeth laughed.

"Okay, I can send it right now, while we're talking."

Rebecca gave Elizabeth her email address, and within a couple of minutes she had the best picture of Jayson's father on its way to Virginia. It was a colored snapshot of Jay and Leslie, actually both looking happy. On Jay's lap was a two-year-old Drew, and Leslie was holding Jayson as a baby. The most important thing was that Jay's face in the photo was clear. Elizabeth could see a strong resemblance to Jayson in his features, and she prayed that Rebecca would see in that face her long-lost brother.

"Okay, it's here," she heard Rebecca say, and her heart began to pound. "I'm opening the file. It's downloading." Then she heard nothing.

"Rebecca?" Elizabeth finally said, fearing that she would say it wasn't the same man.

She heard a loud sniffle just before Rebecca barely managed to say, "It's him. That's my brother. I can't believe it." She sobbed through a burst of laughter. "And what a sweet little family. You must tell me about them."

Elizabeth had a difficult time telling Rebecca what little she knew about Jayson's early childhood and the divorce, and how Jayson had only seen his father once after their move to Oregon.

"And where was that?" Rebecca asked.

"Well, Jayson is—"

"Jayson?"

"My husband."

"His name is Jayson?" she asked with pleasant amazement.

"That's right."

"Like my ancestor," she said.

"Yes, but . . . it's spelled Jay-son, as in the son of Jay."

Rebecca laughed again. "Oh, that's wonderful. Keep talking. I'm sorry."

"It's okay," Elizabeth said, laughing with her. "Jayson was working in Montana, in the area where he'd grown up, and lo and behold his father found him at the hotel where he was staying. I don't know that it was a very pleasant experience for Jayson, but . . . a couple of years later Jayson was informed that his father had died. I can get you a copy of the obituary."

"Oh, that would be nice," Rebecca said. "But tell me more about your husband and his brother, and about your family. What does Jayson do for a living?"

"He's a professional musician."

"Really?" Rebecca said, sounding pleasantly surprised. "What does he play?"

"Piano and guitar are his specialties," she said. "I can tell you all about that when we have more time. I need to let you go, I'm certain, but . . . Jayson's older brother is Drew. He's married and living in LA and has a new baby. He was single until last year. Jayson and I were high school sweethearts and—"

"And you've been together since then? That's—"

"Actually," she interrupted, "we both went our separate ways, but always stayed in touch. He was divorced some years ago, and my husband was killed more recently. Jayson and I were married last year. He has one daughter, Macy, from his first marriage, who is living with us and doing well. I have a son who has passed away, and a son and daughter with us. And we have a new baby."

Rebecca kept getting more thrilled as the conversation went on. She insisted that they needed to meet and soon. Rebecca said that she would like to have Jayson surprise her mother, rather than telling her about it now. Elizabeth told her she would talk to Jayson and see when they could make a visit. Rebecca said that Ruth would be having her ninetieth birthday celebration next month, and they would like to have Jayson and Drew meet her before then, and hopefully they could meet everybody else at that time. Elizabeth put the date on the calendar, relieved to see that Jayson had nothing scheduled for that day, or the day before and after.

She finally got off the phone and went to the studio to find Jayson rehearsing on the piano. In preparation for the tour, he needed to be able to play every piece with perfect finesse, and without any thought. Repetition was the best way to accomplish that. She sat down and waited for him to finish the piece he was playing.

Jayson turned to see Elizabeth looking almost smug. "Guess who I just talked to for more than an hour?"

"Who?" he asked with a mock excitement that made her laugh.

"You'll feel bad for that kind of attitude when you hear what I have to say."

"Okay, who?" he asked more normally, toying with the piano keys.

"Your Aunt Rebecca," she said, and his heart began to pound. While he'd rehearsed, he'd honestly forgotten that they'd been talking about her calling his possible relatives.

Elizabeth saw Jayson's countenance change, then he stopped what he'd been doing as if he'd been quick-frozen. "Are you sure?" he asked.

"I emailed her a picture while we were talking. Her brother, Jay, left home when he was young and they never heard from him again; they thought he'd died soon afterward."

"I can't believe it," he said breathlessly. Elizabeth gave him some time to absorb the news, then heard him say again, "I can't believe it."

"Well, it's true."

"So . . . what is she like?"

"She likes to talk," Elizabeth said with a little laugh. "She's delightful, Jayson. She and her sisters—your other two aunts—are active in the Church. They sound like great people. Apparently your father was the black sheep, not the norm."

"I can't believe it," Jayson said again.

"I haven't told you the best part."

"What?" he asked, wondering if he could take any more.

"She wants you to come to Virginia and surprise your grandmother."

Jayson gasped. "My . . ." He could only get one word out.

"Grandmother," Elizabeth said for him.

Jayson said he needed to think about it. They talked for a while longer, then he returned to his rehearsing when Elizabeth could hear on the baby monitor in her hand that Derek was awake. Nothing more was said until that evening when Elizabeth found him helping Addie with her homework. "Come here," she said. "You need to see this."

Jayson followed Elizabeth to the computer where she showed him five different pictures that Rebecca had emailed of his father as a child and a youth—including one that was of the family.

"I can't believe it," he said still again.

"You look like him," Elizabeth said. "At least when he was younger."

That night Jayson couldn't sleep. His life had been so good, so rich and full, that he'd never even contemplated the absence of extended family. He had everything he could ever want or need. But *a grandmother?* Aunts and uncles, cousins. He couldn't believe it. While a part of him felt apprehensive to step into such unknown territory, something deeper ached to make this connection. He prayed fervently about the situation, and by the following afternoon he knew that he needed to meet these people—most specifically his father's mother. He called Drew with the news, hoping they could go to Virginia together. Drew was pleased and as surprised as Jayson, but he didn't have the deep excitement for the connection that Jayson felt. He felt he needed to be at home with Valerie and the baby, and said that they'd plan on going to the ninetieth birthday thing if the initial visit went well for Jayson.

Jayson exchanged a couple of emails with Rebecca and made arrangements for him and Elizabeth to go to Virginia, taking the baby with them. Will and Marilyn eagerly agreed to come and stay with the children. Rebecca made it clear that they had plenty of room at the house for them to stay, and not to worry about a thing except getting there. Jayson left that open, thinking they could get a motel if they arrived and found the situation uncomfortable.

Throughout the long series of flights, Jayson was so nervous that he nearly drove Elizabeth crazy. She was grateful, however, that Derek was such a good baby, and that he mostly slept through the journey. In Virginia they rented a car, and with the detailed directions Rebecca had emailed, they found the house with no difficulty. Jayson parked the car and took in what he was seeing. Never in a million years would he have imagined his father growing up in such a home. It was like something from a movie—a place where a perfect family would live. The home was two-story, white with dark blue shutters, huge trees, and a big porch surrounded by a white railing. He wondered why his father would ever leave such a home to become a drunken derelict, and then he thought of his own addiction to drugs, and a new perspective settled into him that he'd never considered before. If his father had been genetically vulnerable to substance addiction, perhaps the alcohol had simply overtaken him beyond any hope.

"Are you going to just sit here and look at it?" Elizabeth asked.

Jayson said nothing. He just got out and removed the baby carrier from the backseat. Elizabeth got the diaper bag and her purse, and they headed up the walk. They had barely stepped onto the porch when the door swung open and Rebecca appeared. They recognized her from pictures she had sent. She had graying curly hair, a pleasant face, and she was almost as tall as Jayson and slightly heavy. For a long moment they just looked at each other, then she said, "You must be Jayson."

"That's right," he said, and she put her arms around him in a firm, warm embrace.

"Welcome home," she said with tears in her eyes, then she turned to greet Elizabeth. Then her eyes went to the baby seat that Jayson had set at his feet in order to hug her. She fussed over the baby, who was sleeping soundly, then silence fell momentarily.

Not knowing what to say, Jayson was relieved when Rebecca began to talk. "I told Mother I had someone coming over that she would want to meet and she should get dressed up. She said that she was going to work in the garden, and if whoever it was didn't want to meet her as she was, then she had no interest in meeting them."

Jayson laughed and tightened his hold on Elizabeth's hand. Already he liked the sound of this woman. He said, "Well, I wouldn't want her dressing up on my account."

Rebecca smiled at him and motioned toward the door. "Come inside. Would you like some lemonade or something? Are you hungry?"

"I think we're fine," Elizabeth said when Jayson made no response. She turned to see him standing just inside the door, his eyes glazed over.

Jayson could hardly breathe as the screen door closed behind him. There in the little front parlor, clearly visible from the door, was a very old, incredibly beautiful upright piano. It was so much like the one they'd had to sell when they'd moved to Oregon, except that this one had obviously received much better care.

"Come on through," Rebecca said, heading down a long hall toward the back of the house. Elizabeth followed her, and Jayson pulled his attention away from the piano and carried the baby, following after Elizabeth.

They stepped out onto the back porch, which was as large as the front and well equipped with wicker chairs and a round table. "Mama?" Rebecca called as the screen door slammed shut. "There's someone you need to meet. Could you come up here where it's not so hot?"

The woman's head was covered by a large hat, and she was kneeling in a flower bed. She muttered, "Just give me a minute."

"Jayson, Elizabeth," Rebecca said, "this is my mother, Ruth Wolfe."

The older woman absently removed her gardening gloves as she said, "Try to say that five times fast and I bet you'll trip over your tongue."

Jayson couldn't hold back a chuckle as he set the baby down at his feet, glad that Derek was still sleeping. He'd known this woman ten seconds, and already he liked her. He'd expected some old, frail woman, barely able to stand. But she came to her feet with only minor difficulty and moved toward the porch. She tossed her gloves down on the bottom step and pulled off a wide-brimmed straw hat to reveal a head of curly silver hair. His heart quickened as he saw a resemblance to his father. This was his grandmother! He couldn't believe it. He simultaneously wanted to sit down and cry like a baby, and run and take her in his arms just to see how it might feel. All he could do was stand there and wait for something to happen.

Ruth put a foot onto the bottom step and a hand on the white-painted banister before she looked up at Jayson and Elizabeth standing on the porch. Her eyes passed quickly over Elizabeth and came to rest firmly on him. "Hello," he said when their eyes met. He saw her expression go from passive to intrigued in the breadth of a heartbeat, and his own heart quickened further.

"And who might you be?" she asked with a voice that indicated she was more than mildly interested.

Jayson glanced at Rebecca and realized she intended for him to break the news. He cleared his throat carefully and said simply, "My name is Jayson Wolfe."

Ruth smiled and walked up the stairs. "That explains the family resemblance, then. With all of my cousins' children having children and grandchildren, who can keep track anymore?"

When Ruth was on the same level as Jayson, he realized she was about the same height as Elizabeth, which was taller than average. She leaned against the porch rail and folded her arms. "So, who do you belong to, Jayson?"

Jayson noted Rebecca discreetly moving to her mother's side, as if she suspected the older woman might need some physical support once he answered the question. He prayed for the right words and was surprised at how quickly they came. He said simply, "I belong to you." He saw her eyes narrow and the intrigue deepen in them just before he added, "Your son is my father."

Jayson watched her closely as her bewildered expression turned to a startled enlightenment. She absently reached for Rebecca just before her eyes filled with tears that quickly spilled down her face. She unsteadily straightened from her leaning position, still holding to Rebecca, then she let go and moved toward Jayson, looking directly into his face. "You wouldn't tease an old woman about something like that, would you, young man?"

"No, I wouldn't do that," he said and watched her become blurry through the moisture in his own eyes.

The old woman reached a hand up to touch his face just as his tears fell, and he was able to see her clearly again. "I never imagined," she said with a serene smile, "that he would have married and had a son."

"Two sons, actually," he said. "I have an older brother."

Ruth let out a little laugh, then took his face firmly into her aged hands. "Oh, my boy," she said. "It's a miracle."

"Yes, it certainly is," Jayson said, and they embraced, holding to each other tightly while they each cried almost as much as Rebecca and Elizabeth, who were looking on.

Derek began to make noises that indicated he was working up to a cry. Ruth's attention was drawn to the baby in the little infant carrier near Jayson's feet. "You have a little one!" she said with obvious pleasure. Jayson bent over and unbuckled the baby, lifting him into his hands for his grandmother to see. She laughed softly and touched the baby's little hands just as he began to squawk, making them all laugh.

"Let's go inside," Ruth said, "where we can visit."

She led the way back to the parlor where they all sat down, and Elizabeth discreetly nursed the baby beneath a blanket thrown over her shoulder. Ruth was full of questions that Jayson answered easily, and he had a few questions of his own. The baby finished eating, and Elizabeth turned him over to his father to be burped. Once Derek was content, Jayson stood and placed him in Ruth's arms. She cooed at the baby and fussed over him, then Rebecca took him and did the same while they continued to visit. Jayson enjoyed the conversation, but felt torn between his fascination with the piano and his fascination with his grandmother. She asked about Drew, and he told her about his recent marriage and new baby. When she asked more sensitive questions about his father, Jayson apologized, saying it might be better to leave certain things unsaid. Ruth assured him it was alright; Jay had given them a great deal of grief as well, and she wanted to know the truth. As he told her an overview of the story of his parents and his own association with his father, a few tears were shed, but Ruth said she was grateful to know that he and Drew had been blessed with such a good mother, and that they had turned out so well in spite of their father's difficulties.

At a lull in the conversation, Jayson finally asked, "So, who plays the piano?"

"Oh," Ruth laughed, "nobody. Absolutely nobody. I tried and tried to get my children to play, and none of them stuck with it enough to do much good. I told them to play anything. Ragtime. Rock and roll. Whatever. Just play. My father played the piano rather well, and I so wanted music in my home, but I just have to play it on the stereo. I certainly didn't get any talent." Jayson glanced at Elizabeth and saw her discreetly smirking. Ruth then added, "Jay was the only one to play at all, but he soon lost interest in it when he couldn't stay out of trouble."

"My father played the piano?" Jayson asked, astonished.

"He did," Ruth said firmly. "He never could read a note, but he could play by ear. He had a unique gift; there's no doubt about that. And if he'd been able to stay away from his drinking, he might have been able to do something with it."

Jayson was assaulted by unexpected tears. Ruth asked with alarm, "What's wrong, dear?"

Elizabeth answered for him. "You have to get used to this. He has what we call a high water table. He cries easily, and he's worked very hard not to get embarrassed over it."

"I haven't mastered that last part very well," Jayson admitted, wiping at his tears.

"He has a sensitive spirit," Ruth said, and Elizabeth nodded in agreement, holding Jayson's hand.

"I'm sorry," Jayson said. "It's just that . . . oh . . ." Emotion overcame him so completely that he jumped to his feet. "I need a minute. Forgive me."

He rushed out to the porch, and Elizabeth followed, leaving the baby in Rebecca's arms, saying quietly, "Don't go away. We'll be right back."

She found Jayson at one end of the porch, attempting to get control of his emotions. "They probably think I'm crazy," he muttered.

"No, I don't think that's the case."

"I just . . . I can't believe it. All these years I . . . I believed that he'd never given me anything but grief. I didn't want to have any part of him in me, but . . ."

"Now you realize that through him you have this gift of music."

Jayson nodded, unable to speak. She hugged him tightly and let him cry for a couple of minutes, then she wiped at his tears, saying, "I think you need to go back inside and tell your grandmother what you just told me."

Jayson nodded again and struggled for composure. They went back inside and sat down. Jayson cleared his throat and said, "Sorry about that."

"Don't you worry about it," Ruth said, then she started talking about trivial family things, as if she purposely intended to distract him from whatever had upset him. She talked about all of her children and grandchildren—and even a few great-grandchildren—and their interests and hobbies, their talents, their occupations. He couldn't help noticing that music didn't come up once. He thoroughly enjoyed listening to her talk while it began to sink in that she was talking about *his* relatives. He had a family. A great, big, amazing family full of successful and happy people. It just seemed too good to be true.

"So, tell me more about your brother," Ruth said. "What does he do for a living?"

Jayson smiled at Elizabeth, then at his grandmother. "He's a professional drummer."

He wondered if she might be put off by that, or perhaps think it was odd, but her face brightened as she said, "Really now? Perhaps he got something of a gift from his father without even knowing it."

Jayson reached for Elizabeth's hand. "Perhaps he did," he said, wondering how to tell her that Drew wasn't the only one. "He's great."

"Well, I'll look forward to meeting him—and hearing him play for me. Do you think he'd do that for me?"

"I'm sure he would," Jayson said.

Ruth then said, "We've talked about everyone but you, Jayson. I do believe you have a way of maneuvering the conversation away from yourself. You must tell me what you do; tell me everything."

"Well . . . I . . . uh . . ."

Elizabeth interrupted his stammering by asking, "Is the piano tuned?"

"Oh, no," Ruth said. "Nobody's played it for years and we—"

"Yes, it is," Rebecca interrupted, and Ruth looked at her in astonishment. "I had it tuned last week while you were visiting Mabel." Rebecca winked at Jayson, then answered her mother's astonished gaze by explaining, "I knew Jayson was coming." She then added, directing her words more to Jayson, "Your wife mentioned that you play the piano . . . and guitar, I believe she said."

"That's right," Jayson said, and Ruth looked at him with the same expression she'd worn when he'd told her Drew was a drummer.

"So you *both* have music in your blood," she said as if she'd just been awarded a million dollars.

"Yes, that's true," Jayson said humbly.

"And do you do it professionally as well, or is it just a hobby?"

"Both," he said firmly. "Music is a very big part of my life."

"The first time I heard him play," Elizabeth said, ignoring Jayson's embarrassment, "I was so stunned I couldn't talk for a week."

Jayson gave a scoffing laugh at her exaggeration. Ruth looked at him just as she'd done when he'd first told her they were related. There was a distinct sparkle of intrigue in her eyes. "So what do you play?" she asked. Her nose wrinkled slightly, and she added, "Not that classical stuff like . . . Mozart or Beethoven?"

Jayson chuckled tensely. "No . . . I *can* play that kind of stuff a little, and I admire their gifts, but . . . I'm afraid my specialty is a little more . . . contemporary."

"Oh, good," Ruth said. "I *hate* classical piano. It's so . . . oh, I don't know. I just don't like it. So, what do you play, Jayson?"

Jayson chuckled. "Well . . ." he said, "most of what I play is the kind of stuff that teenagers would listen to on the radio, although my own generation seems to appreciate it as well and—"

"Rock and roll, you mean," she said eagerly, and he couldn't hold back a little laugh.

"That's what I mean," he said.

Ruth clapped her hands together and let out a delighted laugh. "Well, make my dreams come true, my boy, and play some music."

"I can certainly play some music," he said, "if you're sure. I can tend to be a little loud."

Ruth laughed again. "That way I can hear it better."

Jayson chuckled and had to admit, "You know, if we weren't related, I'd be tempted to ask you to adopt me." This made Ruth laugh louder, while Rebecca grinned as if she were having the time of her life.

Jayson sat down at the piano and lifted the cover off of the keys. Memories of his youth came rushing over him, and he had to turn back toward his grandmother and tell her the story of the upright piano, the birthday gift he and Drew had given their mother, and how they'd had to sell the piano to move. She got tears in her eyes when he said, "This is the first time I've played an upright since I was sixteen." He went on to tell her how the song he'd played for his mother had come to have profound meaning for him. It was the song that had first drawn Elizabeth to him when she'd heard him play it. It was the song Derek had loved, and he'd begged him to play it at every opportunity. It was the song he'd played at Derek's funeral—and his mother's. And through the years it was the song he would play when he was all alone and needed to come to terms with anger or sorrow or fear. "That's the song I want to play for you first, Grandma." He smiled to hear himself say it. He'd never said it before except to his mother after Macy was born. "It's called 'Funeral for a Friend.'"

Elizabeth watched Ruth and Rebecca closely as Jayson played this song she knew so well. They were not only visibly pleased, they looked downright excited—especially when the music picked up tempo and complexity. When the song was done, they applauded, then Ruth came to her feet and walked over to Jayson. She put out both her hands. He took them and stood up.

"I'm so proud of you," she said and hugged him tightly. He thought of how she had no idea of his fame, or the fact that he currently had a hit on the top ten. But she was proud and happy. His gift had rarely given him more gratification than in that moment.

Ruth sat on the piano bench and motioned for him to sit beside her. "I want to ask you something," she said, still holding one of his hands. "And I hope you won't be offended."

"I won't be," he said. "I promise."

"Did you know that your father belonged to the LDS Church?"

"I had known that he came from a Mormon family, but I knew nothing more than that until recently. I confess that my opinions of the Church were not good. But that's all changed now. I was baptized last year."

Ruth's joy was evident as she said, "Oh, that's about the best thing you could have told me. And knowing that, I know you'll understand something I want to share with you. You see, Jayson, after your father left home, I was brokenhearted. He had given the family—and especially me—a great deal of grief. I couldn't deny that there was a certain degree of peace in his absence."

"I'm afraid I can relate to that," Jayson admitted.

"Yes, I'm sure you can. But my mother's heart worried so deeply for him. At a time when I was especially upset and needing comfort, I was given a priesthood blessing. In that blessing I was told that my son would come back to me, and his gift of music would touch many lives for good."

Jayson saw tears in her eyes just before he felt them come into his own. An intense warmth filled him as his spirit seemed to recognize that their reunion had been the fulfillment of that promise.

With emotion in her voice, she went on to tell him that when years passed and he never contacted the family, they had assumed he was dead. She could see now that he was just too drunk most of the time to even think about who might be wondering over him.

She had only been able to find hope in thinking that the promise of that blessing would be fulfilled in the next life, that they would be reunited and he would yet be given a chance to undo whatever it was inside of him that had caused such confusion. And she believed that such gifts as musical talent carried over into the next life. Her belief on that count hadn't changed, but she added with conviction, "I have seen in the last hour that God's promises are indeed fulfilled, even if it takes nearly fifty years to happen."

Again Jayson hugged her tightly, then he told her more about his gift, and how he'd felt it in him from a very early age. Rebecca went to the kitchen to work on supper, and Elizabeth left the baby sleeping and went to help her, leaving Jayson and Ruth alone to have a long, private conversation. Rebecca's husband, Ben, came in from some errands he'd been doing. He was pleased to meet Jayson and Elizabeth, and soon afterward they all gathered around the table for a supper of fried chicken and potatoes and gravy and cooked vegetables. Jayson took in the experience, feeling again as if he were in a movie; it all seemed so surreal. He felt so thoroughly blessed.

CHAPTER 14

When dinner was over Jayson insisted on helping with the dishes. They all pitched in, talking and laughing as they worked together, and Ruth sat at the table drying the freshly washed pans. When the kitchen was cleaned up, Ruth insisted that Jayson play some more for them. She wanted to hear "Funeral for a Friend" again, and she insisted that Ben needed to hear it. After he'd finished, Ruth commented, "Little Derek doesn't seem to mind the music."

"He's heard it from the womb," Elizabeth said, noting how the baby was looking around the room, perfectly content in her arms.

"What will you play next?" Ruth asked eagerly.

"Well," Jayson said, "this is something I wrote myself."

"You write music, too?" Ruth asked with proud astonishment.

"I do," he said with a little chuckle. "It's a form of insanity, Grandma. I've heard music in my head for almost as long as I can remember. This song is actually the title track from my new CD."

He immediately started to play before they could question him on that.

Elizabeth listened with pleasure to the song he had written for her when they'd married. On that occasion he had played it on the guitar, and now he played it on the piano with intricate handwork. On the CD it was a combination of both. After the first couple of phrases, he adjusted his seating and his feet at the pedals without missing a note. The song showed off his incredible vocal range, and she loved the way he often closed his eyes when he sang. She also noticed how he leaned forward each time he sang, a habit that sprang naturally from putting his mouth to the microphone. When his head almost met with the top part of the piano a couple of times, she realized why performers used grand pianos.

When he was finished, they all applauded and made a fuss, and Jayson graciously laughed it off. Elizabeth asked him to do "Harmony." He said, "Only if you'll do the backing vocals." She reluctantly agreed, and he told his new family members that this was another of his mother's favorite songs and it was by the same artist who originally wrote and performed the first one he'd done. After "Harmony," he did a couple of other originals, then he insisted that they'd probably heard enough for one night.

As Jayson moved from the bench to a chair, Ben said, "Forgive me, but. . . what did you mean by the title track to your new CD? Are we missing something here?"

While Jayson was trying to think of the best way to answer and not draw attention to himself, Elizabeth reached into her purse and pulled out a copy. Jayson looked startled and said to her, "What are you doing with that?"

"You never know when you might need one."

Jayson made a disgruntled noise as Elizabeth handed it to Ruth, and the others moved closer in order to see it.

Jayson actually felt his heart quicken as he waited for his grandmother's reaction. He wondered if the approval of anyone had ever mattered more to him than hers did in that moment. In a matter of hours she had became a part of his heart and soul, and he wanted her to be pleased, not by his fame, but with what he had accomplished with the gift that had come through her blood in his veins. Never had he felt more grateful to know that there was no music anywhere in the world with his name on it that was questionable or offensive. Never had he been more grateful for his clear conscience with the life he'd led. He'd struggled, he'd suffered, he'd made mistakes, but he was here now, facing this incredible woman, wishing he could tell her that he somehow believed his instincts had been leading him to this moment from his birth. He saw her eyes widen and her countenance brighten, then she turned her sparkling gaze toward him, and a smile filled her face. He wondered what she would say, and wondered why he felt as if the words that might come out of her mouth next would be priceless and precious to him. A glisten of moisture appeared in her eyes just before she said with conviction, "You followed your heart. You honored the gift inside of you. You made your dream come true."

With a rise of emotion he nodded and said, "Yes, I did."

The remainder of their visit passed all too quickly. The following day they went to the cemetery where many relatives were buried, then they looked at photo albums and genealogy records. Jayson was surprised to realize that Elizabeth had packed his career scrapbook. He had to admit that he enjoyed looking through it with his grandmother and aunt, while answering their questions.

When they finally had to leave, he promised that they would be at the big birthday party, along with their children, and that Drew and his wife would be there as well. Ruth thanked him profusely for sharing his gift and asked if he and Drew might play something at the party, so that the rest of the family could have the privilege of sharing their gift. Jayson said he'd get back to her on that. He wasn't sure he wanted his first encounter with his new relatives to be associated with music.

By the time they had arrived home, there was a lengthy email from Rebecca, thanking them for their visit and for the light they had put into her mother's eyes. She said they had been listening to the CD and enjoying it. She said that she kept finding her mother in her room, listening to it over and over. Jayson found the idea endearing and wondered if any other grandma in the world liked rock and roll enough to listen to it over and over—even if it was her grandchildren playing.

Jayson let Rebecca know via email about his upcoming television appearances. He actually found that he was less nervous about the interviews if he thought about his sweet grandmother sitting in her armchair, watching him with pride and pleasure.

During a lengthy interview with a national morning news program, Jayson wasn't surprised to have the interviewer say, "So, I hear you've found religion since Gray Wolf disbanded."

"Well," Jayson chuckled, "I had religion in my youth, and I've always had certain core beliefs concerning God. But yes, I have since found a religion that is completely fulfilling."

She didn't come right out and ask which religion he was talking about, but she did ask how his beliefs had changed his life for the better, and he gladly told her, knowing that millions of people were watching. He hoped that some of them would be curious enough to go to his personal website, which linked to the Church website. If nothing else, perhaps people might become a little more educated and open-minded about Mormonism.

Ruth's birthday party came in the middle of intense tour rehearsals, but Jayson just gave the guys a few days off while he and Drew and their families all flew to Virginia. He'd let Rebecca know that they were going to decline playing at the party, and he'd tactfully told her their reasons about not wanting music to interfere with getting to know their relatives. She understood completely.

The party ended up being a huge success. He and Drew both thoroughly enjoyed getting to know a mass of aunts, uncles, and cousins, and they were all wonderful people. Elizabeth and Valerie and the children also had a marvelous time. Jayson noticed Macy having a long conversation with Ruth, and he couldn't help being struck with such an incredible family connection.

There was conversation at the party about Jayson's new CD, which made it evident the word had spread. While many of them seemed amazed with the connection, no one seemed aghast over their fame, or treated them with any deference—which he and Drew both appreciated greatly. A few cousins admitted that they had been big Gray Wolf fans, and they'd often joked about being related, never dreaming that they actually were. They all stayed for a day after the party, and Jayson was glad for the private time his family had with Ruth. She truly was a remarkable woman, and he loved her dearly.

Returning home, they jumped headlong into intense rehearsals, but Jayson felt like it was going well. The single of "Second Chance" was released and also hit the top forty. As the beginning of the tour crept closer, Jayson had an idea that he discussed with Drew and then made some calls to arrange. He was pleased to find out that the plan was going to work. Since tickets hadn't actually yet gone on sale for the venue where they would perform closest to his grandmother's home, he was able to reserve an entire balcony section that would be more than adequate for the entire family, if they chose to come. He made the arrangements, then got the family mailing list from Rebecca and sent out an official invitation, with more than two months' notice. He said on the invitation that rooms had been reserved at a particular hotel for those traveling from out of town, and the band would foot the bill. It was his gift to his new family for accepting him and his family with open arms. He hoped they would all be able to make it—especially Ruth.

During the brief break before the tour began, Jayson was able to go to the Salt Lake Temple with Elizabeth, where they were sealed for time and all eternity. Ruth and his aunts and uncles actually flew to Utah for the event and were present in the sealing room. Jayson could, without question, say that it was the most profound experience of his life. After they were sealed as husband and wife, Macy, Trevin, and Addie knelt at the altar with them, all dressed in white, and Derek was placed on the altar. The legalities had been taken care of previously so they could all be sealed together as a family, and later Will acted as a proxy for Bradley so he could be sealed to them as well. While the experience itself was beyond compare, Jayson had the distinct impression his parents were there—both of them. That could only mean that his father had made a great deal of spiritual progress on the other side of the veil. While there was so much in Jayson's life that was good and gave him cause for happiness, this was the frosting on the cake.

Afterward, they had a family picture taken on the outside stairs of the temple—and they were all dressed in white. Elizabeth had a huge print ordered and framed, and she hung it in the living room, on the wall opposite of the painting of Christ. Jayson loved the way he could sit at the piano and see it clearly. It represented all that mattered to him.

The official kickoff of the tour was in Salt Lake City. A great deal of hype had gone out about this being Jayson Wolfe's new home-town. He'd been very careful that nothing specific about where he lived had gotten to the press, and the impression was given that he actually lived in Salt Lake City. While Jayson was backstage, waiting for the show to begin, he closed his eyes and absorbed an experience that had once been so familiar to him, a sensation that he'd believed he would never feel again: the anticipation in the air, the sights and sounds of the arena from this perspective. He knew that Will and Marilyn, Macy, Trevin, Addie, and Valerie were all in the audience, as well as Aaron's family. They'd been warned that it would be loud. He hoped they weren't too overwhelmed.

"Wow, you look great," he heard, and he turned to see Elizabeth standing there, wearing a silky red dress—and high-heeled red shoes.

"*You* look great," he said, realizing that before him was the evidence of a dream come true.

Elizabeth took in Jayson's appearance once more. He wore exactly what he'd worn on the CD cover, but on his feet were white lace-up shoes that he'd ordered custom-made. He had the entire outfit in triplicate, so he could wear it at every show, and she had three different but similar versions of the red dress.

"I love you, Jayson Wolfe," she said, if only to distract herself from her nerves.

"I love you too, Mrs. Wolfe," he said, then pointed out the obvious. "You're nervous."

"Nervous? I'm terrified. Do you have any idea how many people are out there?"

"Sold out," he said with a little chuckle. "And once you get out there, it's just you and me and the microphone. You'll do beautifully."

"I hope I don't embarrass you," she said. "I've never felt equal to this, Jayson. You were always so amazing, so incredible. I'm just . . . filler."

"You're the missing ingredient," he said and kissed her. "And I want to thank you for doing this. I know it's not easy, but it means more to me than I could ever tell you. If you . . ." He stopped when the lights went down and the crowd went wild. "Okay, this is it. You can relax back here for a few numbers."

"Relax? Are you kidding?" She kissed him again. "Good luck," she said, then stood where she could see him but not be seen. The stage was so dark that only the little flashlights the musicians were using to move into place could be seen. The crowd was so hyped that the arena seemed to rumble. The darkness remained as the first guitar chords of "Predator" broke the air, and the crowd's enthusiasm magnified to a deafening roar. She knew Jayson had made the decision to start the show with a well-known, longtime hit. And it was obviously working. As the drums and bass came in, the lights went up, and the show commenced.

That song merged right into one from the new album, then Jayson stood at the microphone and bellowed with enthusiasm, "Hello, Salt Lake City, my new hometown!" The crowds went wild. When they'd calmed down he said, "I need to tell you guys a story." Applause. "You see, there was this girl, back in high school, and . . ." Applause again. He laughed and said, "I haven't told you anything yet." Laughter and more applause. "She was hot," he said. More laughter. "And she had talent. I saw her in this school play and . . . oh, man! It was love at first sight. But she was Miss

Highbrow, you know what I mean? Orchestra, student officer, straight-A student. And me? *Me?* I was the rebel who played screaming guitars." The audience cheered. "And, oh . . . she wore these great red shoes. How I wanted to talk to her, but . . . I was . . ." he paused for emphasis, "tongue-tied." The applause merged directly into another old hit; obviously the audience was familiar with his music, and they were eager to hear the song.

Following their performance of "Tongue-Tied," Jayson said into the microphone, "There was this girl, you see." Applause. He laughed. "If you guys don't give it a rest, we'll be here all night." This really brought on the noise from the crowd. "As I was saying," Jayson said with mock impatience, and the crowd became quiet, "there was this girl. Funny thing, she loved me too. And we were in this band together. Did I say she wore these great red shoes? But eventually . . . she dumped me." Drew did a dramatic drum roll, provoking laughter. "She said she'd still be my friend, though," he said with exaggerated delight. "And eventually," he strummed the guitar, "she became," he strummed it again, and the crowd cheered with anticipation. "Oh, wait a minute." He pretended to be confused and handed the guitar to a member of the stage crew and moved to the piano, which brought up a huge cheer. He hit a dramatic chord. "Eventually," he repeated and hit another chord, "she became . . ." He shouted into the microphone, "The missing ingredient." The response threatened to bring the house down.

They played one of the recent hits while Elizabeth marveled at her husband's energy, his interaction with the audience, his unfathomable talent that kept the audience fully engrossed. When the song was done, he stood and moved to the microphone. "Thank you," he said. "I appreciate you people humoring these guys. They've worked hard." He made a sweeping motion toward the band, and the crowd cheered. He introduced them, ending with the declaration, "And that's my little brother on the drums. Drew Wolfe!" The crowd cheered as they had for the other musicians.

Drew jumped off his stool, ran to the front of the stage and gave Jayson a high-five before he returned to his seat. When the applause died down, Jayson said, "You want to know the rest of the story?" Loud cheering. "Okay, well . . . you asked for it. There was this girl, you see, with red shoes. She stuck with me through the good times and the bad, she was my best friend, and she gave me a second chance." The audience cheered, and he chuckled. "No, that song's coming later." They cheered again. In an exuberant voice he said, "Ladies and gentlemen, the missing ingredient, Elizabeth Wolfe."

She walked onto the stage amidst huge applause and took up the violin. Jayson said, "Isn't she beautiful?" Again there was cheering.

Elizabeth said into the microphone, "Get on with the song, Jayson."

"Okay, fine," he said, pretending to sound insulted. He moved back to the piano and began to play "Second Chance" with great approval from the audience. The show progressed with growing excitement, and when the encores were finished, Jayson found Elizabeth backstage, pulled her into his arms, and kissed her. He laughed and said, "You were incredible."

"*You* were incredible," she said and kissed him again. All things considered, she thought, touring with Jayson Wolfe had its appeal.

Reviews hit the papers, and they were good. The headlines read: *The Wolfe Is Back and He's Wearing White.*

"You'd better believe it," Jayson said when he read it.

The tour progressed according to plan, and the children actually did very well. Even little Derek. Macy thoroughly loved the tour experience, grateful for the opportunity to see this side of her father's life and all that she had been unaware of when he'd been touring during her childhood. While the younger children were with them, Trevin ate up the music scene and occasionally he actually jammed in a hotel room with the band. Jayson could see potential in him—and a certain drive—that exceeded the norm for a boy his age. Addie became the band mascot, adored and teased by every member of the band and crew.

In August the date finally arrived when they would perform with Jayson's family in attendance. Rebecca had let them know that every single member of the family would be there, except for the children who were too young to do anything but cause commotion. Jayson couldn't help feeling pleased, and an extra excitement filled him as the show began. He did all the usual songs and monologue, and got the usual response, while he was intensely aware of the blur of faces in the balcony of a smaller-than-average but very elegant concert hall.

After the intermission, Jayson sat on a stool with his guitar, while Elizabeth sat on another with her violin. He looked over at her and smiled before he said into the microphone, "I want you to know I have roots in Virginia." The crowd went wild, and he laughed. "I didn't know I had roots in Virginia until a few months ago. You see, my father left his family in his youth, and I never knew about that connection. Now I have a balcony full of relatives here tonight." He pointed at them, and they all cheered and screamed and whistled. "They're Drew's relatives too," he said, and Drew did a little drumroll before he shouted, "Hi Grandma!" Laughter and applause. "So, before we go on with the usual show, I hope you will bear with me as I express my gratitude to my new family for loving me, and for humoring me, and for coming to share this night with me. And, Grandma, I want you to know that you are one of the most amazing women I've ever known. My mother, my wife, and my daughters are in good company with your example." He blew a kiss, then said more lightly, "And you people need to know that my ninety-year-old grandma loves rock and roll." The audience cheered, and he laughed. He strummed the guitar and added, "I wrote this song after I found my new family. This is the first and last time I will be performing it publicly." He pointed again toward the balcony. "This is for you, Grandma."

He played a few intricate bars on the guitar before the violin came in with perfect harmony. Jayson put his mouth to the mike and crooned, *"Wrapped up in my child's bed, I heard voices in my head, singing always singing. Drowning out the voices I heard down the hall, through the wall, shouting always shouting. Raging with hot-blooded youth, the voices sang to me of truth, luring me, assuring me, curing me of every pain, wooing me into the rain that bathed my aching soul. The voices singing in my mind; they call to me, call to me. From another place and time they seem to say, 'One day you'll see . . . some day you'll see . . . that true love lasts forever, that no heart beats alone, that a mother's care reaches out across the sea and sky and brings the wanderer home, brings the wanderer home. The voices calling in my mind; they sing to me, sing to me . . . that music flows like water . . . turned to wine . . . in perfect rhyme with seasons gone before me and seasons yet to cross.*

"In the wavering sands of manhood I hear the voices in my head, they sing to me, sing to me, luring me, assuring me, curing me of every pain. The hands of time hold me securely . . . as surely . . . as darkness turns to light, daylight turns to night and reaches out toward another dawn. And reaching to the east I feel your hand in mine, finding me, reminding me . . . that true love lasts forever, that no heart beats alone, that a mother's care reaches out across the sea and sky and brings the wanderer home, brings the wanderer home. The voices calling in my mind; they sing to me, sing to me . . . that music flows like water . . . turned to wine . . . in perfect rhyme with seasons gone before me and seasons yet to cross."

Epilogue

At the close of the U.S. tour, Jayson and Elizabeth were at home for several weeks while the children settled back into school. In the fall, they went to Europe on three different occasions to do some selected shows, then they declared the tour officially done, and they were able to settle comfortably into the life they'd always dreamt of sharing. The royalties poured in, and Jayson sent most of them to the Church to support the humanitarian, welfare, and missionary efforts. He started working on some spiritual music at a slow and easy pace, and when Elizabeth discovered that she was pregnant again, he put most of his focus into helping her take care of the children. Pregnancy was harder on her this time, given her age and the brief time it had been since she'd had a baby. But they were thrilled with the prospect of having another child.

Jayson began getting invitations to do firesides, and he found it was something he dearly enjoyed. Elizabeth usually went with him, and he started inviting her to share a few thoughts as well that added to the impact of seeing his story from her perspective. He was called to be the pianist for the choir, and also to teach the seven-year-olds in Primary. And he loved it.

Five months into the pregnancy, Rebecca called to tell them that Ruth had passed away in her sleep. Jayson was grateful that he'd taken the family to Virginia during the holidays some weeks earlier, and even more grateful that he'd had the privilege to know her. The entire family, and Drew's family as well, went to Virginia for the funeral, and Jayson gladly agreed to play the song that he'd written for his grandmother. He could give her no better tribute than that.

Returning home, Jayson settled more fully into a life he considered ideal. They had their little challenges, as any family would. But they were together, and they had the gospel.

In spite of Elizabeth being pregnant, she insisted that they were going to plant a garden as soon as the weather warmed with spring. It was something Jayson had never done before, but he found he enjoyed it, and getting the family involved made it even better, even though the children were often reluctant.

The same week that the kids got out of school for summer vacation, Aaron came home from his mission. It didn't take long for it to become readily evident that he and Macy were right for each other, and a wedding date was set for early September. In the middle of July, a girl was born to Jayson and Elizabeth, healthy and strong and beautiful. Since Addie's middle name was Elizabeth, and Macy's middle name was the same, Jayson was firm on giving this little girl the same middle name to make it a tradition. They debated over the first name. Jayson had wanted to name a daughter Leslie, after his mother, but Drew had already taken it for his daughter—and Jayson couldn't begrudge that. After trying several names, only one felt absolutely right to both Jayson and Elizabeth, even though Jayson admitted it sounded a little funky for musicians to give their daughter such a name. But looking at her little face, they just knew her name was meant to be Harmony Elizabeth Wolfe. Harmony's presence in the home added a completeness that was difficult to describe. Jayson and Elizabeth both knew they were finished having children, and now they could focus on raising their beautiful family.

At the end of the summer, Jayson did a concert for a local charity benefit. It was just him and Elizabeth, doing simple versions of some of his popular songs, and fitting in some of his more recent compositions that were of a spiritual nature. He decided this was something he could enjoy doing once in a while, if only to keep his performing skills sharp and his creative juices flowing. He wasn't against doing anything big in the future, but for the time being he was content to take life more slowly and stay close to home.

Macy and Aaron were married in the Salt Lake Temple, and the largest sealing room available was filled to overflowing with family and friends. Jayson watched Elizabeth closely while his daughter exchanged eternal vows with this wonderful young man. He pondered the legacy his children would have that he'd not grown up with, and he was deeply grateful.

When the ceremony was over, they went outside and took pictures for nearly an hour beneath overcast skies. After the bride and groom had changed out of their wedding attire, they realized they all had some time to kill before the wedding luncheon would begin at the Joseph Smith Memorial Building. Jayson suggested they go into the visitors' center and take some pictures in front of the *Christus*. Elizabeth asked a woman standing there if she would take the picture so that the whole family could be in it, and the woman eagerly took on the task. She snapped a couple of pictures, then handed the camera back to Elizabeth. Jayson was preoccupied with keeping Derek out of trouble when he felt someone tap him on the arm.

"Excuse me," a young man said, and Jayson turned to look at him. He had a ponytail and an earring. His eyes looked hard, weary, confused. "I'm sorry to bother you," he went on, "but . . . you have a beautiful family. How do you get a family like that?"

Jayson smiled and put a hand on his shoulder. "If you've got a minute, I'll tell you all about it."

Elizabeth noticed Jayson sitting on one of the benches, talking rather intently to a young man she'd never seen before. Will and Marilyn took the kids and said they'd meet them at the luncheon in a few minutes. Macy and Aaron followed after them. Elizabeth waited for Jayson to finish his conversation. She saw each of them writing something down, apparently exchanging email addresses or phone numbers, then they shook hands, and Jayson returned to her side.

"What was that all about?" she asked.

"He asked all the right questions, and I gave him the right answers."

"I see," she said, noting the smile of gratification on his face.

They gazed once more at the statue of Christ, then walked hand in hand out into the Square where they gazed up at the temple spires, neither of them having anything to say.

Jayson moved his gaze from the temple to take a long look at the woman he loved. He thought of the first time he'd seen her, and how his heart had responded with the belief that they were destined to be together. He felt freshly humbled by how their lives had been brought together. He loved her beyond all description, and miraculously, she loved him too. It started to rain, and people all around them scurried for cover. He expected Elizabeth to do the same, knowing they were headed to a wedding luncheon. But she lifted her face heavenward and closed her eyes.

"You're getting wet, Mrs. Wolfe," he said.

"So are you." She looked at him and smiled.

"It'll make your hair curly," he said.

"It already is."

"So it is."

"It was raining the first time you kissed me."

"How could I ever forget?" he asked and kissed her in a feeble attempt to bridge the years from then to the present moment. He touched her rain-dampened skin and smiled.

About the Author

Anita Stansfield, the LDS market's number-one best-selling romance novelist, is a prolific and imaginative writer who wants her readers to know that she is "real." She and her husband, Vince—whom she calls "her hero"—have three boys and two girls: John, Jake, Anna, Steven, and Alyssa. She loves butterscotch chip cookies, long walks, and romantic movies. She loves to go out to eat, especially for seafood and steaks. Her favorite color is black. She loves lemonade and French fries with fry sauce. She loves her husband. She loves her kids. She loves her sisters, her brothers, her dad, and her friends. She loves her house and her neighborhood. And she loves Alpine, the little town she lives in. And—oh, yes—she loves to write stories.